Further Praise for *Capitol*

"Javitt has melded his professional and pol[illegible] chilling thriller that should alert every reader to the very real dangers we face in the twenty-first century. His characters are compelling and realistic, very much like the dedicated people who served with me during my tenure as Surgeon General. His plot, while (hopefully) fictional, could just as easily be a headline from tomorrow's newspapers."

—Dr. C. Everett Koop,
former U.S. Surgeon General

"Javitt has written a grab-you-by-the-throat thriller that could easily be tomorrow's lead news story. Under the guise of a compelling read lurks a keep-you-guessing plot that should cause any intelligent reader to worry about the safety of us all. An intrepid female physician, a town full of bad guys, and the safety of the American people at stake. Seems like a surefire recipe for success."

—Janet Rehnquist, former Inspector
General, Health and Human Services

"A fast-moving, medical twist-and-turner, written with a knowledgeable pen and a creative wit."

—Fran Kritz, *Washington Post* &
Los Angeles Times columnist

"Compelling and terrifying. This book is a must for mystery and adventure readers—and for everyone concerned about what he puts in his body."

—Ben Stein, bestselling author,
Emmy-winning TV host, and national
commentator

"*Capitol Reflections* may read like fiction, but the truth should scare us more. Our food safety laws were written long before we ever imagined, much less created genetically-modified food. Within the guise of a great thriller, Jonathan Javitt has vividly illustrated the danger that confronts us all if we don't act soon."

—Wayne Pines, former Associate
Commissioner, U.S. Food and Drug
Administration

"Author Javitt, a well-known epidemiologist, physician and health advisor to three presidents, presents this frighteningly believable first novel of a health crisis, political corruption and cover-ups; the work brings Robin Cook and David Baldacci to mind."

—Author Online

CAPITOL REFLECTIONS

JONATHAN JAVITT

Dedicated to the memory of Capt. Henry Krakauer, M.D., Ph.D., M.P.H., of the U.S. Public Health Service, Gwen's true mentor and an inspiration to the rest of us.

The Story Plant
The Aronica-Miller Publishing Project, LLC
P.O. Box 4331
Stamford, CT 06907

Cover and interior design by Barbara Aronica Buck

ISBN-13: 978-0-9816087-1-6
ISBN-10: 0-9816087-1-X

Visit our website at www.thestoryplant.com

Sterling & Ross Hardcover Publication: January 2008
First Story Plant Printing: September 2008

Printed in the United States of America

10 9 8 7 6 5 4 3 2 1

PART I
MAY 2005

1

Marci Newman, coiffed, petite and impeccably dressed in a gray business suit, picked up her briefcase and left the new Pequod's coffee bistro in SoHo, clutching her double skim latte by its cardboard sleeve. She carefully wove her way through an obstacle course of vendors, deliverymen, and pedestrians. As usual, she had just inhaled a salad, along with a few guilty puffs of the cigarettes she'd "given up" years ago, during her all-too-short lunch break before heading back to the daily grind of the city courts in Foley Square. She was especially pressed for time, having walked an extra three blocks and passing four other espresso bars for her daily dose of Pequod's. The additional stress was worth it, though; ever since the new chain took New York by storm, nobody else's latte tasted quite as good. Marci knew she wasn't the only one who felt this way. In the months since Pequod's entered the city, the lines at the ubiquitous Starbucks shops dwindled to a trickle.

Marci's friends and colleagues claimed she needed to eat more and find time for rest and relaxation. Her college roommate, Gwen, now an epidemiologist for the Food and Drug Administration, was forever preaching to Marci about slowing down, getting exercise, reducing her caseload, maybe even getting out and dating occasionally. Marci smiled at the thought of seeing Gwen tonight for dinner, even though it would lead to a reprise of this ongoing lecture. Marci loved Gwen dearly and even loved the fact that Gwen never got off her back about her lifestyle.

Of course, she was never going to do anything about that lifestyle. So what if she was "professionally overextended"? She wasn't soccer mom material, anyway. She wasn't about to give up the *pro bono* work she added to her caseload at Denniger, Sachman & Wayne even at the risk of exhaustion and spinsterhood.

Marci's latest *pro bono* cause was Anh Nguyen. Ms. Nguyen was being evicted from her apartment by a slumlord looking to turn a quick profit by flipping the tenement to a developer who, in turn, intended to convert the property to condos with a trendy boutique on the ground floor bordered by a bookstore and gourmet coffee shop (probably a Pequod's, though Marci didn't want to let that sway her). To the real estate crowd who traded property like Monopoly cards, Anh was just another nuisance holdout, a pothole on the road they called "urban renewal." Anh had lived in the building—apartment 5B—since coming to New York in the early seventies as a refugee from America's adventures in Southeast Asia. Her first home, a Vietnamese village surrounded by fecund rice paddies was turned into a napalm-fueled sheet of flame, along with her husband and five of her seven children. The thought of losing the only remaining point of constancy in her life was more than this seventy-six-year-old Hmong woman could bear.

Marci would do her part to save her. Right now, Marci felt as though she could save anyone—she was invincible. She was playing a vital role in the greatest city in the world on one of its picture-perfect May days—seventy-five degrees, blue skies, and lots of sun. She felt good. Superb, in fact. The street sounds overwhelmed her like a symphonic orchestra at its climax. She was a modern day Walt Whitman taking in the poetry that was Manhattan's lifeblood. Everything was clear and sharp; every pedestrian, taxi, pigeon, and store sign in perfect focus. She was definitely "on," which she knew would not have been the case had she eaten a large meal. A full stomach doesn't win cases. Lettuce and litigation made a much better combination.

She continued walking, still thinking of Anh. The case was perfect for her. The law was against her, the facts were against her, and the New York judges played golf with the real estate boys every Saturday morning. All Marci had going for her was Anh's sincerity and her own social-grievance-engendered spunk. Oh yes, and one other thing: yesterday the slumlord was indicted for bribing a public official. Marci knew that the slumlord's crime and her particular case were separate legal situations and that it was also possible the slumlord had already bribed the judge on her case. On the other hand, ever since Joan Salzman became chief prosecutor to the city's ethics board, city officials were thinking very carefully about doing favors for their old cronies. Suddenly, Marci and Anh had a fighting chance. That was usually all Marci ever needed.

"You help Anh."

Marci remembered the first words she had heard from the frail woman with passion in her eyes. She was waiting outside Marci's office building. Marci would later learn that Anh had waited for hours. The receptionist for the firm did not make a practice of admitting anyone without an appointment, certainly not an elderly woman wearing a faded housecoat. But Anh Nguyen had stared down hundreds of automatic weapons in her village when the camouflaged A-teams surreptitiously stepped from the edge of the jungle; she was both persistent and tough. She crouched on the sidewalk, head resting on knees tucked close to her body, waiting for a lawyer with a sympathetic face to emerge from the glass high-rise.

"Landlord tell Anh 'Move out. No want. Building change owner.' But Anh no go. Anh no leave home." She paused, and Marci studied her face. At that point, Marci knew nothing about the woman, but she knew her eyes had seen more than its share of darkness. "Husband, children, brother, sister—leave, die, move way. Not here. Help Anh. Please."

In actuality, the speech lasted quite a bit longer and was punctuated by tears and more pleading. As the distressed stranger clawed at her Donna Karan jacket, Marci listened to every word. She knew long before the tiny woman had finished that she would handle the matter. Denniger, Sachman & Wayne expected Marci to represent a number of New York City landlords and developers. She was well aware of the bottom-feeders among them. She was going to take one on today.

Stopping at a light, Marci raised her head and beheld the Brooklyn Bridge spanning the waters of the East River in its turn-of-the-century majesty. Beautiful, she thought. Absolutely spectacular. She wished she could stop and muse over its architecture, its intricacies, its history—even speculate on the lives of the people who built it and those who died in the attempt. Not now, though. She had a client to send home, happy and content, to apartment 5B. The bench trial that morning had been short and sweet. Marci clearly demonstrated that Anh's landlord was selling the property after years of neglecting various building codes, not to mention the fact that he broke any number of clauses in Ms. Nguyen's lease. The judge would summarily render his verdict and Marci would be back in her corner office with its commanding view of the city. Within two hours, she would be ready to see at least three more clients before surrendering to the close of another business day and meet with Gwen and Jack Maulder for dinner.

Caught up in her thoughts, she barely noticed the man in a rumpled suit heading straight for her. He was dark-complected, with black, oily hair combed straight back above an unfashionably early five o'clock shadow. He smiled, revealing nicotine stains on his uneven teeth. He planted himself squarely in Marci's path.

"So," he whispered into Marci's ear, "are you ready for me to show you the night of your life?"

Marci stopped dead in her tracks.

"Fazio, if you had the equipment to back up your offer, I might actually get outraged enough to complain to the Bar Association about your pathetic desperation to lose your virginity. Last I heard, however, people couldn't find your package with tweezers." Marci smiled sweetly, as if she'd just complimented his tie. "Go find more slumlords to defend. And for God's sake, try topping off your Chinese food with some Altoids. You reek."

"Is that any way to speak to a colleague in the world's second oldest profession?" asked Joseph Fazio, attorney-at-law.

"As I see it, Counselor, you only joined the second oldest profession in order to represent relatives who have the dubious distinction of belonging to the world's first oldest." Marci was pleased with the comeback; that double-latte had her firing on twelve cylinders. She stepped aside and strode intrepidly up the courthouse steps and through the main entrance, hoping to lose Fazio. She always felt the desire to take a shower after speaking with him.

"Loosen up, Counselor," urged Fazio, who unfortunately thought Marci was interested in continuing their exchange. "You're obviously not getting any, and I'm just offering to help you with that problem. I'll even buy dinner."

Marci pivoted sharply. "If you want to help me, tell your slumlord to fix up his building. Oh, right, he can't because he's too busy trying to figure out a way to stay out of jail at the moment. Otherwise—"

"Yes, yes," Fazio interrupted. "Otherwise, I should go fuck myself while you simultaneously defend the poor and keep corporate criminals safe over at Denniger, Sachman."

"I would never suggest an anatomic impossibility. That's just your filthy mind at work." Smiling coldly, Marci continued toward the nearest open elevator, turned, and watched Joseph Fazio stop abruptly, unable to push his considerable girth into the small cubicle.

"Next car," she called our cheerily as the doors slid closed.

■ ■ ■

Marci stepped from the elevator directly into a wall of heat and humidity on the third floor. The building engineer was supervising workmen crawling through access panels in the ceiling, and it was obvious that the air conditioning wasn't combating the eighty-degree temperature in the hallway. Marci silently cursed the city councilman who had shepherded the air conditioning contract through the process and the unknown relative of the councilman from whom it had been procured.

She opened the door of the first courtroom on the right, noticing Fazio once again hot on her tail. The sight of the frail Vietnamese woman sitting at the back of the room immediately renewed her sympathy. Anh looked nervous and she wore the same housecoat she'd worn when she first encountered Marci.

"They'll probably call our case in a few minutes," Marci whispered reassuringly as she slipped into a seat next to Anh and lightly touched her forearm. "Looks like another case is dragging a bit. Don't worry."

Fazio sat down with his client, a man in his fifties, on the opposite side of the courtroom a few rows ahead. The disheveled tenement owner was wearing wrinkled navy-colored pants, a faded herringbone jacket, and workman's shoes. Looking over his shoulder, he scowled at Anh and then began whispering something to Fazio.

The courtroom was even warmer and stuffier than the hallway. Marci was beginning to perspire. She took a tissue from her purse to wipe beads of moisture from her forehead. The heat notwithstanding, her senses were still attuned to everything around her. She was able to follow two conversations being held in low tones far back in the room, as well as the more audible exchange between a lawyer and the judge.

I guess this is the true meaning of multi-tasking, she said to herself, immodestly in awe of her own ability to follow the threads of so many simultaneous situations. Then, as she wiped her forehead again, she inhaled deeply. Something more than air seemed to escape from her when she exhaled. Suddenly, without warning, she felt drained.

"Nguyen versus Lazlow," a voice rang out. "Step forward and be heard."

Marci took another deep breath, trying to regain her spark. She looked up and saw that the bailiff was staring at her. She started, suddenly aware that she had lost track of time. That never happened. She chided herself for the lapse, wondering if she should have gotten another shot of espresso with her latte.

No time to think about that now. She took Anh by the hand and led her to the front of the courtroom. The bailiff read the case number while the judge casually shuffled papers.

"Very well," Judge Walter T. Jacobs declared, finally looking over glasses resting on the tip of his nose. "I've considered the testimony from this morning and I'm prepared to put this issue to rest. Does anyone have anything else to say?" His tone was that of a man who had little interest in what he was doing, someone who listened to dozens of petty disputes every day while his mind was on the putting green, gauging how far to the left a six-footer would break.

Marci smiled very slightly as the phrase "turnstile justice" floated through her mind. *You're in, you're out, slam bam, thank you, ma'am*, she thought. *Next case. Hi everyone! Welcome to the show!*

If that was the way things were, Marci believed the little guy—or gal, as the case might be—deserved to win one once in a while. And there was something in the judge's eyes when he looked at Lazlow. Jacobs seemed repelled by the man, as though Lazlow got on an airplane seat next to him with a runny nose and a hacking cough.

"Yes, your honor," Marci said, reaching for a paper in her briefcase. "There's one final document that— "

Marci's hand began to shake, the paper making a thin, high-pitched rattling sound. She was perspiring heavily now.

"Are you okay, Ms. Newman?" inquired Judge Jacobs.

Marci wasn't okay. Her eyes rolled up beneath her eyelids. She tried to speak, but her tongue seemed to have a mind of its own. The fingers of her right hand began to rhythmically pull at the silver chain around her neck, as if it were too tight and prevented her from breathing. A heart-shaped pendant, a Christmas gift from Gwen, dangled from the chain as Marci tugged hard on the small silver links.

Seconds later, she fell to the parquetry of the courtroom floor, her arms and legs moving spasmodically like those of a marionette whose strings are being pulled by a sadistic, unseen puppeteer.

2

Marci slipped in and out of consciousness on the way to Bellevue, only occasionally managing to pry open her eyes to look at whatever appeared directly above her head—a hand, the head of a male paramedic, and IV tubing coiled in an overhead storage rack. Something—she guessed Valium—had broken her seizure, but she could only keep her awareness focused for seconds at a time, and even then reality was a series of unrelated slides in an out-of-focus carousel projector. Just when one image began to make sense, she would start to slip away again, alternating between memory and reality. Pictures of herself on the beach swam through her brain as she spiraled into unconsciousness.

Now, overlapping voices clamored for attention. Multiple conversations—the kind she'd always been able to decipher—scrambled together. She was being rushed through a corridor on a gurney, and the overhead fluorescent lights were blinding. Doctors and nurses seemed to float about her in the awful luminescence, and either their speech was garbled or they were speaking in tongues. The fuzzy outline of a head appeared and asked if she knew her name, but Marci was too tired to answer.

Got to hang in, she thought. Keep your head in the game.

■ ■ ■

Gwen Maulder was relaxing with her husband Jack at the bar of The River Café, waiting to be seated. She was drinking a glass of Chardonnay, happy to get away from work early. This was one of those rare trips when her workload, Jack's traveling schedule, and her best friend's day planner all meshed. The subdued lighting over the bar created a lovely ambience of both peace and elegance. It was a good feeling. Gwen wished she could get Marci to understand that. Careers didn't need to own your life. You could have it all if you performed the balancing act perfectly. She glanced over at Jack and smiled at him softly. No—career didn't need to own your life.

Gwen was in town to review current stats with people at the New York FDA office. She could have done this via download back at her computer in Rockville, Maryland, but she always relished a chance to see Marci. Gwen's deceased father, Dr. Fitz McBean, had been an old-style family practitioner who put great emphasis on personal contact with people. Indeed, Gwen took over her dad's practice when he died, but found she couldn't run it alone. No one wanted to make house calls like Fitz, and using a minimal office staff to deal with HMOs had become oppressive. ("It's not managed care," Fitz had remarked. "It's mangled care.") So Gwen decided to use her considerable diagnostic skills in a different venue at a time in history when the federal government needed real doctors, not bureaucrats, to take the pulse of the nation's health. Terrorism, anthrax, flu, AIDS—these factors and so many more demanded that competent physicians assess health concerns from a broader, more comprehensive perspective. So here she was in New York City, a public health official, a division chief in the U.S. Food and Drug Administration and a captain in the U.S. Public Health Service. Yet, she was still very much the daughter of Fitz McBean, only two generations removed from making house calls in a horse and buggy.

And she couldn't wait to see Marci.

The conversation at the bar revolved around medicine, politics, movies, and a mutual friend whom, both Maulders were convinced, was having an affair with a decadent artist in SoHo, a man named Ernesto—no last name. She and Jack were laughing one moment, challenging each other at another, and ruminating the next. She loved that she could do that with him.

Just as she loved the energy required to fill her role at the FDA. Every new drug carried with it the risk of unintended consequences, complications not detected in the pre-market testing. One-in-a-thousand atypical responses just don't show up that often when only a few thousand patients at most are tested before drug release. Constant diligence—and the patience to withstand endless bureaucratic meetings—could be draining. Fortunately, Chardonnay and soft lighting could be so restorative.

Gwen was having a harder-than-usual time relaxing, however. Marci had not been her usual self on the phone this morning, and Gwen felt a little on edge waiting for Marci to show up and explain why.

"I really need some quiet time with you, more than just a long bathroom break at dinner," she had said. Gwen tried to pry the subject out of her and managed only to ascertain that it had nothing to do with a current romance, Marci wouldn't talk about it over the phone, and that it had her somewhat unnerved.

■ ■ ■

In Marci's twilight consciousness, the ocean looked bluer than it ever had before. Seagulls wheeled over the dunes as water gently washed across her feet before sinking into the sand. The wind pressed a blue dress of the lightest cotton firmly against her body while she peered into the hazy distance. A ship was slowly becoming invisible as it lumbered away from shore, finally disappearing over the horizon.

How far had the water between her toes traveled, she wondered. Five miles? Five hundred? A thousand? What midnight constellations had ruled over these small trickles when they had been part of the immense depth that was the Atlantic Ocean? Had freighters cut through the waves that were now breaking onto shore, or had the swells been lonely and isolated?

■ ■ ■

Gwen groaned as her pager relayed a phone number. She slid off the bar stool, walked to the restaurant's foyer, and removed the cell phone from her purse. She didn't recognize the telephone number on the pager, but she dutifully punched her keypad until she heard the ring tone of whoever wanted to speak with her.

"This is Captain Maulder," she said, hoping that the disturbance was nothing more than someone who couldn't locate her last report on sub-clinical infections.

Moments later, the blood drained from her face. She closed her flip-top phone with a flick of the wrist, went back to the bar, and took her husband's hand.

"We have to go," she said, trying to keep the panic from her voice.

"What's up?" Jack Maulder asked, as Gwen pulled him onto the street, her legs almost breaking into a run.

"That was the ER at Bellevue. It's Marci. She's had some kind of seizure."

"Is she going to be—"

Gwen shook her head nervously. "They don't know."

Jack stepped off the curb and hailed a taxi. Moments later, the vehicle's red taillights faded into the gray twilight as a slight drizzle dampened a street warm from a day of sunshine and the friction of ten thousand tires.

■ ■ ■

Marci felt a sharp prick in her right forearm and opened her eyes. Five minutes later, her pupils were not quite as dilated as before thanks to whatever was dripping through the tube snaking into her arm. She could see more clearly now and stared at the dots on the suspended ceiling. She felt slightly better and thought she might not die after all. All around her, machines were beeping and people were talking. She couldn't actually see anyone since her peripheral vision was constricted, but she was alert enough to know that there was a steady flow of traffic in and out of the cubicle where her gurney was parked.

"Anh," she said. "Anh Nguyen. Tell her things will be okay."

"Don't talk, Ms. Newman," said a female voice. "Just lie still."

The beeping from one of the machines suddenly sounded faster and louder.

That can't be good, Marci thought. *Not good at all.*

It wasn't. Marci felt a sharp pain in her chest as her heart started beating more rapidly than it had ever beaten in her life. She thought the sensation might be similar to what a hummingbird felt as its wings fluttered faster than the human eye could possibly detect. The bird's heartbeat, she recalled, was also incredibly fast, and she closed her eyes as her own heart hammered against her ribcage. She sensed more activity around her, doctors and nurses speaking in rapid-fire, staccato jargon.

"Hi," said a familiar voice.

"Hi, Gwen," said Marci, not opening her eyes. Her heart rate slowed a little when she heard the voice of her old friend.

An argument followed, during which the medical team told Gwen she needed to leave the room, and Gwen informed them that she was a physician and a friend summoned to the hospital twenty minutes earlier.

"Gwen?" said Marci, opening her eyes.

"Yes, honey. I'm still here." Gwen leaned directly over the gurney so Marci could see her face.

"I love you."

The two women looked at each other, Gwen's hand wrapped around Marci's small, pale fingers.

"I love you, too."

"Ond . . . dee," said Marci.

"What did you say, honey?"

"Ondee," Marci whispered again.

"*Ondine*?" Gwen said, a single tear rolling down her cheek. "Your favorite ballet. We'll see it again soon."

Marci tilted her head slightly, and for a brief moment her focus seemed sharper as she stared directly at Gwen. "Ondee," she repeated.

Gwen shook her head. "I understand."

Gwen's eyes were filling with tears. *Ondine* was about a water sprite. Marci had always loved the tragic ballet. Perhaps it was her love of the ocean. Perhaps Marci identified with Ondine's inability to find love. Either way, she had listened to its sad *pas de deux* over and over again.

Suddenly Marci's entire body went rigid. The beeping sound was replaced by a steady whine, terrifying to anyone who knew its significance.

She was flatlining.

At the beach, a hummingbird was carried far out to sea by a strong wind.

A new adventure, the little bird thought. *A brand new adventure*.

And then the bird was gone.

3

An attendant led Gwen and Jack through a maze of corridors to a small, carpeted room with a sofa and three chairs. A stately picture of the Hudson Valley hung over the sofa, and a standard-issue ficus plant rose in the corner, giving the room a bit of color in contrast to the sterile surroundings of the hospital. Gwen was stunned she could even notice this, stunned that the world had any detail for her at all at the moment. Marci was gone. Inexplicably gone.

"What the hell just happened?" Gwen asked, sitting on the sofa.

Jack Maulder, tall and broad-chested, pulled his wife close. He didn't say a word and Gwen didn't expect him to. He gave her what she needed just then—a place to cry for the conceivable future.

"I can't believe it," she said when she'd regained a modicum of composure. "This isn't possible."

"She literally worked herself to death," Jack commented sympathetically. "You warned her for years to slow down, but Marci couldn't resist the adrenaline rush of a high-powered career."

"Yeah, but she was pretty healthy, Jack, all things considered."

"People die unexpectedly every day even if they don't lead stressful lives."

Wiping away fresh tears, Gwen ran her fingers through her hair. "I know, I know, I know," she said with exasperation in her voice. "But I knew Marci, and . . . well . . . this shouldn't have happened."

"What are you suggesting?"

"I don't know what I'm suggesting, but people don't die of

seizures. Not the first time, when they're in the prime of life."

"Sometimes they do, honey."

There were exceptions to everything. Gwen knew that. But the exceptions were extremely rare. It was virtually impossible to believe that Marci was one of them.

Once again, a wave of tears crested on top of her. Marci had been Gwen's best friend for most of two decades. She was as essential to her life as her heart and lungs. How do you survive that?

Pulling herself together, Gwen rose abruptly.

"Where are you going?" Jack asked, rising with her.

"I have to call Marci's family, hopefully before a stranger here at the hospital finds their number." She pulled out her cell phone and started to walk away. Jack seemed confused by this, so she said, "I just need to be alone for a few minutes."

Gwen called Marci's parents, people she felt as close to as anyone in her own family. Her mind flashed on holiday visits. When Gwen's dad humorously battled her for the Thanksgiving wishbone, could either of them ever have imagined the conversation they were about to have?

The call rapidly devolved to single syllables, incoherent fragments, and, ultimately, wails of grief. When it was over, Gwen leaned against the nearest available wall for support and sobbed against it because Jack's chest was too far away.

She had no idea how much time passed before she was capable of drying her eyes. When she did, she cleared her throat and scrolled to another number on her phone's contact list.

"Dave?" she said, unsure of how she sounded. "Captain Maulder, USPH. I'm going to be over tomorrow morning. You're going to be getting a new customer shortly—Marci Newman's the name. I want you to save a blood sample for me, but don't accession it in your lab system. I want to take it back to Rockville with me, okay?"

Dave Dardenoff was one of the assistant coroners at the New York State Medical Examiner's Office across 32nd Street from Bellevue. Dave had worked at the FDA's New York office for a while, but he fancied himself to be Quincy, the medical examiner from the old TV series. He preferred a real life medical mystery to analyzing charts and graphs and going on the occasional plant inspection. Dave and Gwen had always gotten along well, and he would provide her with a sample of Marci's blood, no questions asked and strictly off the record.

Gwen began walking back to the quiet room to rejoin her husband. He'd be worried about her by now, but he knew better than to come to look for her. Somewhere else in the hospital, Marci's lifeless body lay. Everything in Gwen's medical training told her that Marci shouldn't be dead. She wouldn't forgive herself if she didn't do something to figure out what had just happened to her very best friend.

4

Mark Stern sat at his desk, playing Space Invaders on his Dell flatscreen. He took his job as a top reporter for the *Wall Street Journal* very seriously, but that didn't stop him from sneaking in a little R & R during a day otherwise devoted to profiling the bluebloods who controlled the blue chips. He'd just turned forty, but part of him was always going to be a kid, and he had learned years ago that a complete surrender to adulthood was just too difficult for a man who still kept R.E.M. T-shirts and a jean jacket in his closet. He had attempted the quantum leap to responsible, dashing, GQ status; the most notable example being when he tried to placate his old girlfriend by wearing Brooks Brothers suits and attending elegant East Hampton parties, complete with string quartets, champagne, and caviar. He always left depressed, feeling like an imposter. He'd go back to his apartment, smoke a little dope, listen to bootleg Clash CDs, and dream of the Pulitzer he was going to win someday.

In Mark's dreams, that Pulitzer would come from a multi-part investigative piece on the plight of the tamarin or the spider monkey published in the *Nation*, but if it had to be about a next-generation globalized billionaire, that would work as well. Mark knew the Pulitzer thing really was more than just a dream, even if the subject matter probably was. He'd started his career by writing for various small town papers in upstate New York ("Police Chief Election To Be Held Saturday") and gradually moved up to the *New York Times*, going after the kind of local stories buried on page four of the Metro section ("Priest Talks Jumper Off Whitestone Bridge,"

"Chimpanzees Found In Bronx Apartment—Owner Pleads Ignorance"). Stern was a ringmaster in the word circus where reporters used prose style aimed at seventh-grade syntax. While his editors never took the stories seriously, the paper's marketing department started noticing one reader poll after another in which Stern's stories and byline were the only ones readers could remember. The publisher, well aware of the importance of selling newspapers, ordained that the *Times* give Stern his own column.

For Mark, this was a personal emancipation proclamation, freeing him to be an iconoclast who stylized the eccentricities of the frenzied, dispirited commuters who poured into the New York City subway system every day so they could make a few bucks, go home, sleep, wake up, and do it all over again.

The column went platinum when the paper suggested he collect his observations into a book, *Sterner Stuff*. It spent a few weeks on the bottom of the bestseller list and spawned a sequel, *Latitudes and Attitudes*, that landed Mark on Letterman and Charlie Rose. The liberal management of the *Times* certainly gave Mark healthy latitude to lampoon everything from what he called "the Neanderthal nature of twenty-first century man" to the myriad verbal blunders of a sitting president. In short, he had achieved celebrity status, with his name and picture on the sides of hundreds of city buses. And he had done it all while keeping a few posters of whales and condors on his apartment walls.

Reporters like Stern didn't usually get calls from the *Wall Street Journal*, regardless of talent. The *Journal* was famous for supporting presidents and political potentates who were always optimistic, even if the Dow suggested that the nation's financial roller coaster was bottoming out. The paper was decidedly conservative, always bullish, and rewarded writers who regarded William F. Buckley as a thoughtful moderate. Stern, however, had written eloquently on the Enron scandal while at the *Times*, championing workers while simultaneously skewering the likes of Ken Lay and company. And he had done so with less irony in his prose, showing compassion for the countless employees who lost a lifetime of savings to executives and their golden parachutes.

Articles on corporate greed, coupled with Mark's high profile and clear ability to build readership, coincided nicely with the *Journal*'s sudden feelings of guilt over their deification of Lay and other recently fallen robber barons. In a moment of self-expiation, the publisher of the *Journal* called Mark and offered him the plum assignment of reporting on the movers and shakers who the *Journal* highlighted on page one, far left column. If your byline appeared in that coveted space, you had arrived. Mark extracted the promise of total autonomy, but wondered just how many sacred cows he would be able to gore before the publisher forgot his promise.

His lawyer, always the realist, negotiated a million-dollar termination clause into Stern's contract. Thus, each time Mark received the inevitable phone call from the publisher attempting to smooth over the roughing-up of yet another Wall Street deity, Stern would glibly ask, "Did I do a mil's worth of damage yet?" So far, the answer was no, although over the years he had learned how to hone his journalistic dagger into a stiletto and slide it into his victim without a sound.

Even so, his trademark attitude was still visible to his loyal following that saw an undercurrent of dark satire hiding beneath the sometimes seemingly benign commentary. Stern saw himself as a modern-day Mark Twain, who was regarded as a humorist and children's author when, in point of fact, he had been darkly pessimistic about humanity, even in works such as *Tom Sawyer* or *The Adventures of Huckleberry Finn*.

Mark hit the exit key and Space Invaders disappeared from his screen. He was doing a piece on Gregory Randall, whose father, Charles Carson Randall, had been killed the previous month when his Lear 65 slammed into a mountain in the Peruvian Andes. Gregory Randall was the heir apparent, with Randall, Inc. coming in at number thirty-two in the Fortune 500. Randall was no Bill Gates, but he would now command an empire with enough subsidiary holdings to keep thousands of accountants and lawyers busy number-crunching year-round.

Stern opened a file on his computer titled, "Lifestyles of the Rich and Randall." The Randall family had made its initial fortune—"the first of many," Randall, Sr. had often bragged —by developing software that enabled mainframe computers to communicate faster and more efficiently with thousands of smaller PCs connected within a company network. The technology arrived at a time when desktop computers were first proliferating in the mid-eighties. That alone had given Charles Randall a net worth of twenty million dollars. But Randall became a player by buying several start-up tech companies in Silicon Valley and putting them on a par with Hewlett-Packard, Cisco Systems, Yahoo, Symantec, and a dozen others. His new meta-search engine, InfoTech, was beginning to rival Dogpile and Google.

Always savvy, Randall sold most of his dot-com stocks right before they went belly-up, causing Stern to wonder if Randall and Martha Stewart had the same basic approach to maintaining wealth. He also wondered why Martha drew the heat for selling off a few hundred thousand dollars worth of shares while Charles Carson Randall had dumped more than fifteen million dollars worth of dot-com holdings.

Well, some people covered their tracks better than others—he'd learned that during the Enron debacle.

Randall, Inc. had also become a telecommunications giant, owning fifteen newspapers and eleven television stations. This part of his empire was called, according to the FCC documents scattered across Stern's desk, Informed Sources, Inc., a corporate entity looking to expand even farther. Proposals were on the table in six states to acquire four more papers and three additional television stations. This grabbed Mark's attention in and of itself since he had learned that some CEOs thought media-related companies were good investments—people were no more going to stop gobbling up information and entertainment than they were going to stop guzzling Coke—while others sought to control the population's beliefs and spending habits through news and advertising.

Curiously, Randall, Inc. moved into produce in the early eighties. The company owned a hundred orchards in Florida and California, with the Grove Fresh label appearing on juice cartons in supermarket freezer cases in all fifty states. Randall also owned several banana plantations in Honduras, Panama, and Belize, and the scantily-clad woman highlighting the oval sticker on his bananas, "The Yellow Senorita," was starting to rival Juan Valdez in recognizability.

Stern wondered why a man interested in tech stocks and media would be attracted to produce. Simple diversification? Greed? Lust for power? Perhaps. But any agribusiness was subject to fluctuating temperature and rainfall, and CEOs usually stayed within what was called "the corporate aggregate." While a company might have dozens of subsidiary holdings, the typical mindset of the parent company's board was to stay focused on related industries. There were exceptions among the super-giants of the corporate world, of course, such as R. J. Reynolds merging with Nabisco, or Phillip Morris acquiring General Foods and Kraft. To be sure, tobacco and macaroni 'n' cheese made for strange bedfellows, but Charles Carson Randall, as far as Mark Stern could tell, had not been the kind of person to dabble in both bananas and computer chips. Ultimately, Mark knew that's why the *Journal* hired him. He had good instincts. After all, he titled a chapter in his second book with one of his favorite sayings, "Everyone is Naked Under a Double-Breasted Suit." He knew what made people tick and his profiles always succeeded in showing the more human side of a man masked by a well-groomed corporate image.

Mark Stern would do a little digging to find out more about the younger Randall. After all, that was what he did best.

5

Gwen Maulder was up most of the night. Jack did his best to comfort her and the conversations she'd had with friends gave her a bit of solace, but the force of what had happened seemed to have an increasingly greater impact on her. She hadn't even begun to consider what she'd lost in Marci. All she understood for now was that her dearest friend was gone forever—and Gwen refused to believe it was something that "just happened."

She entered the New York Medical Examiner's Office the following morning looking for Dave Dardenoff , whom she regarded as tops in forensics. She had hated to see him leave the FDA but respected his decision considering that more than a few people still wondered why Gwen had made the jump from old-fashioned "doc with a lollipop" to epidemiologist. She found the tall, imposing medical examiner sitting in the lounge, feet propped up on a Formica table next to a soda machine.

"Well, bless my soul, if it isn't Captain Maulder!" Dardenoff proclaimed as he jumped up to greet his visitor.

"Morning, doc," said Gwen, pulling together the energy to smile broadly. "I think we can drop the formality. When the PHS gave me that fourth stripe, I realized that even I didn't have big enough shoulders for it, so I had to settle for those Army eagles instead. You, of all people, should know that rank and intelligence are usually inversely related. But enough about me. What's with you, Dave?"

Dardenoff, attired in green scrubs, returned the smile and shrugged. "I can't complain, Gwen. The city gives me the stiffs and I do my thing. I like to call it 'reading the bones.' I stayed late last night so I could perform your autopsy personally. I figured you had a special interest in this one given your request for . . . well, you know." They were alone in the lounge, but Dardenoff walked to the doorway and looked up and down the corridor.

"Marci was a good friend," Gwen explained, and the smile that had blossomed during their exchanged pleasantries evaporated entirely.

She paused, steeling herself for a series of questions she could not have imagined asking when she'd left Washington two days ago. "Did you find anything unusual?" The question was extremely general, but given the decidedly personal nature of her investigation, it was the only way she could think to begin.

Dardenoff took a deep breath and ran his fingers through brown, wavy hair that was slightly tamped down from being under a surgical cap. "Not really," he said. "Ultimate cause of death was from cardiovascular collapse."

"I'm not interested in 'ultimate.'"

Dardenoff shook his head. "Then I'm afraid I'm not going to be of much help. Your friend only weighed ninety-five pounds. She had the typical mitral valve prolapse seen in many young, thin women. That, by itself, can cause sudden cardiac death once in ten thousand cases, but this just isn't the right picture for prolapse as a cause of death. The convulsions don't fit, either. On the other hand, the prolapse might have made her heart more vulnerable, and the resulting convulsions might have been the straw that broke the camel's back. Your friend also had low potassium and sodium levels, and her stomach contents didn't go beyond some lettuce, carrots, and a few shrimp, all of it coming, I suspect, from a lunchtime salad. And speaking of the stomach, it looks as though she was a worrier. I noted some early ulceration, but nothing advanced. I'm guessing the obvious: high stress and poor diet, on top of an h. pylori infection. Workaholic?"

Gwen sighed and looked vacantly at the far wall as she answered. "That would be an understatement, though she was supremely confident and not given to worrying. Successful lawyer with an aversion to exercise. Virtually no social life." The last statement caused

Gwen to jerk her head back and look quizzically at her former colleague.

"Any— "

"Nah," the medical examiner said with a dismissive wave of his hand. "No semen on the vaginal swab."

"Alcohol or drugs?" Gwen knew that Marci, consummate professional that she was, would not have taken a drink while working, not even at a power lunch with other legal gurus, and she had never known Marci to indulge in any kind of drug other than a little marijuana as an underclassman. She nevertheless had to ask these fundamental questions—not only for her own peace of mind, but for that of the Newmans, with whom she'd be speaking at greater length after the funeral. They would want answers. Marci had been an only child, and Lawrence Newman, a retired lawyer of considerable reputation in mergers and acquisitions, reveled in his daughter's accomplishments.

"Blood and urine were clean," Dardenoff replied. "Compared to other young, attractive women who come through here, your friend was a veritable Girl Scout. Any history of anorexia?"

"None at all. She was a picky eater, but she never starved herself."

Gwen sighed and sat down in a plastic chair, frustrated. Dardenoff eased his large frame into a matching chair across the table. "What did you find?" she asked. "Anything at all?"

"Here," Dardenoff said, taking a tube of unmarked blood from his floppy green shirt pocket and handing it to Gwen. "Spin it down and you'll find the same things I did. There were trace amounts of aspirin and caffeine, plus the usual chemicals one sees in a smoker—nicotine, nitrosamines, cyanide, urethane, acetone, formaldehyde, butane, various metals— "

Gwen held up her hand as she took the vial of blood and slipped it into her purse. "I know the list, Dave, although I didn't know Marci still smoked. I thought she gave it up years ago."

Dardenoff folded hairy arms across his muscular chest. "Goes with the territory, Gwen. Stress, poor diet, heavy workload . . . " He shrugged, as if the conclusion were a no-brainer. "And the cigarettes; I see it every day."

"What did her lungs look like?"

"Pretty clean, actually. She couldn't have been smoking for too long. As for the brain, kidneys—"

"Just send the report to my office in Rockville," Gwen said, holding up her hand a second time. She didn't want to hear any of the gorier details that would conjure up autopsy procedures in her mind. She would indeed look at the full report, but only after a few days had passed and she'd had time to say good-bye to Marci in her own way, and then again, properly, at the funeral.

"You wanted all this on the q.t., right?"

"Yeah," Gwen replied, feeling horribly fatigued. She knew it wasn't because of her lack of sleep. "Send it to my attention and add 'eyes only.' You kept all this out of your office's files, right?"

"I'm afraid that's not so easy to do, at least not completely. I can't pretend the body wasn't here, but I entered your friend's name, time of death, and a few other rudimentary details into the database, and then cross-referenced the computer's basic autopsy template, which would usually list chapter and verse for the whole procedure, with a Jane Doe brought in last week. The file shouldn't raise any eyebrows, but if anyone gets curious—highly doubtful—it'll look like nothing more than a computer glitch. As for any paperwork, I've accidentally on purpose sent the hard copy to Syracuse. Just another minor screw up. Happens all the time in the city that never sleeps. Even dedicated public servants like *moi* get a little careless while pulling an all-nighter."

"Thanks, Dave. I owe you."

"You could always make the IRS lose my Social Security number."

Gwen smiled. First real one of the day. "Dream on. I don't mess with the revenuers."

Gwen stood, shook hands with Dardenoff, and left the lounge. On the way out, she stopped at the ladies' room. She stared at herself in the mirror. She looked dreadful. Did Dave notice? Did Dave ever notice the "little things" about the living? The thought of Dave, and what Dave had spent several hours doing last night, brought the immediacy of Marci's loss back to the forefront. Caring little about her appearance or where she was, Gwen bowed her head and cried.

6

Why did it always rain at funerals? The downpour at a gravesite while mourners held black umbrellas had become a Hollywood stereotype, and yet the stereotype held true for the funeral of Marci Elizabeth Newman. Family and friends, together with at least fifty lawyers and DS&W colleagues, gathered at the cemetery as a rabbi recited words few could hear. Rain slapped their umbrellas and the tarp over Marci's grave. Black-clad figures huddled for shelter under shared umbrellas. Marci's casket was protected by a flimsy green canopy. The Jewish funeral customs observed only enhanced the stark reality—a plain pine box, no flowers, an unadorned mound of earth, and shovels wielded by the mourners themselves. Nothing to prettify death or avoid its finality.

When the service concluded, Gwen felt numb. Nothing she'd done or considered since Marci's death had helped to make any sense of it. She stared at the somber crowd making its way across soggy grass to limousines and town cars. Determined to be the last to leave, she even asked Jack for a moment alone.

"Good-bye, Marci," she said. "I wish we could have seen *Ondine* one last time." She brushed away a single tear from her cheek and knew the good-bye wasn't near enough. "I'll always love you."

She turned and walked into the rain.

■ ■ ■

Back at the Newman home, a three-story red brick mansion on Long Island, Gwen mingled with Marci's extended family—cousins, aunts, and uncles she'd known from the days when she and Marci could get themselves into some healthy mischief—as well as a good many lawyers who had decided to take the afternoon off and imbibe some of the Newmans' excellent scotch. Gwen forced herself to smile, nod, and make small talk, all the while repeating in her mind what had become a mantra since she and Jack had been ushered to the quiet room at Bellevue immediately after Marci's death: This shouldn't have happened.

The one person with whom she was genuinely interested in speaking was Susan Parks, Marci's paralegal. Parks was middle-aged—maybe late forties—and had been responsible, to a large extent, for creating order out of the maelstrom of activity that was Marci's professional life. Gwen knew—because Marci bragged about her endlessly—that Susan herself had frequently put in overtime to find the legal precedents necessary to keep Marci up to speed on the dozens of cases she juggled. No one else saw Marci as regularly as Susan Parks did.

"Had Marci been feeling okay during the last week?" Gwen asked the paralegal as they stood by themselves in a small room toward the back of the house.

"If she was feeling bad," Parks answered solemnly, "I didn't pick up on it. She was her usual energetic self to the very end. I expected to see her stride into her office from the courthouse, ready for another ten rounds."

"Was her color good?" Gwen felt as if she were back in family practice, questioning an attending ER physician about a recently admitted patient.

Parks knit her eyebrows. "Color? Uh . . . yeah. It was fine."

"What was she working on? Anything unusual?"

"I could get in real trouble talking about her cases, Dr. Maulder. I mean, well, I want to help, but . . . " Parks paused, looking out the window at a side garden as rain pelted the panes of glass. Then she seemed to make a decision. "She was helping a Vietnamese woman, one of her *pro bono* cases, the afternoon she collapsed. I guess there's no harm in mentioning something that didn't fall directly under her work for the firm."

Gwen nodded appreciatively. "I know these questions are difficult, and may even seem a bit odd, but as a doctor and Marci's friend, I'm curious. I know she worked hard, but she had youth on her side, and . . . " Now it was Gwen's turn to pause and consider the dreary afternoon for a few moments lest her voice break. "Did you know that Marci smoked?" she continued.

"You know, it's funny you mention that. I never saw her actually holding a cigarette—not ever. But lately she left the building every morning at exactly nine-thirty and eleven, which is when all the smokers head for the sidewalk to light up. There's no smoking in the building—you know, the Mayor made that decision—so most smokers hit the pavement for their breaks. Workers in the building call them "the elevator people" since they're always riding up and down for a nicotine fix. You think smoking had something to do with—" Parks stopped abruptly, clearly not wanting to finish the sentence with the words "her death."

"No, not really. It's just that somebody told me she'd started again recently, and it caught me off guard."

A moment later, Lawrence and Jennifer Newman, both in their late sixties, entered the room and hugged Gwen warmly. Parks excused herself after politely expressing condolences to Marci's parents.

"You're a godsend, Gwen," said Mrs. Newman. "Having Marci's best friend at the hospital when it really counted means more than Lawrence and I can express in words."

"Please." Mr. Newman motioned toward a wingback chair in the small sitting room. "If anyone can make sense of this, you can. What happened?"

Lawrence and Jennifer Newman, sitting on a sofa opposite Gwen, puzzled countenances on their faces, sat waiting for the most important revelation of their lives. They said nothing more as they waited for Gwen to speak.

"As far as I can tell," Gwen began, looking from the oriental carpet to the faces of her friend's parents, "Marci suffered a seizure for reasons nobody has figured out. Usually a seizure in a young person is pretty benign and either doesn't recur or can be controlled with medicine. Fatal seizures are incredibly rare, but unfortunately, Marci was the one-in-a-thousand exception to the rule. I'm sure you know that she put herself under a great deal of stress at work. It turns out that she also had a slight defect in her heart valve. We still don't know why everything went wrong all at once. We may never know."

Gwen was not willing to let her private doubts compound the grief for Marci's parents.

"Is this what the autopsy revealed?" Marci's father asked, leaning forward slightly. "Heart trouble?"

"I'm afraid the medical examiner found nothing conclusive either way. There was a little bit of floppiness to one of her heart valves—what we call valve prolapse—but that's seen in many young, thin women. It almost never causes problems, but this might have been one of those 'almost never' cases. There was naturally some damage to the heart muscle given cardiovascular collapse, but that unfortunately would mask any other preexisting damage."

This was actually untrue in a majority of cases. For someone with Dardenoff 's skill, a tissue sample could speak volumes about the body's cardiac history, but Gwen didn't know what else to tell Lawrence and Jennifer Newman. She certainly wasn't going to confide that she suspected something was very wrong with the entire scenario of Marci's collapse at city court. People don't die of seizures unless there are drugs involved—and she knew there weren't.

Why, then, did Marci's seizure act like it was drug-induced? There was more to this story.

"I was wondering," Gwen said, breaking an awkward silence, "if I could go to Marci's apartment and look for a keepsake. I'd like to have one or two things from our college days. I would naturally ask your permission for anything I chose."

"Of course," said Jennifer as her husband put a comforting arm around her shoulder. "Marci would certainly want you to have something special. We'll give you a key to her apartment before you leave today."

"Thanks. It means a lot to me."

Finding memorabilia was not exactly what Gwen had in mind, though she was sure the apartment would bring back a flood of memories and Gwen would love to have a token of those memories. However, her primary motivation was to search the apartment for something that would help explain the tragedy. She'd been Marci's friend, but she was also Dr. Gwen Maulder, and any epidemiologist worth her salt was part detective. She would go through with a fine-toothed comb.

If something were even slightly amiss in Marci Newman's apartment, Gwen Maulder would find it.

7

Mark Stern read the *New York Times* religiously every day. Without the success of his column in the *Times* and the books it had spawned, he wouldn't be writing his *Journal* column today, complete with stipple portraits by artist Noli Novak. After all was said and done, he enjoyed keeping his fingers on the pulse of New York City, from Broadway to the bag ladies and schizophrenics who slept behind dumpsters. Gotham provided the perfect microcosm for Stern to practice his mojo, part journalistic, part metaphysical.

He paged through the Metro section first every day since the real stories were there—stories that took place on crowded streets with millions of pedestrians going everywhere and nowhere. On page three, he read "Subway Traffic Halted—Woman Proclaims End of World." That was right up his alley. He had always thought that crazy people could teach everyone else a thing or two. Wasn't the normal response to an absurd world to go a little wacko? Of course it was. And who knew? Maybe this woman was on to something. Elijah and Jeremiah must have seemed pretty far out in their day. Stern often wondered how one could distinguish prophecy from lunacy.

The brief half-column story explained that a Brooklyn woman started to scream, alarming a carload of commuters at 8:07 a.m. the previous morning. Two men finally managed to restrain her before the train pulled into the next station where the Transit Authority Police waited to remove the maniacal "prophet." She wailed that Jesus was coming back any day now. She'd seen the Great Beast from Revelation, seen the Four Horsemen of the Apocalypse, seen the great Harlot corrupting the powerful leaders of the world. With a bloodstream full of righteous adrenaline, she had attacked a woman, shaking her hard enough to cause a mild concussion when the woman's skull bounced off the thick glass window of the subway car.

Stern turned next to the obituary section, a morbid habit he'd developed since turning forty. With a slight grin, he'd dismissed the black balloons he'd received from friends along with birthday cards declaring that his life was over, but the stark truth was that Mark Stern, kid in residence at the *Wall Street Journal*, did not like the idea of growing older. He had way too much to do with his life—there were the tamarin and the spider monkey, the rainforest trip he still hadn't made, the dozens of bands he hadn't seen live yet, and maybe even the so-far-elusive woman to share his soul with.

There. Page five, column four. The brief obit caught his attention immediately. Marci Newman, prominent lawyer and daughter of Lawrence and Jennifer Newman, had collapsed in city court two days earlier and died at Bellevue. He remembered Marci vividly as Gwen McBean's roommate. Something that reminded him of Gwen just moments after thinking about "soulmates" had to have some cosmic significance. Gwen was the flame Mark had never quite given up on, even after her marriage to Jack Maulder. She must be hurting badly right now. He remembered how close Gwen and Marci had remained even while they pursued stellar careers.

Mark looked wistfully out of his window. Gwen. He could still measure the time between thinking about her in hours. And each time, he'd never been anything less than mystified over how Gwen had so completely subtracted herself from his life. Gwen had Jack, the FDA, and no place in her life for a man she once must have loved.

Gwen was in town, for she would have undoubtedly come up from D.C. to attend Marci's funeral. "I know you're out there somewhere," he mumbled, echoing a line from an old Moody Blues song.

He moved his gaze to the bookshelves opposite his desk and located an edition of Wordsworth's poetry. He got up, walked across his office, and picked up the book, carefully opening the faded, embossed cover.

Gwen knew that Mark liked to read poetry from old editions since he believed slightly yellowed pages had more character than pristine white stock purchased at Barnes and Noble. He looked at the inscription and smiled: "To Don Quixote. All my love—Gwen." Yes, they did love each other once. Even if only one of them remembered it now.

At least she'd understood who he was. "Don Quixote?" Yeah, that was as good a description as any. Gwen was sympathetic to Mark's mission on behalf of the underdog as evidenced by her Herculean effort to make a go of her father's practice, but Mark's personal style was simply too anachronistic for the more practical and scientific Dr. McBean. "Grow up and join the rest of us," Gwen had told him. "You might actually enjoy the experience."

"Bingo, Gwen," he uttered, placing the volume back on the shelf.

For a brief moment, he considered trying to find her and meet her for a drink. He could locate anyone he wanted, even in a city the size of the Big Apple, but tracing her through the Newmans would be inappropriate at such a time. There were other ways to do it, but the timing was a mistake. Gwen would be shattered by losing Marci. And then there was her husband to consider. While Jack Maulder wasn't the jealous type, he was a former Secret Service agent and too tightly wound for Stern's liking. Federal cops always reminded him of Big Brother.

"Though nothing can bring back the splendor in the grass, we will grieve not," Stern said, philosophically quoting a snippet of Wordsworth.

Let it go. How many times had he told himself that?

He needed to get back to work. The reporter turned back to his computer screen and to his examination of Gregory Randall's dynasty. Why in the world, he wondered, had Randall spent the last week globe-trotting? Wasn't he officially in mourning for his father?

Yeah, right. More than likely, Randall had found himself a pretty, young woman—Asian, no doubt—in some exotic location. Mark wondered if the younger Randall gave the elder a moment's thought, while some nubile lovely performed acts on him no Western woman knew.

■ ■ ■

Gwen did not expect to find what looked like a tornado debris field in Marci's Fifth Avenue apartment. Marci was a neat freak, maybe even a tad bit obsessive-compulsive. Her precision of thought was matched by a precision in most everything she did. She was an avid reader, but leaving an open book on the sofa? No, that wasn't Marci Newman. A place for everything, and everything in its place; now that was Marci.

The apartment Gwen saw as she walked through the front door had not been cleaned for weeks. Books, legal briefs, empty Diet Coke cans, and clothes were everywhere. Black, rotten bananas sat on the kitchen counter next to an open jar of lowfat peanut butter, which Marci probably used as energy food when she didn't have time to eat a proper meal—and Gwen was starting to wonder exactly how many proper meals Marci had eaten recently, if any.

An open pack of Virginia Slims Light was lying on the glass end table by the couch in the living room. Gwen considered Marci's choice of brand to be morbidly appropriate given her ninety-five-pound weight. At least ten cigarette butts were visible in a mound of ashes.

Gwen scoped out the rest of the apartment, but the same domestic litter was everywhere—clothes, partially-eaten food, books, and ashtrays. She next examined Marci's desk. The little ivory seagull Marci got at the shore and loved so much sat next to her PC, where Gwen imagined she enjoyed seeing it so much of the time. When Gwen touched the mouse, the screen came to light, the cursor still blinking. She sat down in front of the screen, put her purse on the floor, and tapped a few keys. Nothing. The entire system was password protected.

"Piece of cake," Gwen said to the empty apartment. First, she tried Marci's birthday, her name, and her parents' names, all without success. Absentmindedly (but admitting to a little nudge from her ego), she typed "Gwen"—and Marci's personalized desktop floated onto the screen. Gwen's pleasure at guessing the password was muted by the realization that she would probably never again be blessed with such a close friend. A picture of the dunes at Montauk covered the screen, a background to the many scattered icons. Gwen went straight to the directory and looked at the list of documents.

There were hundreds, but she didn't have time to inspect so many files or even print them out for later inspection. Highlighting the first line, she pressed the "arrow down" key and scrolled through the document titles, looking for something that would raise the proverbial red flag. Most of the files were related to her cases—Aaron v. Thompson, Brown v. Altman, and so on—and Gwen didn't bother to open a single one.

Haydn104—now that was a file she would open.

Marci had loved all the symphonies of Josef Haydn and regarded them as musical "uppers" in college, always playing them when she had to pull an all-nighter to write a paper due the following day.

Gwen clicked on the file, only to be rewarded with a password prompt. Of all the files for Marci to lock, why this one? She tried a variety of passwords but each attempt generated, "password incorrect, enter password." Displayed ad infinitum. She saved the file to CD. She would have Jack, a specialist extraordinaire in the matter of computers and the cyberworld, take a look at the file to see if he could find a way inside.

Marci's "Personal" e-mail folder was filled with letters from Gwen and memos from Susan Parks. Nothing unusual in the least.

Turning off the laptop, Gwen put the CD in her purse and headed for the front door. Her hand was already on the knob when she turned around and looked at her friend's apartment for the last time. She walked back and picked up the ivory seagull. So many of Marci's happy times had been spent at the ocean side, watching the waves roll onto the shore, sometimes for hours at a time.

Gwen decided this would be her keepsake. She took the seagull and deposited it in her purse along with the copied CD. She needed to rendezvous with Jack at the hotel and then get to the airport. It was time to go home.

PART II

FALL 1977

8

The Cottage Club was ensconced in an antebellum mansion on Prospect Street, a tree-lined lane that served as the address for all of Princeton's eating clubs. Admission to Cottage was highly selective; the athletically-inclined scholar needed the right family background, membership on a suitable sports team, and grades respectable enough so as not to leave the club financially strapped after February's typical flunk-out season. Cottage men were known for entering in coats and ties, out-drinking the lower life forms in other clubs, and never waking up in their own detritus.

Henry Brome was the quintessential jock—golf, crew, hockey, soccer, and rugby—and he spent far more time in Cottage's taproom playing poker than he did taking notes in class. Such was his stature, his strength, wit, and ruthlessness, that he was invariably surrounded by a group of fawning vassals known as Broome's Brigade.

Like most undergrads headed for the family business, Henry chose one of the soft majors—in his case, history. His brushes with academic censure were usually swept under the rug following a phone call from the Alumni Office to an understanding dean. Princeton was in the habit of getting a new building from the Broome family, owners of the small Hawaiian island of Lanai, once every generation. Those entrusted with the growth of the university's endowment had no intention of strangling that golden goose.

Unbeknownst to the university's chancellors, said goose was in extremis, since the family's sugarcane and pineapple crops had failed four years in a row. The stock portfolio of Henry's father, Henry Bramwell Broome III, was good for little more than lining the cage of the family's macaw, thanks to his habit of swimming around in gin and tonic from noon to eight o'clock each evening. While attempting to keep up appearances, the Broomes had become convinced that any hope of rebuilding their small Pacific empire lay in Henry's following the path trodden by his ancestors since Henry Broome, family progenitor, had taken his theology degree at Princeton and shipped out as a missionary to convert the heathens of Hawaii. In those days, missionaries went to do good . . . and usually ended up doing quite well.

Henry IV's parents had less lofty hopes. Nevertheless, they prayed that their son, who favored quite a different kind of missionary position, would somehow acquire the skills to rehabilitate the island, the crops, the portfolio, and, most importantly, the Broome family name. Henry III, though a consummate lush, still had a few markers he could call in after his son graduated. He planned to place Henry with any one of a dozen companies where his heir could hone his entrepreneurial skills, be ushered into the boardroom in record time, and parlay the Broomes' declining reputation back into solvency with an infusion of capital. Hopefully, their son would not only shore up the dwindling portfolio, but also return to run the plantation full-time. First, however, it would be necessary for Henry to run the corporate gauntlet in order to acquire experience.

Though the elder Broome placed an awesome responsibility on his son's shoulders, Henry had an uncanny way of making things happen. From earliest childhood, he had been a leader, an organizer among his cadre, and heaven help the boy—or occasional girl—who didn't fall in line with Henry's plans for a game of football, a party, or a day-trip to Maui. Loud and strong, he was persuasive to an extreme, a one-man wrecking crew if the situation warranted.

By age sixteen, Henry supervised virtually all the plantation's workers during the summer, earning a reputation as a taskmaster among people four times his age. The Asian workers would glumly chant, "Yes, Mr. Henry" or "No, Mr. Henry" as they chopped, bundled, and loaded sugarcane onto flatbeds destined for the docks at Kaumalapau on the island's southern coast. He'd pull off the family's plan to stay in the social register all by himself if necessary.

The senior, class of '78, therefore felt entirely justified in loudly regaling his Cottage coterie with his latest accomplishments. He'd led Princeton's soccer team to a decisive victory over Brown earlier in the afternoon, three of the four goals attributable to Henry. Soccer was a rough game, and Henry played to win.

Always.

The slight-framed Bruce Merewether was a prime example. Bruce was a Classics major and captain of the men's equestrian team. While riding horses barely met Cottage entrance requirements, the presence of Bruce's grandfather on Cottage's Board of Governors rendered the issue moot. Bruce made it clear—foolishly, on this particular evening—that people of Henry's ilk lacked the aptitude to excel in their studies.

More precisely, Bruce had muttered that, "Jocks like Henry Broome were placed on Earth to make Neanderthal Man seem intelligent by comparison." Having injected this acerbic gem into the pub's pulse of activity just loudly enough for Henry and his comrades to hear, he resumed holding forth on Chaucer's rhyming couplets.

Henry could hold six beers and still walk a straight line for the campus police, which he'd had to do on more than one occasion. He had chugged ten thus far tonight, and his not-so-considered opinion was that Bruce's remark had slighted the honor of all true Princeton athletes, past and present. "At least I don't spend my time reading a lot of queer poetry," he stated, strutting over to Merewether and his two companions.

Bruce pushed his chair back with a screech and stared blankly up at the muscular figure of Henry, who, at six-foot-four, towered above a literary discussion that dwindled with each passing second. "I don't believe you were invited to join our group," Bruce said confidently. "And to assume that Chaucer's poetry is more queer than a group of grown men in shorts dancing around a spotted ball, giving each other love taps on the ass . . . " Bruce concluded the rebuttal with a mocking grin.

Henry smiled, leaned over, and clapped Bruce Merewether on the shoulder as if the two young men were old friends, a couple of buds having a few brewskies. His ruddy complexion and dirty blond hair were just inches away from Merewether's face. "Aren't we Cottage men all one group, one family?" he asked rhetorically, his eyes gleaming with mock goodwill.

"A bit of a generalization," answered Bruce. "Some people here are part of the group, as you put it, because their parents cut a few dozen extra checks every year and grease the palms of the right administrators and athletic directors. Besides, ailing Hawaiian pineapple entrepreneurs really don't have much in common with the rest of us, wouldn't you agree?"

The noisy conversation in the bar abated quickly as several dozen people directed their attention to the imposing Mr. Broome and his seated rival. The sharp crack of a pool cue breaking freshly racked balls sounded in the corner and then faded as silence claimed lease on the pub for several tense seconds.

"I think you owe the true gentlemen-athletes of this university an apology," Henry said emphatically, grabbing the front of Bruce's white polo shirt and lifting him from the chair. "The last time you competed in anything, all you succeeded in doing was tiring your horse."

"You're just a dumb-ass jock," Bruce asserted smugly. "You're an insult to Cottage. You may get away with some sneaky elbow punches on the soccer field when the refs aren't looking, but you're neither a gentleman nor a scholar."

"Maybe you're right, Mr. Merewether. In fact, maybe I'm just a janitor. I must be, because I just realized that it's time to take out the trash."

Henry lifted Merewether over his head and headed for the front door, already propped open by a fawning member of Broome's Brigade.

Angling sideways, Henry carried his load into the crisp, blue New Jersey evening and walked down the alley on his left.

"Put me down, Broome!" Merewether demanded. "One more step and the honor committee is going to find out who really wrote your junior essay."

"You have Mommy and Daddy do whatever they like," Henry

said, heaving Merewether's body into a corroded green dumpster with a single thrust of his powerful arms. "And tell them Henry Broome sends his warm regards."

Broome's Brigade burst into applause and cheers.

Henry bowed ceremoniously. "*Dei sub numine viget*!" he bellowed, reciting the school motto, Under God's name she flourishes. "Cottage rules!"

"Cottage rules!" the students echoed.

Henry walked casually toward the bar's entrance, ready to put away a few more beers, but first he stopped and faced the dumpster.

"Didn't think I knew Latin, did ya?" he called to the now invisible Merewether.

Laughter followed the indomitable Henry Broome back into Cottage's leather-lined lair.

■ ■ ■

Eddie Karn was the lone bystander on the sidewalk that night. Karn was on his way back to the library to put in a last hour before closing. He stood there, transfixed at the sight of Broome's disregard for another's humanity. Though there was nothing he could do, he felt compelled to bear witness. Karn didn't hang around Cottage types and wasn't impressed by demonstrations of power. Or by Henry Broome, for that matter. He would remember the night Bruce Merewether got dumpsterized for a long time.

A very long time.

9

Jamie Robinson, hunched over the low handlebars of his bright red Schwinn ten-speed, cut through the chilly air and fallen leaves as he rode to Princeton's Biochemistry Department, a little nub of architecture tacked onto the biology building. To enter, one had to walk past dinosaur bones and mounted animal specimens discovered by renowned biologists into a realm where test tubes and DNA were rapidly threatening to eclipse the rudimentary practices of the various biological disciplines. The biochemistry department was starting to realize that molecular biology was the wave of the future.

At one end of the campus, the old-line biochemists fiercely defended their turf and methodology in the chemistry building. At this end of the campus, however, amazing things were happening, and quickly. Destined to become world-class academics, young professors like Raju Kucherlapati and Arnie Levine were busy unlocking the secrets of how genes really worked.

Jamie couldn't wait to get to the lab each morning, realizing that he was in the middle of a paradigm shift in scientific thinking. He couldn't take his mind off the pace at which molecular biology was moving, especially last month's landmark discovery by Montagu and Schell. Jamie dismounted and wheeled the Schwinn's slim tires into the metal bars of the bike rack. He was probably the only cyclist on campus who wore a protective plastic helmet, the strap of which he now looped around the handlebars in his morning ritual while simultaneously glancing down at his shirt to verify that all seven of his colored ink pens were still neatly lined up in his pocket protector.

His roommate found Jamie's habit of constantly checking his

shirt pockets annoying in the extreme, but the biochemistry major needed to sketch molecules in his black marbleized notebook every day, and he enjoyed color-coding the various organic groups he studied. Drawing carbon rings, proteins, nucleic acids, alkaloids, terpenoids, and phenolics in black and white? Unthinkable.

Jamie was the first member of his family to go to college, having matriculated to Princeton from a family of steel workers in Scranton, Pennsylvania. Robinsons generally worked hard, stuck close to their kin, and died early. But Jamie had demonstrated an intellectual aptitude since kindergarten that amazed his parents and teachers alike. "His superior intelligence is a gift from God," Father Ignatius had told Mr. and Mrs. Robinson when their son was in third grade, "and you are obligated to cherish that gift and develop it." From then on, Jesuits filled Jamie's head with as much knowledge as they thought the boy could absorb while his friends were tackling one another at recess.

The good priests of the Society of Jesus weren't disappointed. Jamie's appetite for learning was insatiable.

Predictably, Jamie's aspirations extended beyond the foundry and the slag heap. He was college bound, and despite becoming class valedictorian, he declared his independence at the last minute, turning down a full scholarship to Notre Dame in favor of a work-study program at Princeton. Recognized as the prodigy that he was, he managed to get the best of both worlds. His campus job was glassware cleaner in Professor Kucherlapati's lab.

"Morning, Raju," Jamie said, beaming upon entering his mentor's office on the second floor of the building, nicknamed the Mobio. In the matter of academic protocol, Kucherlapati cut his students considerable slack owing to the fact that his name, following the title "professor," had more syllables than most people could comfortably swallow. The microbiologist was a short man with a dark complexion, black hair, and unusually large, Ghandi-like probing eyes. Humming a wordless acknowledgment as he looked up from a stack of graduate term papers, he said with a slight, yet comforting, smile, "What have you got to show me this morning . . . as if I don't already know?"

Jamie put a sheaf of papers on the desk.

Kucherlapati inspected them briefly, sighed in frustration, and leaned back in his leather chair, hands clasped behind his head.

"Genomics. It's an interesting theoretical approach, blindly analyzing the entire genome. Personally, I just don't believe it will amount to anything until we understand the basic mechanisms of how DNA works and how proteins are made. The future, Mr. Robinson, is in somatic cell hybridization. Now we can move human genes from one cell to another. Devastating human illnesses, like Tay-Sachs and sickle cell anemia are caused by a defect in a single gene. I am arrogant enough to believe that my students will contribute to the cutting-edge research that will one day control, and maybe even eradicate, these diseases."

Jamie knew that genes were just instructions coded in the four-letter alphabet of DNA that enabled the human body to synthesize all of the proteins necessary for life. As Kucherlapati hinted, some diseases had been linked to defective instructions in that DNA and early attempts at therapy involved manufacturing and administering the gene product at enormous expense. Kucherlapati imagined the day in which missing or defective genes would simply be implanted.

His students pictured him walking onto the stage in Stockholm to accept his Nobel Prize.

Jamie had to admit that somatic cell hybridization was interesting work, and to study with Kucherlapati was an opportunity that any Biochemistry major with the correctly folded proteins in his cerebral cortex would not pass up. The brainiac from Scranton had some other ideas. Kucherlapati might be out to save the few with rare genetic disorders. Jamie was out to feed the world.

Jamie had produced some astounding results in his very own dorm room, in fact. His roommate Henry wasn't fond of the many plants growing under high-intensity lamps, but then Henry generally ran a blood alcohol level that would fell a mere mortal, so things balanced out. Jamie conducted his research well into the night while Henry either slept off the booze or shacked up with some bimbo cheerleader behind the screen that the incorrigible Mr. Broome unfolded so he could have token privacy.

Jamie had all the folding and unfolding he could handle.

10

Henry returned to his dorm in 1901 Hall around eleven, pleasantly anesthetized but not drunk. The university was fond of Princetonian neologisms; hence, everyone on campus referred to the building as "Oughty-one."

Henry walked into the dorm room, plopped his two-hundred-twenty-pound frame onto his bed, back against the wall, and studied his roommate.

"What the hell are you doing now?" he asked Jamie Robinson.

It seemed to Henry that every time he entered the room, there were more plants growing under the long banks of lights hanging from every available source of support: bookshelves, the ceiling, a towel rack, and Jamie's bed frame. "I feel like I'm living in the freakin' Amazon." Henry punctuated his comment with an exceedingly long belch that introduced the odors of Cottage Club into the room.

Jamie laughed without looking up from his Apple II computer.

Henry still couldn't believe that Jamie spent all of his money—literally all of it; he had nothing left for new clothes, trips home, or meals out—on a machine.

"What the bloody hell are you growing, anyway? A little grass maybe?"

"Grass?"

"Weed, kiddo. Marijuana, Mary Jane, reefer."

"Hardly. I'm growing a variety of peas and beans, with a few herbs on the side."

Henry laughed at his geeky roommate. "Lemme guess. You're

gonna make us a kick-ass salad for when we get the munchies."

Even though Jamie was forever entering data into his stupid computer, Henry sort of liked the skinny nerd. Despite his squeaky-clean image, Jamie was not above doing much of Henry's classwork. The kid was a goddamned Einstein when it came to calculus, plus he didn't seem to mind young coeds giggling and moaning on the other side of the room when Henry's libido kicked into overdrive, which was at least three times a week. Hell, Jamie was so absorbed in becoming the Emperor of Agriculture that Henry wasn't sure if the kid even noticed the sweet young things that the leader of Broome's Brigade brought up to the room and bedded behind the constantly folding and unfolding screen.

"What did you say?" asked Jamie.

"Geez," sighed Henry, rolling his eyes. "Do you live on Jupiter? I asked if you were going to make some salad with all this shit you're growing."

Jamie swiveled around in his chair and faced Henry Broome squarely, his demeanor serious. "When man progressed beyond the hunter-gatherer stage approximately thirteen thousand years ago, he grew cultivated cereal grasses, mostly barley and wheat, in the fertile crescent. He always saved the biggest seeds from the stalks for both eating and planting. The result? The new plants also had bigger seeds. Without realizing it, man had produced the first genetically modified foods in history. This worked with livestock as well. Only the healthiest goats and sheep, for example, were chosen for breeding."

Henry could barely tolerate lectures in lecture halls. Getting one in his room was like swallowing a handful of sleeping pills. His head fell onto his right shoulder, his eyes barely open.

"In the nineteenth century, a monk named Gregor Mendel performed some extraordinary experiments with pea plants," Jamie continued while Henry tried his best not to listen. "Long story short: a plant or animal inherits a gene from each parent for any given trait. If the two genes—alleles, to be specific—are different, then the dominant allele is fully expressed in the new organism's appearance. The other remains recessive but may assert itself in future generations. It's called Mendel's Law of Segregation."

Henry was curled up and sound asleep within minutes.

■ ■ ■

Jamie smiled and turned back to face his Apple. The machine had a regular typewriter keyboard embedded in an off-white plastic shell, with a monitor housed in the same plastic casing sitting on top of the flat surface behind the keyboard. Jamie ditched his Apple I, little more than a motherboard hooked up to a keyboard and television screen, as soon as the newer version went on the market because the Apple II had eight expansion slots. A kid who tinkered with electronics instead of playing catch with Dad back in Scranton, Jamie added a few special devices to the computer, one being a piece of hardware that Apple inventor Steve Wozniak had surely not envisioned for the average user. Jamie constructed an interface to connect a thumbprint recognition pad to one of the expansion slots. A regular password didn't give Jamie enough peace of mind. His research would one day knock the sandals off Kucherlapati's small feet. Folding protein chains were all well and good, but the real action was at the atomic and molecular levels. For security, therefore, Jamie used his jury-rigged thumbprint recognition system in addition to always locking the machine with a key that he kept on a chain around his neck.

Jamie glanced at a row of plants directly to the right of his desk. Casually, he picked a couple of leaves from the nearest stem, popped them in his mouth, and chewed. Henry hadn't been far off the mark. Jamie liked to nibble a little salad fresh from his narrow gardens from time to time.

He continued to transfer data from his notebooks to the green computer screen. It was two in the morning when he shut down the box and locked it after saving new info to a floppy drive, another of Jamie's innovative uses of the expansion ports. He would grab a few hours of sleep, go to a couple of rudimentary classes the next day, and then return to his real love—the research that Kucherlapati thought so frivolous.

11

Henry could no more stifle his curiosity than he could stop screwing coeds or inflicting punishment on the soccer field. He had to be in the loop, and it irked him that Jamie Robinson worked late into the night seven days a week, doodling cryptic pictures in his notebook or tapping computer keys and munching on leaves like a rabbit. The kid even wore a lab coat, like he was some kind of Jonas Salk cooking up a vaccine to save the world, and he was apparently unaware that Henry was not always asleep after slouching on his bed. What bothered Henry the most was that Jamie destroyed his notebooks after transferring their squiggles and chemical formulas to his computer. What kind of secrets did Jamie harbor in that box?

He didn't know a lot about the Apple, but he was savvy enough to know that whatever Jamie was storing in its guts might be important. In Jamie's absence, Henry tried several times to break into it. He'd attempted to unlock the computer with several small keys and had even pressed his thumb onto the recognition pad, thinking it was some kind of "open sesame" device. None of this worked.

The info on the machine might turn out to be crap, but if Jamie thought it was important enough to Fort Knox, then Henry needed to know about it. The most important thing he had learned from his father, besides how to make a perfect martini, was that information was more valuable than money, not that the latter should be neglected.

In fact, if used correctly, information could lead straight to the bank vault. But how could he break into the damned computer?

Sadly, he couldn't simply crack the thing open. Henry didn't know much about computers, but he did know that it would be useless if he smashed it.

He'd have to use a subtler form of entry—ones named Carol and Heather, two sophomores from Ryder College down the road. They had come by the Cottage Club party last Saturday night and Henry, being his social self, naturally befriended them. He'd know what was stored on the computer soon enough.

■ ■ ■

At ten o'clock, Jamie Robinson was doing what he did every night: meticulously recording data about the successes and failures of various mutations he attempted. One had been particularly successful. The mutation was certainly interesting, but the plant was virtually the same.

Well, almost the same.

The mutation seemed to have rather unusual properties discovered through trial and error in Kucherlapati's lab. Through selective breeding, Jamie was able to amplify the mutation, although the native gene sometimes asserted itself and caused the original version of the molecule to reappear.

Intriguing. Jamie bypassed the breeding process entirely and isolated the mutation on a DNA segment. Then he used one of Kucherlapati's prize-winning techniques for inserting it into the natural DNA of the plants. Now the mutation replicated itself every time.

Jamie was convinced that his work had potential applications in the real world and was far too sensitive to show anyone, at least for the time being. Not even Kucherlapati. Like any good, budding scientist, Jamie would duplicate the results and then expand his testing. If the experiments continued to yield consistent results, there were people who would pay a great deal of money for Jamie's discovery.

Kucherlapati could have his Nobel Prize. Jamie wanted to cash in and give his blue-collar parents a beautiful home as a retirement present.

■ ■ ■

Henry was his usual ebullient self as he squired Carol and Heather into his Oughty-one digs. Carol was a tall blonde with sparkling blue eyes; Heather was brunette, five-foot-five, with deep brown eyes and a tan worthy of a *Sports Illustrated* model. Both girls wore haltertops that barely contained their assets and displayed them to maximum advantage. In the fifteen minutes they had already spent talking with Henry, they had imparted only the information that Carol was majoring in physical education and Heather planned to go to hotel management school.

When it came to women, Henry was a devotee of décolletage and had minimal appetite for intellect. The two girls wanted nothing more than an invitation to Cottage for House Party Weekend. Henry promised them that if they could pass the "Jamie test," they were in.

"It's time to take a night off, Mr. Robinson," declared Henry in an insistent tone of voice as he entered their room. "If I see you screwing around with those plants for one more minute, I shall thrash you to within an inch of your life." Henry feigned drawing an invisible rapier from his belt and lunged forward, left arm poised above his head for balance, right arm straight and perpendicular to his body, as if ready to skewer his roommate. Henry was also a member of the fencing team.

"Come, come," he said. "Let our mirthful endeavors begin."

Carol and Heather giggled . . . and then giggled again.

"Actually, Henry," confessed Jamie with a forced smile, "I'm at the critical phase of seeing if I can crossbreed two kinds of pea pl—"

"Wonderful!" shouted Henry. "I'm glad you're in the mood."

Henry grabbed Jamie's wrist and yanked him from his chair.

"But I can't—"

"Yes, I know!" interrupted Henry. "You can't say no! It's party time! Girls?"

Heather reached into one of the bags she and Carol carried up to the room and produced two bottles of vodka and one of tequila.

"What's your pleasure, sweetie?" she asked Jamie. "Or would you like me to mix them together with some fruit juice?" Heather began pouring some Hawaiian Punch over crushed ice in a tall glass, adding equal amounts of the two clear liquors. "Just think of me as your slave for the night, okay?"

"My slave?" said Jamie, swallowing nervously.

"You talk too much, Jamie," Henry remarked good-naturedly. "Shut up and drink."

"Well, uh, I dunno. Maybe I could—"

Heather interrupted Jamie's stuttering by bringing the tall, cold glass to his lips and placing a straw in his mouth.

"That's pretty good," Jamie admitted. "But I don't taste any alcohol."

"That's the idea!" said Heather.

"I think we just found a party animal!" squealed Carol, drinking straight from the tequila bottle while handing the second fifth of vodka to Henry.

"Be careful, Heather," cautioned Henry. "Beneath that lab coat beats the heart of a genuine Don Juan."

■ ■ ■

Jamie blushed. He took a long pull on his drink. "I guess a little break wouldn't hurt anything," he said, eyeing Heather's long, tanned legs.

Looking up into the girl's face, his blush grew deeper.

"You can not only look, sugar—you can actually touch if you want to." Heather pushed Jamie backward gently until he fell clumsily into his chair. She then proceeded to sit on his lap, stroking his hair and face, occasionally scratching his skin with long, manicured fingernails. Jamie felt things he barely imagined before.

Henry and Carol had meanwhile made a serious dent in the contents of the vodka and tequila bottles respectively and were comfortably entangled on the athlete's bed, lips pressed together, legs locked. Henry hadn't bothered to unfold his privacy screen.

Heather stood up, stepped over to Jamie's bed, and curled her index finger coquettishly, coaxing the light-headed Jamie to her side. She refreshed Jamie's drink, poured one for herself, and then slipped her arm around his waist, drawing him tightly against her body. Jamie was practically airborne. No woman had ever come on to him like this before.

For the next fifteen minutes, the room was absent of all speech.

A far older, universal language was spoken as sheets and blankets were pushed into disarray by eager arms and legs.

Jamie didn't know any women like this in Scranton. Tonight, all of his experiments would be on a decidedly different life-form.

■ ■ ■

Henry sat up in bed and looked around. The only lights in the dorm room emanated from the eerie glow above Jamie's plants. He climbed carefully over Carol's limp body and crossed the room to inspect Heather and Jamie.

Perfect. All unconscious, thanks to the Quaaludes he ground up and put into the liquor earlier that afternoon. His little bacchanal had finally wound down, and the two girls slumbered on either side of Jamie like babes after their favorite bedtime stories. Since Henry's vodka bottle contained only water, he was as fresh as a new day.

Henry Broome smiled like a man about to open a bank vault. He slipped the chain with the computer key over Jamie's head, unlocked the computer, and hit the "ON" button. The Apple's motor hummed as the monitor screen glowed bright green. The words next to the cursor requested a password. Henry laughed and typed in "d23&if5#al@2r." He'd glanced over Jamie's shoulders a dozen times during the semester, pretending to do other things when his roommate was booting the computer, but he knew that a password alone wouldn't unlock any files. He studied Jamie for weeks before he finally knew what he needed to know—the drill for making the machine surrender its knowledge.

He lifted the strawlike body of his roommate—the kid couldn't have weighed more than 110 pounds—and dropped him on the desk chair facing the Apple. He then placed Jamie's right thumb firmly against the recognition pad until the computer screen flickered twice and displayed what appeared to be a directory. Henry replaced Jamie next to Heather and sat down, inspecting the column of files.

"Jesus Lord Almighty," Henry said lowly, shaking his head. "What the hell is all this crap?"

Having observed Jamie's fingers carefully while the geek nightly tapped the keyboard like a mini-piano, Henry knew which keys would scroll through the files. The list was extremely long and the scientific names would normally have put Henry to sleep faster than a keg of beer. The first few lines read:

Adenosine
Agrobacterium Tumefaciens
Alpha Helix
Arganine
Beta sheets
Carbon Rings
Chiral Compounds
Climatology
Cyclic Hydrocarbons
Cysteine
Ethylpropane
Glutamic Acid
Isomers

Farther down, one file in particular caught Henry's attention. It said, "Experiments, spring thru fall, 1977."

Henry was happy to see familiar words. Though he was not well-versed in science, he immediately recognized the names of two molecules listed in the file that were, in fact, household words.

"Interesting," he said. "Very interesting. I think the little weasel is actually on to something here."

There was no need to copy the information by hand. Jamie had hooked the computer to a daisy wheel printer. It was a noisy contraption—it spit out words like a typewriter on speed—but it wouldn't wake his companions thanks to the booze and the 'ludes. They would remain in the drug- and alcohol-induced black hole until the following morning, when they would awaken feeling like they'd been run over by a Peterbilt.

Despite his considerable knowledge of potent spirits and pharmaceuticals, however, even Henry Broome sometimes miscalculated where the threshold of consciousness lay.

"Hey, wuss goin' on?" asked Carol, trying to lift herself on wobbly elbows. "What ya typin' on that . . . that . . . con . . . smuter?"

No response was necessary, as Carol quickly fell back onto the bed in a stupor.

Having been spooked for a second, Henry relaxed. "Now that's just a pity," Henry declared to himself. "A real pity. All you had to do was stay asleep and you would have lived out your little cheerleader life in suburban bliss."

He looked back at the computer as it printed out the file and several others that Henry thought might be related. Though often underestimated by the likes of Bruce Merewether, Henry Broome was quite thorough.

■ ■ ■

Jamie opened a bleary, bloodshot eye—the other felt as if it were glued shut—and surveyed his room. Trash littered the floor—empty liquor bottles, textbooks, crumpled chip bags, and a half-dozen foil condom wrappers, all opened.

"Gotta clean up this place," Jamie mumbled, sitting up.

That was when the first wave of nausea hit. In an attempt to stagger to the communal bathroom four rooms down, he got as far as the hallway before he threw up on the tile floor.

Henry emerged from the bathroom as Jamie straightened up, weak and pale.

"Steady there, little buddy," said Henry, sounding like the Skipper addressing Gilligan. "You and Heather had a pretty wild time last night. You have to kind of ease into the day. Come on back to the room and let ol' Henry fix you up."

"Ol' Henry" couldn't have been more in the pink—freshly shaved, towel wrapped around his neck, hair combed, and whistling Oklahoma's "Oh, What a Beautiful Morning." Jamie's head throbbed with each cheerful note passing through Henry's oval-shaped lips.

Heather and Carol were starting to rouse, their smudged make-up giving them the appearance of two very hungover raccoons.

"Good morning everyone," proclaimed Henry, beaming. "Time for Dr. Broome's wake-up special, complete with a little hair of the dog."

"Hair of the what?" asked Jamie.

"The dog that bit ya, sonny boy Jim. Sit down until you get your sea legs, pal."

■ ■ ■

Jamie stumbled to his bed and sat next to the disheveled Heather while Henry removed the top from a blender and poured in tomato juice, two raw eggs, powdered ginseng, and vodka from a two-ounce airline bottle. The appliance's buzzing sound caused Heather and Jamie to flinch and they covered their ears.

"Jesus," Heather complained. "Sounds like a fuckin' swarm of bees."

Henry noted with interest that Carol, while a little haggard-looking, was perking up faster than the others. That little episode last night while he was at the computer might very well be sitting in her pretty little head waiting to be revealed at the least propitious time.

"Okay, everyone," Henry said. "Drink ye of this potion and the cobwebs in your brains will be blown away like a piece of trash in the hands of a nor'easter."

Fifteen minutes later, Henry's party companions were standing and stretching. "Quite a party we had last night, eh?" Henry said, elbowing Jamie in the ribs.

"Uh, yeah, I guess," Jamie blushed profusely. He looked at Heather and added, "I mean yes, it was great. Really great. Thanks."

It took all Henry could do not to laugh in Jamie's face. "I'm going to escort our guests to their car. You just relax."

"Okay. Think I'll grab a shower."

Henry chuckled as he led the girls out of the room. Down in the dorm lobby, he gave each a hundred-dollar bill, patted their rear ends, and told them he'd be calling them in the next day or two. Squinting, they walked into the sunlight toward Carol's Ford Mustang. Carol turned around and blew Henry a kiss.

"What a shame," Henry sighed. "A prize piece like that. A damn crying shame."

■ ■ ■

"What's eating you, kid?" Henry asked Jamie when he returned to the dorm room. The athlete's face was more businesslike as he addressed a clearly disturbed Jamie Robinson. He pulled a rugby shirt over his shoulders and began lacing up a pair of cleated sneakers as he spoke. "Hell, didn't I show you a good enough time, or do you need more airheads to screw?"

"It's my computer. It shows one more access than I have in my computer log." Jamie scratched his head, brows knit. "But that's impossible. My records are never wrong."

Henry stood and rolled his outstretched arms in circles. "Listen, kiddo, you were pretty messed up last night. You ever drink that much before?"

Jamie paused. "I'm not sure how much I drank, to tell you the truth."

"Well, there you go, Jim-boy. You probably hit that whatchamacallit button and turned on the thing by accident. May have been right after you and Heather did some horizontal cha-cha. For the record, you also howled like a wolf. You ought to cut loose more often. All work and no play, as the saying goes."

"Dancing? Howling?"

"Take it to the bank, kiddo. Anyway," Henry said offhandedly as he headed for the door, "it's not like you have the secret for the A-bomb in there. It's just an undergrad thesis, right?"

"Thesis? Yeah, that's all."

"So long, Casanova," said Henry, his trademark grin reappearing. "You behave yourself. See ya later."

12

At nine-fifteen, Jamie pedaled home in the dark after putting in three hours of research at the library. He was trying to find out if anyone else had successfully produced any of his mutations. After searching several databases, he came up empty, which was most definitely a good thing, especially in the case of one of the little beauties he'd produced in his room. He was really pumped and in a hurry to get back to what he'd come to regard as the seat of his soul—the desk chair in front of his Apple.

Jamie stood up, straddling the ten-speed's crossbar, waiting for a break in the traffic on Washington Road, a Princeton municipal street that cut straight across campus. He was about to jump up on the narrow seat and resume pedaling when a large hand gripped his left shoulder. Jamie cringed, a cry of fright escaping his throat, and his entire body shivered from the unexpected touch.

"Hey there, roomie," greeted Henry, standing on his roommate's left side. "Been to the library again, I see."

"Jesus, Henry! You scared the shit out of me."

"Sorry, buddy." The athlete's fingers formed a viselike grip on Jamie's left shoulder.

"No problem, but I really have to get back to the room, Henry. It's late, and I haven't even begun to record today's data."

A delivery truck was approaching from the right, headlights spreading a wide cone of light that illuminated the tableaux of bicycle, Henry, and Jamie.

Henry's grip was excruciating. It was as though the big man's fingers dug right into the bone. "Come on, Henry. Let up, will ya?"

"Okay, pal. Anything you say."

With that, Henry shoved Jamie out toward the street.

Stunned, Jamie lost his balance, fell, and looked up in horror at the approaching vehicle.

■ ■ ■

Brakes squealed and tires screeched as the truck rolled over the aspiring scientist and rendered his bicycle into a twisted heap of aluminum that Henry thought resembled a Picasso sculpture.

Henry knew his next move was to go instantly to his knees over Jamie's lifeless body. While he was there, he made sure that Jamie was gone. He couldn't afford the risk of a deathbed utterance.

The driver jumped out from the cab of his vehicle and ran to Jamie.

"Aw, Jesus," said the driver, a man in his early thirties. "I didn't . . . I mean, God Almighty, I was just . . . You're my witness, mister. That kid started to cross the street when I was almost on top of him."

Henry nodded with understanding. "It all happened so quickly, and with the light so bad."

The driver nodded his head slowly.

"Leonard told me you were a standup guy. Just tell the police how there was no way to stop it and I'll stand behind you."

The driver startled. "You mean this is why Leonard told me to drive down this hill when he flashed his headlights. He told me it was just to scare somebody and nobody was going to get hurt. I don't want nothin to do with no . . . "

Henry put his muscular arm around the man's shoulders and pulled him to the side. Washington Street was otherwise deserted. "Let's you and me have a talk, okay, pal?"

The driver merely nodded.

Henry fixed him with a hard stare. "You and I know that if you go down as an accomplice to anything, you're looking at twenty years at least. All this needs to be is a simple pedestrian accident with an absentminded kid who couldn't wait for the light."

Henry's demeanor magically transformed as he reached up to

wipe away a tear. "Kid was a like a brother to me." His chest heaved spasmodically several times. "Was . . . my roommate. I grabbed his left shoulder and told him not to be in such a hurry, but— " Real tears now rolled down the face of Henry Broome. "But he wanted to get back to our room. I think he was expecting a phone call from his mom and dad."

13

Henry sat on his bed, a somber look etched across his face. Puffy spots beneath his eyes indicated that he'd been crying. Tom and Alice Robinson sat side-by-side on Jamie's bed, facing Henry. Neil Rudenstine, dean of the college, sat in the deceased boy's desk chair.

"We've made numerous safety improvements to the campus," Rudenstine explained, using his most sympathetic voice to diplomatically convey that the university was not inclined to accept culpability for the accident. "In fact, there's a traffic light and crosswalk not thirty yards from where Jamie was hit. But sometimes these things happen. Kids are always in a hurry."

Mr. and Mrs. Robinson shot a stern look at the dean.

"Please pardon me," Rudenstine said. "I meant no disrespect to poor Jamie, who was thought of highly by all his teachers. What I'm trying to say is that tragedies just happen, and only God above knows why. In fact, two cheerleaders from Ryder College were killed just yesterday after their Mustang had a blowout and veered out of control while crossing a bridge. Their car jumped the guardrail and the girls drowned in the river below."

The dean shook his head and sighed heavily as Alice Robinson broke down and began to sob.

"It's been a dark couple of days for the university, I can assure you," Rudenstine declared in a carefully compassionate tone. "The entire campus is in shock."

Tom Robinson leaned over, looking at the floor vacantly and clasping his hands. "Jamie was the first member of our family to go to college. We thought he'd become a doctor or scientist or something like that."

Henry got up and seated himself next to Tom Robinson, putting his large arm around the distraught father. "I want you to know that Jamie was a wonderful friend to me—very studious and conscientious. He inspired me to work harder. Sometimes we went out for a burger together. Jamie always talked about how important his family was and how he wanted to make the both of you very proud of him."

"You were a good friend, Henry," Alice Robinson declared. "Thank you for being here today." She looked around the room and shook her head. "It's going to be hard to pack up Jamie's belongings."

"I'll send two of our dorm advisors up to help," Rudenstine volunteered. "They'll bring all the boxes you need and will remain at your disposal for as long as it takes. If there's anything more that I can do, please don't hesitate to contact me."

The dean dismissed himself and disappeared down the hallway.

Two upperclassmen arrived thirty minutes later. One put Jamie's computer into a large box, while the other packed books and clothes.

"What do you want to do with all these plants, ma'am?" the first student asked respectfully.

Alice looked at her husband uncertainly and then at Henry.

"Goodness me, I'm not sure. Jamie always liked to perform experiments, but I really don't know what to do with all these plants."

"Your son worked very hard on them," Henry said. "It would be a shame to just throw them away. That's just my own opinion, of course. He put his heart and soul into his work."

Tom rubbed his chin thoughtfully. "Jamie mentioned in a letter that you live on some tropical island. I don't suppose you could—" The grieving father paused.

"I'll be happy to help you in any way I can," Henry said, anticipating Tom's request.

"Well, I was wondering if you could take the plants to that island of yours—Leeki, I think Jamie said it was called—and plant them there. Kind of like a memorial."

He looked at his wife, who nodded in agreement.

"We'd feel like a part of Jamie was always alive if those plants could actually take root and grow," Tom continued. "If it's no imposition, that is. We'd pay for the shipping."

"The island is called Lanai. My family has owned it for generations." Henry said politely, "I would be honored to plant them as a tribute to your son. But I won't hear of your paying for anything. It would be my privilege to handle all the details. After they're planted, I'll send you pictures regularly so you can see how they're doing."

"I think I'll take just one plant," Alice said. "If it doesn't grow, I'll find some way to preserve it." She lifted a single green plant, which was growing in a small container that had the consistency of an egg carton.

Henry and the Robinsons stood as the two dorm supervisors hauled away boxes and headed for the elevator.

"You're a blessing," Alice said, standing on her tiptoes to kiss Henry lightly on the cheek. "I hope you'll visit us one day at our home in Scranton."

"It would be my pleasure."

"Is there anything of Jamie's you'd like to have?" asked Alice, glancing at her son's desk, which still had a few personal effects that had not yet been packed.

"No," Henry replied. "I assure you that Jamie has already given the greatest gift a friend can give."

PART III
JULY 2005
14

Jack Maulder regarded himself as a patient man. A former Secret Service agent, he'd served on the White House protective detail for ten years. Before that, he investigated counterfeiters, potential threats against the First Family, and high-profile homicides with possible government connections, the kind that caused Washington insiders to play super-sleuth and point fingers at one another. He had met his wife, Gwen, in connection with one such case—a case that was nearly the death of them both.

Jack was methodical, analytical and thorough. He did things by the book—mostly—and prided himself on knowing when to break the rules. An agent didn't get the call to ensure the safety of residents at 1600 Pennsylvania Avenue without having the ability to survey hundreds of people at a glance and pick out the one person who just didn't look right—a man holding an unusual-shaped package or a woman wearing a winter coat in October. Sometimes it was an individual with a scowl or an unkempt appearance that prompted an agent to speak into his cufflink, alerting sharpshooters on nearby rooftops or plainclothes detail mingling with a crowd as POTUS (President of the United States) pressed the flesh along a rope line. An agent had to be able to make split-second decisions and yet remain cool enough to prevent a rifle from taking down someone who was simply an overeager veteran trying to shake hands with the commander-in-chief.

Maulder had lived a life of high drama, literally rubbing elbows with the powerful and elite men and women who controlled the destinies of nations around the globe. He had resigned his position, however, in order to show Dr. Gwen McBean, old-style family practitioner, that he was serious about staying in one place and putting down roots.

The house on Twin Pines Lane was located in Garrett Park, a small community midway between Rockville and Bethesda. Fortunately, Jack handled a keyboard and mouse with the same finesse as he handled a Glock. He became a computer security specialist, helping companies stay several steps ahead of the latest hacking technology. Today's outdated firewall was tomorrow's disaster, and Jack's innovative ideas were effective because he could think from a hacker's point of view. As an innate programming genius, Jack figured he'd gotten the best of both worlds: he could remain close to home while still dabbling in a bit of intrigue.

Ironically, Gwen realized that she couldn't bring house calls and eighteen-hour workdays into the twenty-first century without incurring exhaustion and daily doses of righteous indignation at the ludicrous decisions made by insurance companies and their managed healthcare plans. She simply couldn't deal with bean counters deciding whether or not a patient needed a CT scan. Shortly after she married what she regarded as a new-and-improved Jack Maulder, she found herself drawn to the Commissioned Corps of the U.S. Public Health Service in order to continue living her dad's ideals: enhancing people's quality of life through medicine. She wasn't going to cast her lot with a medical partnership that double-booked patients into five-minute time slots costing eighty-five dollars a pop. She decided to apply her doctoring skills to the nation as a whole, rather to one patient after another.

It was classic role reversal; Jack leaves public service, Gwen signs up. Their marriage was nevertheless solid, with Jack, by virtue of his first career, understanding the demands and rigors of having to keep unusual hours or pick up and travel at a moment's notice. Secretly, he thought he was more understanding of Gwen's lifestyle than she would have been of his if he had remained with the Service. Even solid marriages were subject to personal prejudices.

Jack Maulder, rightly or wrongly, believed patience to be one of his strong suits. That said, he was more than a little concerned about

Gwen's ongoing obsession with the circumstances surrounding Marci's death. The problem, as Jack saw it, was that there were no circumstances. The young lawyer had died of exhaustion and stress. Period. Maulder was certainly no expert in forensics, but agents of the Secret Service were well-versed in conspiracy theories and suspicious circumstances. In the case of Marci Newman, there was no smoking gun. Nothing to indicate murder most foul. Nothing to suggest a public health hazard.

Zilch. Nada.

Gwen had brought home a vial of Marci's blood obtained from a New York Medical Examiner. On their first day back, Jack caught her surreptitiously transferring the vial from her coat pocket to the briefcase she brought to the office each day. Speaking somewhat defensively, Gwen claimed that she intended to store the blood at FDA headquarters in Rockville in the event that some significant detail occurred to her, something that warranted further examination of Marci's collapse in municipal court. Jack didn't believe her for one minute. He was one hundred percent certain that his wife was going to analyze the blood sample, and this was troubling in the extreme. Not only was he skeptical of the need to pursue analysis in the first place, but, more importantly, she'd never lied to him before.

To pursue peace and domestic tranquility, Jack decided to back away from the confusing signals his wife was sending, but still offer to participate in her search. He even agreed to examine the Haydn104 file that Gwen copied from Marci's laptop. He'd looked at the file a dozen times now, and nothing whatsoever aroused his suspicion. Granted, the file was unusual, but Marci had been reclusive—even a bit quirky—and Jack thought there might be any one of a thousand explanations for the creation of Haydn104 that no one was apt to guess. Humoring his unrelenting wife, he examined the file carefully, putting the rows of numbers through a dozen different encryption programs. He saw no pattern, no rhyme or reason lurking in the numerals. It didn't appear that Marci had been playing Nostradamus, couching dire warnings in coded format. He even applied sophisticated musical software to the problem, exploring the possibility that the seemingly random digits might correspond to Haydn's work if the melodies, harmonics, or compositional keys were converted into mathematical equivalents.

Thus far, Jack had found nothing.

He looked at the oak table in the corner of his office, a ground floor utility room adjacent to the kitchen. On the table was the classic brown Wilson fielder's glove he bought in the hopes he might one day have a son. Like many childless husbands, he often dreamt of electric trains and games of catch. The mitt, purchased in the spring, was also a not-so-subtle hint to Gwen.

Gwen was actually starting to warm up to the idea of having children. The couple was even beginning to debate which upstairs room would be the best candidate for a nursery. But all discussion of having children had ceased since the Maulders had returned from New York in May.

Jack was firmly convinced that it was time for Gwen to consult a therapist for grief counseling, obsession, or both. She'd lost her dearest friend and she couldn't get through the pain of it alone.

And nothing Jack did seemed to help.

15

Mark Stern left the Main Street offices of the *Washington Post*, a newly emancipated man. No longer would he have to camouflage his trademark journalistic attitude or profile elite moneychangers residing in modern-day temples where express elevators went straight to the penthouse. He had enjoyed his stint with the *Journal*, but he now wanted two things desperately: renewed contact with ordinary people, and the opportunity to dig deeply when he came across a potential scandal.

His colleagues, who did not yet know the details of his departure, said he was foolish to give up his position at the *Journal*. He was a regular guest on economic and political talk shows on PBS and he was invited to weekly soirees where he mingled with celebrities, senators, and CEOs. What the hell was he doing? Even harsher critics maintained he would never regain his preeminent stature in journalism, but Mark knew this to be rubbish. The *Post* had helped bring down a president and countless congressmen. Stern was still a best-selling author with a loyal following. He was iconic, and he would, with well-turned phrases and an engaging personality, work his way into the mythos of Washington just as he'd done in New York.

Not that second thoughts were an option. No, they definitely were not.

Mark had called the editor-in-chief at the *Post* to offer his services only after he received a call from his lawyer saying, "Welcome to the Millionaire's Club, Mark! Your termination clause with the

Journal is finally being enforced since you did that surreal piece on the privatization of social security and how the ghost of FDR is giving our current president nightmares. Your editor obviously didn't read the column before putting the paper to bed or it wouldn't have been printed. I'll give you this much: you must have earned a helluva lot of trust to sneak that one by. But let me ask you one question, my friend. Are you crazy? You had to know—had to—that the *Journal* wasn't going to swallow a fantasy piece on the biggest hot-button issue in all of politics. Jesus—it doesn't take a brain surgeon to figure out that privatization is something the *Journal* and its readers favor—and favor strongly!"

Mark stopped listening at this point, holding his cell phone at arm's length from his ear so that his lawyer's voice sounded like the annoying drone of a mosquito caught behind a microchip. Yes, he was crazy. And yes, he most definitely knew that the *Journal* would invoke his termination clause before the ink on page one had time to dry. He had finally done a mil's worth of damage by crossing a line big-time.

He couldn't understand his lawyer's whining, though. It was a win-win situation. He would get a cool million for saying what needed to be said on behalf of aging boomers, and he would land on his feet given his previous success. After all, Woodward and Bernstein hadn't achieved fame by being Boy Scouts.

The controversy, in fact, would actually work in his favor. Naughty journalist goes south . . . to Washington! The inherent curiosity of readers, coupled with Stern's recognizable moniker, would sell a lot of papers as liberals and conservatives alike turned to his column to see what he would tackle next. The *Post* was more conservative than the *Times*—he probably wouldn't be drinking Shiraz with Tony Blankley on summer evenings—but the paper's management liked his moxie.

Controversy sold papers and kept stockholders happy. Long live the free press.

If anyone had asked Mark whether his career move was prompted by thoughts of Gwen Maulder living in Maryland, he would have vehemently denied it. Hell, he'd denied it to himself a dozen times. He wasn't a homewrecker, and a friend of a friend had informed him that Jack and Gwen seemed reasonably happy.

In point of fact, Mark would have gravitated to the *Post* even if Gwen lived in Peoria or Pretoria for that matter. He nevertheless thought of her from the moment he made the decision to live and work in D.C. It was, he reasoned, natural enough to wonder what an old girlfriend was doing. He couldn't help it if he still had feelings for her, but that didn't mean he was prepared to act on his fantasies.

Garrett Park. There was no harm in looking up where she lived, was there? Anyway, what were the odds that he'd ever run into her.

16

Senator Henry Broome IV detested photo ops with his constituents. He considered root canal preferable to posing with thirty-four pimple -faced students from Honolulu High on a class trip to Washington.

"Let's get this over with, Ms. Chang," Henry declared, marching down the hallowed halls of Congress with a resolute stride, his polished black wingtips hitting the marble floor loudly enough to cause an echo. "A few smiles, a couple of class photos—no singles—some hand disinfectant and I'm done. Got it?"

"Got it, Senator," said the very efficient Roberta Chang, a stunning Chinese-American woman and Henry's chief aide. "You'll be back for your 11:15 phone call with minutes to spare." Chang was petite, with lustrous black hair that fell to her waist and swung like a satin stage curtain with each turn of her head. She kept up with her boss with quick, energetic steps as she consulted a sheet listing Henry's schedule for the remainder of the day.

Five minutes later, Henry Broome stood on the steps of the Capitol, smiling, as a dozen shutters clicked and the Honolulu High Civics Club stared in awe at a man who was on network news, not to mention *Meet the Press* or *Face the Nation*, at least five times a month.

Henry's basso profundo voice boomed across the small crowd of students and onlookers. "It's great to see you here today! It's heartening to see young adults like yourselves taking an interest in government and coming all the way to our nation's capitol to watch democracy in action. Please allow me the privilege of taking a picture with your class so that I can be reminded continually that future generations will keep America great! I'm sure your teachers will see to it that everyone gets a copy."

There was a burst of applause as students lined up on the steps, Henry standing in the middle of the back row, towering above everyone. A teacher with a digital camera took two pictures before Henry broke ranks.

"Thank you all!" called the senator, waving grandiloquently as a broad smile revealed a set of dazzling white teeth. "Enjoy your stay in Washington!"

Roberta Chang escorted Henry away from awestruck students, their pens and pads at the ready, before they could start clamoring for autographs.

"Slam bam, thank you, ma'am," chimed Henry as he walked up the Capitol steps. "It's a beautiful morning."

Right before he entered the stately building, Henry turned around and looked carefully back at the throng. A blond girl, probably a senior, had caught his eye during his close encounter. She could easily have passed for twenty-two or twenty-three, and her miniskirt revealed long, smooth thighs. He would have bet an even grand that she was head cheerleader at her high school.

"Damn, but life is good, isn't it, Ms. Chang?"

"Yes, Senator. Very good."

Back in the privacy of his office, he looked at his chief aide. Behind closed doors, the senator's relationship to his aide was on a far more personal basis.

■ ■ ■

Although he was the junior senator from the Aloha state, Henry was also the chairman of the Senate Agriculture Committee and, by sheer dint of his charisma, a powerhouse on the Hill. When he graduated from Princeton, all records of Henry's academic probation and his less-than-stellar 1.4 GPA had mysteriously disappeared from the university Registrar's Office. With an Ivy League diploma tucked securely under his arm, Henry stood as President Bowen intoned "admitto," Broome's Brigade applauding loudly in the wings. He knew instinctively at that moment that he had to toughen up, get serious about grad school, maybe replace soccer and rugby practice with some mental aerobics.

Daddy Broome was going to place him on a completely different playing field soon, and he needed to be ready. Accordingly, he took his MBA in 1981 and became Vice President of Sun Valley Microsystems, an Arizona tech company, by 1984. Moving up to President and CEO after the unexpected retirement of Sun Valley's head honcho, Henry delegated power judiciously, allowing himself time to attend Stanford University Law School, and passed the bar in 1989. It was in 1991, while working for Peterson, Hewitt, Drake & Keyes, a Los Angeles-based firm specializing in maritime law, that Henry decided to run for a state legislature seat in Hawaii after the incumbent bowed out of politics due to a mysterious illness.

The year 1996 saw Henry's ascendancy. He ran for the U.S. Senate and won handily. His campaign slogan, "A New Broome Sweeps Clean," was trite yet effective. The Broome family was once again held in high esteem, even though both of Henry's parents had died in the mid-eighties. Lanai was now ruled by King Henry IV, as the plantation workers referred to their irascible boss. Since 1980, in fact, he made time to return to the island occasionally to oversee the cultivation of a new cash crop to replace pineapples and sugarcane. With the aid of a botanist and a molecular biologist working full-time on the Broome family payroll, the plants thrived.

New Jersey, Washington, or Hawaii—only the location changed. The plain truth was that Henry knew how to get things done.

■ ■ ■

It was 11:15 sharp. A green light and a low beep from the desktop communication system indicated that the senator had a priority phone call. Henry reached for the slim black receiver and took a deep breath.

"Henry Broome," he said in a formal manner reserved for very few.

"Good morning, Henry."

"Good morning, sir."

"How are you? All is well, I presume?"

"I'm fine, thank you, and yes—operations are completely nominal."

"I heard we had a visitor."

Henry was nonplussed. "Visitor?"

"Tropical Storm Beverly. It's in the Pacific and is expected to reach hurricane force by tonight. Projected landfall is anywhere from Costa Rica to Panama."

Henry breathed a sigh of relief. His caller was sometimes terse and often enigmatic. "Yes, sir. I've been in touch with the manager of operations for Central America. We've doubled shipments over the past week in case we experience any downtime."

"Very good, Henry. Have a pleasant day."

The call ended abruptly, which always irritated the hell out of Henry.

He also hated having to call anyone "sir," but protocol demanded that he treat the gentleman on the other end of the line with utmost politeness. Indeed, Henry was a member of what was commonly regarded as the most exclusive and powerful club in the world, the United States Senate, but his caller wielded a good deal of power himself.

And if he chose, he could have Henry killed in a heartbeat.

17

Gwen retested Marci's blood upon returning from New York, and the results matched those of Dave Dardenoff. The sample contained chemicals found in cigarettes, plus aspirin, caffeine, and trace amounts of the carcinogens that humans in industrialized areas are exposed to on a daily basis: pesticides, herbicides, household cleansers, and a dozen others that most people other than environmentalists and vegans wouldn't recognize. None should have been responsible for seizure or premature death. As for Marci's mitral valve prolapse, it was fairly common in the general population, and most people who had the condition were unaware of it. They were either asymptomatic or experienced transient dizziness and arrhythmias that they ignored or attributed to stress. Even if diagnosed, MVP was not always treated with medication. Physicians often opted for a regimen of diet, exercise, and stress reduction.

Maybe Dardenoff was right. Marci was an underweight workaholic with unbalanced electrolytes. Add smoking, poor nutrition, and mitral valve prolapse, and she became the one in ten thousand who suddenly dies. Perhaps it was synergy, a combination of factors that, taken together, shouldn't surprise anyone, least of all an epidemiologist.

Except it didn't make any sense.

"Dammit!" Gwen said, throwing the folder with Marci's lab results on her desk. It was ten minutes after five, time to head home and throw some stir-fry into the wok, but she wasn't in the mood to talk with Jack this evening. A confrontation was looming, and she already knew what the methodical Mr. Maulder was going to say: "It's time to let Marci go, honey. We need to move on, do the things we've been talking about doing." "The things we've been talking about doing" was code for starting a family. Jack thought his little thing with the baseball glove was clever—and she had to admit it had some charm—but since Marci died, the glove seemed like a taunt of sorts, a way of nagging Gwen to let go of Marci, to seek psychiatric help if necessary, and get on with their lives. She couldn't do that. Not now. Not until she knew what really happened to Marci.

Gwen took a deep breath. She was torn. A good epidemiologist looked at patterns, made connections, examined trends. If the case of Marci Newman had come across her desk under some other name, her professional opinion would have been that the deceased was an unfortunate statistic, one well within predictable parameters, all variables taken into consideration. But she was approaching the case not as a public health officer, but as Gwen McBean, Marci Newman's college roommate and best friend. Her dad taught her to look past reports and charts and to trust her instincts. Fitz Rule Number One: Textbooks and lab procedures are only starting points. The human part of the equation couldn't be denied in medicine, and Gwen felt certain beyond any reasonable doubt that Marci shouldn't be dead because . . . well, because Marci wasn't ready to die. If that wasn't scientific, so be it.

The human equation. Terminally ill patients with an optimistic, feisty attitude almost always lived longer than those who picked out a casket, closed the drapes, and waited to die. Like Fitz, Gwen believed in the mind-body connection. A person's health was affected to a large degree by what he or she believed. The mind produced endless peptides that could cause disease or work miracles, and the plain fact of the matter was that Marci Elizabeth Newman was high on life and loved her job.

Underweight? Yes. Minor heart defect? Yes.

Waiting to die? No way.

As far as Gwen was concerned, Marci should still be alive. She accepted Jack for what he was: a rational man who gathered facts and then chose the most logical explanation that fit existing data. She couldn't fault him for that, and yet they had gone out at a time when he relentlessly pursued the truth, even playing the occasional hunch when following a lead in the course of a baffling murder investigation. Had he grown into a boring conservative? If so, could she blame him? Hadn't she wanted him to quit the cops and robbers routine so they could have a shot at a "normal life?" Wasn't she being hypocritical?

Yes, but that didn't change her intuition about Marci, and what her gut was telling her. She couldn't go home yet. She needed to be here and she wasn't sure what to do if she was there.

She picked up a copy of the *Washington Post*.

"Holy shit," she said under her breath.

Unfolding the paper and spreading the pages wide, she saw that the *Post* was running a new column by an old pro.

"Confessions of an Iconoclast" by Mark Stern.

Hadn't he moved from the *Times* to the *Journal*? What was he doing in D.C.?

Reading the column, she couldn't suppress a smile. Mark's premier piece for the *Post* was pure, unadulterated Stern, the quintessential observer of human foibles. His debut column was titled "Franchising the Full Moon." It claimed that incidents of public madness were on the rise—a lady on a New York subway train screaming that Jesus was returning any day now, a man at the Guggenheim taking off his clothes and exhibiting himself as free-standing art, a seventy-year-old woman jogging around the reflecting pool in Washington wearing nothing but an American flag. According to Stern, aberrant behavior was spreading like a virus and was a natural response to a political administration that courted madness. "The country is ruled by paranoia," the columnist wrote in the last paragraph. "Acts of lunacy are being produced by a climate of fear and uncertainty that the administration uses to maintain its Orwellian hold over the population."

Gwen looked at the ceiling and laughed. How simplistic Mark could be . . . and how endearing. Though she'd grown a bit more politically moderate over the years, she admired her former beau's boyish passion and naiveté. In Gwen's estimation, even now, however, these qualities alone could not sustain a long-term commitment. She decided long ago that he was never going to grow up, and their relationship, despite some enjoyable times, had nowhere left to go.

Gwen got up, stretched, and grabbed her purse. Sooner or later she'd have to make that stir-fry. Maybe a bottle of Merlot would keep the dinner discussion from heading down the wrong road.

She turned off the overhead lights and smiled. "Nature Boy working right here in Washington. Interesting."

■ ■ ■

A million bucks hadn't changed Mark Stern's spartan lifestyle one iota. He stood in his one-bedroom apartment carved from a once-grand townhouse on the corner of 31st and R Streets in Georgetown, staring at the four cork bulletin boards on his living room wall. He didn't store much info on computers in the preliminary stages of working up a story. He made notes in nearly illegible longhand on yellow legal pads and pinned interesting newspaper articles to the bulletin boards. Staring at a computer screen didn't cut it. He needed to feel the muscles in his fingers grip a Paper Mate, needed to see the words drip from the pen onto the yellow paper. That was journalism—real writing, raw and fresh.

Likewise, when it came to weighing facts, scrolling down a list on a PC monitor simply didn't engage his gray matter. He needed to stand, pace the floor, rearrange articles, look from one board to the other. Blood had to pump and muscles had to move in order for the right idea to poke its head from some sleeping synapse and say, "This is what's important."

His first column for the *Post* had been well-received despite the fact that more than a few conservatives thought he should pack up and go back to New York. Stern welcomed such criticism, for when people started to attack, he knew he had drawn blood. Over the years, he'd learned that there were two kinds of criticism: valid and malicious. When readers turned nasty, it was because they saw the truth and didn't want to deal with it. They'd been exposed. Game, set, and match to Mark Stern. He hadn't gotten into the field to make people feel comfortable.

He glanced from one board to the other. On the top left, six articles chronicled people going a little wacko, four in New York and two in D.C. He had seen several more, but these were the ones that most interested him. But did they mean anything? On the bottom right were ten articles, all from obit sections in New York and Washington papers. Young adults dying from unexplained or natural causes. They were aggressive young professionals and politicians. The ten thousand dollar question was this: Was there some kind of connection between people acting loony and the premature deaths?

The trend in New York had begun in early May and then ceased by the first week in June. The same kinds of articles were now appearing in Washington during the month of July. Was there some kind of full-moon madness hovering over parts of the country? Had someone spiked the water supply?

Perhaps there was no connection at all. Going postal certainly wasn't a new phenomenon. He knew it might just be a statistical anomaly that more people were freaking out in New York and D.C. Mark's stock in trade, however, was charting patterns in the general population. He always believed that a good reporter was a good sociologist.

He paced the floor, scratched his head, and halted in front of the clippings. He stared at them for a while and shook his head. "There's definitely a disturbance in the force."

■ ■ ■

Dinner with Jack was not the somber proposition that Gwen had anticipated. When she stepped through the door, Jack's face wore that "Let's talk—let's really communicate" expression on his face. Gwen was determined to elude confrontation. She simply gave her husband a long, sensuous kiss, opened a bottle of Merlot, and started the stir-fry. As soon as Jack began his litany of reasons for Gwen to abandon her investigation and start breeding little Maulders, Gwen launched a preemptive strike.

"You know, Jack, I don't think the guest room would be a good choice for a nursery. My upstairs office would probably work better since its closer to the master bedroom. I think we should renovate the basement and move my office down there. Whatya think, Mr. Secret Service Agent?" Despite her relaxed demeanor, Gwen employed her ceramic-bladed Japanese chef's knife with lightning speed, reducing whole vegetables to small piles of perfectly symmetrical cubes in moments.

Completely flummoxed, Jack could barely stammer, "Fine by me. I'll take a look at the basement and see what might be involved. I think I could do most of the work myself."

Gwen knew that her husband, like many men, liked to play with his toys—drills, table saws, sanders, and anything metal that could hang from a tool belt. She stepped over to the kitchen table and planted a small kiss on Jack's forehead before moving back to the stove. "Catch any cyber crooks today?" she asked matter-of-factly.

"Uh, no. So how was your day, honey?"

"Same ol, same ol," Gwen replied, scooping the wok's contents onto two plates she carried to the table with an ever-so-subtle sway to her hips. "Bugs and drugs aplenty, but not to worry. They won't triumph on Captain Maulder's watch."

Jack finished his glass of wine and continued to smile. To Gwen, he looked like an unmoored buoy at the mercy of conflicting tides. She knew he wanted to say something to her about Marci and she also knew that she'd short-circuited him. Long-term, this wasn't the best thing for a marriage. For tonight, though, it was just what she needed.

Gwen sipped a second glass of wine after she and Jack washed the dishes. A slight buzz was fine, but postprandial drowsiness was not in the offing. As Jack dried flatware, she decided to do something more productive for her marriage. She quietly slipped upstairs and returned minutes later wearing one of Jack's flannel shirts . . . and nothing else.

Trial and error had taught her that Jack was not a Victoria's Secret kind of guy. He could not resist L.L. Bean, however, when it was modeled with a flair not exhibited in the catalog. With urgency and red wine governing hormones, the long climb upstairs was not an option. Gwen wondered if her grandmother's couch had ever seen this kind of action before. Although she doubted it, she did remember that Fitz was one of nine . . .

Later, as Jack drifted off, Gwen whispered, "If it's a girl, can we name her Marci?"

■ ■ ■

The red numbers on the digital clock said 2:00 a.m. Gwen opened her eyes and glanced at the nightstand, her brain racing at the sight of the red "2" just inches away. Jack was fast asleep, having been led upstairs with great difficulty shortly before midnight.

Slipping into her silk robe, Gwen crept downstairs and sat on the living room sofa, legs tucked beneath her.

"I'm a complete idiot," she said to the quiet room. "I could kick myself."

Her mind was clear from what amounted to a power nap, and the nocturnal epiphany now brewing in her brain stemmed from remembering Fitz Rule Number Two: When baffled, turn the world upside down. Rotate a problem 180 degrees. Look at things differently.

She was an epidemiologist, and she needed to start acting like one. She needed to step back and look at the problem from a wider perspective. It's what she did for a living, for God's sake. Jack had his manly tools down in the basement, but Gwen had her own set of tools at the FDA. She also had contacts at the Centers for Disease Control and Prevention in Atlanta, people with very sophisticated tools that might be helpful in getting to the bottom of Marci's death.

Marci's dead, and there's nothing I can do about it.

Gwen paused. In her grief, the words had been streaming through her mind like the updates at the bottom of a cable news screen—they were there but not necessarily assimilated. Marci was dead and Gwen would always cherish the memory of her former college roommate. But she had finally reached the all-important stage of acceptance. She would be able to work more effectively now. Grief and confusion would be replaced by action and an attention to detail. There was something she could do after all.

Gwen went back upstairs, knowing exactly what steps she would take at work in a few hours. She would call Jan Menefee, a medical school classmate and director of the BioNet Surveillance Project down at the CDC. A relatively new system, BioNet was a highly sensitive computer network comprised of more computing power distributed around the globe than was ever conceived for even the largest supercomputer. The goal was to use everyday clues in order to provide early warning for disease outbreaks or bioterrorism events by searching for subtle anomalies, minor blips on the radar screen that could help the medical community stay one step ahead of potential disaster. With such a sophisticated database, perhaps BioNet would be able to provide some clues as to whether Marci's death was truly a random tragedy or part of some larger picture.

Gwen slid under the sheet next to Jack and fell asleep immediately.

For the first time in two months, she had peace of mind.

18

Eddie Karn was having trouble sleeping after a long day treated to Washington's *auto-da-fé*.

Dr. Edward Jason Karn, graduate of Princeton, 1979, had been nominated by the president for the position of commissioner of the Food and Drug Administration. The nomination came as a mild shock to Eddie, whose outspoken insistence on the need to subject certain genetically modified foods to premarket approval by the FDA had met with considerable resistance, and the agency was obviously an anathema to the entire grocery lobby. Dr. Karn did not hesitate to speak out on the elimination of rBGH (bovine growth hormone) from the food supply, nor did he temper his opinion on chemically-altered feedstock given to chicken and pigs to make them fatter and meatier. He didn't believe enough long-term testing had been conducted on chemical additives, and as far as genetically modified foods were concerned, scientists were just beginning to understand gene sequencing in humans, enabling them to isolate certain genes that might predispose certain individuals to illness. How could anyone be sure that genetically modified foods were not causing illness by disrupting normal gene functioning? Karn also believed that mutations in the very structure of DNA might result from such modifications.

But his gastronomic conservatism didn't end there. A bachelor, Karn shopped at the Whole Foods Market, eating products without preservatives, hormones, colorings, or bleached flour. Eddie Karn talked the talk and walked the walk.

So why had he been nominated by a conservative administration? One reason. Politics, plain and simple.

The sitting president was quickly losing his political capital, with approval numbers falling into the low forties. Things were not going well at home and abroad, and the White House chief of staff decided that the Oval Office needed to score a few victories. Supreme Court nominees, for example, might be easier to confirm if the administration threw Congress a bone in the form of a liberal FDA commissioner. It was a show of bipartisanship that might provide even the most stubborn senators with enough incentive to confirm High Court nominees while making some good old-fashioned pork barrel trades on the side. A Supreme Court seat was for life. FDA commissioners usually came and went with administrations. The White House was far more interested in restructuring the court than battling feeble attempts, doomed to failure, aimed at changing the entire food industry. It was doubtful Karn could affect FDA regulatory processes which had been in place for years without new laws that the right would never allow. It was a win-win situation for an administration with other agendas.

Aware of political realities, Karn was completely at ease with the rationale behind his selection. If becoming a political pawn enabled him to put some ideas into public awareness, even if he couldn't implement them, then so be it.

Over and above the odd alignment of political planets that led to his selection, Karn was certainly qualified for the job. After five years in private practice, the well-known oncologist spent four years as president of the American Cancer Society. He spent another seven years with the CDC, monitoring the incidence of various diseases in southern states bordering the Mississippi River, where cancer rates were unusually high since industry used the Big Muddy as its primary means for the disposal of toxic waste. Phenol levels alone were off the chart. The last ten years of his career were spent overseeing research at Sloan Kettering and Johns Hopkins respectively, where he had investigated how human genes were affected by chemical agents and preservatives. His research convinced him that Americans had no idea what they were ingesting.

Political or not, Karn was exhilarated over his nomination. Then he learned that Henry Broome was on the Senate Committee on Health, Education, Labor & Pensions. Karn never forgot the night he witnessed Henry Broome dumpsterize Bruce Merewether back in college, and had kept a watchful eye on him, out of simple curiosity at first. Subsequently, he found Henry's career moves rather suspect.

Henry Broome IV always prospered after people unexpectedly retired or succumbed to mysterious illnesses. The naturally wary Karn didn't trust the braggart ex-jock. As a matter of fact, Karn thought Senator Broome was downright dangerous.

Karn had been wise to curtail his enthusiasm. During Karn's courtesy visits to the Hill, Broome was habitually "called to the floor." This left Karn at the mercy of Henry's staff, comprised to a large extent of twenty-four-year-olds dressed out of the Talbots catalog who were even less articulate on food and drug issues than on the novels studied—though not necessarily read—in college lit seminars. The inanity of the questions from Henry's staff during preliminary interviews gave Karn virtually no opportunity to prepare for Henry's own issues and inquiries—or rather those of the lobbyists who kept him fed and watered—which he would have to address when the actual hearings finally began.

In the hearing room, Henry greeted Karn off-camera like a long-lost friend. A traditional two-handed grip and a string of reminiscences from college days led Karn to the witness seat. Having seen Henry's ruthless behavior at Princeton firsthand, Karn detested this false show of camaraderie. And false it was. The moment the chairman's gavel opened the proceedings, Broome grilled the physician mercilessly on his positions regarding the possible danger of chemical additives and genetically modified foods. Karn's confirmation hearings were as acrimonious as those for Robert Bork in 1988, when Bork had been recommended for a Supreme Court seat.

Henry was not the only senator to adopt an attack posture, however. Despite Karn's attractiveness to the left, liberal senators suddenly realized that they represented America's breadbasket. It was one thing to get up close and personal to visit voters at home, but they didn't expect to see constituents unceremoniously bumping up and down past their offices in tractors, trucked in overnight thanks to the grocery lobby, and waving distinctly unfriendly signs such as

"KEEP KARN OUT OF THE BARN." One or two who actually served on their senators' finance committees scraped enough mud off their shoes to mosey upstairs into the rarified offices of the Senate in order to explain to their representatives that reelection should not be regarded as a given no matter how much money was stashed away in the local party's war chest.

The committee vote was 17–4 against Karn, a doleful political lynching of the first order. Karn's White House handlers professed the proper amount of shock and betrayal at the hands of conservative Senate leaders, while most pundits thought the president should have withdrawn the nomination to save the very respectable oncologist considerable humiliation at the hands of his questioners. Thanks to Senator Broome, the hearings had become an inquisition, making Dr. Edward Karn look like a New Age lunatic who would disrupt the country's entire food chain, spiking prices in the process because of his hard-line stance against what most people regarded as scientific progress. Consumers wanted to see products moving swiftly along the supermarket's conveyor belt, not a warning leaflet from the paranoid Dr. Karn.

And that was how Eddie Karn knew that Henry was still the same monster he'd known in college.

■ ■ ■

As morning broke, Gwen felt renewed, invigorated. Adrenaline flooded her bloodstream as she put on her PHS uniform while Jack slept peacefully in the gray dawn. She left his favorite cereal on the counter—Cap'n Crunch (boys will be boys, she figured)—and was out the door by 7:30.

Gwen flipped on the fluorescent lights of her office at exactly 8:15. She hastily reviewed some trivial reports littering her desk, grabbed a cup of coffee, met with a coworker to discuss projected flu stats for the coming winter, and then impatiently waited for the digital clock on her desk to register nine o'clock in green block letters.

A few minutes before nine, her phone rang unexpectedly.

"Gwen? Dardenoff here."

"How are you, Dave, what's going on?"

"Something a bit puzzling at this end. Not quite sure what to make of it . . . After we spoke, I decided to run some of your friend's brain tissue for advanced testing in the hopes of finding something."

"And?" Gwen asked.

"No other traces of foreign substances, but the cyclic AMP level in the brain was off the charts. I see that sometimes in cocaine-related seizures and the crystal meth that those bikers like to cook up. I haven't seen it before in a plain old overworked smoker."

"What do you make of it, Dave?"

"I'm kind of at a loss here. It's not a test we do very often because it doesn't really help establish any kind of cause. On the other hand, it's a pretty unexpected finding and I thought you would like to know."

"Do you think there was some sort of foul play?" asked Gwen.

"I really don't know what to think. I'll call again if anything comes up."

Dardenoff 's call shook Gwen to her core. There was just no way she was going to leave this one alone. Marci deserved more of an explanation than "worked herself to death." It was time to play her strongest card.

Gwen's fingers practically dialed by themselves. "Is Jan Menefee in?" Gwen asked.

"One moment please," replied the passionless voice of a receptionist.

Gwen nervously tapped a ballpoint pen against a coffee cup with PEQUOD'S glazed around its surface in large letters. In the thirty agonizing seconds before a familiar voice announced its presence at the other end of the line, she pictured Jan in her mind—brilliant scientist by day, flirt and party girl by night.

"Menefee."

"Hi, Jan. It's Gwen Maulder. How are you?"

"Other than shocked, fine. I haven't heard from you since last year when you called about that botulism hoax. What kind of deadly disease warrants a call from my old friend today?"

"Okay, guilty as charged, Jan. Sorry I've been out of touch. Can I blame my lack of social graces on my husband by any chance?"

"Is he being a pain?"

"Not really, but I thought it was worth a shot."

"Then what can I do for ya this time, Cap'n?"

Gwen paused and closed her eyes. She would lay out the story as best she could and hope that Jan would understand the urgent nature of her call. "A good friend of mine died in May. Marci Newman."

"You talked about her a lot in medical school. Your undergrad roomie, right? That's pretty awful."

"Thanks. It was very . . . unexpected. There was no history of disease whatsoever except for mitral valve prolapse." Gwen related the details to Jan, as few as they were, anticipating the response.

"Sounds like another victim of stress in the twenty-first century," lamented Jan. "At Marci's age, I doubt smoking contributed to her death, but then hey—I don't think Big Tobacco has come clean yet on what kind of additives go into cancer sticks. I don't know what to think about those cyclic AMP levels. It's not the kind of thing that gets measured routinely at autopsy and you sure can't take brain samples in normal healthy living people for comparison. I can understand why you might be a bit suspicious, though. Hey, on a different subject, it's a shame that Eddie Karn wasn't taken seriously as a candidate for your front office. I heard the word 'additives' causes him to bristle, which didn't play well at his confirmation hearings."

Gwen scratched the words, "cigarettes/additives" on a memo pad. Upon awaking that morning, she'd decided to make a list of any and all possibilities. Fitz Rule Number Three: Leave no stone unturned.

"Yeah," Gwen said. "Karn's a decent guy from what I've heard, but I don't know that it's feasible to start looking in every box of chocolate chip cookies to see if the chemicals that extend shelf life will cause us all to grow an extra finger. We have to find a happy medium or we'll all go completely bonkers."

"Point well taken. But how can I help you with the death of Marci Newman? Is there something you haven't told me yet?"

"Actually," replied Gwen, "I was hoping there was something you could tell me."

"I'm not following."

"BioNet. Word up here in Rockville is that it can track small trends in large populations."

"Absolutely. It passed its trials with flying colors, although it really hasn't had any serious test of its potential, which I suppose is good when you remember that it's designed to pick up signs of bioterrorism—exposure to powders, gas, viral and nerve agents—things like that. It can also key on symptoms of something out of left field, like SARS. Hopefully, it won't be detecting anything at all if the supersnoops at the FBI and CIA are getting their act together. At present, we're just beginning to do regular surveillance runs to see what's out there."

"What if you programmed BioNet to look for cause of death in people in the thirty-to-forty age group, people who were thought to be otherwise healthy?"

"I'd say you were casting an awfully big dragnet. Too many young people die everyday, Gwen. I don't have to remind you of that. BioNet is sensitive, but I can pretty much guarantee that it's going to spit out a normal morbidity and mortality curve for any segment of the population."

Gwen leaned back in her chair, fingers laced behind her head.

"What if we narrow it down and look for people who died after a seizure episode?" Gwen realized that if cigarettes were involved, young people wouldn't be the only ones affected, although teens and twenty-somethings were indeed smoking more than older people during the past decade, with seniors turning to nicotine patches and gum in droves. Tobacco aside, the idea that the mysterious trend for which she was hunting involved only younger members of the population was an unwarranted assumption. She was, after all, trying to look at things from a greater perspective, Fitz Rule Number Two.

"Seizures?" said Jan. "Very doable, since seizure activity, as luck would have it, has already been programmed into the system. Many chemical agents used by terrorists push people right over the seizure threshold, so it's an integral part of the project."

"What kind of statistical breakdown can BioNet provide?"

"Let me give you a mundane but very accurate example. Every community in the country with public sewage can measure the volume of refuse processed by its treatment plant on a minute-by-minute basis, providing an extremely accurate measure of toilet flushes per minute. Big deal, right? Actually, a sudden spike in flushing might indicate a possible attack of the runs on a community-wide basis. This might signal nothing more than beef poisoning from a bad fast-food chain, but it could just as easily point to something far more insidious, such as the introduction of a deadly viral agent to the community's water supply. Thanks to Homeland Security, BioNet is linked to an unbelievable number of information sources, with sewage plants being just one example among thousands. If a threat were to be identified, the system could tell you age, gender, race, geographical location, preexisting medical conditions—could tell you almost anything, in fact, except whether or not a patient attends church regularly."

"Damn," said Gwen. "It's that good?"

"Yep. The joke down here is that it should be able to predict the stock market by next year. Let me give you the short version of BioNet's capabilities. I already told you that BioNet is first and foremost an amazing data bank that has amassed more information than any previous computer or record-keeping system in history. That alone makes it worth its weight in gold. For starters, BioNet can search its database for routine patterns, such as where certain disease outbreaks usually arise or what age groups are most susceptible to certain kinds of infections, but that's just the tip of this cyber-iceberg. It can correlate different sets of variables, be they geographical location, ethnicity, symptoms—you name it—and show possible relationships within a matter of seconds, whereas old-fashioned medical research could take weeks, months, or even years to establish patterns. That's just Level I, however."

Gwen chuckled. "What is Level II? A computer from Star Trek?"

"Actually, you're not far off the mark. Level II is what makes BioNet a quantum computer, the very first of its kind."

"Quantum?"

"Yes. Follow along, and I'll forego the lecture on Boolean algorithms, which, in a nutshell, give computers the ability to process yes-no and either-or statements. We've all seen messages displayed such as 'Do you wish to quit this application?'—yes or no—or 'Choose drive C or drive D as file destination'—an either-or decision. Here's where it gets creepy, though. In a Quatum computer, each bit—or quibit—can have a value of zero, one, or anything in between, exponentially increasing the power of computation."

"If you say so, Jan."

"I say so, Gwen. What BioNet is programmed to do at Level II is to decide which probable realities are most likely to exist given a set of variables, and what realities might be expected to exist in the future. It takes the entire yes-no, either-or computer logic to a level of programming based on quantum physics. Theoretically, it can actually predict outbreaks before they happen. Likewise—and here's the real beauty of the entire system—it can assign a preliminary diagnosis to a set of symptoms and then extrapolate backward to find the agent responsible—environmental, viral, bacterial, what-have-you. Does that mean BioNet is perfect in using quantum probability as its programming foundation? Let me just say this: in simulations, it hypothesized heretofore-unknown viruses as the cause of a disease by deciding on the probability of viral mutations. Yep, I'd say we're most definitely in Star Trek territory, my dear Dr. Maulder."

"To say I'm impressed would be an understatement," Gwen admitted. "I could also ask a million follow-up questions, the answers to which I wouldn't understand. So the bottom line is this: will you run my data at Level I, Jan? On the q.t.? Depending on results, we can move to Level II."

"Sure, but no need for secrecy. With seizure frequency built into the program, I can run it at will. Shouldn't raise a single eyebrow. And since I'm the director, who's going to tell me I can't play with my own toy? As far as I'm concerned, this is what BioNet was designed to do. You're an FDA epidemiologist with a concern. Period."

"You're a peach, Jan. I owe you."

"Hey, I'm a Georgia gal, Gwen. Of course I'm a peach. And all you owe me are a few more calls from time to time. Deal?"

"Deal."

Gwen hung up and sat back in her seat, feeling a sense of accomplishment that had eluded her for too long. For the first time since Marci died, Gwen felt that she might finally know what happened to her.

Her good mood lasted until 5:15 that afternoon. That was when she got an e-mail from her boss, Ralph Snyder. Gwen had been around the agency long enough to know that no end-of-the-day e-mail was a good harbinger, particularly when it came directly from above rather than through the bureaucratic chain of secretaries and administrative assistants. The note was terse and to the point. It read, "Can we review your current workload, recent accomplishments, and job priorities in my office Monday morning at eleven?"

The seemingly straightforward question was a bad omen. In bureaucratic parlance, "review" was a sure indication that something was going to change. Snyder couldn't fire Gwen without citing an incident of gross negligence or incompetence, but he could make her life hell by dumping paperwork in her lap, reducing her to nothing more than a secretary compiling stats.

Why would he suddenly be on her case? Gwen knit her brows and tried to recall something—anything—that would have caused the anal-retentive Snyder to single her out for reassignment. No, there was nothing she could think of. Her duties had remained constant except for work resulting from the occasional request from Snyder himself to supervise fieldwork in various cities for limited periods of time. What interest, she wondered, could Snyder possibly have in her "job priorities"?

She left the building and then stopped dead in her tracks. "Oh shit," she muttered, her legs suddenly feeling weak. She slid into the driver's seat of her trusted blue Nissan Maxima and lowered her head onto the steering wheel.

The call to Jan Menefee. Snyder must have somehow learned of her request to use BioNet.

"Dammit," Gwen said, raising her head. "It's a valid inquiry. It's what I'm supposed to do."

Gwen could hear Snyder's high-pitched, whining voice lecturing her on the need to separate her actions on behalf of the agency from a single case, and one without a great deal of merit, involving a friend.

Gwen turned the ignition key and backed out of her parking space, attempting to parse the matter in her thoughts as she began her drive back to Garrett Park. How could Snyder possibly know of her call to Jan—and know so quickly . . . unless she was under surveillance. She was alone when she made the call, and even if a secretary had overheard her, the subject of her conversation was routine. She was conducting medical business, which is why the FDA cut her a paycheck every two weeks. The only logical conclusion was that someone didn't want her investigating Marci Newman's death.

She would tell Jack about Snyder's e-mail as soon as she walked through the front door. If anyone knew about being under surveillance, it was a former Secret Service agent.

No. That was the one thing she definitely couldn't do. Jack would say that enough was enough. He would tell her to back away—safety first—and then he'd recite a dozen other maxims. Being a former special agent, he would probably do some snooping, but he wouldn't bend over backwards to find out why Snyder was unhappy. On the contrary, he would be secretly elated that the agency itself stamped the death of Marci Newman out of bounds as a legitimate avenue of inquiry. He'd also be supremely pissed that she had called Jan Menefee in the first place.

The deep green foliage of a late summer afternoon drifted by the car window. She had to confide in somebody. But who could help her? Perhaps more importantly, whom could she really trust?

I can trust Mark. The thought surprised her as soon as it came to her. Mark Stern? Was there some cosmic reason why she'd read his byline just yesterday? Was there even a bigger cosmic reason why he was in Washington at all? Gwen wasn't sure she believed in such things, but she also didn't believe in accidents. It wasn't an accident that she flipped open the paper the way she did last night. Maybe she needed to know that Mark was there.

And regardless of how she felt about their time as lovers or Mark's ability to ever join the adult segment of the human race, she knew one thing absolutely—she could trust him with anything. But should she contact him? If she did, she wouldn't be able to let Jack know for any number of reasons. Did she really want to do this behind Jack's back?

No, she didn't.

Not yet, anyway.

19

Two days after Edward Karn's nomination had been expertly torpedoed, Senator Henry Broome appeared on *Washington One-On-One*, a weekly political talk show hosted by Keith Caldwell, preeminent pundit of the airwaves. The show was taped at WETA studios for airing the following Sunday.

The senator from Hawaii settled into the chair opposite Caldwell, his large body still in fighting trim thanks to workouts at the Senate's private gym. He was relaxed. Caldwell was no pit bull, but he had a reputation for being politely aggressive. Henry, however, had become quite a rhetorician over the years, and his seamless segues from one topic to another were more than sufficient on most occasions to change the subject of conversation or, in true political fashion, obfuscate it altogether. Henry knew what Caldwell's agenda would be once the cameras started to roll and he regarded the coming show as nothing more than a sparring match.

"Three, two, and one!" announced a voice in the dark recesses of the studio.

"Good morning, and welcome to *Washington One-On-One*," the fifty-two-year-old Caldwell spoke in a halting manner reminiscent of David Brinkley. "Today our guest is Senator Henry Broome of Hawaii who, besides being chair of the Senate Committee on Agriculture, is also a member of the Senate Committee on Health, Education, Labor & Pensions." Caldwell then added the signature line he used at the beginning of each taping: "Let's get right to it, shall we?"

The host promptly turned in his chair to face Henry squarely.

"Senator Broome, Washington is talking about little else than the Senate's refusal to confirm Dr. Edward Karn as commissioner of the Food and Drug Administration. It's believed by most observers that your influence was responsible for Karn's defeat. Would you say that's an accurate assessment?"

Henry smiled affably and crossed his legs. "Not entirely, Keith. I'm only one member on the committee, and the vote of the committee naturally involved my twenty colleagues."

Henry's opening gambit was always to answer a question as simply and as briefly as possible, offering up the obvious in order to give him time to read his interviewer.

"But your questioning of Dr. Karn was 'grueling, malicious, and partisan' to quote Mark Stern of the *Washington Post*."

"I'm disappointed that Mr. Stern can't see past his own biases, Keith." Henry looked straight at the camera and smiled. "Karn's defeat was very painful to me personally. I've known Eddie since college and have always thought of him as a friend, but friendship has to take a backseat when the needs of the nation are at stake. I regret that Mr. Stern is unable to make that distinction. I bear no malice whatsoever toward Dr. Karn. What Mark Stern calls partisan and malicious is nothing more than thoughtful examination of important issues. Perhaps Stern's fame has gone to his head, causing him to lose the objectivity that is so essential to his profession."

Henry was warming to the subject—and to his imagined audience. He'd gone on the offensive while simultaneously voicing his disdain for liberal reporters. He would love to have gone further, labeling Stern as a former pot-smoking hippie, but a shrewd politician knew where to draw the line. He possessed plenty of information about the redoubtable Mark Stern that he could discreetly leak if the *Post*'s latest wonder boy became too vociferous about matters Henry considered off-limits for public discussion.

"Besides," Henry continued, preempting Caldwell's next question, "my constituents elected me because I'm a conservative—not ashamed of that, Keith—and it would be irresponsible of me to support someone like Dr. Karn for an important position if he can't be trusted to stay within the legal guidelines that Congress, in its wisdom, has established for the FDA."

"Elaborate on that, if you would, Senator. Why would Dr. Karn's confirmation as FDA commissioner present such a danger to the country? His record and credentials are impeccable."

"I'm not calling Dr. Karn's credentials into question, Keith. He's done exemplary work as an oncologist, but we need to understand the precise role of the FDA in the regulatory process, which is something the good doctor fails to grasp. Among other things, Dr. Karn is against genetically modified foods, or GMOs. So let me give you the simple facts regarding the regulatory process governing GMOs. The EPA evaluates a genetically modified plant for environmental safety. The USDA determines if the plant is safe to grow. Lastly, the FDA decides whether or not the plant is safe for consumption in food products."

"I believe the FDA has a slightly larger mandate than that, Senator," interjected the liberal Caldwell with a hint of sarcasm, attempting to throw Henry off balance. "I think you may be simplifying the role of the FDA considerably."

Henry was unfazed. "Keith, I think I see where you're going with this, but we have to compare apples to apples, oranges to oranges. It's certainly true that the FDA is charged with ensuring the safety of pharmaceuticals, cosmetics, and other chemical agents that could impact our health—not just food products per se. When it comes to food, however, the FDA is charged with guaranteeing the safety of processed foods, not whole foods and crops, once they enter the food chain, Keith. The FDA regards GM crops as natural foods."

"Such as?"

"Let's look at corn versus cornflakes. Cornflakes is a packaged food that has undergone a great deal of processing. An ear of corn is a whole food, Keith. Cereal is a food product, while fresh corn, right off the stalk, is, beyond any doubt, a natural food. Historically, the FDA's stance has been that GM foods are equivalent—and let me repeat that—they are equivalent to natural foods and therefore not subject to regulation."

"Don't you think that we're counting how many angels can dance on the head of a pin, Senator Broome? Let's be candid. Whether we modify a food product before or after it's harvested is of little consequence, isn't it? I think your argument, Senator, begs the question."

"In that case, Keith, I need to beg your indulgence, for we need to start at the beginning. Do you like Silver Queen corn?"

"Yes, I do. My whole family does. When Silver Queen comes in every year, my children can't get enough of it. Sometimes they even eat it raw."

Caldwell had let his guard down, and Henry was ready to go in for the kill.

"That's my point, Keith. Just about everyone likes it, and yet 350 years ago, it didn't exist. What the Pilgrims found in the New World was Indian maize, which isn't sweet at all and is today relegated to decorating homes at Thanksgiving. It's really not considered edible. After a few centuries of genetic modifications through simple farming techniques, however, we have a completely different product."

"Wait just a minute, Senator. Are you equating the planting of corn with genetic modification?"

"That's exactly what I'm doing, Keith, because that's what genetic modification is. People regard it as some evil, arcane process, when the reality is that crossing one plant with another to select a certain trait has been done for thousands of years. Just as dog breeds have changed over time because breeders chose to emphasize longer noses or shorter tails, humans have, both knowingly and unknowingly, attempted to maximize the expression of plant genes to affect taste, color, size, and numerous other traits that we desire. Scientifically, we say that farmers or breeders are selecting a dominant gene over a recessive one. Whenever you select the healthiest animals to mate, you're engaging in genetic modification in an attempt to ensure that the most desirable genes are reproduced in the offspring. What could be more natural? It really makes no difference whether you select a gene in the lab or on the farm." Henry had a good memory, good enough to remember certain facts that his buddy Jamie Robinson recited way back in 1977.

"I'll concede that your argument has some merit, Senator," stated Caldwell, "but then why are European populations so upset about genetically modified foods?"

"It's a complex question, Keith, but basically it boils down to politics. European countries have experienced two food-related scares in the last few years: mad cow disease in Britain and dioxin-tainted foods in Belgium, but neither case has anything to do with genetic modification. These concerns, while valid, undermined consumer confidence, and many European governments used sleight-of-hand to divert attention to imported American products so as not to take responsibility for problems originating on their own turf. The reality is that, after fifty years of progress in agriculture, we in the United States can bring better food to market than European nations can. Then they criticize us sharply because they must otherwise either pay for our seed stock or, as is the case now, suffer the consequences and produce fewer crops. I might add that the crops they do produce are not high-yield or disease-resistant in a good many cases. The truth is that European farmers have been compensated with subsidies and restrictive import policies because of their governments' irrational attitudes toward agricultural technology. That doesn't give their governments the right to expect farmers here in the U.S. to use the same methods as they did in the 1950s. It's just not a realistic expectation, Keith."

Henry reveled in the disappointment evident in Caldwell's expression. Few *One-On-One* guests were able to disarm the show's suave, well-prepared host so easily.

"I'm not sure everyone agrees with you, Mr. Chairman, but you're certainly well-versed in agricultural matters, both domestic and abroad. Do you have any final statements?"

"Only that American farmers work hard and deserve a lot more credit than they get. In conjunction with science, they help our country produce the safest food in the world."

Keith Caldwell swiveled back to face the camera. "Senator Broome, thank you very much for stopping by today. In just a moment, we'll be joined by Senator Ted Kennedy, a ranking member of the Judiciary Committee, who will discuss Supreme Court nominations."

"Clear!" somebody called from behind the cameras. "Ready for segment two!"

Henry removed his lapel mike, stood, and shook hands with

Caldwell. He passed Senator Kennedy on the way out, but the Massachusetts legend said nothing, and he left the studio feeling more than satisfied with his performance.

Henry got into his Caddy and sped toward the Hotel Rouge, where Roberta Chang would be waiting for him, dressed in a negligee and holding two fluted glasses of Dom Perignon.

Henry would be back home with his wife and family in time for dinner.

20

Gwen was fixing grilled cheese sandwiches late Saturday morning when the cell phone on the kitchen counter chimed, the melody a ridiculously fast rendition of the first fifteen notes of Pachelbel's Canon in D.

"Hello?"

"It's Jan, Gwen. I've got some results for you, and they're gonna knock your socks off."

Gwen looked at Jack, who was sipping a cup of coffee and perusing the morning paper at the kitchen table. A tool belt hung on the coat rack behind him since he intended to start on the basement after lunch. Initially, all he needed to do was clean up and take some measurements, but he certainly seemed to be starting this project with gusto.

"Hey!" Gwen said enthusiastically into the phone. "Tell me what you've got." She turned off the range and looked at Jack, mouthing the words, "Going to check the mail."

Jack nodded and continued scanning the Sports section.

Outside, Gwen spoke more freely. "Sorry, Jan. Jack would think I'm a little nuts to be pursuing this, so I had to move outside. He was just a few feet away."

"Well, he wouldn't think you're nuts if he could see the data that I'm looking at now."

"That's debatable," Gwen said, "but more to the point, tell me what BioNet found."

"BioNet shows definite seizure spikes in New York City during an extremely short period of time. Keep in mind that our system has been running for less than a year, but the data is pretty conclusive. What it means is another matter altogether."

"Give me some specifics, Jan, before I go out of my mind."

"Okay. Here goes. The week Marci Newman died, three other New Yorkers died in emergency rooms, all having suffered seizures. Furthermore, from the second week in May to the first week in June, BioNet registers four, three, six, and five deaths per week, respectively, for a total of eighteen in New York City."

Gwen let out a low whistle under her breath. "That's incredible."

"It gets scarier. During that same time period, 126 people were admitted to ERs with seizures that didn't prove fatal. The patients were discharged uneventfully."

"What other symptoms did the fatalities present?"

"I can only give you info for fifteen. According to BioNet, no postmortem exam was conducted for three of the deceased. Their families were probably very well-placed and pulled some strings since most people would rather not think of their loved ones lying on an autopsy table. Of the fifteen, however, one had diabetes and one had seriously occluded coronary arteries. The rest had no prior medical history to speak of."

"Toxicology reports?"

"I'll give you the overview so we won't talk for the next four hours and cause poor Jack to think you're having an affair. I can e-mail the specifics to your office later. Here's a quick breakdown of substances identified by labwork and how many of the fifteen had them in their systems at the time of death. Marijuana, three. Sudafed, one. Antibiotics, four, tetracycline and Bactrim. Blood thinners, one. All fifteen had either aspirin, ibuprofen, or Tylenol. Caffeine, fourteen. Thirteen were smokers, which is a bit high since people are cutting back these days, but young professionals in big cities still have a higher incidence of tobacco use."

"Young professionals?" asked Gwen.

"The stats are definitely skewed toward young adults. Eleven of the fifteen were under thirty-five. Most had high-powered jobs. Turns out age is a part of this bizarre trend after all."

It was time for the million-dollar question. "What does BioNet say about the statistical probability of this kind of seizure activity in a city as large as New York?"

"Factoring in the 126 patients who were discharged—and 74 percent of them were fairly young, too, by the way—BioNet The All-Knowing says that there's only a 4 percent chance of such an occurrence during the four-week period. That's low by anyone's standards. Seizures happen for various reasons in the general population across all age groups, but for a total of 144 patients to be treated at medical facilities for seizures in that short a time is pretty unusual. Hell, you know that better than anyone, Gwen. But we can refine the stats even further. Factoring out the one person who had occluded arteries, and assuming the other three for which no data was available were healthy, BioNet calculates a probability of only 3.7 percent that seventeen seizure fatalities would be recorded in predominately young patients without known complications or serious preexisting conditions, with a margin of error of 0.2 percent."

"So what the hell went wrong in New York back in May?" asked Gwen. "This sure as hell sounds like a health hazard to me. Does BioNet have any predictions as to possible causes?"

"Whoa there, Captain. I've only given you the tip of the iceberg. The phenomenon isn't confined to New York City."

There was a long silence on both ends of the line.

"That's right," Jan continued. "In 2004, eighty-six seizure patients were admitted to emergency rooms in Denver between October 3rd and December 10th, with twelve of those reported as fatal. Seizure spikes also occurred briefly within the past year in the metro areas of Boston, Chicago, Kansas City, Trenton, Miami, Detroit, Los Angeles, Milwaukee, St. Louis, Phoenix, and numerous smaller cities that have a large enough population for which data was fed to BioNet."

"Without chapter and verse, what's the general story in these cities?" asked Gwen, whose mind was in computer crash mode.

"The scenario is pretty much analogous to New York in every single city. A few people were older or had some recognizable medical condition, but not many. Most were treated and released, with a certain percentage of those admitted—5 to 15 percent—listed as fatalities. According to BioNet, the statistical probability of the New

York scenario playing out again in so many other places is about one in a trillion. It's just not in the realm of possibility. The odds are about the same as a meteor hitting the Earth tomorrow morning. We've got ourselves a mystery, Dr. Maulder."

"Any similarities in toxicology reports?"

"It runs the gamut, Gwen. There were a lot of legal and illegal drugs in people's systems, including both OTC and prescription medicines. Almost all patients were caffeine users—big surprise—but a whopping 78.8 percent of these people smoked. That's way above the national average, even for younger people who still think it's cool to smoke or that there's time to quit before their lungs are charred."

"What's the protocol, Jan? This is big. The CDC is surely going to send out field investigators to start interviewing ER doctors, survivors, and relatives of the deceased, right? Maybe start taking air, water, and soil samples?"

Jan took a deep breath. "I submitted the findings to my superiors, and the official response was 'collect more data and regard the findings as highly confidential.' The CDC obviously doesn't want to start a panic, but I would think some pretty thorough investigations should be forthcoming."

"Simply incredible," said Gwen. "I need to get back inside before Jack thinks I've gone missing, but let me know if BioNet comes up with anything else. Thanks for everything, Jan."

"No problem, Doc."

Gwen pressed a button to end the call and walked up the driveway.

The grilled cheese sandwiches had gone cold. Jack was still reading the paper and hadn't bothered to touch the one she'd already set before him when the phone rang.

■ ■ ■

Down in the basement of the Maulder home, Jack occupied himself by measuring the wall studs for Gwen's new office, while his brain continued to cycle over a confusing set of developments. Gwen was being secretive. She'd come back inside with no mail, looking pale as a ghost. When he asked her what was wrong, she said she'd been talking to someone from the CDC about a report that Chinese passengers arriving at U.S. airports were complaining of high fevers. Jack knew that Gwen would never discuss serious business in her shorts out by the mailbox on Saturdays.

She was obviously hiding something. But what the hell was it?

21

Mark Stern strolled down Pennsylvania Avenue after meeting with an old friend, United States representative Rick Mecklenberg, a thirty-eight-year-old Democrat from Denver, Colorado. Both Rick and Mark had attended the Columbia School of Journalism, but Rick's righteous indignation had grown with each passing scandal until he could no longer sit on the sidelines. "I've decided to stop covering the news and become the news," he told Mark years earlier, sitting at a corner bar in Greenwich Village.

Rick had been one of Mark's best confidential sources for the past five years, although representative Mecklenberg's services had not been in much demand when Mark was profiling aristocrats for the *Journal*. Mark was in Washington now, however, and wanted to check in with his old classmate and colleague to find out if anything juicy was currently traveling the political grapevine.

"Nothing terribly unusual at present," Rick told Mark over lunch. "A prominent senator will quietly check himself into rehab next week for prescription drug abuse. He's the third one this month, by the way. Technodyne Systems will be investigated by the Appropriations Committee for kickbacks regarding the hang fire missile it's producing for the army. Just routine stuff that's normal for this town."

The two men laughed as they devoured turkey club sandwiches.

"But keep an eye on Senator Henry Broome," continued Rick.

"There are those in the GOP who think Broome may be the party's presidential nominee in 2012, depending on what happens in

2008. Some observers think Broome might even get the nod for Veep next time around. The guy steamrolls his competition. He's charming, suave, and absolutely ruthless. Also a ladies' man—which could be his undoing if he's not careful."

On the way out of the restaurant, Rick turned to Mark and said, "Hey, are you seeing anyone? Wendy has this friend, met her during a fundraiser a few years back. Really politically active, with legs that don't quit—"

"Thanks," Mark replied. "I'm still settling in. Maybe in a few months."

"Okay, pal, but you're not getting younger."

"Thanks, you bastard," Mark said jokingly. "Keep in touch."

"Give 'em hell in your column," Rick said as he got in his car.

Mark decided to walk around a bit. He'd been in Washington often before, but he wanted to take some extra time to wander the streets, maybe even stroll down the Mall to get a whiff of the intangible life of the city.

But first, he needed to assuage his thirst. The restaurant only served Pepsi, and Mark was an unmitigated Coke-a-holic. Coca-Cola was, in fact, the only stock in which he'd invested since he was convinced that people were never going to stop drinking "the real thing." Coke was a proven winner on Wall Street and as conservative an investment as one could make. The rest of his money, including what remained of his million-dollar termination bonanza after the taxman had cometh, was in CDs and T-bills. His lawyer had once remarked, "You must be the only employee of the *Journal* to be thoroughly bored by the subject of investment strategies and portfolios."

He came across a soda machine one block away. Feeding it a dollar bill, he jabbed the Coke button—classic red with caffeine and a ton of sugar, no diet please—but the machine stiffed him. Mark engaged in the great American reflex of hitting the machine, following the gesture with a swift kick to the plastic casing. The large machine, cold to the touch and humming with electricity, maintained its mechanical aloofness and withheld Mark's Coke.

"*C'est la vie,*" the reporter sighed, only to have his aimless wandering arrested by a Pequod's sign in his peripheral vision.

Pequod's. Mark wasn't much of a coffee drinker, but it was time to head on back to the office, and he needed a jump-start since his digestive system was claiming his brain's much-needed blood supply.

Reluctantly, he went into the store and ordered one of their espresso-caramel-whipped cream concoctions. He felt like a yuppie, but sometimes necessity caused you to do things. If only Gwen could see him in a Pequod's store, she would—

"Not gonna go there," he said aloud, censoring his thought process. Mark made his way to the long table opposite the coffee bar to get a napkin and a spoon. He stopped, his attention snared by a photograph on the wall a few feet away. Billy Hamlin, chairman and CEO of Pequod's, smiled confidently from the picture, causing Mark to speculate that Billy boy was also smiling from the walls of several thousand other Pequod's stores. It was dangerous to judge people by appearances, but Mark prided himself on his ability to size people up very quickly, and Hamlin seemed like a decent fellow. Odd, thought Mark, that such a young man had been able to make Pequod's coffee America's premier eye-opener.

He left the restaurant, took three sips of the coffee concoction, and pitched the cup into the first wire trash receptacle he saw.

The ads were right. Coke was the real thing.

Mark started walking again but stopped abruptly and looked back in the direction of Pequod's. Billy Hamlin, at the helm of a growing American phenomenon, would be a great interview. The coffee boom was most definitely a Mark Stern story since Mark was, after all, a student of culture in the good old U.S. of A. He'd put in a call to Pequod's corporate headquarters in Seattle and see if Hamlin's smile was as inviting as the picture implied.

■ ■ ■

Gregory Randall, CEO, was slender, with jet-black hair parted perfectly above an aquiline nose and narrow jaw. He dressed impeccably. His Armani collection required an entire closet of its own. He wouldn't be caught dead in shoes that cost less than a thousand dollars, and his ties, like most of his women, were imported. Several publications had named him the most eligible bachelor in the Western Hemisphere (though he would categorically deny interest in any assessment made by publications such as *GQ* or *Vanity Fair*).

His manner, terse and to the point, was the reason that his board meetings rarely lasted more than thirty minutes, a rarity in the world of mega-corporations. The thirty-nine-year-old chief executive officer of Randall, Inc. gathered his board of directors more as a formality than a policy-making necessity. He was not averse to entertaining suggestions, but he preferred them to be sixty seconds or less in duration. He wasn't interested in graphs, pie charts, or PowerPoint presentations. He had all the figures he needed in his head.

"I'd like to thank all of you," Randall said at the start of the 2005 meeting of the Board of Directors, "for your kind words of sympathy regarding the death of my father. He was an estimable man and such losses are never easy." Randall cast his eyes downward for an extended beat. Then he rose from his chair and assumed his traditional posture for board meetings—pacing back and forth at the head of the long mahogany table on the eighteenth floor of the Randall Building in New York City.

"We have three matters before us today, so we need to move briskly." He looked closely at the ten men and two women seated around the table. He switched eye contact from one board member to another every fifteen seconds or so, forcing his twelve listeners to stay sharp. "First, our fourth generation Acceleration Chip—AC IV—will be market-ready in just a few days. It will be the fastest operating chip ever used in a personal computer, making Intel look like Aesop's tortoise. Even dial-up Internet users will see their PCs moving at the speed of light. As CEO of our Friendlyware subsidiary, Ralph Stefano will naturally be our point man in making sure we start to make Intel a bit uncomfortable. Right, Ralph?"

A white-haired gentleman in his early sixties nodded and smiled compliantly.

"Comments, anyone?"

There were none.

"Next, there's the matter of expanding Pequod's into different markets. We have hundreds of stores in every state, and our coffee is achieving cult status. We'll be taking our product right down to the grassroots level, with coffee bars in bookstores, airports, and malls. Furthermore, the complimentary coffee served to shoppers by grocery stores in twenty-two states will shortly become Pequod's. We're also going to test-market iced coffee beverages in glass bottles, placing them in the dairy cases of at least three grocery chains in five states."

Billy Hamlin, CEO of Pequod's, leaned forward, hands clasped on the polished table. His dazzling white smile disappeared, and a frown suddenly recast his boyish features—square jaw, fair complexion, light blue eyes, and blond hair—into a study of polite, respectful confusion.

"You and I have discussed this for a while now, Gregory. I think we're looking at possible market saturation. Of course we need to continue to expand, but the most prudent thing to do at this point is slow the process down."

"Normally I'd agree, Billy, but the fact of the matter is that Pequod's outperforms its competition in every state, and that's in no small part because of your expert leadership in using PR to make Pequod's a household name. The other big boy in the market doesn't know what hit it. They're hemorrhaging market share to us. Meanwhile, the smaller chains that try to expand and take us on never make any serious headway. They start local and stay local. Personally, I'm comfortable with that. I'm sure that with you overseeing the expansion, we'll continue to not only thrive, but also keep the competition at a very comfortable distance."

Hamlin's face relaxed, allowing an "aw shucks, just doin' my job" grin to replace his momentary look of concern. "Just playing devil's advocate, Gregory. I'll do my best."

Randall smiled. Hamlin was just as good as he needed to be. "I have every confidence that you will, Billy. Now then, does anyone else wish to speak for the devil?"

There were a few chuckles around the table.

"Very well, then. The last item of business concerns the company founded by my late uncle, James Compson Randall, namely Compson Tobacco, Inc. Compson is doing well in virtually every targeted demographic market, which is precisely why I want to step up our obligatory antismoking commercials and programs. It pays to be proactive, and if we're doing well without simultaneously trying to demonstrate that we're withdrawing from addiction, if you'll pardon the mixed metaphor, then we may draw some attention down the road from *60 Minutes* or *Dateline*. We'll have the usual: TV spots—those heartwarming thirty-second pieces showing parents and children discussing demon tobacco—as well as posters for school bulletin boards and an expanded Website on ways to kick the habit. Statistics show these programs have no significant effect on sales in any region, so I think we cover ourselves and stay ahead of any public criticism. Agreed?"

Nods of approval appeared around the table. Randall wondered why he gathered the board at all.

"Great. Now if you'll excuse me, I have a date with a golf ball in less than an hour. The helicopter's already warming up on the roof, so I bid you good day, ladies and gentlemen."

There was polite applause in the room as Gregory Randall slipped through a side door into his office. The guru of Randall, Inc. expected a duly appreciative audience and they dutifully obliged him every time.

They regarded it as job security.

22

Gwen walked into the Parklawn Building on Monday morning with a bit less enthusiasm than usual. A meeting with Ralph Snyder could do that to a person. Gwen deliberately wore her PHS dress whites. There was nothing like gold eagles on a woman's blouse to keep a man like Snyder mired in his insecurity. She was going to act professionally and she considered dressing the part to be essential for a possible confrontation with this pencil pusher.

When she reached Snyder's pallid office suite, Snyder's secretary motioned for Gwen to sit, shrugging apologetically. Did the man have anyone who truly respected him?

The magazines on the end tables were predictably sterile. Gwen absentmindedly leafed through twenty pages of *Public Administration* when Snyder's door opened, revealing a man whose comb-over was less convincing than usual, strands of hair clumped on his all-too-visible bald pate.

"Good morning, Dr. Maulder," he said thinly.

He motioned her toward the famous "victim's chair" in his office. Rumor had it that he'd shortened one leg of this chair to keep his subjects uncomfortable during their encounters with him, a trick he'd likely learned from a correspondence course on leadership and intimidation. The chair kept tottering on its uneven legs, forcing Gwen to spend much too much attention on keeping her balance. She flashed on Fitz Rule Number Four: Don't let the morons of the world cause you to compromise your beliefs.

"Bring me up to date on your work in the Epidemiology Division, if you would," Snyder began, settling into his armchair. He was a thin man, and his baggy suit was obviously straight off the rack.

Gwen realized instantly that Snyder was playing games, asking her to state what he already knew. She obliged him, however, by going through the general protocols for her department. She explained that her division of the Center for Drugs was a support unit for the entire Center, the mission of which was to track underlying disease processes in the general population. She often received assignments that went beyond these parameters, but this explanation encompassed the main mission statement of her department. If the FDA were considering approval for a new cholesterol-lowering drug, for instance, her unit could provide up-to-the-minute information on how many people in the country had high cholesterol and to what degree. Along these lines, she related to Snyder the results of a recent study on the prevalence of asthma in inner-city children.

Snyder clasped his hands, elbows resting on the arms of his chair. "That's all very interesting, and I'm sure it's invaluable to the scientific community, but my job, Dr. Maulder, is to make sure that our manpower is used to the taxpayers' maximum advantage. I'm afraid I'm going to have to shift the focus of your efforts, at least temporarily. Your colleague, Dr. Wayne Spitzer, will be overseeing your division's studies for an unspecified period. I've gotten complaints from the front office that we're two years behind in reporting out our Adverse Event files from the Medwatch system—you know, the voluntary reporting database. It's all about the 9/11 Commission Report. Someone upstairs is worried that we may have some data buried in those files related to bioterrorism. Expertise like yours is our only hope for catching up. I'm assigning you to examine these files."

Gwen had prepared for many different scenarios for this meeting, but not this one. "But those AE reports and Medwatch belong to the Office of Drug Safety. That has nothing to do with my mandate. Everybody knows that the stuff in that database is useless from an epidemiologist's perspective."

"I understand your concern, Dr. Maulder, but this request comes from the highest levels. We have increasing intelligence that terrorists might attempt to tamper with the pharmaceutical supply chain in order to harm Americans. Rumors have surfaced that there have been some dry runs. Perhaps the FDA already has evidence that it has overlooked. Given the post 9/11 climate, we have decided that we need to examine certain files to be sure that we haven't overlooked anything that might indicate terrorist activity."

"But the CDC has BioNet to handle that kind of job, sir. With all due respect, I think we'd be wasting the taxpayers' money."

Snyder flashed a humorless smile. "BioNet is certainly a valuable new asset, but I still think there's no substitute for old-fashioned human intuition. I can think of no one better qualified than you to give our retro-analysis that indefinable human touch. Moreover, the CDC budget is grabbing a disproportionate share of the new Homeland Security allocations. It's time we got some of that money to come home to Rockville."

Gwen's throat went dry. This was the bureaucratic equivalent to being sent down to the minors. What was going on here? She burned inside, but she maintained a calm, professional demeanor. "Mr. Snyder, there are thousands of AE files. There's no way I could do this job in less than a year. It deserves a staff of several people and should be handled by a separate division with its own administrator."

"I'm afraid the FDA is not budgeted for that at present. If you want to use an assistant, I have no problem with that."

"One assistant?" Gwen asked incredulously.

"Yes, Dr. Maulder. One assistant."

"But—"

"Be thankful, Doctor, that I'm not assigning you to liaise with the Army on their combat virus control program. They want to start doing their own vaccine trials for diseases the civilian sector has never heard of. The only problem is the assignment will take that appointee to Somalia for six months. I haven't figured out on whom to spring that little nugget. I thought I was actually doing you a favor, as well as selecting the best person for the job. Your files show that you were a master diagnostician while in family practice."

Gwen felt a migraine sliding into her brain like a warm front scorching the Midwest. This didn't make sense. Assigning a captain in the USPH to go over Adverse Event files? That was the kind of drudgery first year medical officers had to endure. This had to be about something else. She was on the verge of asking Snyder if he knew about her call to Jan, but decided not to show her hand. She would follow Fitz Rule Number Five: Act, don't react. She'd find out later what was behind Snyder's ludicrous orders. In the meantime, she had ways of continuing her investigation in a more clandestine fashion. It might be risky, but she fully intended to find out what else BioNet had to say about the seizure stats. She would call Jan from home and suggest that they both open an account with iPrive.com to communicate only via secure mail.

"I guess my only answer is 'aye-aye, sir'" Gwen said innocently. "I'll start immediately."

"I appreciate your cooperation, Doctor," Snyder said smugly. "Your service has always been exemplary. I'll note your cooperation in your file. With any luck, you'll be back to your regular duties soon."

What did that mean? More than ever, Gwen sensed that this new assignment was all about keeping her from doing other work.

■ ■ ■

BioNet was malfunctioning.

Jan Menefee sat at one of the many computer terminals connected to the medical surveillance computer, a cup of coffee next to the monitor. She'd been named director of Project BioNet because she was both an excellent physician and a master at the computer keyboard, thanks to some undergrad classes in programming. It was 2:30 in the morning, and after several hours of prep work, her general plan was to search for more info on the seizure trends, hoping that BioNet might have explanations or predictions at its quantum level. All of this was surreptitious, of course, and she'd have to cover her tracks. She knew she couldn't erase the computer's boot log completely because there were too many security features built into the system, but she could shunt the log of the night's clandestine activity to a sub-directory that no one was likely to check.

But the damned system wasn't cooperating. She received repeated error messages more appropriate to a PC running Windows 95 with a Pentium I:

Input error
Bad command
Data not available
Requested file does not exist
Programming error: If problem persists, please contact system administrator.

Jan folded her arms and sighed. In the universe of bytes and RAM, BioNet was one of the Seven Wonders of the World. The problems that BioNet encountered during trial runs presented in numerical codes, not outdated error messages. The designers of BioNet did not imprint Microsoft jargon in its state-of-the-art chips.

Jan got up and stretched, walking into the adjoining room where the mainframe—BioNet's brain—was kept.

"Damn," she muttered. Several digital readouts indicated that the system was not only in optimal condition but was actually in the process of carrying out various commands. Large spools of tape spun behind a dark glass casing. "I'm being shut out of the freakin' system. This is nuts. Okay, Hal 9000, let's see why you're acting pissy."

The room was dark except for the glow coming from the computer screen. Jan returned to the desktop terminal. "We'll try something simpler," she said. "No programming commands. Just a straightforward question."

She opened the system's main diagnostic window and tapped a few keys in order to determine BioNet's current operating mode. The following text appeared on the screen: UPLOADING FILE 23789.626.

"No, goddammit," she cried. "Stop!"

File 23789.626 contained every byte of information she'd gathered about seizure activity around the country. But if it was uploading, where was it going?

She frantically opened another window and typed in DESTINATION.

The reply from BioNet was swift: PLEASE WAIT UNTIL UPLOAD IS COMPLETE.

Frantically, Jan tried to cancel the upload, but the system ignored her efforts. Something was overriding.

"Okay, let's do things the hard way."

She took a sip of coffee and called up a hidden file on her desktop computer. Jan had been part of Project BioNet from the beginning, but even as director, she was not familiar with every single command that could be given to the supercomputer.

The file, available to administrators only, appeared on her screen, but the options displayed on its panel were anything but user-friendly.

Programmers naturally had to adjust the highly complex system on a daily basis and she couldn't stay on top of every single bit of techno-jargon. Jan studied a line of programming code and saw "&whoR594job!enteradclear." Did the "adclear" refer to "administrative clearance?" Was the panel requesting what amounted to a password?

She pulled open a drawer to her lower right and found a floppy handbook titled BioNet Administrative Job-Control. After several frustrating minutes, she found an entire directory of "&who" commands. Her index finger slid down the page until she found the entire line currently displayed in the panel. Next to it was a password.

She typed in "biodestination/operator27" and got an immediate response. "Yes!" Jan proclaimed, throwing her right arm up in victory.

UPLOAD 45D
120,887 KB SUCCESSFULLY SENT TO:
user9187@network.iceland.net

Jan was stumped. Why should BioNet send the file to an anonymous re-mailer in Iceland? What had triggered the upload? More importantly, who had triggered it? She was confident that the system hadn't been zombied by an outside party. As director, she had ordered the same level of security as the National Security Agency—and even more secret "shops"—to prevent outside hacking. The source, therefore, almost certainly had to be internal.

The BioNet director buried her face in her hands. She could

hardly believe the implications of what she just saw. Jan rolled her chair back to the nearest BioNet terminal to determine what other uploads, if any, had been sent in the last forty-eight hours. Thankfully, there had been none.

She would get CDC security people on the problem first thing in the morning, and she had a hunch that the investigation into the upload would go even higher. This kind of penetration was exactly what the executive branch of the government had been worried about. But here was the catch. There were many reasons that might drive someone to steal CDC files, and yet the hot topics on the CDC agenda—Ebola, avian flu, and other viruses that could turn someone's face to mush—had been neglected. Out of thousands of available files, the intruder chose number 23789.626.

Still, why had any file been uploaded and sent anywhere outside the CDC network?

It was a sobering question and Jan decided it would be prudent to wait awhile before calling in the agency's security division. Once they started an investigation, everyone, including the perpetrator, would run for cover in a general atmosphere of paranoia. The leak would be plugged with sophisticated patches and firewalls, rendering any hope of finding the responsible party virtually impossible. She owed it to Gwen to keep things quiet for the time being.

There was another option, however. In March, she'd been a fly on the wall in the White House Conference Center at a meeting of the president's Information Technology Advisory Council. PITAC was especially interested in security around cutting-edge antiterror computer programs, and Jan was there because of her top-level position with BioNet. One of the presenters, Peter Tippett, had made a great deal more sense than most of the people babbling for the sake of recognition in their various fields.

"The most important action after a penetration has been detected," Tippett remarked, "should be no different for computer spying than it was for the old-fashioned kind. It's crucial not to let the adversary know you are aware of the penetration. Use the adversary's own conduit to trap him."

It took Jan all of fifteen seconds to Google "Tippett" and find his contact information. She'd call him in the morning.

As originally planned, Jan sent her boot log to the predetermined sub-directory and then went home. There, she retrieved a voice-mail from Gwen that said "iPrive.com" and nothing else.

It was difficult to believe that was coincidental. She recalled a line from Sir Arthur Conan Doyle's famous detective: "The game's afoot, Watson."

What kind of game was another matter altogether.

23

Mark Stern's mentor at the Columbia School of Journalism once told him that a reporter without sources usually ends up covering the county fair. Mark understood the implications and maintained his contacts in Washington while he worked at the *Times* and the *Journal*. Now based in Washington, he kept in touch with his old colleagues at the New York papers with equal care. Today, he decided, was time to call in a marker from an old friend in Gotham.

He dialed the number of Charlie Nicholls, city desk lead at the *Wall Street Journal*, and waited for the voice of his former comrade-in-print. As far as Mark was concerned, Charlie was the only other colorful character in a sea of gray at the *Journal*. They weren't exactly Woodward and Bernstein together, but they goaded each other on, sharing information and doing their best not to scoop each other.

"Charlie, it's the Sternster. Got a few minutes?"

"For a fallen hero like you?" said Nicholls. "Absolutely. You have balls, my boy. People here are still shaking their heads about the manner of your exit from this rich man's rag. What can I do for ya?"

"Know anything about Billy Hamlin?"

After a short pause, Nicholls delivered one of his trademark snorting laughs that Mark always found mildly irritating. "Why am I not surprised by your timing, Mark?"

"What do you mean?"

There was another brief pause. "You're telling me you don't know about one of the biggest forthcoming announcements in the corporate pantheon of Randall, Inc.?"

"You got it, Charlie. Don't have a clue, but I think I'm about to get one."

"Whoa, partner. The *Journal* is about to do a three-part series on Hamlin and what's shaking at Pequod's. How the hell can I just hand over that kind of privileged info?"

"For one thing, I doubt that the *Journal* is the only organization that has info on something going on at Pequod's if the revelation is as big as you say. For another, you know me. The news is not my beat—I cover the personalities. Besides, you know you're dying to tell me, Charlie."

"Of course I want to tell you."

"Then do it. We never had this conversation, and I'll pay you back in spades. There's enough political shit in this town to empty out your toner cartridge every two weeks. So?"

Charlie Nicholls sighed heavily. "Well, I'll give you the big picture. You fill in the details as you're able, assuming you can get within a mile of Hamlin or any other source. Plus, you don't have the luxury of time since this story is about to come out the gate like Seabiscuit."

"Whatcha got, amigo?"

"Hamlin's going to announce that Pequod's is expanding its markets."

"Expanding? Where? To the restrooms in two-star restaurants? You can't walk your dog without running into one of their stores."

Nicholls chuckled and snorted. "Restrooms? I wouldn't mention it to Billy Hamlin. It just might fly. For starters, the company is going to put coffee stands in airports, malls, and bookstores. It's also going to have some drive-thru java joints as well as vendors in 'coffee kiosks' in parks. You can count on that little two-word phrase working its way into the vernacular pretty fast. They're also planning to go toe-to-toe in the packaged iced coffee business."

"This sounds like the declaration of an all-out turf war. Gotta feel for the smaller companies, though."

"As far as less visible coffee chains are concerned, mom and pop would do well to cash in and move to Florida," Nicholls said grimly.

"Progress, my friend. It will be the undoing of us all."

"No argument here. Thanks, Charlie. Like I said, I owe you.

Anything else going on up there?"

"Betty Bannister is getting laid by Floyd Harkins from the advertising department."

"Floyd wears a pocket protector. I thought Betty had better taste."

"Women these days look past such things, Mark. They're not shallow like us men."

"Speak for yourself, you chauvinist pig."

"You getting any down in D.C.?"

"I naturally can't name any sources, but Mr. Stern is always in demand."

"In other words, no, right?"

"You always were good at reading between the lines. Bye, Charlie."

"Take care, Mark."

Mark hung up the phone and glanced at the notes he'd taken. This wasn't what he expected at all.

Now he needed to track down Billy Hamlin.

■ ■ ■

Subj: *RE: compromised*
Date: *7/27/05 8:03 a.m. Eastern Standard Time*
From: *biodoc107@iprive.com*
To: *captainepi323@iprive.com*

Got your voicemail. BioNet is compromised. File in question uploaded to re-mailer outside U.S. Calling in outside party for advice. Problem appears to be internal, which is scarier than the seizure stats. Can only trust "I & thou." What's going on in Rockville?

Subj: *RE: reassignment*
Date: *7/27/05 9:27 a.m. Eastern Standard Time*
From: *captainepi323@iprive.com*
To: *biodoc107@iprive.com*

Have been reassigned to Adverse Event files. No real explanation. Best guess: someone knows I asked you to use BioNet to uncover information that's supposed to remain buried. Public health just took a hard jab in the solar plexus. I concur on use of third party. Pretty sure Jack thinks I've gone round the bend. Maybe he's right. Start looking over your shoulder. Any idea where the file's final destination was?

Subj: *RE: sources*
Date: *7/27/05 11:30 a.m. Eastern Standard Time*
From: *biodoc107@iprive.com*
To: *captainepi323@iprive.com*

I'm hoping the third party will be able to answer your last question. (He's quite handsome, btw.) May take time.

Have also rethought tobacco angle. You may be right. As Ray Bradbury said, something wicked this way comes. A major investigation should be taking place. Obviously, it isn't. I'm slowly becoming a conspiracy theorist. Help!

Subj: *RE: hypothesis*
Date: *7/27/05 1:07 p.m. Eastern Standard Time*
From: *captainepi323@iprive.com*
To: *biodoc107@iprive.com*

Agree on tobacco. Hypothesis: additive, maybe legal, or else modified tobacco plant. Perhaps the bastards found a way to circumvent lab inspections and are manipulating nicotine levels again. (And to think private practice seemed stressful!) Keep me informed on your progress as time permits. Inquiring minds want to know.

Subj: *RE: ???*
Date: *7/27/05 3:44 p.m. Eastern Standard Time*
From: *biodoc107@iprive.com*
To: *captainepi323@iprive.com*

Are we in danger?

Subj: *RE: (no subject)*
Date: *7/27/05 5:26 p.m. Eastern Standard Time*
From: *captainepi323@iprive.com*
To: *biodoc107@iprive.com*

Probably.

24

Gwen sat at a computer networked with Medwatch, the FDA Safety Information and Adverse Event reporting program. The FDA instituted the reporting of adverse events for patients taking approved drugs in the 1980s as a part of its drug safety initiative. Every physician and medical staffer was duty-bound to report adverse events suffered by a patient taking any medicine. Medwatch even had a slick website the public could use to report and to gather information on drugs and other medical products regulated by the Food and Drug Administration. Reality, of course, was quite different. Reports on adverse events were sporadic and poorly policed. Searching through Medwatch was like searching through a haystack for the proverbial needle.

Gwen stared at the form for reporting problems stemming from hundreds of drugs, including heart medications, birth control pills, cholesterol-lowering drugs, and acid reflux meds. For every ailment, there was a drug and for every drug, there were unintended consequences—adverse events—not identified in the original testing. The Office of Drug Safety was supposed to identify those adverse events and protect the public's safety. Unfortunately, since all of the reports in Medwatch were anecdotal, there was no real way to link particular problems with specific drugs.

Gwen perused the standard reporting form, her mind in free-association mode. All the routine info was there . . . age, sex, and weight of the patient, outcome of the event—death, life-threatening illness, hospitalization, or disability. Items five and six asked for a description of the actual adverse event and relevant laboratory data. All basic stuff.

Box number seven, however, reminded Gwen of Fitz Rule Number Six: Turn adversity into strength; turn disadvantage into advantage.

7. Other Relevant History, Including Preexisting Medical Condition (e.g., allergies, race, pregnancy, smoking and alcohol use, hepatic/renal dysfunction, etc.)

That could be an opening. Maybe she could use Medwatch to help in her investigation of Marci's death. Instead of searching the AEs one by one, she could compile a list of all AEs that involved seizures in healthy people and start to look for patterns. She could even match the Medwatch database to the cities Jan had listed in BioNet's findings. It might be time-consuming, but at least it was a place to begin.

Since her superiors assumed they'd assigned her to an exercise in tedium, Gwen didn't think they'd monitor her computer. To be safe, though, she reset her computer for one-time passcodes. It was simple, once you got the hang of it. The password would always be the day of the year, minus the day of Gwen's birthday. Simple, but nearly impossible to crack.

Snyder and the "higher powers" had no idea what they'd done by putting her on this project. "Bureaucrats," Gwen said to herself, smiling. "Once in a while, they actually do you a favor."

■ ■ ■

Jack Maulder sat at his desk in Garrett Park, staring blankly at Haydn104. If Gwen wasn't going to be honest with him, he would redouble his own efforts and find out why his wife had gone from preoccupied to deceitful. He assumed that whatever was claiming her attention had something to do with the death of Marci Newman. Had Gwen found something? If so, she might be hiding it because he had been so adamant about her dropping the investigation. That didn't say good things about the trust levels in their marriage. Jack was going to have to do something about that. He didn't want genuine concern for Gwen's emotional health to put up walls in their relationship.

He went back to Haydn104, which, truthfully, had him stymied. He prided himself on his ability to find patterns in even the most random information typed, coded, and double-clicked into the cyber world, but there just didn't seem to be anything here. Spammers, hackers, and phishers were able to disguise their activities in a dozen different ways, and the world of cyber spying was infinitely more sophisticated than the viruses and worms used by these online nuisances. Jack had encrypted files for defense contractors, and decrypted codes used by foreign governments trying to forward messages to terrorist cells through the pixels of a photograph. If there was something to Marci's ridiculously simple list of numbers, he should have detected it by now.

Suddenly, Jack sat up. As with all epiphanies, Jack's came out of the blue. What if Marci's series of numbers was just a red herring, meant to fool someone into thinking there was nothing more in Haydn104? He gave himself a quick slap with his palm on the side of his head, reminding himself to be a little less immodest next time.

Humility keeps a person in the game, he reminded himself.

It couldn't be, though. Marci was a lawyer, not a programmer.

Jack studied the rows of numbers on his computer screen. "She was a bookworm, though, wasn't she, and smart as a whip. Little social life. Reclusive. Or might have gotten some info on hiding and retrieving files from a barrister buddy." Jack was aware that lawyers encrypted information all the time. Opposing counsel was sometimes very naughty, in fact, trying to hack into confidential files to gain a competitive edge.

It was a long shot, but if the numbers were a decryption program, what file or files would it open? And what was so important that Marci had felt the need to bury information?

On the spur of the moment, Jack decided he had to go to New York to have a look at Marci Newman's computer.

■ ■ ■

The phone rang as Roberta Chang applied the last bit of make-up to her cheeks. She usually got to Henry's office by 7:30, a full hour before the senator himself arrived, in order to brief her staff on scheduling, appointments, policy changes, e-mail responses to constituents, and a dozen other matters that made for a hectic workday. A call at 6:20 in the morning wasn't unusual given that Henry was one of the most important people in the country.

There was nothing routine about this call, however. Roberta's father, his voice quivering, said that her mother had died unexpectedly during the night. The preliminary indications pointed to a heart attack. That was all he knew now. Understandably, he wanted to know if Roberta could come home as soon as possible.

"Of course, Daddy. I'll be there on the next plane."

Roberta placed the cordless phone on the table with a trembling hand.

And then she cried long and hard, spasms of grief gripping her stomach muscles until she had to run for the bathroom.

She returned to the bedroom and looked out the window of her fifth-story condo at a sky covered by an even layer of stippled gray clouds. Her mother, fifty-eight years old, had been a robust, healthy woman. She drank a few cocktails on weekends and snuck a few cigarettes every now and then, but otherwise she was in top form. She ate a diet rich in fish (omega-three fatty acids were excellent for the heart, she always said) and some research actually indicated that occasional drinkers lived longer. There was no excuse for indulging, but Roberta knew that one or two out on the patio wouldn't cause a sudden heart attack. As for stress, her father had been a successful securities broker, and they were enjoying an early retirement in Connecticut.

Her mother should be alive.

An hour passed before Roberta Chang had the energy to pick up the cordless and punch in the number for the office of Senator Henry Broome.

"Dave?"

"Hey, Roberta. What's up?"

Roberta paused in order to hold back a fresh wave of tears. She inhaled deeply and steeled herself.

"I won't be in for the next three days, starting today. There's been a death in my family. Tell the senator, please."

"Aw gee, Roberta, that's terrible. I mean— "

"Good-bye, Dave. Thanks."

She couldn't bear to listen to condolences just yet. There would be dozens over the coming weeks. Right now, she needed to cry again.

And do some serious thinking.

25

The penguins and their mates, newly emerged from rented limousines, entered the great hall designed and built by General Montgomery C. Meigs. Completed in 1887, the National Building Museum was a massive structure that had witnessed gatherings and elegant dinners for more than a hundred years, including several presidential inaugural balls. Tonight, the hall was the scene of the annual one-thousand-dollar-a-plate Senate Committee Gala. It was an occasion to fill the party's coffers, catch up on gossip, flirt, and drink the very finest wine and liquor. Despite the party's identification with the average working joe, it did not cater its events with beer and peanuts.

Henry Broome entered the hall with his wife, Anne Davidson Broome. Henry was in his element, for this was where policy met champagne and caviar. In attendance were congressmen, aides, lobbyists, lawyers, and most importantly, the party's corporate and private contributors. This was the heart and soul of the party, from bleeding heart liberals to moderates. Male party members hobnobbed in tuxedos while their women, decked in sequins and diamonds, imbued the museum with as much light as the candles sitting on round dining tables. There was ample room for both dinner and dancing, with the interior space of the cavernous hall surrounded by a balcony laced with open archways. Eight enormous Corinthian columns surrounded a large round fountain at the center of the complex. The museum was large and elegant—no mere convention center to house delegates for a trade show.

Henry moved freely across the floor with his wife. Anne's grandfather, Brian Davidson, had been an Oklahoma wildcatter who brought home the dust and grime of the prairie each evening, at least on nights when he came home at all. Establishing an oil empire was not a job for the faint of heart or people who punched time clocks at nine and five every day. It was an adventurous enterprise for those who were willing to risk everything in order to jump over social strata and claim a larger-than-average share of the American Dream.

Brian's son Daniel—Anne's father—had been able to assume a more traditional role in the boardroom of what became the Great Midwest Petroleum Company, which had been acquired by Exxon-Mobile in the early nineties. Daniel Davidson had been a friend and fraternity brother of Henry Bramwell Broome III while at Princeton. When Henry III realized he could further rehabilitate his family's fortune by playing matchmaker, he was quick to invite Anne to the island. Anne frequently visited Lanai in the days before her future husband became rich and powerful, the days when Henry IV knelt in the fields working with plants he'd brought back from Princeton and planted, he said, as a lark.

With Anne at his side, Henry worked the room as if campaigning. As the dream couple glided across the pink tiles and pressed the flesh, Henry received accolades for his work on the Hill during the Karn hearings and for his performance on *Washington One–On-One*. Many of the cognoscenti regarded Henry as the uniting eminence in an otherwise fractious political party. Henry was revered for his ability to keep party eccentrics at bay—the "tree-hugging" element, as he called them, who would rather preserve a snail darter than an American job.

It was Phillip Trainor, the forty-eight-year-old representative from Arizona, who managed to usher Henry into an unoccupied space under the balcony for a few private words. Many saw Trainor as the party's future, with charisma and a political posture just slightly to the left of center. Some compared him to John Kennedy in terms of general likeability, and the party's leadership considered him very electable.

Many assumed that both Henry and Trainor would be on a very short list for vice president in 2008 regardless who received the nomination for president. Outwardly, they were congenial, closing ranks to preserve longstanding sacred cows of the party, such as Social Security. Behind closed doors, they would have just as soon grabbed pistols and stepped off twenty paces.

"Well, well, well, Henry," said Trainor. "I see you're in top form tonight."

"Form?" asked Henry. "It's just your basic, portable Henry Broome. I'm the same everywhere. The voters expect consistency, wouldn't you agree?"

"Most definitely. But speaking of consistency, I don't see your lovely aide, Ms. Chang, this evening. Have you lost your taste for Chinese food?"

"I do believe my honor has been slighted, Phillip. What an unkind remark."

"I'm just your basic, portable, and politically correct Phillip Trainor. Always there for the people . . . and always honest. A family man, of course."

"I do believe someone has tattooed '2008' across your ass, Phillip. Are you trying to make a point here?"

"Of course not, Henry. You do great work for the Democratic Party. It's just that people talk, and it doesn't take much gossip to do a lot of damage. I'd hate to see your career blighted for any reason. You'd also be a liability to the party if your personal proclivities came to light."

Never taking his eye off Trainor, Henry brought a fluted champagne glass to his lips and smiled. "Your thoughtfulness, Phillip, is truly appreciated. Frankly, I worry about the party's future as well. The Republicans still have enormous political capital with the ongoing terrorist threats around the world. It would be a shame, just a crying shame, to see something happen to anyone in our party who can advance its core ideologies."

"Happen?"

"Phil, there are quite a few misfortunes that can affect a career in this town."

"I do believe I've been threatened, Henry, though I'm not sure what the nature of your threat is. A warning shot across the bow perhaps?"

"I don't fire warning shots, Phillip. They're a waste of ammunition. Have a wonderful time tonight."

Henry clapped Phillip Trainor on the shoulder and rejoined his wife near the fountain.

In the course of the evening, Henry shook a hundred hands, kissed a hundred cheeks, and shared a hundred embraces. If his right hand occasionally slipped a bit too far down a woman's waist—into the small of her back, or even lower—it was only because Henry was so busy and people were in constant motion, smiling and greeting each other with the warmest of words.

■ ■ ■

Gregory Randall smiled cordially. In the months ahead, he would attend the RNC Gala as well as this gathering for the Democrats. Like many corporate CEOs, he liked to hedge his bets by contributing to both parties. Access was everything, and Randall's political agenda was what he liked to call "fluid."

His personal style was just as amorphous, for Randall didn't walk across the ballroom as much as glide effortlessly through a throng of well-wishers. He could engage in a thirty-second conversation, slowing his stride slightly while the aura of his presence literally pulled his listener across the floor.

His escort? There were several, but each one drifted onto his arm as if on cue, staying with him for a brief fifteen minutes before another replaced her. They were all Asian beauties with dark silky hair and deep, mysterious eyes. Their gowns tastefully revealed contoured bodies sculpted and toned at Randall's private gym.

As could be expected, the company of a man who considered Trump and Gates to be annoyances was much in demand. Some patrons of the party simply wanted the honor of being seen with the great Gregory Randall. Others foolishly hoped they might actually entice him into granting a favor, from forming a business partnership to hiring a new son-in-law fresh out of college. Most of these social suckerfish were unaware that at the highest levels of Randall's companies applications were not accepted. Rather, Randall used his own team of headhunters to find the right man or woman for a particular job. These professionals kept a careful eye on people prominent in their fields or academically outstanding in graduate schools throughout the country, though the methods employed to find and screen candidates were usually surreptitious, not to mention illegal.

Randall happened upon Henry next to the fountain. The juxtaposition of the two larger-than-life men caused some stir, with people casually drifting to within a few yards of where they stood in the hopes of overhearing a snippet of conversation. It was as if two heads of state, both equally influential, were coming face-to-face for the first time at a summit meeting.

"And where is that charming aide of yours?" asked Randall.

"I'm afraid she couldn't make it," Henry replied. "A death in the family."

"What a pity. I was hoping she would meet me for a drink later in a more private setting."

"Roberta has always enjoyed the pleasure of your company, Gregory. I'm sure there will be other occasions. What's mine is yours."

"In more ways than one," Randall said with an enigmatic smile, every word and gesture choreographed for the admiring crowd.

■ ■ ■

Edward Karn had been a loyal party member since the first time he pulled a voting lever. Nothing over the years had ever tempted him to change party affiliation, and given his predilection for government control and regulation in the area of food and drugs, he felt Republicans could not be counted on to rein in large pharmaceutical companies or food manufacturers. He was, therefore, a regular contributor to the party and attended the DNC Gala yearly. While Henry received congratulations for demolishing the very liberal Dr. Karn, the oncologist received his fair share of condolences from party members further to the left who thought it was high time for the FDA to start making serious noise about genetically modified foods and a host of other issues that affected the nation's food and drug supply. These condolences came, of course, from those who either didn't hold public office or weren't up for reelection in the near future.

It was after midnight. Dessert had been served and sobriety had long ago fallen by the wayside. Eddie Karn sat at a table by himself, surveying the thinning crowd. It was his way to study public activity from a discreet, if somewhat lonely, vantage point, just as he had done at Cottage all those years ago. He was getting ready to depart for home, an empty yet comfortable condo, when he spied two figures emerging from a private room adjoining the main hall. Senator Henry Broome and Gregory Randall.

Karn shook his head and walked away, his gait slowed by fatigue rather than alcohol. That Broome and Randall shared some common interest was not in the least bit surprising to him, but he would have given anything to have been a fly on the wall moments earlier and find out exactly what that common interest was.

26

Perky as ever, Katie Couric interviewed Billy Hamlin, who smiled a great deal and talked of how it felt to be at the helm of a company with one of the most recognizable names in the country. There had been much joking as Couric, in the course of her questioning, picked up a cup of coffee, looked off-camera, and declared, "I believe I'm drinking Pequod's at this very moment, isn't that right, Sid?" In keeping with the show's lighthearted informality, an invisible assistant producer gave her a thumbs-up and a "Yep."

Hamlin talked about his wife and family, his belief that America's economy was as robust as his company's coffee blend, and his first-class education. He'd graduated from Stanford's Young Entrepreneurs Program and had been recruited by Pequod's, a company he'd never heard of at the time.

"You are the great American success story," proclaimed Couric. "Do you ever wake up and say, 'This can't be happening to me! It's too good to be true?'"

"I've been blessed in many ways, Katie. Not only have I been very successful, but I'm head of a company that produces a fantastic product."

"Do I hear a little of the pitchman coming out?" Couric asked with trademark enthusiasm.

"Absolutely," replied Hamlin, laughing. "Pequod's coffee helps this nation get moving every morning and, more than that, it tastes great! But I think our greatest accomplishment has been to offer diversity to people who want a good cup of coffee. We have seventeen different flavors, all based on the same terrific roasted beans, and we can add numerous toppings for coffee drinkers who would like to be creative when ordering their morning eye-opener."

"Yes, the pitchman has definitely arrived," said Couric with her signature smile. "Thank you, Billy Hamlin, for joining us this morning. It's 8:47. Stay tuned, everyone, for more of *Today*."

■ ■ ■

Mark Stern clicked off the TV in his hotel room, tossing the remote on the rumpled bed behind him. The interview had failed to cover anything substantive, and Couric's questions were nothing more than softballs lobbed at the CEO. Fortunately, there had been no announcement about Pequod's plans to expand, so there was still time to make a pitch for the interview. Mark suspected that Hamlin had been booked on to the show by the PR gurus at Pequod's as a way of increasing visibility and awareness of the company, a critical small step before the company's latest marketing barrage.

The reporter waited ten minutes, giving Hamlin time to get clear of the studio at 30 Rockefeller Center. An important guest usually had a limo waiting close by to ensure the precise execution of a tight schedule.

Mark had done some of his best investigative work in recent memory with the intent of throwing a kink into Hamlin's seamless itinerary. He dialed the CEO's number, his cell phone programmed to appear as if the call was emanating from a Pequod's corporate phone number in Seattle. After two rings, Mark heard, "Hamlin here."

"Good morning, Billy."

"Excuse me? Who's this?" Hamlin's tone wasn't indignant, just curious.

"Someone who's in possession of a great deal of knowledge about your announcement to take Pequod's into new markets."

"Wait just a second. I won't— "

"Calm down, Billy. I'm a reporter. My name is Mark Stern and I'll write the story one way or another, but I'd rather have your input before doing a piece on how Pequod's is making it harder for many of its competitors to stay in business. Looks to me like 'Corporate Coffee Giant Stamps Out Competition.' But, hey, if you can convince me that Pequod's is in the best interest of the consumer and that other chains are not being muscled out, then the story might have a completely different feel to it."

"And if I decline your request, you'll write a story," Hamlin replied personably enough. "Big deal. You wouldn't be the first person to criticize us, Mark."

"That's true," responded Mark, "but if you decline, I'll have word out in less than sixty seconds that Pequod's is going to steamroll what's left of local coffee chains. You'll be doing damage control for weeks, maybe even months."

"You'll be leaking proprietary information, Mark, and that's against the law."

"People talk, Billy. I found out because a little bird told me. It's a free country, and my being a reporter doesn't mean I can't pass on information like anyone else. First Amendment, and all that. But I'll tell you what. I believe in playing fair. You talk with me privately and I'll make sure the *Post* won't run the story until you've made your announcement. I'm not trying to steal your thunder."

There was a pause. Mark could tell that Hamlin was talking with someone nearby, but the words were unintelligible.

"I'm curious, Mark," said Hamlin when he came back on the line. "Why didn't you just come out and ask for an interview. We at Pequod's are extremely proud of our product."

"You're not talking with Katie anymore, Billy, so save the taglines. Are you trying to tell me that if I'd just said 'please' you would have opened your arms and embraced me before making your announcement? I've never ridden in a turnip truck in my life, so I sure as hell didn't just fall off one."

"You speak like you write, Mark. I like that. Would it surprise you to learn that I'm one of your fans?"

"I'm not wearing my hip boots, Billy, so try to restrain yourself."

"You can believe it or not, Mark, but I've read many of your columns, as well as your first book."

"Which was called?"

"*Sterner Stuff*. I have *Latitudes and Attitudes* in my home library, but I've never gotten around to reading it."

"I'm impressed," admitted Mark.

"I also liked the column you did on full-moon madness."

Mark wasn't thrown off balance very easily, be he had to admit that Hamlin had surprised the hell out of him. "Okay, so you like my ink. Maybe you're not a corporate robot after all. What do you say we sit down and talk? I'm looking for a story. If you know my work, you know that I deal in pop culture and societal trends, and nothing is trendier than Pequod's right now."

"Of course I'm going to speak with you, Mark. You play racquetball?"

"As a matter of fact, yes."

"Good. Tomorrow at two. After the game, we sit down and I'll answer your questions as long as we agree that your story is kept under wraps for one week."

"That's acceptable."

"Deal. I'll have my assistant give you the address of my favorite racket club in New York."

Mark clicked off the cell after he'd gotten the necessary address.

"Damn," he muttered. "He knew my work. This might be my best interview since I asked Bloomberg why there were two rats in New York City for every child under ten."

27

Where to begin?

After consulting the partial list of cities BioNet listed in its search for seizure activity, Gwen typed in her private password of the day. She was looking for any kind of geographical pattern to seizures reported as part of the AE forms. The problem was that populations were ever-changing and mobile, and people were still exiting urban areas for the 'burbs. The seizure events, if there was a pattern, could well have spread beyond a neat, well-defined geographic area.

There were a few cases in Ann Arbor, Michigan. Ann Arbor was near Detroit, so Gwen summoned up AE files from the Motor City.

"Crap," Gwen mumbled. More than a thousand AE files recorded seizure activity as part of the patient's history. Those patients had taken dozens of different drugs in all sorts of combinations.

What would Fitz do in such a situation?

Pick a drug and a year and start reading.

She examined Pfizer's trials for medications to treat arthritis and ulcers. Zilch. No reports of seizures were included on any of the hundreds of forms she scanned. After three hours of tedious reading, however, she began browsing adverse events stemming from trials of various birth control methods, including pills, injections, and skin patches. The patients in a test for a skin patch had all been young, sexually active women. While it wasn't clear whether the women were aggressive professionals like Marci, the company reported that three of the women had seizures resulting in one fatality and two hospitalizations. Box number seven on the reporting form indicated that all three had been smokers, but otherwise had enjoyed reasonably good health.

Gwen leaned back and carefully studied the computer screen. Three women out of one hundred. That was highly anomalous. Birth control meds didn't lower the seizure threshold the way other drugs did, such as SSRIs like Prozac. While they increased the chance for stroke or heart attack, especially if the woman was a smoker, seizure was not a normal precursor to such events.

As in Marci's case, she heard her dad whisper.

Three women out of ten thousand? Maybe. Three women out of one hundred? Much less likely.

Gwen checked the dates of the seizures in the trial against the dates Jan had provided from the Detroit BioNet scan.

They matched perfectly.

Could the birth-control skin patch have been responsible? The thought warranted further investigation, but if Gwen saw similar trends in other cities associated with other drugs, the skin patch would become increasingly unlikely as a suspect.

Next stop: Chicago.

Gwen keyed on a cluster of reports submitted in association with a new antibiotic. She discovered that seven patients in a trial of 500 subjects had died from seizure episodes in Chicago during the five weeks that BioNet reported a seizure spike for the area. One of the fatalities, a forty-one-year-old man, had a history of angina. The others, including a twenty-six-year-old woman, had no prior medical history worth noting. All were smokers.

"Damn," said Gwen. "This is too bizarre."

This is old-fashioned detective work, Fitz's voice reminded her, and it's paying off.

"One more time," the intrepid Dr. Maulder declared, summoning up new files. This time, she went straight to reports for the timeframe BioNet had specified for seizures in Trenton, New Jersey. Unbelievably, nine people out of five hundred in a test for a long-acting acid reflux pill had experienced seizures. One had died, a thirty-two-year-old woman previously treated for depression and anxiety. All of the patients were under forty. Three were smokers.

"Smoking has to be the common thread," Gwen said aloud, "but if that's the case, then why not four out of four?"

Maybe the other smoked and didn't report it, either by accident or because some people aren't always honest. Gwen had amassed an amazing amount of information in the course of one day's work. She was willing to bet that she would find similar trends in other cities where drug companies tried out their pills and potions. Medwatch was turning out to be a valuable asset. She fired off a memo to Jan.

Subj: *RE: AE files*
Date: *7/27/05 9:27 a.m. Eastern Standard Time*
From: *captainepi323@iprive.com*
To: *biodoc107@iprive.com*

Seizures reported in drug-testing facilities, not just emergency rooms! Direct correlation between seizure activity in clinical trials and BioNet's findings as far as time frames and locations are concerned. Can you believe this?! What's going on down in Atlanta? Is the quantum wizard up and running?

■ ■ ■

Peter Tippett entered Jan's office at the CDC with a plastic visitor's pass dangling from his neck. He was at the Center unofficially, ostensibly visiting a friend he'd met at the PITAC conference and nothing more.

Sitting at her desk, Jan looked up, saw him, and let out a sigh. "Thank God you're here. Strange things are going on—off-the-chart strange, in fact—and they just got stranger according to an e-mail from an epidemiologist friend up in Rockville."

Tippett covered his lips with an index finger as if signaling naptime for a room full of kindergartners. "Not here. Let's go out for a bite to eat."

"Sounds good to me, Peter. My treat."

"You'll get no argument from me."

They left and headed for a café on the other side of town, in the new chic pedestrian mall.

"If your computer is compromised, then there could also be electronic bugs no bigger than a pinhead in your office if someone wanted to listen to our conversation," Tippett stated as they drove. "But now that we're out on the road, tell me what's up."

"What I'm about to say to you, I never said. Right?"

"Scout's honor."

"Okay, then," said Jan, merging into traffic on the interstate. "Our new top-level security computer for detecting bioterrorist events—"

"That would be BioNet."

"You're not supposed to know that name, Peter."

"At my clearance level, Jan, I know what the president had for breakfast this morning."

Jan smiled and proceeded with her reasons for calling the computer supersleuth. "BioNet has picked up seizure activity way above the norm in certain cities during the past year. The spikes last about a month give or take. The statistical probability for such occurrences is so remote that 'coincidence' isn't worth discussing."

"Sounds downright intriguing, but that's your department, Jan. What do you need a computer security specialist for?" Tippett was an American citizen but had lived in London from the age of five until he graduated from Cambridge University. He enunciated perfectly, speaking with a slight English accent that Jan found appealing.

"Because BioNet is not functioning correctly to begin with. When I called you a few days ago, it was completely down as far as normal operations were concerned, although it uploaded the seizure files to a re-mailer in Iceland. I'd naturally like to know where the ultimate destination was."

"What about BioNet's current activity?"

"Back to normal, but something's not right. I'm the director, and nothing should have been uploaded without my knowledge and consent. The info we collect is just too sensitive. And for BioNet to simply stop functioning and then start again, with no log entries reflecting temporary downtime—there's just no way that should have happened."

"You suspect the project has been compromised from the inside."

"Has to be. Too many safeguards in place for this to be a breach from the outside. If I call security, then the possibility of tracking down whatever is going on is shot to hell."

"Agreed."

"So, feel like snooping around?"

"The larger question is, how can I snoop around without anyone getting too curious?"

"Good point. Any suggestions?"

"I can install a router in your office and have wireless access to the system from outside the premises."

"You have to be kidding. We have so many microwave towers and wireless communications systems already in place that you'd be detected in a heartbeat."

"Oh ye of little faith." Tippett had a childlike grin and a mischievous twinkle in his eye. "Consider the average wireless laptop. You can grab someone else's signal if you're close enough—a dream for ID thieves—but I can install thirty-digit passwords for both the router and the program I'll use. My own equipment will be similarly protected. We'll be completely invisible. Never underestimate a low-tech approach to gaining access to high-tech systems. It's a fundamental mistake made by governments and big business."

"What kind of program can you run?"

"First, I can run a trace to see where Iceland sent the file. After that, we'll see if we can run BioNet and refine the seizure stats at Level II without anyone else knowing what we're doing."

"That's impossible. I had to shunt my activities to a sub-directory after running the seizure stats. The system is designed to keep careful track of every user and data run. You can hide activity for a while, but all users are recorded one way or another."

"And yet, as you just pointed out, BioNet's downtime wasn't logged. I don't foresee any problems. Trust me. There's a simple solution if one knows how to go about it."

"Which is?"

"I'll never log in."

Jan burst into laughter. "You can do that?"

With a decidedly British air of surety, Tippett said, "With your help, I most certainly can. If you provide me with a few passwords, I can bypass certain directories by using what is called a JDM patch."

"What's that?"

"JDM stands for 'Just Dare Me.' I can literally bypass some of BioNet's programming protocols. Think of it as putting a patient to sleep for surgery so that he's unaware of what the surgeon is doing. I'm the anesthetist of the cyber world."

"Peter, I think this is the beginning of a beautiful friendship."

"I was rather hoping you'd say that."

28

To Jack, Lawrence and Jennifer Newman appeared as somber as they had on the day of Marci's funeral. They were nevertheless cordial, if a little subdued, and welcomed Jack into their home without hesitation. They'd removed Marci's belongings from her apartment by mid-June, and Jack had correctly assumed that her laptop was now at her parents' home. He was less than candid about his need to see the PC, however, since Mr. and Mrs. Newman might think it strange that Gwen had looked at Marci's private files, their long friendship notwithstanding.

"Gwen's still devastated by Marci's death," Jack explained, "and I was thinking the other day that maybe—just maybe—there might be something on Marci's computer—a journal or a file—that might describe the way she was feeling physically before she went to court that day. I don't want to intrude on her privacy, and I'll understand completely if you'd rather I not look. Gwen's awfully busy these days, and since my specialty is computers, well, I thought I'd stop by since I was in the city on business." Jack was indeed in New York on business, but it was confined to investigating Marci Newman's death. He hated telling half-truths to these people who were obviously still in mourning, but he convinced himself that what he was doing might help them in the end as well.

"You're welcome here anytime," Jennifer Newman said warmly. "And of course you can look at Marci's computer. I'm only sorry Gwen couldn't come with you today."

"We don't particularly want to know Marci's personal affairs," Lawrence Newman confessed as he ushered Jack inside the foyer, "but if there's anything in her computer that might shed some light on her death, we'd naturally like to know about it. After the funeral, Gwen said that Marci had a minor heart defect that was probably exacerbated by stress. Does she think there may have been something more?"

Not having been privy to Gwen's conversation with the Newmans back in May, Jack had painted himself into a corner. "She's not sure what to think," he said. "She's been over the tragedy in her mind many times. I think she's looking for a little more closure."

His last statement was much closer to the truth, making Jack feel a bit more at ease in his clandestine effort to uncover the cause of his wife's erratic behavior.

"In fact, she doesn't even know I'm here today," Jack confessed. "I think she feels that if she'd kept in closer touch with Marci, she might have picked up on something that could have, well, maybe changed the course of events."

Mrs. Newman gently put her hand on Jack's forearm. "We certainly don't want Gwen to feel responsible for Marci's death. Marci was a very busy woman, as is Gwen, and it troubles me that Gwen is having so much difficulty with this."

Lawrence and Jennifer led Jack to Marci's old room, where her laptop was sitting on one of the many cardboard boxes the Newmans had obviously not had the courage to unpack. Jack found himself humming the same melody Jennifer had been humming as they walked up the stair, the same melody line from the symphony playing in the background, elsewhere in the house.

"What is that music, anyway?" He turned to Jennifer with a quizzical look, "Haydn. Am I right?"

"Yes, it's his London symphony. Marci loved to listen to it and I just can't get it out of my head these days."

"'London?"

"Actually, Haydn just numbered it '104' but his patrons immediately named it London."

As usual, Jack was amazed by his own inability to grasp the obvious. The Newmans left, and Jack moved the laptop to Marci's desk, which had two pictures on its polished oak surface: a shot of

Gwen ten years earlier, and an enlargement of a seagull hovering over waves against a backdrop of wide, open blue sky. Jack felt a deep sense of irony. The likeness of his wife was right there in the room, as if keeping tabs on him. He looked at her picture again. "I'm doing this for both of us, honey. I love you, but there's something you're holding back."

He sat down at Marci's computer and clicked on the troublesome file one more time. When the password window opened he hurriedly typed "London."

Incorrect Password

"Piccadilly."

Incorrect Password

"Thames."

Incorrect Password

And then, "Bridge."

Within seconds, Jack found dozens of filenames scrolling across Marci's screen. He couldn't keep himself from chuckling quietly.

"Everything okay in there?" came a voice from the living room.

"Just fine." Jack coughed, loudly this time, to try to mask his momentary amusement.

Jack copied the now-open files to the CD he had brought. Most of the legal files were straightforward, documenting litigation involving dozens of influential clients and companies. A few, however, pertained to tobacco. During the past year, Marci had represented several people in suits against various tobacco companies—Phillip Morris, R. J. Reynolds, and Compson—for wrongful death or severe impairment of health and the inability to work. The individuals had smoked for years, and the suits focused on the manipulation of nicotine levels, making it far more unlikely that the plaintiffs could kick the habit regardless of what gum they chewed or patches they put on their skin.

One of the files alluded to a suit against Compson Tobacco. The suit brought against the tobacco company was by a twenty-seven-year-old CPA named Virginia Rampling, a woman who, like Marci, had smoked for a brief time. The file listed the woman's name, address, and telephone number.

The next file was even stranger. It contained a series of e-mail exchanges between Marci and Ambassador Jon Cohen at the State Department. Cohen apparently ran the State's program against trafficking of human beings. Marci was asking for information about human trafficking between Vietnam and other Asian capitals in the 1970s but, so far, Cohen had been of little assistance.

There was no obvious smoking gun here. Haydn104 was just a mixture of Marci's concern about security on the one hand and humor on the other.

Fifteen minutes later, Jack bid the Newmans farewell and thanked them for their kindness. He told them he hadn't seen anything unusual and was sure that Gwen's original explanation was correct; Marci was the unfortunate victim of stress and a minor heart defect. It was easy to sound convincing because Jack believed it completely. That had to be the explanation. Nothing else made sense. Jack hugged Lawrence and Jennifer and got back into his rental car.

Despite his pessimism, all of Jack's training told him to leave no stone unturned. The suit against the tobacco company intrigued him. Those folks could play rough when they felt threatened. Taking out his cell phone, he punched in the number of the woman named in the one of Marci's files. The phone rang repeatedly, but no one picked up, nor was there an answering machine or voice mail to handle the call.

"Okay, so now we do the necessary legwork," Jack said to himself, feeling very much the private eye. He would never admit it to Gwen, but this case had captured his imagination.

■ ■ ■

Jack Maulder pulled up to a modest home in Yonkers. He jumped out of the car, walked up a short walkway, and rang the bell at the address he'd obtained from the laptop.

No answer.

He rang again, and after several seconds, the door opened a few inches. "Yes?" said a young woman.

Jack knew from his experience as an investigator that he might only have seconds to explain his presence before the door shut in his face. "My wife and I were friends of Marci Newman, who represented Virginia against Compson Tobacco."

The young woman, standing in the dark recesses behind the front door, knit her brows and looked more closely at Jack. "Marci?"

"Yes. Marci Newman. My wife and Marci were friends back in college."

The woman paused. "How do you know about the suit? Did Marci tell you anything?"

Jack rubbed his chin as he fished for the right words that would keep the stranger engaged in conversation. "Only indirectly. We've been trying to put her affairs in order, and we found a brief note that referred to the suit. I don't mean to meddle, but it seemed that the case must have had special importance to Marci." Jack was skirting the very edge of the truth in saying "note" and "we" but he wasn't prepared to go into details that would only confuse his listener. "I was wondering if Virginia were at home, and if so, if I could have a word with her. Again, I don't want to intrude, but— "

"Ginny died two weeks ago."

Jack stood stock-still. "I'm terribly sorry," he said after several seconds. "I had no idea."

"And I'm sorry about Marci," the young woman said. "She was handling the case on a *pro bono* basis for Ginny. Her firm called us back in May after Marci died. Nobody else in the firm was willing to continue."

Jack shook his head. "It's terrible what cigarettes can do."

"Ginny had only smoked for two years, but she was starting to have arrhythmias and shortness of breath."

"And Marci felt these symptoms were somehow related to cigarettes in someone so young?"

"I guess so. Ginny had only been a client for a couple of weeks before Marci died."

"Did Virginia have any history of heart problems?"

"Nope. I would have known since . . . well, let's just say I would have known."

In other words, Jack reasoned, Virginia and the young woman behind the door had been more than just roommates.

"I see," Jack said, though his inner vision was more clouded than ever. "May I ask what Virginia died of? I'm guessing it must have been sudden."

"She had a seizure one morning, and the doctors at the ER couldn't stop it." The woman was crying now.

"I'm sorry," repeated Jack. "I can tell I've upset you, so I'll be going. Thank you for your time."

"Wait a minute," said the tearful woman. "You're not some attorney or detective from the tobacco company, are you? I mean, I'm not looking to sue anybody, okay? I just want to be left alone."

"No. Like I said—just a friend of Marci Newman's. I'm sorry to have bothered you."

"Good luck." The young woman closed the door, leaving Jack standing in the bright sunshine of an otherwise baffling morning.

Back in his automobile, Jack had the same urge he'd been having for weeks—to light up a cigarette. He'd smoked heavily while in the Secret Service—protecting the president was a stressful assignment—but he'd quit two years ago. It wasn't easy then, and it still wasn't. Like most ex-smokers, he still experienced the urge to light up at certain times—after dinner, when drinking, or when under stress. He was grateful that getting his hands on a smoke meant taking an out-of-the-way trip to a convenience store to buy a pack. And after what he'd just heard, that would be just plain stupid.

What in the hell were tobacco companies putting in their cigarettes now? Marci Newman and Virginia Rampling—two young women dead from seizures after smoking for relatively short periods. He could easily have chalked it up to coincidence but for the fact that Marci had the Rampling file on her PC.

Jack was more puzzled than ever. There was a bigger picture that Gwen wasn't sharing with him. Today in Yonkers, he thought he might have stumbled on to a fragment of that picture. This private eye would have to keep the investigation going, at least for the time being.

29

"You're in pretty good shape," commented Billy Hamlin, wiping the sweat from his face with a towel, a large "E" monogrammed at the top. Lean but muscular, he wore white shorts and a yellow polo shirt with "Pequod's" stitched in red beneath the left shoulder.

"So are you," said Mark Stern, "even though you kicked my ass."

"But it wasn't easy kicking. Most of my opponents tank the game so they can ask me for a favor."

"You've already promised mine. The interview."

"Right you are. Why don't we shower and sit down in the lounge?"

"Sure. Nice digs, by the way."

"Thanks. The club is pretty picky about its members and I can exercise and do a little business without getting buttonholed by every wannabe venture capitalist."

"I would think Randall would have his own gym at the Randall Building."

"He does, plus another one on the floor below his penthouse, but this suits me fine."

Mark wondered if Hamlin's strategy was to impress the reporter with the fact that he was his own man and not a Randall puppet.

"I always used the New York Athletic Club when I lived here," said Mark.

"That would be ideal under normal circumstances. More people, more noise. I generally don't like the isolation that goes along with this kind of a position of responsibility. But the N.Y.A.C. wouldn't work schedule-wise. Crowds slow me down. Although one of my greatest pleasures is to mingle with Pequod's customers when I do a PR tour."

A man of the people, thought Mark. Was it hype?

The Excelsior's lounge was empty and the two men sat near a window that gave them a commanding view of East 57th Street. A waiter wearing a white linen jacket approached them silently.

"Anything to drink, Mark?" asked Hamlin.

"Coke, please."

"I'll have a Muscle Punch, Charles," Hamlin told the waiter, who returned five minutes later carrying the beverages on a silver tray.

"Shall we start?" asked Mark, putting a tape recorder on the glass table where they sat.

"Yes, but sorry, no recording devices. Words are easily taken out of context. Not that you personally would do that, but tapes can be lost or stolen."

Mark had run into this objection hundreds of times in his career. The reason, of course, was far different from what Hamlin stated. A taped remark couldn't be disputed. The accuracy of a reporter's notes, on the other hand, could always be contested.

"No problem," said Mark. "We'll do it the old-fashioned way."

Hamlin struck Mark as a protagonist from the pages of Horatio Alger. The rugged jaw, blond hair, and clear blue eyes created a dual impression of strength and innocence. The Pequod's chief executive was a composed, articulate man who spoke with an easygoing cadence and a slight Midwestern accent. Farm boy makes good. The perfect corporate image.

"I've read your bio on the Pequod's website, so I don't need you to tell me that you're thirty-eight, grew up in Oklahoma City, and have a wife and two kids."

"Don't forget the dogs. Two beagles: Roxie and Dynamo. Haven't the faintest idea how the kids came up with the names."

"There's something *Post* readers need to know," Mark said with a grin while jotting down the names. "Now tell me about your professional life before Pequod's."

"There was none, really. Gregory picked me straight from the Stanford program to run Pequod's. The interview process was lengthy and grueling, but when Gregory Randall comes calling, a grad student sits up and listens. I certainly did."

"That's not SOP for a conglomerate like Randall, Inc. You're telling me that Randall took a twenty-eight-year-old man with no experience and put him in charge of a company that would rise to national prominence in a decade?"

"Yes, and you're right. It was totally unorthodox, but Gregory was interested in someone with no preconceived notions about how things should be done at Pequod's."

"That's sometimes done for low- to mid-level management positions, Billy, but never for the top spot."

"Gregory Randall is an unusual man, and if his business practices seem equally unusual, all I can say is that the success of his various companies speaks well for his instincts. Gregory gave me the blueprint for what he wanted and, together with his management team, looked over my shoulder for a couple of years. I don't mind telling you that the scrutiny was pretty darn intense. But after that, Pequod's really took off, and Gregory gradually stepped into the background."

"It must have been a pretty futuristic blueprint that Randall handed you."

"Actually, it was a step back in time—say, about 350 years. Until 1659, coffee was little known in Europe. Coffee berries made their way from the Indies via the spice trade but were only considered suitable for medical compounding into various prescriptions. An enterprising Portuguese Jew, who fled the inquisition to Amsterdam, figured out how to roast the dried berries and brew something akin to today's coffee. The combination of the aroma and the kick of the caffeine took Amsterdam by storm. Coffee bars proliferated on every corner, and people traded their beer for Kaffee. The Europeans have traditionally savored coffee in a way Americans never have, with the accent on 'savor' since we know America loves that first cup every morning. Our friends across the pond have always had the corner coffee bar where they could drink espresso and read the newspaper. American coffee was mostly swill served in a diner, little more than dark dishwater with no real taste. All Pequod's has done is teach America to savor coffee in the same manner the Dutch did hundreds of years ago."

"You weren't exactly the first on the scene with that. There's, you know, that other megachain."

Hamlin laughed. "Yes, there is. But our product is the first that really captures our European cousins' love affair with the beverage."

"And an empire is born. You and Randall never butted heads on anything?"

"We've had our disagreements, Mark, but Gregory has proven himself to be a man of compromise time and time again. With such a clear vision of what Pequod's could become, he wanted someone who could understand and accept his game plan. He nevertheless wants an executive to be his own man or woman."

This assertion didn't quite tally with what Mark knew of Randall. Of course, no one wanted to regard himself as a lackey. Hamlin certainly took great pride in what he'd accomplished. "Can you give me an example of Hamlin trumping Randall on an executive decision?"

Hamlin nodded, took a long sip of his Muscle Punch, and sank deeper into the brown leather chair. "Gregory wanted to introduce all the flavors at once. I convinced him that people would be more likely to be repeat customers if we introduced new flavors every six months. I told him we'd create more ongoing excitement about the product that way. He agreed."

"Would you say then that Gregory Randall is maybe a bit impatient at times?" Mark already knew this to be the case from his *Journal* profile of Randall, but he wanted to see how Hamlin would respond.

"Well, you're putting words in my mouth, Mark. It goes without saying that Gregory is aggressive. I think that's a more accurate word than 'impatient.'"

Hamlin had clearly paid attention during media training sessions.

"So it's clear sailing at Pequod's headquarters in Seattle?"

"Generally speaking, but this is the real world, of course. We have problems like any other company. We have the occasional lawsuit by people who claim to have found a dead mouse in their coffee, as well as the ever-popular 'my coffee was too hot and spilled all over me' suit. That kind of thing is inevitable. I also have to manage my managers, so to speak, and there are personalities to be dealt with in any corporate setting, but I have to say that our management team is professional and a pleasure to work with."

"Who does the hiring at Pequod's?"

For the first time, Hamlin hesitated. "The Personnel Division of Randall, Inc. oversees the hiring for all of its subsidiaries, but it's always done in conjunction with liaison teams from the various companies."

"Does Pequod's have veto power over hiring and firing?"

"Absolutely."

Mark wasn't sure if Hamlin was being truthful. The CEO had looked away for a split second before his last answer. Mark was an excellent judge of body language, but perhaps some movement on East 57th Street had claimed Hamlin's attention.

Or perhaps not. Large parent companies never interfered in the hiring of personnel at a subsidiary. Never. However, Randall, Inc. was not your usual large parent company.

"Tell me about your coffee, Billy. What makes it so different from all other brands? Why has the country gone crazy for Pequod's?"

"Because people have good taste, and we serve the best coffee in the country."

"Your honor, please instruct the witness to address the question."

Hamlin smiled broadly. "Okay. Guilty as charged. The truth, Mark, is that we use excellent, quality beans that are roasted by one of the finest roastmasters in the world."

"What kind of beans? Colombian, I presume."

"That's proprietary information, which is the norm for all food and beverage companies. If you wrote Celestial Seasonings and asked how much ginseng went into their Ginseng Plus tea, you'd get a polite letter thanking you for your interest, but the company wouldn't answer your question."

"Does Pequod's get a lot of letters asking for information on the beans?"

"All the time, and to be truthful, most are probably honest queries from individuals who like our coffee. Others are no doubt from competitors."

"Who's the roastmaster?"

"Dieter Tassin. Undoubtedly the best in the world at what he does."

"What's his background?"

"Dieter worked at a world-class restaurant in the California wine country before joining our team."

"So you found Tassin by accident while dining there one evening? Kismet?"

"It was Gregory who actually convinced Dieter that his future was at Pequod's. It was a chance for Tassin to devote his talent to a nationwide enterprise rather than confine it to a single establishment."

"What about your competitors? Do they stand a chance against a juggernaut like Pequod's?"

Hamlin looked the reporter in the eye. "There are hundreds of brands out there, and most turn a healthy profit. We're certainly never going to put Maxwell House or Folgers out of business. As for small chains, some are quite successful, and they can thank Pequod's for that. If someone wants gourmet coffee and happens upon another store while riding down the street, our competition is going to get that person's business. We've enhanced the image of the entire gourmet coffee industry, not just our own."

"With the expansion, however, it's going to become more and more unlikely that people won't be able to find a Pequod's while riding anywhere," the reporter continued. "Or walking, for that matter. We're talking airports, bookstores, park kiosks, shopping malls, drive-thrus, to name just a few, right?"

"I think you may be overstating the case a bit. First of all, there's that other big chain. More importantly, though, people have free will. No one is forcing consumers to buy our product. If someone can find a better cup of coffee elsewhere, then go for it. The fact is that people like our product better."

Mark tilted his head and scratched his cheek. "You and I both know that taste and perception can be shaped by advertising and availability."

"Our marketing campaigns are designed to do one thing: get people to try our product. Beyond that, what people do is out of our hands. We're grateful for our customers' loyalty, of course, and hope that they'll continue to patronize our stores. We have good coffee and good PR. We're naturally not ashamed of either."

Hamlin was handling each question like a pro. Mark didn't necessarily agree with Hamlin's assessment—hell, he was on the side of the small guy—but he had to admit that Hamlin's answers were right down the center of the pipe: capitalism, free will, and competition. It came down to the old adage: if someone can build a better mousetrap, then let 'em do it.

"Any plans to move into grocery stores?"

"Yes and no. We'll never vacuum-pack our coffee and sell it in a grocery setting."

"Why not?"

"People can't get the same kind of great hot coffee with chocolate, caramel, cinnamon, or whipped cream, to name just a few of the extra ingredients we use, except in our stores, where each cup is individually served according to a customer's preference. 'A little extra of, this, please, a little more of that.' There's an art in how we do that that would be difficult to replicate at home."

"You make drinking coffee sound almost mystical."

"It is. The ritual has been around for a mighty long time. Pequod's has simply made it more enjoyable by taking it to a new level."

Mark put down his pen and looked vacantly at East 57th Street. He had hoped to come away from the interview disliking Billy Hamlin, but that wasn't going to happen. The Pequod's CEO was a charming, open man who cared deeply about his product. The story on Hamlin was nothing more than "honest guy graduates and catches a break with a company that sells a part of American culture." When it was finally time to submit the column on Pequod's to his editor, the piece would probably express the opinion that there was hope for America yet. There were still good companies out there run by good men. In fact, Pequod's sold a product that actually helped people say "hi" to each other in the morning. Mark felt there was no harm in giving his acerbic wit a vacation in order to do a "feel good" piece occasionally. If he stumbled upon a hopeful trend in a country where people were growing more alienated, wasn't he bound to report that, too?

"So," said Hamlin, "care to join me for dinner tonight?"

The question jolted Mark from his musings. "Um, sure. Dinner sounds fine."

"Eight o'clock?"

"Deal."

30

"I'm shut out of the system," said Peter Tippett, a sheepish grin and hangdog expression on his face. He and Jan were having mid-morning coffee at the new Pequod's minibar in a park bordering world-famous Peachtree Street in Atlanta.

"You're kidding, right?"

Peter watched Jan's concerned expression. She was an unusual woman—she actually became more attractive when she looked worried. "I'll deal with it. It's just that I tried to access BioNet, and ran into a gatekeeper program that even monitors internal maintenance accounts. Not quite impenetrable, but it sure does slow a guy down. I simply can't get into it at present. Have you tried any routine runs lately?"

"Not since yesterday morning. And we already have numerous firewalls."

"Gatekeepers are a bit different. I'm guessing this one was installed sometime after your last run yesterday."

Jan's brow furrowed. "That means somebody is noticing us."

"Perhaps. But if the system is compromised from the inside, you would expect the powers that be to do something like this sooner or later. I suspect it's actually good news."

"How so?"

"It means that the system is, in all likelihood, functional, though only for a select few."

"But I'm director of the whole damn project!"

As appealing as she looked in this intense state, Jan had to calm down. Peter touched her arm. "I said I'll deal with it. I'll simply remove the gatekeeper and replace it with one that is almost identical."

"Almost?"

"Yes. I can neutralize the gate with a program called X-Vader. I then insert a new gatekeeper that looks exactly like the original, except that it will have one very minor but important difference—the replacement will have a lock that recognizes our key as well as theirs."

Jan smiled. Her face was actually quite lovely with any expression.

"You really are a genius, aren't you?"

Surprisingly, Peter found himself blushing. "So I've been told," he said off-handedly.

"So when do we do this?"

"In the dark of night, of course."

Jan sipped her coffee and held him with her eyes. It dawned on Peter that there were multiple mysteries to solve in this project.

■ ■ ■

Panting and sweating, Jack rolled away from Gwen on their king-sized bed. Was it just his imagination or had Gwen become a more passionate lover since they made the decision to have a child? For all he knew, Gwen found some research that suggested that children conceived during vigorous sex scored higher on the SATs. No, she would have told him if she had. She told him everything. At least she used to.

"Love you," Gwen said dreamily.

Jack kissed his wife gently on the forehead as she drifted off to sleep. "Love you, too."

Gwen normally liked to cuddle after lovemaking, but she dozed off quickly tonight. A man more concerned with his talents as "a swordsman" might have bragged to himself that he'd literally knocked his wife out with pleasure. Jack wasn't that guy, though. And he knew that Gwen's early slumber probably had more to do with a heavy work schedule.

That assumed, of course, that Gwen was actually working at work. These days, she rarely said anything about it.

Jack stared at the ceiling, his breathing returning to normal. He closed his eyes, but fifteen minutes later found himself still tossing and turning, unable to sleep. He couldn't stop thinking about the secret he knew Gwen kept from him. Or the one he kept from her.

Finally, he got out of bed and tiptoed downstairs, carefully closing the French doors behind him as he stepped onto the patio and pulled a cigarette from a crumpled pack he had started to hide in the bottom drawer of his desk ever since that day at the Newmans.

His decision to investigate Marci's death independently was the first time he had ever acted behind Gwen's back. Still, at least in his case, he had good intentions. He wanted to crack this case so Gwen could hand it off to the appropriate superiors at the FDA, and maybe even the FBI, depending on what he found. His objective was to present his wife with clear answers, all neatly contained in a single file, and say, "It's over, honey! Your very own Secret Service agent solved the mystery!" He knew if he gave her only preliminary leads, however, that she would want to go down all sorts of avenues that might take months to explore. That wasn't going to work. If Gwen became pregnant, he wanted her searching for baby accessories and color schemes for a nursery, not criminals.

But aside from a bizarre encounter in Yonkers, New York, Haydn104 still yielded nothing. There was nothing on Marci Newman's PC to decrypt.

The only thing that calmed him was to light a cigarette and take a long drag, letting the smoke swirl deep inside his lungs.

He stood in the cool air for a while, pondering how to proceed. His discomfort dissipated. He crushed the butt of his second cigarette and headed inside to brush his teeth and wash his face and hands in the hopes of getting the tobacco smell off before returning to bed.

Suddenly, he heard the sound of an automobile engine coming from the front of the house. Walking through the side yard, he positioned himself behind a large rhododendron and surveyed the street from a crouching position. An unmarked white van was slowly rolling past his neighbor's house. Jack knew that it had been in front of his own moments before, engine idling.

Were they under surveillance?

"Nah," he muttered. "Probably just somebody lost. I stayed in the damned Secret Service too long. A van is a van is a van."

■ ■ ■

At the end of the block, the white van turned the corner. The driver flipped open his cell phone and punched its speed dial. "Subjects appear to be alone. The house is dark. Ops Two clear at 2300 hours."

Without waiting for a response, the driver closed the phone.

The van picked up speed and left the neighborhood. It would return two hours later to check on the Maulder home.

And two hours after that.

31

Peter and Jan sank into the plush captain's chairs in the rear of his van, positioned in the parking lot of a fast-food joint down the street from the CDC. It looked like a miniature version of the interior of the Starship *Enterprise*. Jan thought this was slightly hilarious—she encountered a lot of "geekdom" in her line of work, but this beat it all—and more than a little dazzling. From what she'd come to know about Peter, she guessed there weren't any extraneous bells and whistles here. Just raw technological power. Rows of wireless laptops lined both sides of his vehicle. A chair installed on a track ran down the center of the van so its occupant could slide freely from one computer station to the next.

"This is utterly amazing," said Jan, gazing in wonderment at the almost supernatural glow emanating from the ten laptop screens that surrounded them. "It's like something out of a sci-fi movie, or James Bond."

The security specialist turned to her and smiled confidently. He had a great smile.

Jan laughed as Peter unlocked a cabinet at the front of the van and selected several CDs from its shelves. The CDs shared space with laptop batteries, cables, routers, and other equipment arranged neatly on dozens of small metal shelves. The man seemed prepared for anything.

"What now?" asked Jan.

"Keep your eyes on the magic fingers at all times," he said, imitating a carnie huckster running a shell game. He put disks into the three laptops directly in front of him, two of which he hooked together with a slim cord. His hands moved with quickness and agility, indicating supreme confidence in his abilities. "I'm going to knock on BioNet's door again. I'll be denied, of course, but that's no problem. I just want to establish an interface so that I know BioNet is communicating with the laptop, even if it's merely to say 'Go away.'"

"And then?"

Peter didn't answer. He performed his digital ministrations, then turned to Jan and said, "Okay now. Ready to see where File 23789.626 ended up?"

■ ■ ■

Gwen stared at the Medwatch computer in her office. She rubbed her eyes and yawned. It was late, and the corridors outside her sanctuary were empty. She'd spent the entire last week searching Medwatch's database like Diogenes searching for an honest man, ostensibly looking for evidence that terrorist cells within the United States were contaminating the nation's drug supply.

Rolling her chair back from the terminal, she concluded that she'd found everything she needed in the AE files, although she would continue to massage them in order to satisfy her superiors. The seizure patterns Gwen noted in Ann Arbor and Trenton were not isolated events. Seventeen drug companies and 352 physicians had independently reported seizures in 789 patients. She discovered that sixty-three of the reported seizures had fatal outcomes, fifty-seven required hospitalization, twenty resulted in long-term illness, and the rest were resolved through intervention and short-term treatment. Although each adverse event was associated with a particular drug taken by the seizure victim at the time, there was no discernable pattern. Most of the drugs had no real potential for causing seizures. With numbers like these, though, Gwen didn't need any more corroborative data from Medwatch to know that something strange was happening. The signal was off the charts. There was a massive cover-up underway, and what she wanted to know more than anything was who in the FDA was responsible for shutting down a legitimate investigation into what could potentially be the greatest health risk to affect the country since the AIDS epidemic.

Gwen heard a light tap on her door, as if someone had accidentally brushed against its surface. She got up, opened the door, and peered into the corridor. It was empty.

Turning around, she noticed the miniature china bird she kept on the table near the doorway had slipped to the carpet. That must have been what she heard—not a brush against the door.

She was becoming more than a bit paranoid lately.

But perhaps with justification. Had the china bird been tipped over by someone snooping in her office? Had she simply not noticed it until now? If so, maybe someone had brushed up against the door a few minutes earlier.

Returning to her chair a little more subdued, she once again focused on the cover-up. She shot an e-mail to Jan.

Subj: RE: access
Date: 8/03/05 10:14 p.m. Eastern Standard Time
From: captainepi323@iprive.com
To: biodoc107@iprive.com

Need advice on getting into the personal filing cabinet of my boss's PC. Have any interesting toys that might be of help? Seizure stats are widespread according to Medwatch. I need to find out who's trying to divert my attention.

Gwen received a reply thirty minutes later.

Subj: RE: toy
Date: 8/03/05 10:44 p.m. Eastern Standard Time
From: biodoc107@iprive.com
To: captainepi323@iprive.com

Your timing is impeccable. I'm with the third party now and just checked my mail using one of ten PCs here in the . . . well, later—long story. Should have info on BioNet soon. In the meantime, try this upload. But you can only use it once. Hope it helps.

The attached file was named "Gwen's Toy." Gwen assumed it came from Jan's computer whiz, Peter Tippett. She opened the file and saw the name PASSBREAK. The instructions were simple: "Type name of PFC user into box and hit ENTER. When results appear, make hard copy or transfer to floppy or CD."

With adrenaline removing any trace of her former fatigue, Gwen typed "Ralph Snyder" into PASSBREAK's box and hit the ENTER key. A few seconds later, Ralph Snyder's PFC appeared as if by incantation, with a column of dates, senders, and subject headings.

Gwen wasn't particularly interested in reading Snyder's correspondence, especially when she learned that her boss actually had e-mail from porn sites on his work computer. Well, if he needed to add a few inches, that was his business. She didn't have to scroll very long to find a subject line that pertained to her.

7/19/05 gmcmjr@fda.gov . . . . . . re: Dr. Maulder

Gwen double-clicked the highlighted line and stared, mouth open, at the memo. "The goddamned bastard," she said, shaking her head in disbelief.

Remembering the file's instructions, she printed out a hard copy of the message. Snyder's PFC disappeared from the screen five minutes later. She would like to have checked other memos sent to or from "gmcmjr," but the self-destruct mechanism kicked in too fast.

Gwen looked over her shoulder at the china bird. First, reassignment. Now, a breach of her privacy.

"That goddamned bastard," she repeated. "Unbelievable."

■ ■ ■

"Know anyone in Panama?" Peter asked Jan.

"Is that where the file went?"

"Take a look for yourself."

Jan read the results of Peter's handiwork on the nearest laptop.

The destination for BioNet File 23789.626 was 9546transfer @panama/transpac.gub. "What do you make of it?"

"Hard to say. Let me cross-reference the Panamanian address with a file of foreign outfits known to be operating illegally."

A few taps on the keys of a fourth laptop revealed nothing.

"Did we just hit a deadend?"

"There aren't any real deadends in my line of work. I need to see if the Panamanian address is the ultimate destination, or just one more stop along the—" Peter broke off his remark abruptly.

"What's the matter?" asked Jan.

"Everything." Peter looked alarmed, which chilled Jan immediately since she had never seen this expression on his face before. "The blinking red light on that laptop at the end of the row—that's trouble. The laptop is essentially a wireless scanner to make sure no one knows what we're doing."

"You mean—"

"I'm afraid it has detected an RB, probably GPS in origin."

"Huh?"

"It means that we've been had, to use the vernacular. Somebody's figured us out. They used a Global Positioning Satellite to establish an RP—a reverse probe. We have just gone from hunters to hunted."

"We need to get the hell out of here!"

Peter had already climbed into the driver's seat and started the motor. "Indeed!" he shouted. "Hold on!"

Only seconds behind, a Chevy Caprice with blackwall tires followed them out of the lot and onto the road.

■ ■ ■

Gwen paced back and forth across her office. She couldn't believe what she was reading. "Gmcmjr" was none other than Gene McMurphy, Jr., the associate commissioner for policy at the FDA. His memo to Ralph Snyder had been brief and to the point. It read, "Assign GMM to Adverse Event files. Present duties temporarily suspended pending investigation of recent activities."

Recent activities? This was an obvious reference to her contact with Jan and their use of BioNet. But what interest did the commissioner's office have in the Epidemiology Division? That particular office was staffed with political appointees who generally came and went with each administration and worried about broad policy issues, not the type of research in which Gwen was engaged.

Furthermore, how did McMurphy find out about her request to use BioNet in the first place?

But the million-dollar question weighed heaviest on Gwen's mind: why was the commissioner's office seemingly oblivious to the seizure stats? If anything, McMurphy should have been grateful that Gwen had brought a serious problem to light. It seemed unlikely that this was a simple case of bureaucratic wrangling over divisional jurisdiction. It was a downright obfuscation of the truth. And the truth was that people were dying. Gwen felt that she was going farther and farther down the rabbit hole.

Her pacing picked up speed.

The only working hypothesis Gwen could come up with was ludicrous: the FDA was protecting tobacco companies.

But maybe "protect" wasn't the right word.

Had Big Tobacco first cowed the feds by getting the courts to declare cigarettes off-limits to FDA regulation and then done the unspeakable—juiced up the product to hook even more smokers? It was true that Big Tobacco often played it close to the edge. One company tried to circumvent regulation only ten years earlier by growing many of its plants in South America, outside FDA jurisdiction. The plants had extremely high nicotine levels and were used to regulate the chemical's strength in particular brands by using greater or lesser amounts of the South American leaves in their blending process.

Were tobacco companies once again experimenting on customers and causing the occasional seizure breakout in the process?

She had to admit the scenario seemed unlikely. Chemical additives interacted with each other, and such interactions were part of FDA scrutiny. There had to be some larger picture here—maybe larger than she could imagine—that involved government, big business, or possibly even intelligence agencies. Gwen ran the options through her mind. Maybe terrorists had infiltrated the tobacco industry. Maybe the federal government was secretly working with Big Tobacco to eliminate some toxic ingredient from its product without alarming an already vulnerable post-9/11 populace. But maybe not.

"Next," Gwen said to herself, "I'll be going online to read the latest news from Area 51. I must be losing it."

For each question that came to mind, Gwen thought of a hundred more. There were numerous hypotheses, most of them outrageous, but no answers seemed to fit. She would need the help of someone who knew how to work back channels and take some shortcuts. It couldn't be Jack. He tended to be rather conservative in his investigative techniques, a product of his many years of government training and service. Gwen needed someone who was willing to take a few risks and think outside the box.

She knew who that someone was. She did not know, however, whether she was ready to see him again, even under these circumstances.

■ ■ ■

"What are you doing?" Jan asked as Peter parked the van in a strip mall a mile away from the CDC.

"I'm going to use a jamming program and then boost the gain on my wireless equipment. I still have the frequencies I need to access BioNet. We won't have another opportunity unless I act quickly.

By tomorrow night, they'll have discovered the new gate—if they haven't already. The reverse probe has probably alerted them that I've been tampering with their equipment."

Jan's face fell.

"This may be game, set, and match," Peter warned, "but I'll leave it up to you. It's your call."

Jan sighed. "How long will it take?"

"Ten minutes. Fifteen tops."

"Go for it," she said resolutely. "But make it quick."

"Okay then. I'm going to have BioNet send a different file to the Panamanian address. This time, I'm going to try to see where the little bugger goes. There may be an automated program running down in Central America that bounced the seizure stats somewhere else. Afterward, I'll erase our night's activity, plus I'll make the uploads and downloads run backward so that the final destination, if there is one, won't ever see that he or she received mail."

"All right, but hurry."

Once again accessing BioNet, Peter located a file on avian flu.

He gave the system various commands to upload the file and send it to 9546transfer@panama/transpac.gub.

"The screen's changing!" Jan exclaimed.

"It certainly is. We're watching the file on avian flu that I downloaded to Panama/Transpac get uploaded to a new destination. Look."

"Holy shit," whispered Jan, gazing at the screen. "The seizure stats were forwarded to Rockville." Jan dashed off an e-mail to Gwen, notifying her of the Panamanian address and its cyber connection to the FDA.

"It's time to roll," Peter declared. "We've done all we can do for now."

"I'm feeling light-headed," remarked Jan, rubbing her temples. "Did we eat dinner tonight? I can't even remember."

Peter coughed. "I think we— "

Jan was growing lethargic, her lips quickly developing a ghastly bluish color.

Climbing into the driver's seat, Peter turned to the door and pulled on the handle. It was jammed.

"The bastards work quickly—I'll give them that much," he uttered while reaching into the back and grabbing a laptop.

Peter's coughing worsened as Jan passed out on the floor of the van. Grasping the three-pound laptop firmly, he turned his head to the right and slammed the PC against the driver's window on the left. The safety glass merely cracked, turning it into a flexible but intact sheet with a thousand veins running through it. Peter's arms and legs grew heavy and his thoughts became disjointed. He knew his strength would be gone in a matter of seconds. Tightening his grip on the laptop, he crashed it against the splintered glass again and again, until parts of the glazed sheet finally started to peel away.

Peter reached through and tried the handle of the truck. It was frozen.

"Gonna do it . . . the . . . hard . . . way," he groaned.

With his bare hands, he grabbed chunks of glass and yanked as many as possible from the window's grooves. By the time he was finished, his hands were soaked with blood. He craned his head out the window. Gasping, he took a deep breath. Then another. Then he hurled himself through the jagged opening and fell to the ground, his head bouncing hard against the asphalt.

With his last ounce of strength, Peter pulled a cell phone from his pocket and hit 9-1-1. The phone fell from his hand as his head lolled to the side. The last thing he saw before blacking out was a canister near the rear of the van. A small tube snaked its way from the small cylindrical tank of gas into the exhaust system of the vehicle where Jan lay unconscious.

Before escaping, however, Peter hadn't had a chance to reverse the uploads and downloads. Someone would soon discover that Transpac had sent him a file on avian flu.

Someone with the address gmcmjr@fda.gov.

32

Stone-faced, the senior senator from Hawaii sat behind his desk, elbows on the armrests of his chair, fingers and thumbs of each hand matching their opposites. It was a studied pose, an expression not often seen on the face of Henry Broome IV ever since his colleague's electoral defeat in November. He looked at Roberta Chang, his minion and mistress, as she sat on the other side of his desk, pen and steno pad poised on her crossed legs.

Roberta went over Henry's schedule: meetings with other members from the Agriculture Committee, a one-on-one with Senator Tom DeGenovese from New York, acceptance of the responsible Stewardship Award from the Young Farmers of America, a call from the president, and a late afternoon meeting with party leaders to discuss strategy for the midterm elections.

"Can we squeeze in lunch?" asked Henry.

"I beg your pardon?"

"Me and you. A couple of hours away from the rat race. It would do us both a world of good."

Henry knew the answer before Roberta could respond. He was aware that she'd suffered a terrible loss the previous week. But he knew something else as well. He knew when something wasn't right, when someone was holding out on him, in business or otherwise . . .

Just as he'd known that Jamie Robinson was hiding something on his Apple back at Princeton.

"I'm sorry, Henry. Not today. I'm still not myself yet. I'm sure you understand."

"Of course, Roberta. I wish I could do more to help, but I suppose grief must run its course. Maybe another time."

Roberta simply nodded her head, saying nothing.

"Okay then," said Henry, leaning forward with a faint smile now etched across his face. "Let's start the wheel turning and get down to business. Thank you, Roberta."

The chief aide got up and returned to her office, her steno pad and leather day planner grasped firmly in her right hand.

Henry leaned back again, troubled. There was something on Roberta Chang's mind other than the death of her mother. Otherwise, she would have been subdued, but she would have at least smiled at Henry occasionally or offered him a wink, something that said, "We're still on, Henry—just give me some space." Instead, Roberta was unusually reserved.

Henry suspected that his aide's agenda might no longer match his own.

■ ■ ■

The elite group of six was simply known as Tabula Rasa, Latin for "blank slate." They got the name because they did not officially exist. Neither did the group's missions. There was no record of Tabula Rasa's activities anywhere.

The six were recruited from various branches of the intelligence community, with backgrounds similar in covert operations and the use of deadly force. Once assigned to Tabula Rasa, operatives lost all technical association with the CIA, FBI, NSA, or Secret Service. Their training reflected their exemption from all normal rules of engagement. None of the six operatives even knew who gave them their orders, delivered via untraceable, encrypted e-mail.

The men sat in an underground room inside a building in Virginia that had no address. Outfitted in ordinary civilian clothes, they were the proverbial motley crew: one fat, one skinny, one handsome, one geeky, one dapper, and one grossly unkempt—traits that served to underscore how little they had in common. Op One, sitting in sweats, chewed on a cigar and dealt the next hand of poker.

"Menefee and Tippett have been neutralized," Op Four bragged, picking up his cards on the metal folding table.

"Two and Five have the doctor and her husband under observation. Should we distract them from poking where they don't belong by emptying their bank accounts?" said Op Three.

All of the men laughed.

"Just make damn sure no action is taken on them until we hear otherwise," stated One emphatically.

"The husband's been to New York," said Three.

"It's the doc that's designated as primary," said One, "although hubby is starting to poke around a bit. He bears watching."

No one said a word for a long moment. Then Three broke the silence.

"I fold," he said, throwing his cards on the table.

"I'm out," said Four.

"Come to Papa," said One, pulling in his winnings.

33

Gene McMurphy was puzzled. Why had Panama sent him a CDC file on avian flu? He could understand why Transpac forwarded the CDC file on seizure stats to his PC, for Drs. Maulder and Menefee fell under the heading of damage control. But what was Transpac's interest in avian flu?

It took a few minutes for his call to get through to the small port city of Pedregal, which sat on the edge of the Golfo de Chiriqui on the Pacific coast of Panama.

"Richey, here," said a faint voice at last.

"This is McMurphy."

"Hi, Gene! How's life in the States? It's lonely down here in the boonies." Carl Richey's voice was interrupted by an occasional crackle.

"I'm more interested about life down in Panama, Carl. Why are you people sending me stats on bird flu?"

"What the hell are you talking about? Have you been sampling some of those outlawed drugs?"

"I don't have time for comedy, Carl—not today. Transpac sent me a file that I downloaded this morning. It's on avian flu."

"Hold on, Gene. Let me check last night's computer log."

Several minutes of static filled McMurphy's ear before Carl Richey made it back to the phone.

"Son of a bitch, Gene. You're absolutely right, but I don't have a clue as to what its significance is. For what it's worth, it's another

BioNet file from the CDC, and it went through our computer system last night. I'm guessing our program automatically bounced it up to you since the file originated from the CDC, just like the seizure stats. We have that enhanced AC-IV processing chip in our PCs just like you guys and gals up in Rockville and Atlanta. Works like a charm and forwards all the info lickety-split."

McMurphy sighed. "Yeah. Works like a charm." Richey was an educated man, but his down-home manner aggravated the associate commissioner to no end. He wasn't in the mood for country chitchat.

"Thank you, Carl."

"You got it big guy. Just call whenever—"

McMurphy hung up the phone. He didn't have time for Richey's bullshit.

Without a second's hesitation, he called the head of Tabula Rasa and related how he'd gotten the unexpected file on avian flu.

"Don't worry," came the raspy voice. "A reverse probe detected tampering with BioNet by Menefee and a friend of hers. That fire has been contained."

"Understood."

The line went dead.

McMurphy believed in the goals of the "secret organization" with which he was associated. They were a government within a government with a true patriot for a leader—a man who understood that the good of the many did outweigh the good of the few. Sometimes extreme measures had to be taken, blood had to be shed. After all, most people had no idea what was really good for them. Someone had to step up to the plate to make sure things didn't get out of control.

Still, McMurphy never liked talking to the creepy man with the raspy voice. He preferred watching him on television.

■ ■ ■

Gwen had sent several e-mails to Jan over the past two days in an attempt to notify her about gmcmjr. There were no responses.

"To hell with iPrive," she said angrily. "I'm going to call her up on a landline and talk about the price of rice if I have to."

Gwen's call to the CDC bounced to several different people, each involving five minutes on hold. At last, a male voice said, "This is Watkins. How may I help you?"

"As I told the other four people I've spoken to in the last twenty minutes, I'm calling for Dr. Menefee." Gwen had been careful not to identify herself to anyone on the other end of the line.

The man paused. "I'm afraid she's no longer employed here at the Center."

"What the hell are you talking about? She's the director of—"

Gwen broke off abruptly. No contact from Jan. Jan "no longer employed" at the CDC . . .

The game she was playing had just changed. Adrenaline spiked and Gwen became acutely aware that she could be in real danger. She only hoped Jan was safe. She put the receiver back in its cradle. Further questions were useless.

It was time to call the one person who might help her. She couldn't put it off any longer.

■ ■ ■

The Excelsior's private lounge was relatively quiet at this time of day. Mark and Billy relaxed over their drinks, after another racquetball match that Billy won handily. At least Mark was getting more competitive.

"That was a great piece you did on Pequod's, Mark," commented Hamlin. "We appreciate the compliments."

"No thanks necessary. I call 'em like I see 'em." Mark was never entirely comfortable when a subject liked a piece, even though in this case, he'd found it easy to praise Pequod's. Mark's investigative projects were long-term, though. If there was something darker under the company's impressive veneer, he'd find it, and the innocuous puff piece he'd just published would give him easier access. "Still, I'm flattered by your observations."

Mark's cell phone rang as he began to say something else. "Excuse me for a moment," Mark said, turning away slightly.

"No problem."

Mark's face relaxed into a smile mixed with mild surprise. "Hello yourself," the reporter said. "It's been a while . . . how have you been?"

There was a pause, after which Mark said, "Okay then. I'll be in touch."

"An old flame?" asked Hamlin when Mark had tucked his cell into a Nike bag.

"A good reporter never reveals his contacts," answered Mark.

"That was an old girlfriend all right. And judging from the look on your face, I'd say she was pretty important to you at one time."

"You're working my side of the street, Billy."

"Like you, I have to be able to read people."

"I suppose," Mark said. His interest in exploring Billy Hamlin further had disappeared entirely. "Well, Billy, I have to be running now. When's the next time you'll be in New York?"

"Not for two months. Why don't you hop up to Seattle and mix some business with pleasure. I'll show you Pequod's up close and give you another chance to beat me at racquetball."

"I might just do that," said Mark, standing. "As you can probably tell from how easily I hop up to the City, Washington's a little too claustrophobic for me. I'll use any excuse for a few days away."

"We'll set it up, then."

"I'd like that."

34

Gregory Randall was more than just agitated. "Apoplectic" was a more apt description. He'd tried to call Henry for the past thirty minutes, both at his Senate office and on his cell, a number that only five other people knew. If Henry was busy, all he had to do was push "3" on the keypad to send Randall's assistant a programmed text message explaining that he was in an especially important meeting but would call back as soon as possible. Today, however, the senator was not responding. His office staff said he was unavailable, and there had been no text message.

No one kept Gregory Randall waiting. From Fiji to Vatican City, Randall expected his calls to be answered.

Randall tried Henry's office again and was informed that his call was finally being put through. He sighed and rubbed his forehead. He didn't get many headaches, but when he did, there was only one remedy: a lovely Asian beauty massaging his temples and neck.

"Good morning, Gregory," said Henry. "To what do I owe the pleasure of your call?"

"Cut the bullshit, Henry. Where the hell have you been?"

"I was on the phone. First with the majority leader, then with the president. The majority leader I can blow off for a few minutes. The president? When I get word his call is imminent, I have to keep the decks clear."

"Then why didn't you signal me, Henry?"

"I guess my cell's on the fritz, Gregory. Sorry about that. I'll have to check the vibrate setting. Or maybe the battery's just low.

Technology is so complicated these days."

"Technology is what keeps you and me in business, in case you've forgotten."

"No, I haven't forgotten, but you're going to die an early death if you don't learn to relax. We've been through this before, Gregory. You know perfectly well I provide you with complete access day or night."

"Yes, so let's get to the point and cut the health lecture. Is Karn sticking his nose where it doesn't belong?"

"Karn is dead in this town, Gregory. Why do you ask?"

Randall paused. "I don't trust him. I don't want to hear him babbling his gospel of all-natural products because he's pissed over the confirmation hearings."

"I don't either, but you'd be the first to know if he was causing trouble."

"Are operations proceeding as expected on your end, Henry? As you know, we're at a critical stage right now. Things have to run with clockwork precision."

"They always have and it won't be any different this time."

"Very well. We're done. And get your damned cell phone fixed."

■ ■ ■

Henry knew the CEO, smooth and controlled in front of an audience, was an incessant worrier who often became agitated behind closed doors. His tantrums were as legendary as those of Trump and Turner. Randall's nervous disposition caused the senator to laugh out loud. He'd felt his cell phone vibrate several times during the past thirty minutes, but once in a while he needed to give Gregory a subtle message that they were partners enjoying a symbiotic relationship. Despite Gregory Randall's enormous wealth, he needed Henry—and badly. If a slight delay caused Randall to get a migraine, so be it. Henry was a U.S. senator and intended to sit in the Oval Office one day. Randall was not the only megalith in this relationship.

He pushed the button on his phone bank and spoke casually.

"Roberta, could you come in here for a second?"

"I'm sorry, Senator. Ms. Chang has left for the day."

"All right. Thanks."

Henry's annoyance with Roberta Chang was growing. He had a meeting with party bigwigs in an hour and his chief aide had left for the day without notifying him. And she'd taken all his notes along for the ride.

■ ■ ■

"Is everything okay?" asked Roberta Chang.

Randall hung up the phone and turned over in bed.

"I was getting a headache, but it seems to be dissipating very quickly thanks to you. Your boss can be so aggravating sometimes. Downright smug, in fact."

"He's on your side, Gregory. He's a bit taken with himself, but you can count on his loyalty. He always comes through."

"He damn well better."

Roberta slipped her thigh over Randall's right leg as the CEO ran his hand through Roberta's lustrous hair.

"Here, darling," said Roberta, handing Randall a glass of Chardonnay.

Randall sipped from the glass and handed it back to his paramour. Relaxed, he stared straight ahead for several minutes. It wasn't long before he turned on his side and drifted off to sleep, his back to Roberta.

The senator's aide waited fifteen minutes, after which she slid from under the covers and tiptoed to the upholstered chair where Randall's briefcase rested. With her thumb and index finger, she silently twisted the gold fastener and opened the black case of soft Italian leather. She lifted a manila folder from a slim compartment and took it to a table opposite the bed. Removing a small digital camera from her purse, she carefully photographed each document in the folder before returning them to Randall's briefcase.

Roberta slipped back into bed, gently laying her slender frame down onto the mattress so as not to cause the slightest movement. If Randall had seen her, he surely would have killed her.

35

Subj: *RE: Lunch?*
Date: *8/04/05 11:33 a.m. Eastern Standard Time*
From: *mstern@washingtonpost.com*
To: *gmaulder@yahoo.com*

Meet me tomorrow at 517 E Street for lunch. 12:30 p.m. Looking forward to it.

~Mark

How, Gwen wondered, did Mark get her private e-mail address? Getting her FDA e-mail address off the Internet would have been relatively simple, but he'd chosen to make contact through her personal Yahoo account. She smiled, though, when she recalled how Mark had once gained admittance to a formal White House dinner by forging an invitation and pretending to be the ambassador from Argentina, complete with bogus accent. He was one of the premier reporters in the country and probably had ways of obtaining information that went far beyond consulting online e-mail directories or the phonebook.

She wrote back that she would see him at the designated time, adding, "It's a date."

No. Bad move. She hit the backspace button and deleted the sentence, replacing it with "See you there." It certainly wasn't a date.

Of course she thought of Mark from time to time. Everyone entertained occasional daydreams of running into an old boyfriend or girlfriend, right? And she'd continued to read his columns, though she learned quickly that she couldn't discuss them with Jack. Jack and Mark saw the world differently and Mark's writing irritated Jack to the extreme. Gwen wondered if Jack would be anywhere near as irritated by Mark's writing if she wasn't the journalist's ex-girlfriend.

No, Jack wouldn't approve of Gwen's call to Mark, but she needed someone other than her husband and his federal law enforcement pals to help her. The government obviously had some thick mud caked on its shoes. Since reading McMurphy's memo to Snyder, she'd become convinced that any satisfactory resolution of the investigation would have to come in the form of a journalistic exposé. She just hoped Mark hadn't thrown his lot in with the yuppies. His piece on Pequod's had been awfully soft and bore no resemblance to his usual satiric style. Mark Stern, on the side of a corporate giant? Highly unusual. What she needed was Mark Stern, the quintessential doubting Thomas who would go to any lengths to show how "the man" routinely stuck it to the little guy.

She hoped he still existed.

She'd find out soon enough.

■ ■ ■

Jack Maulder sat at his PC, surfing the web to find out what kind of information people were posting about tobacco litigation. Sure enough, he found details of endless numbers of pending suits despite industry payoffs to millions, as well as company pledges to educate the public about smoking. Big Tobacco had reached a landmark settlement thanks to the tenacious state attorney general of Mississippi, who had put several companies on the ropes in the nineties, forcing the industry to make unparalleled concessions after the discovery that the industry suppressed damning research on nicotine for almost thirty years. Many citizens had opted out of the class action suit, and the settlement had therefore not deterred smokers from continuing to sue the tobacco giants.

Nothing unusual there. Still, two entries on antismoking message boards caught his attention:

My wife was young and had only smoked for a year before she died. What kind of poison are the tobacco companies using now?

I've been smoking for four years and my whole body started shaking like crazy yesterday. What's going on?

Jack stepped into the backyard and lit a Marlboro Light. In the absence of concrete answers, his brain was becoming quite vocal, and rationalization was its loudest song: Give me what I need. If you can't find the necessary information, then give me something else. Nicotine, to be exact.

Jack gave in to his body's cravings more and more with each passing day, though he knew it was crazy, especially given his current subject of investigation. Where was all that self-control he'd prided himself on? He knew his problem was stress and that little by little he was reestablishing an addiction that had taken him forever to kick. But that was his rational self speaking. His other half lit a new smoke with the glowing butt of the last one.

As he exhaled a plume of blue smoke into the summer air, Jack thought of the last message he'd read. Had the person who posted it actually been on the verge of going into a seizure? Was this another Marci? Jack decided it was time to call up a few friends at the Federal Bureau of Alcohol, Tobacco, and Firearms. He'd have them analyze a few different brands of cigarettes, starting with Compson's, and see exactly what was rolled inside the thin white paper.

His attention pivoted. He walked through the side yard and looked at the street. He was sure he'd heard that same vehicle, that same engine, before.

He looked up and down the block. Nothing.

Back at the PC, he cut and pasted the two messages that had caught his attention into a separate file. He then decided to surf a bit more before going outside for what he promised himself would be his last cigarette of the day.

■ ■ ■

Her Public Health Service uniform with gold epaulettes would have stuck out like a sore thumb. Likewise, her own automobile would have been easy to follow if she were under surveillance. So Gwen changed clothes at the office and called a taxi before heading out to her luncheon engagement with Mark.

Finding the address proved difficult. After paying the taxi driver and stepping onto a Georgetown sidewalk, Gwen had no clue where to go. She was on E Street, but there was no #517 in sight. Gwen entered a nearby watch repair shop and asked for directions. The gruff clerk behind the counter, unfiltered cigarette dangling from his lips, gestured to a space between two brick buildings across the street as if he'd been asked the question a thousand times before. "The address is unmarked. Go down the alley and turn left. You'll find it."

Wearing sunglasses, a scarf over her head, and bleached Levis, Gwen felt she might have gone too far with the cloak-and-dagger. She was also more than a little nervous about seeing her old beau after so many years. She walked timidly into the shadowy alley, the heels of her shoes tapping the flagstones with each step. At the end of the narrow pathway, she found herself in a small courtyard with an oversized potted plant as its centerpiece. On her left she saw a restaurant called The Insider.

Opening the door and stepping in, she removed her sunglasses, expecting to see a room filled with faces staring at her suspiciously. Instead, a hostess in a black dress and high heels approached, smiled, and said, "Good afternoon. How many?"

"Two," said Mark Stern, appearing from a waiting booth on the left as if from a parallel universe. "I've reserved one of the private rooms."

"Certainly. Follow me, please."

The hostess led Mark and Gwen through the main dining room into a narrow hallway where the payphone and restrooms were situated, turning at last into a corridor with several small cubicles attached, each containing a table covered with a linen cloth, silverware, and a slender vase with a single rose.

"Thank you," Mark said to the hostess as he and Gwen slid into chairs and faced each other for the first time in eight years.

"Gwen Maulder," he said with a boyish grin.

"Mark Stern," Gwen said, unsure how her voice sounded.

They stared at each other for a long moment before laughing nervously. Gwen hadn't expected to feel this awkward. *Remember, you have something hugely important to discuss with him. This isn't about anything other than that.*

"How did you get my cell number?" Mark asked, breaking her reverie.

"You're not the only one with investigative skills, you know."

Mark grinned again. "Obviously not."

They both chuckled, but then another awkward silence ensued.

Gwen was rarely unsure of herself, but she was having trouble figuring out how to proceed here. Did she just dive into her story? "I can see why they call this place The Insider," she remarked at last. "You have to be one to find it."

"It's where people in this town come to discuss things that aren't meant for public consumption. That's what I've heard from my colleagues. Speaking of which, tell me what's going on."

Gwen was so glad Mark decided to cut to the chase. She told him about Marci's death and about how she had begun a personal investigation based primarily on instinct. She then filled him in on BioNet, the seizure stats, her reassignment to the AE files, and Jan's disappearance. As she started talking about McMurphy, Iceland, and the Panamanian address, Mark interrupted her.

"What cities are we talking about as far as the seizure stats?" asked Mark.

"Chicago, Trenton, New York, Boston, D.C., Milwaukee, Kansas City, St. Louis, to name just a few."

"When did the spikes occur in New York and Washington?"

"May and July, respectively."

"What about Kansas City?"

"Um . . . I think the spike occurred in April. Why?"

"Just curious."

"Personally, I think tobacco is somehow involved in all of this. Almost all of the seizure fatalities were smokers. There's a definite correlation."

"What about the nonfatalities?"

"They're harder to gauge since we can't rely on autopsy reports. I'm still betting tobacco."

"How sure are you that it's not just your do-gooder's hatred of tobacco companies that's driving you?" Mark paused. "With Marci being such a close friend, I can see why you'd go all out with this."

"My best friend," Gwen replied, more than a little miffed. "You're sounding like Jack," she said sharply, realizing immediately that Mark wouldn't know what that meant and that he might even misinterpret it.

"I've given you info from the AE files, and I don't have to remind you that reporters often proceed on evidence that's a lot less substantial."

Elbows on the table, Mark brought his face down against clasped hands. "Tobacco companies have had the feds all over their asses for years now. It's hard to believe they would try anything new."

Undeterred, Gwen laid out her conspiracy theories, from modified tobacco plants that might be legal and beyond FDA control to a cover-up of terrorist activity that had once again killed citizens on American soil, albeit in a more surreptitious manner.

"Anything's possible," said Mark, "but if it were terrorism, somebody would have claimed responsibility. Terrorism has no effect unless someone takes credit. It's how terrorists perpetuate a climate of fear, which is even more powerful than bombs and body counts."

"Maybe they're waiting for the trend to overtake the country before stepping forward. Tampering with tobacco would be a more insidious infiltration of the homeland. They could effectively shut down the economy if Americans found out that an everyday product had been tainted."

"Maybe."

Gwen studied the reporter carefully. How was it that he didn't seem to have aged at all? He was still handsome; his brown beard was very close-cut and trimmed in a perfectly straight line under his jaw. His brown eyes were still very clear, still warm, and his wavy hair had no trace of gray. Was he still a crusader as well? Other than conspiracy buffs, Gwen figured Mark was the only person willing to entertain the possibility that both the FDA and the CDC were capable of working in tandem to cover up statistically anomalous deaths.

"So what do we do, Mark?"

Mark rubbed his chin and hesitated, trying to find the right words.

"I'm not sure, Gwen. I can ask some questions, poke around, make some calls. Stuff like that. But I've got to be careful. If there's a conspiracy that cuts across several government agencies, it's going to make Watergate look like a misdemeanor in comparison. Let me turn it around on you. How solid is this AE thing?"

"Doesn't sound like you're too optimistic."

"You didn't answer my question."

"BioNet stats and AE reports are hard evidence."

Mark smiled weakly. "You've given me a tall order, Dr. Maulder. Ordinarily, I'd be calling you if I had the kind of info that BioNet reported, but I'll do what I can."

Gwen wrote down her iPrive address on a napkin. "E-mail if you come up with anything, but use this address."

"I'll let you know one way or another," Mark said, folding the napkin and putting it in his shirt pocket.

"Is there any way I can get in touch with you if I discover something else?"

"Go to the *Post's* website and e-mail me at the column. I get hundreds of comments and questions every week. Nothing's completely safe in the cyber world, but it's better than e-mailing me directly."

Gwen followed Mark's logic completely, but she still felt as if he were putting her off. They ate in relative silence, reverting to small talk and catch-up. When it was time to leave, there was an awkward moment—it seemed like an eternity to Gwen—when the two started to lean forward as if to give one another a friendly hug. They backed away quickly instead, settling on a handshake.

Gwen walked back through the hallway and wondered if she'd wasted her time.

36

The next day, Mark was still kicking himself over the way he behaved at lunch with Gwen. Why had he been so coy? Why had he been so reserved in his response to her when his reporter's instincts screamed that she was handing him a career-changing story?

He hadn't expected to feel the way he did when he saw Gwen. He'd thought about her a million times since their split, but the vision in his head was a faulty one—one that failed to capture how vibrant and substantial she was. It was as though he'd been listening to nothing but neighborhood garage bands for years and then suddenly received an invitation to a private U2 concert. Seeing Gwen in the flesh again immediately verified that no woman he'd been with since was in her league.

He was so preoccupied with this during their lunch that he couldn't get the right words to come out of his mouth. When he arrived in Washington, he went to his buddy, representative Rick Mecklenberg, in hopes of finding something juicy to write about. Mecklenberg hadn't delivered yet, but Gwen Maulder had just given him his first real shot at a Pulitzer, a story capable of keeping the nation riveted to page one. While his fame as a reporter was largely attributable to the way he chronicled the foibles of human nature, he always felt a bit the impostor for never having published the really big story, the one in which people were cuffed, put in the back of a squad car, and driven to jail. This could change that.

But exciting as a potential government cover-up was, he needed to proceed with the utmost caution. Gwen seemed terribly vulnerable.

She wasn't confiding in her husband and the FDA had removed her from her regular duties. She'd come to him out of desperation and that could mean that she wasn't seeing things as clearly as she needed to see them.

But that didn't mean he wasn't going to do a little digging.

He cleared one of his bulletin boards and mounted a very simple, handwritten pyramid of words to its surface.

Health and Human Services
Public Health Service
Center for Disease Control
Food and Drug Administration

If Gwen were right, two of the most prominent agencies charged with monitoring the nation's health and welfare were involved in an astonishing cover-up. Exactly how high did the corruption go? A year from now, would he be writing the classic, "Who knew what and when did they know it?"

It was early in the hunt, but he felt his heart beating a little faster, his blood coursing through his veins and fermenting fresh ideas. When Gwen had called him at the Excelsior, he'd been telling Billy Hamlin how a reporter had to have a good memory since a random fact sometimes helped shape a story. He recalled the *Times* piece on the Brooklyn woman who had created chaos in the subway by proclaiming the end of the world. Other stories from New York and Washington, all equally bizarre, had resulted in his "Franchising the Full Moon" column at the *Post*. The New York incidents had occurred in May, the ones in D.C. in July, precisely corresponding with the timeframe of Gwen's seizure reports.

Gwen mentioned a seizure spike in Kansas City during April. Mark asked a cub reporter to go down to the *Post*'s archives of U.S. papers and browse the *Kansas City Star* for all of April. He wanted to see a copy of any article, no matter how short, describing aberrant behavior. The reporter subsequently left five articles on his desk. One told of a man who tried climbing a skyscraper with suction cups. Another described a woman who'd sat in a public park for three days straight in order to compose operas. Perhaps due to sleep deprivation and fatigue, the Kansas article theorized, the woman suffered a mild heart attack and was rushed to the ER. The other three articles were of the same ilk: people were going ape-shit for no apparent reason.

"And if I look into the papers of every city that Gwen has on her list," Mark said to the whale poster on his wall, "I'm going to find articles about people going over the edge. I'd bet my million bucks on it."

He wouldn't tell Gwen yet about how his own data seemed to relate to the info from BioNet and the AE files. He still didn't have much to go on.

But was there a story there?

Yes indeed.

■ ■ ■

Was there any better indication of how overwhelmed Gwen was with recent events? With everything going on, she'd managed to ignore the very insistent signals of her own body—until this afternoon when the signs became too obvious for her to ignore. Now she sat with Jack at the kitchen table in their home at Garrett Park and tried to figure out the best way to announce that their lives would be changing forever.

"I'm gonna get some wine," Jack said, rising right after they sat down. "Would you like some?"

"No thanks."

"You sure? I was going to open a bottle of that great Merlot we just bought."

Gwen raised her head and looked straight at Jack. This wasn't exactly the way she envisioned it, but it would have to do. "Pregnant women shouldn't drink, my dear."

Jack's mouth dropped open comically. Gwen knew she'd keep that picture in her head for a long time. "You mean . . . ?"

"Yep. Looks like the Secret Service taught you how to aim after all."

Jack had her in his arms before she could move. When she stood up, he hugged her tighter and more fervently than she ever remembered. Jack really wanted this. That much had been obvious forever. It wasn't until this moment, though, that she understood how completely he wanted this. And it wasn't until this moment that she understood how much she wanted him—them—to have it.

Gwen dissolved into tears. Was Jack crying as well? It wasn't easy to say.

The purity of the moment dissipated all too quickly for her. Unbidden, the thoughts of what her life would be like while she carried this child came into her head. The seizure stats pointed with increasing clarity to a cover-up that was linked to the commissioner's office—and maybe beyond—and Jan was missing. She'd pulled Mark back into her life, though it wasn't clear that he wanted anything to do with the news she brought him. Oh yes, and Jack had started sneaking cigarettes again, though she was certain he didn't know she knew.

Gwen had heard the stories of women entering a state of bliss during pregnancy; she knew that would never be her story.

37

"Active Health Management," said the receptionist. "How may I help you?"

"Lonny Reisman, please. Mark Stern calling."

"Please hold."

A few moments passed as the inevitable radio muzak traveled through the wires. Mark promptly tuned it out, reflecting on the story he'd done on Active Health. It was one of the few pieces he'd written without hurling a single barb, much like the recent story on Pequod's. AHM was a unique company that had convinced both employers and insurers to feed them all their healthcare claims so it could identify medical mistakes and notify the doctors in time to help patients. Insurers were finally waking up to the fact that medical errors were the fifth leading cause of death in the United States. Not only did Active Health avert disaster on a regular basis, they also saved money for their employers who were trying desperately to meet their healthcare premiums.

"Mark?" said a familiar voice. "It's great to hear from you."

"Thanks, Lonny. It's been a while. How's the business going?"

"Through the roof. After that profile you did on us in the *Journal*, all hell broke loose. We were planning to go public sometime in '07, but you touched off a buyer's frenzy. In fact, our largest client bought us out. The pen is indeed mightier than the sword. At least Mark Stern's is."

Mark laughed. "Then why the hell are you at a desk taking my call instead of sunning yourself on a beach somewhere?"

"Believe me, my wife asks me the same question every day."

"Well, before she persuades you to go to Cancun, I need some serious help from you, but I'll need the same level of confidentiality that I gave you when I was investigating your company for the story."

"You got it. I'm not going to be able to violate our secrecy agreements in handling people's personal information, though."

"I'm not looking for personal info. I'm looking at a bigger picture. A close friend of mine who works in the government got a whiff of something very strange. Something to do with seizures breaking out in isolated cities for a few weeks and then disappearing. When she started examining government databases, she got shut down big-time."

"Wow," said Reisman, whistling. "Big Brother is alive and well."

"Exactly."

"No problem, though. None of our data comes from the government. We actually have better data, in fact, if you don't mind my blowing our own horn. The government mostly knows about problems through adverse events and the like."

"That's what my friend was looking into, although you never heard me say that."

"Anyway, we have health-related information for twenty-five million Americans that represent a fair sampling of the entire country. If there's something going on out there, chances are we can detect it. Give me a list of the top ten cities and the applicable dates, and I'll see if we can find a pattern."

"Terrific, but be careful. I don't want you getting hurt."

"Got it. Nobody but my lead analyst and I will know about this. I'll let you know when we have something. Unfortunately, I can't give you a time estimate. Could be anywhere from a few days to a few weeks."

"Anything you can do to help would be great, Lonny. I appreciate it. If this story pans out, I'll pay for that trip to Cancun myself."

"You're on, Mark. I'll call my travel agent to get some quotes."

Mark hung up, energized and ready.

Soon now, the story would show itself.

PART IV

38

Jack Stopped at a 7-Eleven outside of Wilmington to buy a carton of Marlboro lights. "Damn," he muttered. "Talk about expensive." He bought a carton of generic cigarettes instead—RTB was printed on the red and white carton, standing for rich tobacco blend. "Sure, why not," he said. "I'll be quitting next month, anyway."

He also purchased a few packs of cigarettes representing various brands. He was on his way to Todd Gimmler's house to drop them off. Todd was a field investigator for the Bureau of Alcohol, Tobacco, and Firearms who owed Jack a few favors. Since ATF and the Secret Service were both part of the Department of Treasury, Jack had worked with Todd on a few investigations where the link between counterfeit money and stolen firearms had combusted to cause big fires that needed putting out. Jack's assistance had led to more than one promotion for Gimmler, so Jack had no qualms about asking him to analyze the cigarettes, no questions asked. A definitive analysis, reasoned Jack, would satisfy Gwen. Here, honey. You may already have the same figures from FDA lab work on Marci's blood, but I know your secret now, and it's time to start painting that upstairs bedroom and seriously converting the basement into your new office. If the cigarette had a new or suspicious additive, he would personally inform the Office of Drug Safety. On the other hand, if there were nothing in the cigarette, Gwen could either fold or make him privy to any lead she was pursuing. He'd be tough if he had to, but there would be a resolution one way or another.

Jack usually couldn't stand convenience store coffee, but he noticed, to his delight, that this place brewed Pequod's.

He left the store, got in his Ford Taurus, and lit an RTB. It wasn't the greatest smoke in the world, he concluded after the first drag, but it would do.

■ ■ ■

Gwen had been keeping a mental diary of Gene McMurphy's schedule. He usually left for lunch at one o'clock and arrived back at his office no later than two-thirty. On most evenings, he worked until seven, but not a second later.

She needed to get into his office to gain additional information since PASSBREAK dissolved before she could read more of his mail. It was a long shot. McMurphy probably had most of the information she was looking for—the cause of the seizures, his coconspirators, the reason for the entire cover-up—password-protected on his PC. Still, she had to try. She needed to give Mark something to get him fired up—to get him to approach the cover-up with the same passion that had made him a household name. She would try to get into McMurphy's office and leave with some jewel—any clue that Mark could use.

Entering McMurphy's inner sanctum at lunch was far too risky. Evenings were different, however, with the cleaning staff moving about freely, leaving doors unlocked for long periods.

Between seven and eight o'clock at night—that's when she'd make her move.

■ ■ ■

On the Washington Beltway Westbound coming back from Todd Gimmler's house, Jack noted a white '04 Grand Am weaving in and out of traffic about five car lengths back. At first, he thought it was just one of the millions of impatient motorists making the highways of America hell to navigate. Then the vehicle hung back, maintaining a constant speed. When Jack passed two cars, however, the

Grand Am once again began weaving, as if jockeying for a position close to Jack's Taurus.

"May just be a coincidence," Jack said to himself. But there was only one way to be certain. Jack ducked off at New Hampshire Avenue and took University to rejoin the Beltway at the next entrance.

His white shadow remained.

Back on the Beltway, Jack pressed the accelerator, moving his car up to eighty-five miles an hour. The Grand Am remained close, as if pulled along by an invisible towing cable.

"What the hell?" mused Jack, glancing constantly at his two rearview mirrors.

Jack took the next exit and pulled up to a red light. The Grand Am, windows tinted, sat directly behind him.

Jack turned right, accelerated, and then hit the brakes, turning the steering wheel sharply to bring his car into a sideways skid on a residential street. He was going to confront his pursuer.

The Grand Am braked to a sudden stop just three feet from the Taurus's driver's-side door. Jack withdrew the Glock he kept under his seat, scrambled out the passenger side, and rolled onto the street. He knew better than to simply raise his head above the car's body, in case somebody intended to shoot at him. Instead, he crawled on the ground toward the front of the Taurus, craning his head around the front tire on the passenger's side.

"Hey, buddy!" growled a paunchy man in a wrinkled blue suit. "What's the big idea crawling around down there? You playing *Rockford Files* or something?"

Jack stood up, carefully wedging the Glock under his belt behind his back. "You've been following me for miles, asshole. Now who the hell are you?"

The large man looked like an accountant—wingtips, pocket protector, and all. Jack was relieved to see that he was apparently unarmed.

"I'm going to visit my mother, if that's all right with you. What kind of bullshit are you pulling with a skid like that? You're lucky I didn't smack into your door and cream your ass."

"Like I said, you were following me."

"My mother is stuck in her home with cancer, and I was in a hurry. Her nurse didn't show up and she's all alone. If I had more time, I'd knock your fucking head off." The fat man scowled, got back into his car, and maneuvered around the Taurus, parking just a block away. He got out, walked up to a front door, and inserted a key. He was inside within a matter of seconds.

What the hell just happened? Jack didn't know what to make of the last few minutes. How did he get into that house unless he had a . . .

Jack got into his Taurus and moved off slowly. All of his old alarm bells were sounding and yet, he had nothing solid to go on. He wanted to get the license number of the Grand Am, but it was smeared with mud and illegible. He couldn't take the risk of being seen cleaning the plate. Certainly, the man had entered a house to which he had a key.

Jack took out a cigarette, his hand shaking, and drove the rest of the way home.

■ ■ ■

"Don't make a sound," the fat man in the blue suit told his captive.

The forty-year-old woman in maroon sweats stood motionless, her eyes wide and painted white with panic.

"Is anyone else in the house?"

The frightened woman shook her head.

"I'm not especially interested in hurting you," said Op Four, "but I will if I have to. My gun has a silencer, and none of the other soccer moms in the neighborhood will hear a thing. Now here's the deal. As soon as I see what I'm looking for, I'm going to leave. If you call the police, I'll come back and kill you. And trust me when I tell you that I'll know if you make the call."

The woman nodded.

Op Four parted the living room curtains and surveyed the street for Jack Maulder's Taurus.

"Have a wonderful day, ma'am," he told the woman, his face

suddenly lit with a bright smile. "And by the way, your drapes are a little dusty. You need to use your vacuum attachment."

He let himself out the front door, pretending to lock the cylinder he had so deftly forced on the way in.

■ ■ ■

At seven-thirty, Gwen sat in the stall of the ladies' room on the same floor as Gene McMurphy's office. The cleaning staff had already mopped and wiped down the restroom and wouldn't be back in until the following night. The custodial staff was now cleaning offices up and down the hallway.

Gwen had put on her dress uniform as a final touch, hoping that its official aura would minimize the likelihood of a challenge. The whine of a vacuum motor gave Gwen some idea of where the cleaning person at McMurphy's end of the corridor was working. Leaving the stall, she opened the door of the bathroom an inch. Perfect. The cleaner was around the corner, exchanging gossip with a coworker.

McMurphy's door was wide open.

Gwen dashed across the hall and into his office, quickly examining the lock system. Entering the office required an ordinary key as well as a swipe card. Leaving was as simple as turning the doorknob and walking out. The cleaning person had finished cleaning McMurphy's office, but Gwen thought it best to hide, nonetheless. She scooted under the desk and remained still, hardly daring to breathe.

This is definitely not why I joined the Public Health Service.

Minutes passed, but there was no sign of anyone from the cleaning crew.

I still have time to leave. If I'm caught, the show's over. The investigation will be finished. As will my career—and maybe even my life.

Thinking about her unborn child, Gwen wondered if it really made sense to continue to take risks at this level. Her odds of success were terrible and failure could destroy her. She knew Jack would burst a seam if he saw her here. Maybe he was right. Maybe she needed to move on.

But she couldn't. People were dying. Her best friend had died. How much worse would this get if it went unchecked?

She heard the cleaning person coming back down the hall, humming a tune.

Damn. Why is she coming back? I thought she was finished. This really is it. I'm screwed here . . . Game, set—

The cleaning person entered the office. Gwen heard a snapping sound as the woman abruptly yanked the vacuum cleaner's cord from the wall. Moments later, the lights went off and the door closed.

Gwen found herself sitting alone, crouched under the desk in total darkness. She waited another ten minutes as the sound of vacuuming resumed and slowly faded.

Crawling on her hands and knees, Gwen left her hiding place and stood. She searched for the switch to the desk lamp. McMurphy's desk was sparsely covered, with no memos of any kind littered across its surface. She tried opening the drawers and nearby file cabinets, but they were locked.

Okay, then. His PC.

Like most of the staff, he left it on all the time, though the screen was currently in its dark screen-saving mode. She tapped a key at random and the fifteen-inch flatscreen began to glow. Behind the icons, McMurphy's wallpaper was a dark blue ocean. In lighter blue letters, almost invisible on the waves, was the word "Transpac," whatever that meant.

She moved the mouse and clicked on Microsoft Word. PLEASE ENTER PASSWORD appeared in the middle of the screen.

Gwen rolled her eyes and sighed. She wasn't a hacker and didn't have a clue how to gain access to a protected application.

You came this far. Try something.

She typed "transpac" into the password slot, but the expected message appeared: ACCESS DENIED.

It was useless. She could try combinations of letters and numbers all night, but hitting the right one would be tantamount to winning the lottery. As she stood up, her eyes fell on a map of the United States on the wall behind a library table. She noted red dots over cities where BioNet had identified seizure spikes. Gwen got out her digital camera from a small shoulder bag and took two pictures, then moved to take several more since the lower part of the map was obscured by plants on the library table. Putting away her camera, she left the office empty-handed.

"Good evening, Dr. Maulder. What are you doing up here at this hour?"

Gwen's heart began to race. It was Ralph Snyder.

"All the ladies' rooms downstairs are backed up," Gwen replied. "This was the first one I could find with flushing toilets." Gwen walked past Snyder without breaking stride to emphasize the trivial nature of searching for a restroom.

"Mmm," mumbled Snyder as he swiped a card and entered a nearby office.

That was close. Too close.

Gwen returned to her office, gathered up some papers, and left the building. Her hands were shaking, cold, and clammy. This was not her idea of fun.

39

Gwen still wasn't sure what they were doing in the car. When she got home last night, frazzled by her feeble attempts at espionage, Jack told her—he didn't ask her, he told her—that she needed to take the next day off. They were going on a road trip. He wouldn't elaborate on the reasons why, but he was insistent and he seemed uncharacteristically skittish. Gwen's instincts, still on edge from the evening's activities, told her to leave it alone. Now, though, she'd had enough.

"What's going on, Jack? Tell me, and tell me now!"

"I was followed yesterday. At least, I think I was."

"You think?"

"Yes."

"And so we're driving to Virginia?"

"Yes. I've put up with your investigation of Marci's death for a long time now—and don't tell me you're not actively pursuing the matter—so you can certainly give me some latitude here."

"Fine. You want some latitude, you got it. But why are we driving to Virginia?"

"I want to see if it happens again. If it does, I'll head south on 359 and drive to Treasury's training facility at Quantico. My retiree credentials will get us through the gate."

Gwen was so befuddled she said nothing. She'd never seen Jack paranoid. That meant this was bad just about any way you sliced it.

Forty-five minutes later, Jack pulled into the lot of a Pequod's.

"Need a cup of coffee to go with your cigarette?" asked Gwen flatly.

"What?"

"Come on, Jack. Do you think I can't smell the smoke on your clothes?"

"Okay, okay," he confessed. "I sneak a few, but I'm stressed out."

They got their coffee and sat down. Gwen had questions to ask, but Jack preempted her with an explanation.

"You're pregnant and still chasing down your suspicions over Marci's death. You're more distant lately. You don't talk much, but you sure do stick close to your cell phone and PC. Meanwhile, I've started to notice vans cruising by our house late at night. Then yesterday a Grand Am chased me for more than forty miles. So yes—I'm smoking again."

Gwen knew she'd created trouble for herself with the investigation. However, she hadn't thought enough about putting Jack at risk. She'd never forgive herself if something happened to him.

"All right, Jack. But you're going to stop again soon, right?"

"I'll get it under control by the time the baby arrives." Jack took a deep breath. "Look, you need to know something. I've been working on Marci's files and came across a few things. Marci was suing some tobacco companies. There was even a file on her PC that led me to the friend of someone who'd died from a seizure after smoking only a short time."

Gwen's expression darkened. "You've been working on her PC?"

"I went to see Lawrence and Jennifer up in New York. They gave me access to Marci's computer."

"And you hid that from me? If anyone should have access to her private files other than her parents, it should be me. And why didn't you inform me about the tobacco angle?" Her voice was strained as she leaned over the table, her facial muscles taut. "And to top it all off, you start smoking again while you investigate the dangers of tobacco. That's really rich, Jack. Next you'll tell me you forgot about the risks of paternal smoking to early-stage pregnancies."

"Hold it right there," insisted Jack, his face flushed with anger. "You haven't exactly been the poster girl for rational behavior lately.

And as far as my smoking is concerned, you've got some secrets of your own, or am I completely off-base? You've been acting pretty peculiar lately."

Heads in the coffee shop were beginning to turn.

"You made it clear that you didn't approve of my inquiry, so I kept my activities quiet," snapped Gwen. "You know I hate it when you preach at me. And this time you even ordered me to back off!"

Jack took a long sip of his coffee and looked out the window. "I was trying to help, for Christ's sake. I wanted to solve this thing for you so we could concentrate on the baby. I thought I could wrap it up so we wouldn't have to deal with this for the next nine months. You just don't know when to leave something alone, Gwen. Ever since you closed up your father's private practice, you've been on a one-woman crusade to save the world, and I'm tired of it."

Fuming, Gwen shifted in her seat and ran her fingers through her hair. "It's who I am, Jack. If that doesn't meet with your approval, then maybe we shouldn't be having this baby together. I can take care of myself."

Jack's eyes narrowed. Gwen knew she'd struck a nerve. "So you're standing on moral high ground because you're an all-important FDA doctor—one who's putting us both in danger. You can sneak around and investigate, but as soon as I try to pitch in and—"

Jack paused. His face was twisted in a way she didn't recognize.

"And what?" Gwen said impatiently.

His face relaxed. "I was trying to lend you a hand—that's all. When I finally discovered a clue, I thought I'd follow it up and let you know when I found something concrete. But I now think we're both under surveillance—and we could be in danger."

"We could have worked as a team, dammit. I've come across damaging information about tobacco as well. And I don't care what you say—you had no business going to the Newmans without me."

"Damaging information about tobacco! For the love of God, Gwen. If you'd come to me in the first place, we could have worked as a team. I—"

Jack stopped abruptly. Gwen noticed that his right hand was starting to shake. "Look, can I have a cigarette without your going ballistic?"

"It's rather late for that, isn't it?"

Jack was reaching for his pack of cigarettes when his eyes rolled up into his head. He tried to speak, but only guttural sounds escaped his throat.

"Jack!" Gwen screamed. "What's happening?"

In her haste, Gwen knocked her latte over, got up, and knelt next to her husband.

He was lying on the floor. Faster and faster, his right arm flexed and unflexed repeatedly. Meanwhile, his left leg began to dance a jig to a rhythm all its own.

"Jack, can you hear me? Did you take something?" Gwen turned her head sharply. "Call 9-1-1!" she yelled.

"Is everything okay over there?" a barrista called as if Gwen had ordered another latte.

"No, it's not okay! I said to call 9-1-1. Now!"

Jack's movements had slowed as he attempted to speak. "The . . . baby. You . . . "

"The paramedics are on their way. Everything will be okay." Gwen was in tears now. "I didn't mean what I said, Jack. Of course I want the baby. Jack. Jack!"

Jack couldn't answer. The tonic-clonic movements were becoming more rapid. He was going into a full-blown seizure. Gwen bundled several wooden stirring sticks together and placed them in her husband's mouth so he wouldn't bite his tongue.

An eternity seemed to go by as Gwen waited for help. Finally, the door swung open as a female paramedic rushed in, followed by her partner pulling a collapsed gurney along the floor.

"I'm a doctor! Hurry up! Please do something for him!" Gwen cried.

The paramedics started an IV drip and checked Jack's vital signs. Several tense minutes passed before the female said, "We've got him stable for the moment, but we need to get him to a hospital. You can ride in the back, but please try to stay calm. I'll be calling in his vitals to the ER again as soon as we roll."

"Sure. Anything. Is he going to be— "

"Just ride in the back, ma'am."

Gwen, consumed with guilt and worry, felt as if she were in the midst of the worst nightmare of her life.

It's all my fault. I should have told him everything about the investigation. I'm as guilty as he is.

The image of Marci lying on the gurney at Bellevue hit Gwen like a sledgehammer. "No," she sobbed as the ambulance sped through the streets. "Not again."

40

Before he got to work in earnest on Gwen's story, Mark followed up on Billy Hamlin's invitation and took a trip to Seattle. The CEO could not have been more accommodating, guiding Mark on a tour of the inner workings of Pequod's main facility. Mark was relatively certain that he was only getting marginally more access than the average tourist received, but the average tourist didn't get to walk the plant with the company's head honcho. And the standard tour didn't include dinner with that head honcho's family. Hamlin's wife, Cynthia, was fourth-generation Japanese-American and was trained expertly in the art of preparing beautiful food. Clearly, she had gone out of her way to impress Mark. She prepared a uniquely Japanese meal in which each item looked like something it wasn't: scallops pressed and colored to look like miniature apples, vegetables cut and shaped to look like shrimps.

As Mark entered the dining portion of the house, he was surprised by the sight of two dining rooms, one set with a period Duncan Pfyfe mahogany table and chairs, the other furnished in traditional tatami.

"Take your pick, you're the guest," said Hamlin. Mark immediately shucked his shoes and headed for the tatami room. Hamlin pressed a few keys on the small computer monitor in the wall, and the home was flooded with delicate strains of Koto music.

"And if I had chosen the other room?"

"Pachelbel," answered Hamlin without missing a beat.

Dieter Tassin, Pequod's master roaster, arrived moments later, with two of the most striking women Mark had ever seen. They turned out to be his wife, Mei Long, and her sister, Su Chi. All three were clearly far more comfortable sitting tatami-style than Mark, and Tassin in particular seemed to enjoy Mark's constant shifting to accommodate the growing ache in his knees and ankles.

Dinner was polite but stilted. Hamlin and his wife carried most of the small talk with conversation about the environment, the growth around Seattle, and the school activities of their children. Mark managed to learn that Tassin had left Germany as a child and been raised in Bangkok and Saigon. Mei Long and Su Chi were practically mute, despite Mark's best use of his reporter's skills. They certainly seemed to speak English, but dinner conversation simply wasn't part of their agenda. Mark was left wondering a great deal about what exactly was going on between Dieter, his wife, and her sister.

After dinner, Mark went back to his hotel room and changed into a brown jumpsuit that closely matched the ones he'd seen Pequod's warehouse workers wear. He took one of his many picture IDs from his suitcase—never leave home without them!—and attached it to a silver ball-chain around his neck. A quick look in the mirror assured him he passed muster. He rode the elevator down to the parking garage and got into his rented Neon.

Aware that he was about to attempt one of the more brazen stunts in his career, he thought of what he'd tell his congenial host if someone caught him trying to gain access to Pequod's roasting chamber—the heart of their operation. Aw shucks, Billy, I was just doing my job. Snooping around to see if you had been straight with me. He hoped it wouldn't come to that.

He had copped a Pequod's parking permit from the lobby desk at the main building after his private tour. He removed the Enterprise stickers from the windshield of his rental and hung his Pequod's pass over the rearview mirror.

He encountered trouble as soon as he pulled up to the company gate.

"Don't have any record of a Mark Treadwell," the guard inside the small booth said.

"I was only hired three days ago," Mark said, as if startled.

"Finished my orientation session yesterday. Was just me and a fellow named Smith."

The guard looked at the roster fastened to his clipboard. "You mean Ed Smith at the loading dock?"

"One and the same," said Mark, grinning from ear to ear. "He's a character, that one."

The guard shone a flashlight at the pass hanging over the mirror. "I see they gave you a temporary pass, eh?"

"Yep."

The uniformed man swept his beam across Mark's chest. Noticing an ID hanging against the jumpsuit, he shrugged. "Okay. Have a good night." He pushed a button in his booth, and a yellow gate swung open.

Mark was in.

■ ■ ■

"Stop!"

Mark wheeled around to see who was shouting at him.

"You ever hear of punching a time clock?" asked a man with a white coat and a clipboard.

Mark mouthed the word "sorry" and nodded. But where was the time clock? If he walked in the wrong direction, he would be marched into the Pequod's security office within sixty seconds. He needed to guess—and guess right. The only logical place to put a time clock was at an entry point. Aware that the man who yelled at him, probably a foreman, was still observing him, Mark turned around quickly and headed for the wall next to the door he'd entered moments before.

There it was. Several dozen rows of cards sat in metal slots fastened next to the clock. Mark casually chose one at random and studied the clock. It was part of a digital system, with a bar code on the card that was scanned by a beam under the clock. He passed the card under the clock, heard a beep, and replaced the card in its slot. When he turned around, the foreman was walking in the opposite direction.

But now what? Do I just saunter up to the roasting chamber and walk past the guards?

Mark walked toward one of the forklifts so that he wouldn't appear to be wandering around aimlessly. He surmised that somewhere high above him, supervisors looked at the entire warehouse 24/7. Looking up at a distant wall of the enormous complex, he saw two signs. The one on top said SAFETY FIRST! Below it, a blinking electronic sign said ROASTING PERSONNEL USE DOOR 1. Apparently, workers assigned to the roasting chamber were directed to use different doorways depending on which set of machines were up and running at any given moment. Mark headed for DOOR 1.

A large hand gripped Mark's shoulder.

"You don't belong here," said a voice behind him.

Busted! Mark thought, slowly turning around to face his adversary.

■ ■ ■

Dr. Jason Sutherland brought Gwen to a waiting area and sat down, motioning for her to do the same.

"Jack is out of immediate danger, Mrs. Maulder. In the course of the grand mal seizure, your husband suffered a spinal cord injury."

"Look, I'm a physician. Spinal cord injury can mean just about anything."

Sutherland took Gwen's hand, nodded, and smiled. "Jack is doing okay, Gwen. His speech is slurred from the after-effects of the seizure, and he has partial paralysis on his left side. You know as well as I that it could be anywhere from hours to days to see if his speech or motor skills begin to return. Right now, he needs rest. Sorry for the cliché, but I'm sure you're aware that is what's best for him right now."

Gwen managed a weak nod.

"If things remain constant, he'll naturally need therapy," Dr. Sutherland continued. "As I'm sure you know, there are several new mechanical devices that are employed to help spinal injury patients regain mobility. Hydrotherapy is also an option down the line, plus we'll have consultations with speech therapists when we know more."

"Is there any visual impairment?"

"None that I can detect."

"Why did this happen?" Gwen asked. "His hypertension was under control. He'd started to smoke again, but just in the last couple of weeks."

"We can't really say what precipitated the episode, Gwen. I've reviewed the medical history you gave the nurse when Jack was admitted, and frankly, this seems to have come out of the blue. The only time I see this kind of presentation is when some college student or biker shows up with a bad reaction to various kinds of drugs."

"He's been sneaking cigarettes, but nothing more."

"That certainly shouldn't cause a seizure. For now, it's a mystery."

Gwen briefly visited Jack in the ICU, but he was fast asleep. She stayed in the waiting room across the hall, wishing she had paid more attention in Sunday school as she tried to remember snippets of prayers.

She prayed that Jack had heard her say she wanted to have his baby.

■ ■ ■

"I said you don't belong here. Cat got your tongue?"

Still working out what he might say, Mark turned very slowly and saw an old man wearing wireless spectacles. He had white, unkempt hair and a bushy moustache. His hand still gripped Mark's shoulder tightly.

It was Dieter Tassin. Pretty strong grip for an old dude.

At dinner, Tassin had been polite, if not altogether congenial. His countenance now bordered on demonic, his face frozen in an ugly stare that spoke of anger and mistrust. How, Mark wondered, could this man work for the amiable Billy Hamlin?

"You may be Hamlin's guest," he spit out venomously, "but no one is allowed in this facility without permission. That's not even a legitimate Pequod's ID tag."

"I thought it would be okay for me to look around. Actually, I hoped I might run into you here, Dieter. We didn't really get much of a chance to talk at dinner." Mark was sweating bullets. Surely, Tassin wouldn't believe a word he said.

"I see. And 'Billy' authorized you to enter restricted areas of the plant?"

"Well, no, not exactly."

"Let's call him up then, and ask him if you should be here at all, shall we?"

"That won't be necessary. I'll just go since you're obviously upset."

Tassin released his grip on the reporter's shoulders. "I've got a better idea, Mr. Reporter. You wanted to see the roasting chamber, didn't you?"

"Not in particular," Mark lied.

"Oh, sure you did. Everyone wants a peek inside our secret chamber. Let's go inside and see if you have any idea what you're looking at."

Mark started to backpedal but Tassin took hold of his arm, his fingers digging deeply into Mark's bicep.

"I insist," said Tassin.

The roastmaster urged Mark forward. Just ten yards away from entrance number two to the chamber, Mark felt the air getting warmer.

"You're a reporter," Tassin said, his tone friendly, but his eyes cold and calculating. "You like to see things for yourself, right? Let's go in and have a look."

Tassin's grip on Mark's arm eased slightly as they moved forward.

Mark started to feel a little queasy.

41

Jan Menefee had no idea where she was. The last thing she remembered was sitting in the van with Peter, feeling lightheaded. Her surroundings, however, did not resemble a hospital. She was lying on top of a thin brown blanket tucked into an army cot. She started to sit up but immediately lay back down when the room began to swim in circles.

The room? A cell, to be more exact. The area, about ten feet by ten feet, consisted of cinderblock walls with no windows. A low-watt light bulb on the ceiling was covered with wire mesh.

She sat up again, swinging her feet onto a bare cement floor. Her head throbbed, but the clarity of her vision slowly returned.

They didn't intend to kill me. They just wanted me out of circulation.

But for how long? Permanently?

She stood, walked eight paces to the other side of her cell and then back to the bed.

And where's Peter?

The solid iron door of the cell opened, letting in fluorescent light that painfully struck Jan's retinas.

"Who's there?"

The door closed, and an unseen hand switched on the lights in her cell. Jan still could not make out any of the features of her visitor.

"Time for another treatment, Dr. Menefee."

"Treatment? What are you talking about? Who are you?"

Her eyes adjusted to the stark lighting from the overhead bulb.

She saw a thin man standing before her wearing a white shirt and black pants. He had a pocket protector filled with Bic pens, and his black frame glasses and crewcut reminded Jan of every geek from high school.

This geek, however, held a syringe and smiled ghoulishly.

"No way, pal," she protested. "I don't need any treatment. Certainly not from you."

The skinny man took hold of her arm and pushed her down on the edge of the bed. Feeling unsteady, Jan could offer little resistance. With expert dexterity, he looped a rubber tube around her arm and tightened it. The pinprick of the needle entering her bicep was brief. Jan didn't know who the hell she was dealing with but she knew that, whoever he was, he'd done this before.

"There," the man said. "You need your rest."

A warm lethargy spread throughout Jan's already weakened limbs.

Have to stay awake. Can't lose consciousness again.

The cell grew hazy. An aura was forming around the lightbulb above Jan's head. Jan couldn't help but give in to the pleasant sensation taking hold of her body. Her brain was on the verge of shutting down again when she thought she heard a voice. It was almost inaudible.

"Jan? Are you there, Jan?"

In her final moments of awareness, Jan wondered when Peter Tippett had begun to sound like a noisy mosquito buzzing somewhere at the foot of the bed.

■ ■ ■

Mark was disoriented. He'd been expecting a scene from Hades, but the forbidden roasting chamber was surprisingly well-lit, though a little on the warm side. Several employees stopped what they were doing to stare at Dieter and the stranger with him. Clearly, they weren't used to visitors.

"Back to work," Tassin ordered.

The workers did what they were told, but continued to sneak glances when they dared.

"I take it that you've been told the basics of the roasting process," Tassin said. "A part of Hamlin's standard tour."

Mark nodded slowly. Tassin's voice was more genial now. He almost sounded like he thought of Mark as an invited guest. Tassin had an assistant pull out a tray of beans from a roasting machine that was as big as a bedroom in an average American home.

"Behold the precious second crack," he proclaimed. He arched his body so that his nose was only inches away from the hot beans. When he brought his right hand up, palm open, the odor of the darkened beans wafted up into his nostrils. Smiling, he said, "A thing of beauty, wouldn't you say, Mr. Stern?"

"Sure," said Mark guardedly. "Smells fine."

"More than fine, I assure you, young man."

Tassin showed Mark twelve more roasting machines. Mark did not think he could stand a thirteenth. Smiling, Tassin chose that moment to lean over and whisper a few brief words into Mark's ear.

Mark went pale. "I want to go now," he said. He intended his voice to sound demanding, but the croak that came out would not have moved a frog.

"Of course you do," said Tassin. "You know the way out. I hope you've enjoyed our time together."

Mark turned and started to walk in what he assumed was the right direction. He hadn't felt this numb since his last dentist appointment. He stumbled and looked down. Pausing, he knelt to undo and retie the lace of his right work boot. Suddenly everything snapped back into focus. An inch from his right foot sat one lone coffee bean. Acting as naturally as he could, he palmed the bean, tied his shoe, and continued what felt like the longest journey of his life.

Outside the door, he pocketed the bean.

He left quickly.

When Mark returned to his hotel, he immediately threw his clothes into his suitcase. Tomorrow, he'd call Billy Hamlin and inform him that the paper had summoned him home to start work on an important story.

42

Roberta Chang drove to the Mid-Atlantic Credit Union. Henry would no doubt be throwing another fit about her absence, but that was a short-term problem. She knew the senator was dissatisfied with her performance of late and she knew it was just a matter of time before he suggested she seek employment elsewhere. Roberta had no intention of waiting until then; she'd already contacted a prominent congressman about joining his staff.

She eased her Lexus into the parking lot of the credit union and stopped beneath a row of towering pines that, in her estimation, made Virginia one of the most beautiful states in the country. Feeling more relaxed than she had in months, she took the sealed manila envelope lying on the leather passenger seat, exited the vehicle, and entered Mid-Atlantic.

Inside, her business took no more than ten minutes. She was ushered to the back, where an attendant brought her a safe deposit box. She unlocked it, dropped in the manila envelope, and left.

"You roll the dice and you take your chances," she said to herself, walking back to her car. "Let the chips fall where they may."

■ ■ ■

Dr. Edward Karn pulled his fuel-efficient Prius into the parking lot of the Mid-Atlantic Credit Union. He walked through the glass double doors and asked for the safe deposit boxes. An employee checked the box registration card and saw Karn's name listed for box

5728964 right beneath Roberta Chang's signature. After that, she left him in private.

Karn had been surprised to get Chang's phone call telling him she had photographs for him to view, and even more surprised to learn that she wanted to open a safe deposit box with him. She didn't say exactly what he'd be viewing, just that the photographs might be of some help in "rehabilitating his image."

Did he have reason to trust the chief aide of Senator Henry Broome, the man who had humiliated him in front of America? No, but if Broome were going to try to take him down another notch, he wanted to know about it. He also knew that political alliances were as changeable as the wind in Washington, and he was very curious to see what the materials would manifest.

Karn slipped the key into the lock and opened the lid. With a sharp intake of breath, he shook his head as if to clear his vision. This time, he opened the lid the rest of the way and felt all the way to the back. One last shake revealed what he already knew.

The sealed manila envelope Chang had promised him was nowhere to be found.

■ ■ ■

Op One sat alone, drinking a cup of coffee. Things were going smoothly.

Menefee and Tippett were out of the equation. Jack Maulder was in an intensive care unit thanks to a happy twist of fate, and authorities discovered Roberta Chang's lifeless body two hours ago, sprawled on the floor of her apartment. Thanks to Tabula Rasa, D.C. cops found an empty bottle of sleeping pills and a typed suicide note on Chang's kitchen table. The note described how she suffered from a deep depression for more than two years that had steadily gotten worse. The stress of her job, the recent death of her mother—it had all been overwhelming.

"Farewell, cruel world," said Op One mockingly as he looked through the contents of the manila envelope.

43

Mark practically ran through the concourse of Washington's Reagan National Airport after deplaning. He hurried outside and slipped into the back door of the first cab in the pick-up and drop-off lane. He needed to find Gwen—and fast. He called the FDA to learn that she was on temporary leave. He knew that didn't bode well.

Nor did the fact that someone was following him. He spotted an operative with shaggy hair—the man looked like a refugee from the sixties—three different times while in Seattle and again moments earlier at Reagan National.

He ordered the cabbie to head for the Maulders' address in Garrett Park.

■ ■ ■

As ragged as Gwen looked as she opened the front door, Mark said a quick prayer of thanks that she was still in one piece. Clearly, things had happened to her in his absence.

"Throw some clothes together and gather any documents, floppies, or CDs you have pertaining to the investigation. I've been followed, and I'm guessing this house is under periodic surveillance or will be shortly."

"There's something I need to tell you, Mark. It's about—"

"Save it for later," Mark said urgently. "We don't have a lot of time."

Gwen looked ready to collapse, but gathered her wits and

ascended the staircase. She reappeared ten minutes later with an overnight case, a laptop, and a leather bag.

"Let's haul ass," Mark said. "There's a taxi in the driveway. The meter's running, and I paid the driver an extra hundred bucks to wait for us."

"You're scaring me, Mark."

"There's good reason to be scared, Gwen."

They left the house and climbed into the taxi. Mark gave the driver an address and told him there was an extra fifty dollars in the fare if he would use a heavy foot and take as many detours as possible.

"You got it, mister. For money, I don't ask questions—I just drive. My wife says I don't bring home enough dough. Always nagging, that one. Just the other night, she says, 'Dick, you . . . '"

Mark and Gwen faced each other, tuning out the droning cabbie and his marital woes.

"Jack's had a seizure, and there's some paralysis," Gwen said abruptly. "Can we run by the hospital?"

Mark shook his head. "Sorry, Gwen. It's too dangerous, but tell me what happened."

Gwen told Mark that Jack collapsed at a Pequod's and that he had been fighting hard to recover. She also told him that Jack had been investigating tobacco as a cause of the seizures.

"I'm sorry, Gwen. Really. You must be sick with worry. We have a lot of work to do—crucial work, if Jack was on to anything. I'll make a call later and get a friend to check up on him. Meanwhile, we're going someplace where we can lay out everything we've got so far and see if we can piece this mess together."

"Mess?"

"When you're followed by people who don't seem to work for the good guys, believe me—it's a mess. I've got some things to show you, and I'm not at all sure how they add up, but maybe if we work together, we'll be able to figure out what the next step should be."

Gwen turned away at that point to look out the window. Mark could only imagine what she was thinking.

■ ■ ■

The cabbie stopped at the Smithsonian Institute parking lot nearest the Air and Space Museum. Mark handed the driver a fistful of bills and said a hurried thanks as he exited the cab, grabbing his large Nike sports bag and helping Gwen with her luggage.

"What now?" asked Gwen.

"Follow me," Mark said, placing what appeared to be a nickel on the ground as he walked behind the cab. He then crossed several rows of cars in the lot until he came to a dark green Suburban with tinted windows.

"Belongs to a friend of mine," he said, pressing the unlock button on his keychain.

Mark and Gwen climbed into the van and stowed their gear. The large engine roared to life as Mark turned the ignition key. He backed out, headed for the interstate, and looked over at Gwen who still seemed a little shell-shocked.

Sixty minutes later, they checked into a small motel in eastern Virginia. Mark pulled out his cell—the same one he'd used to call Pequod's and Randall, Inc.—and inserted a new chip into the phone.

"I've gathered some interesting devices over the years," he told Gwen. "With this particular chip, the cell's signal will be scrambled and untraceable."

"Is that legal?"

"Not if you're a civilian, but who's going to tell on me?" He punched a set of numbers into the keypad. "I'm going to call an old friend of mine, Congressman Rick Mecklenberg. He's the guy who loaned me the Suburban. Hopefully, he can get some info on Jack."

Mecklenberg promised to keep tabs on Jack Maulder, though not in person. He'd have a friend of his call the nurse's station and pretend to be family.

"Do you think we're safe here?" asked Gwen.

"For a while. It depends on how many goons are chasing us."

Gwen sat on the edge of the bed and put her head on Mark's shoulder. Mark wasn't sure what to do. How many times had he envisioned a scene like this—he and Gwen in a hotel, her head on his shoulder, back together after so many years. Except the fantasy scenes never involved hiding from an unknown enemy.

Or Gwen's sobbing, which she was now doing.

"I'm pregnant," she said. "This can't be happening—not now."

Or Gwen's being pregnant with another man's child.

Mark put his arm around her shoulder. "We'll deal with this. Hang in there."

Her crying eased a bit. Mark wished the rest of their problems would resolve so easily.

■ ■ ■

Op Three listened to the electronic beeps emitting from the black rectangular object on his passenger seat. The gadget looked like a Radio Shack calculator, but it was a tracking device homing in on the signal coming from the magnetic locator he'd placed under the cab's rear bumper minutes before Mark got into the taxi's backseat at the airport. He followed it for several miles until he came at last to the Air and Space Museum parking lot at the Smithsonian.

"Shit!" he cursed. "That lousy SOB knows too much for his own good."

Op Three got out of his car and picked up the magnetic locator, roughly the size of a nickel, lying on the hot asphalt. His call to Op One would be one of the more unpleasant exchanges he'd had in a while.

■ ■ ■

"Let's see what we have to work with," Mark said once he'd given Gwen a chance to orient herself to their new situation.

Gwen got out her hard copy of the seizure stats, some burned CDs, and a laptop onto which she'd transferred all of Jack's files and research via portable jump drive. Mark was relieved to see that her scientific curiosity and inherent strength of character had risen to the occasion as she powered up the laptop and loaded Microsoft Word, which contained something called Haydn104 and Jack's notes regarding his investigations into tobacco.

"All I know is that people are dying," Gwen said with

determination, "and tobacco has something to do with it." Gwen showed Mark the postings Jack had found on the Internet, as well as the file on Virginia Rampling.

"To be truthful, Gwen, I'm still not buying into the tobacco angle. I know Kessler hired you at the FDA, but you have to stop trying to fight his fight. Big Tobacco is always under everybody's microscope. If the seizure pattern is traceable, I don't think the management of R.J. Reynolds, Philip Morris, or Compson would risk moving a high-nicotine cigarette into the market. Do they like what happened in the nineties? No, but they're too smart to put a lethal cigarette into circulation. It would be a wet dream for every plaintiff's lawyer in the country. Anyway, they're not interested in immediately killing their customers—just in keeping them happily and fatally hooked."

"But what if it's not nicotine that's responsible? What if the companies themselves aren't aware of the seizures because of some new additive?"

"They test their brands too carefully to be ignorant of what they're selling. That's what made their manipulation of nicotine levels such an outrage. They knew exactly what they were doing."

Gwen paced anxiously back and forth, massaging her temples. Her head had been pounding for the last two hours. "Are you saying that Jack was pursuing a dead-end lead?"

"He might have been."

Gwen sat on the edge of the bed, arms crossed. "What keeps coming back to me over and over again is the last thing Marci said to me."

"What was that?"

"Ondee."

"What does it mean?"

"She was referring to *Ondine*. I know you've never been anywhere on a Saturday afternoon except a ball game, but Marci and I used to love scoring last-minute tickets to the ballet. Of all the pieces, *Ondine* was Marci's favorite. It's about a prince who marries a beautiful young woman named Ondine, who in reality is a water sprite who emerges from a fountain in the prince's palace."

Mark, who had read every issue of *Rolling Stone*, but had never been near anything as cultured as a ballet, was puzzled. "I'm afraid I don't see its significance."

"Only that Marci really identified with that dance. She saw herself as Ondine, someone a man could never successfully love because she had another calling. She worked so hard to get through school that she put it above everything else. Guys would always be breaking up with her because she never had enough time for them. I guess it was threatening to their egos. Ondine had this signature series of leaps and spins in the final act. Whenever some guy would dump her, Marci would dance into my room that way."

"Interesting—and very important to you and Marci—but probably not tied to anything."

"I guess not. When someone dies, the right temporal lobe fills with electrical activity that causes pleasant hallucinations. Some think the phenomenon is the basis for near-death experiences."

"Which leaves us, for the moment, with only the information from Jack's laptop. Let me take a look."

Mark inspected Haydn104 first. Unimpressed with the rows of numbers, he began to peruse Jack's files that Gwen had imported to her laptop. These, consequently, included all of Marci's files that Jack downloaded.

"Lots of legal files," Mark commented. "There's enough material here to keep us reading for days, assuming we could understand the legalese."

Continuing to scan the directory of Marci's files, Mark suddenly furrowed his brows.

"What is it?" asked Gwen.

"Just looking at what was apparently the last case Marci worked on. Nguyen v. Lazlow. Looks like a woman named Anh Nguyen was challenging a routine eviction by an all-too-common slumlord."

"I think Jack's visit to Virginia Rampling and his research on cigarettes are more germane."

"Patience," Mark said, winking at Gwen as he looked up. "An investigative reporter has to trudge through a lot of muck, sometimes on the street, sometimes on a PC."

Mark read the details about Lazlow. The landlord was breaking

Anh's lease in order to sell his apartment building to a developer. Apparently, Lazlow had not maintained the tenement and the city cited him several times for violations of various building codes. Mark clicked on "N v. L—background info" to see if there was anything unusual about the case since the suit didn't seem particularly noteworthy.

"What have we here?" he said in a low voice.

"You've found something?"

"Nested files. This one file is really a folder that contains dozens of other files. Trouble is, I can't get into any of them."

Mark paused, considering several possibilities. "This Haydn104 file. Jack was never able to do anything with it?"

"Nope, but Marci wasn't the type to create a file for no reason. She was too methodical, too logical."

"I'm no computer whiz," said Mark, "but I wonder . . . "

"What?"

"I wonder if these numbers open up the nested files. How would I connect the nested files with Haydn104? Any idea?"

Gwen pursed her lips. "I've watched Jack work over the years, but I confess I wasn't always paying much attention. Let me see what I can do."

Mark and Gwen traded seats. Gwen clicked the mouse on the nested files, then reloaded the Haydn104 CD. When it appeared onscreen, she highlighted the numbers, brought down a dialog box and clicked APPLY.

The nested files immediately opened into dozens of extra folders.

"Yes!"

Gwen switched places with Mark again, and he began to inspect the hidden files unlocked by Haydn104.

"Got something, Sherlock?"

"Yes, although I don't know what it means. Anh Nguyen was married to someone I met recently."

"Who?"

"The chief roastmaster for Pequod's. His name is Dieter Tassin. I was staring into his eyes less than forty-eight hours ago. He married Anh in 1975, shortly after she arrived in the U.S. Tassin disappeared in the late seventies, according to Anh's affidavit, and she filed for divorce on the grounds of desertion and subsequently reverted to her Vietnamese name since she and Tassin didn't have any children together. Maybe Marci was saying 'Anh and Dieter'—not Ondine."

"I suppose anything is possible."

Mark continued reading. "It just gets better—and weirder."

"In what way?"

"It appears that Marci was trying to do more for Anh than simply securing her apartment. I think she was going to go after Tassin."

"For what? Desertion?"

"No. Get this—he was trafficking in slaves back in the late seventies."

"You've got to be kidding."

"Not about something like this. Tassin actually sold some of Anh's cousins and friends into slavery—as sex slaves, to be exact. Looks like they became courtesans of well-to-do people that Tassin knew. Anh's daughters escaped this nightmare because they were only two and three years old at the time, although Marci says here that Tassin threatened Anh that if she ever left him, she would never see those daughters again. Anh is about seventy-five now, fairly close in age to Tassin."

"Why all the secrecy with Haydn104?" asked Gwen.

Mark stood and paced the room, looking disturbed. "Tassin whispered something in my ear while we were standing next to the roasting ovens. He leaned over and said, 'Don't you just love the story of Hansel and Gretel?'"

"Guy sounds like a lunatic."

"I think a little research might confirm this lunatic was hanging around Auschwitz or Dachau in the early forties. He was alluding to torturing people in ovens, for Christ's sake. And we were in something very much like an oven at the time. Aside from creeping me out bigtime, he obviously doesn't have much of a conscience. Sex slaves? This man is one bad SOB, and if I were Marci, I wouldn't have left the info hanging around." Mark thought about how he'd had dinner with Billy Hamlin and Dieter just the night before. Hamlin spoke about Dieter as though he were a wizard. Was he unaware of Tassin's past?

"I still don't see his connection with seizures, as intriguing as all this is. What do you intend to do?"

"Play a hunch, my dear Watson. Play a hunch."

Gwen laughed. It was nice to hear. "You're still the same old Mark. As weird and wired as you ever were."

"Why thank you, Gwen. It's nice to know you still appreciate me."

44

Trembling, Jan sat on the edge of her cot. Her thoughts were still hazy. She didn't know how long she'd been out this time. She assumed the people standing in the cell with her used some kind of drug to awaken her.

"What do you want?" she asked. It was a little tough to get the words to come out right.

A bald man in a gray pinstripe suit sat in a wooden chair next to the cot. The man who last drugged her, still wearing a white shirt with a pocket protector, stood behind him in the corner.

"We want information, Dr. Menefee." The man was in his early forties. He exuded confidence and his pale blue eyes and reassuring smile did nothing to put Jan at ease. "I know all this must seem very strange, but believe me, there are reasons why you were brought here."

"You tried to kill me and Peter," Jan said tersely.

"Untrue. We needed to ask you some questions, as well as stop your cyber activity immediately. You could have compromised a very serious government investigation."

A third man entered the room, handed Jan a cup of coffee, and left. After a few sips, her trembling subsided.

"I found vital information that the government is trying to cover up," Jan asserted.

The man paused, never taking his eyes off Jan. "Yes, you've discovered certain information, but you're unaware of its context. Terrorists have infiltrated our homeland, Dr. Menefee, and the government needs to address this threat without causing a panic. The truth is that a radical Islamic sect has contaminated our food supply. BioNet would have picked it up within a day or two on its own, but you and Dr. Maulder helped it along. You reported the seizure stats to your superiors, who told you to keep the findings confidential and proceed no further. I fail to see why you felt the need to destroy the gatekeeper and start sending out files."

"And I fail to see why you installed a gatekeeper without telling me in the first place. Or why Gwen Maulder was pulled away from her regular duties and assigned to—" Jan broke off. She didn't want to volunteer any information to the unknown man before her.

"The Adverse Event files," the man said, nodding. "The FDA knew Dr. Maulder was the best person for the job. Gene McMurphy wanted her to uncover episodes that would corroborate our findings, but he couldn't give her any information about the terrorist threat. That issue is beyond her clearance level. Unfortunately, Dr. Maulder began testing crazy theories by researching clinical trials and tobacco companies instead of conducting a straightforward search for terrorist activity, which is what her boss requested. The fact that you and Dr. Maulder spotted the seizures is a testament to your competence, but we simply couldn't let you two wander off on your own. There's too much at stake."

This exacerbated Jan's confusion. Was it possible that the feds were really onto something as serious as food contamination across America? If so, it was plausible—though not necessarily moral—that the FBI or CIA would confide in only the most essential personnel and keep the public in the dark.

"The people have a right to know," Jan protested. "The appropriate warnings should have been issued as to what is safe to buy and what is not. It's the job of the FDA to do this, as well as the responsibility of the government as a whole."

The bald man shook his head and leaned forward. "It's not that simple, Dr. Menefee. The food and drug laws never contemplated issues of homeland security. Imagine an entire nation learning that a hundred different products—both food and beverages—may contain a deadly chemical that's difficult to trace. There could be rioting in the streets. Stores would be looted for 'safe' items. And fear—a paralyzing fear—could spread across the land, the likes of which would make the fear after 9/11 pale in comparison. The country could be shaken to its foundation. Don't you think that we're doing everything possible at this very moment to combat the Islamic radicals?"

Jan didn't know what to believe. BioNet was constructed to detect exactly the kind of scenario being described, and she had to admit that the system was relatively new. It was entirely possible that she and Gwen had gotten the information days—or even hours—before the system would have identified the seizure spikes and recognized patterns on its own. If that had happened, a Compartmented Secret Information Codeword access shield would have gone up instantly. She remembered enough from her last security briefing to know that she would have indeed been ordered to keep the utmost secrecy concerning BioNet's findings.

But that was the problem.

"Something doesn't make sense," she said. "As director of the BioNet Surveillance Project, I would have been in the loop. I have codeword-level clearance for this project. That's why I was hired. BioNet is crucial to any ongoing investigation of terrorism. Why not call me into the office and explain what's going on?"

Jan's interviewer smiled in a way that suggested he was treating her as a naïve child caught in a situation she couldn't possibly understand.

"Dr. Menefee, you would most certainly have been given certain instructions if you had allowed the Center to move forward in its own manner, although you would not have been privy to countermeasures or political ramifications. Even now, I can't reveal all of the pertinent facts to you, but that's not the issue. You signed documents the day you were hired in which you promised to respect the chain of command and not use the database to pursue unauthorized lines of inquiry."

"So now you're showing me the inside of the puzzle?" she mused. "Seems a bit contradictory, to my way of thinking."

"I have no choice but to give you more information than I would prefer, but I have decided it would be in the country's best interest to enlist your help to deal with this crisis."

"Meaning?"

"Meaning I need to know what you, Mr. Tippett, and Dr. Maulder know. What have you and Mr. Tippett uncovered in your computer-related expeditions?"

Jan barely bit back the retort that first sprung to her lips. "You already know everything we know. Hell, you were spying on—or should I say 'monitoring'—us. There's nothing I can add."

"Have you contacted others within the government? Any civilians?"

"No. Of course not."

"And yet your companion sent a file on avian flu to Panama."

"Surely you realize that was unintentional. He hit the wrong key, and the next thing we knew, the file was sending itself out the cyber-door. And what's up with that, by the way? Since when do CDC files go to Central America?"

The man shook his head again. "Has it occurred to you that the United States government has quite a few tricks up its sleeve to combat terrorism? We have several remote stations and outposts that help us transfer or safeguard information. I confess I'm a bit disappointed that you can't trust the government that pays your salary, Dr. Menefee."

Jan knew arguing was pointless. "I don't have any other information, nor was any given to anyone you don't already know about. Go ahead and shoot me full of more drugs if you don't believe me."

Standing, the bald man looked down and smiled the same condescending smile. "That won't be necessary, and I apologize for the heavy-duty meds. It was necessary to keep you calm until I could arrive. Thank you for your time."

Both men exited the cell, leaving Jan alone on the cot. At this point, she was willing to entertain the possibility that she and Gwen were simply in over their heads. There was no way to refute what the man in the gray suit had said. To a greater or lesser degree, all branches and agencies of government lived and died by a code of secrecy.

She desperately wanted to get in touch with Gwen and tell her of a possible terrorist breach. Whatever leads Gwen was pursuing, she needed to remember that things weren't always what they seemed.

Even the most damning or implausible facts sometimes had explanations. A contamination of foods and beverages could well be responsible for seizures across the country.

She curled up and drifted off to sleep, wondering where Peter was. Just before she dozed, another thought entered her head.

Why did the man in the gray suit look so familiar?

45

Gregory Randall looked at the morning paper. It was a pity, he thought, that Roberta Chang had underestimated him. It had been pure stupidity on her part to think that after making love to the Asian beauty he would simply leave her to her own devices in his quarters. He couldn't deny, though, that he'd been disappointed in the way she betrayed him by sneaking around and taking pictures of the documents in his briefcase. To Randall's way of thinking, the loss of Chang was a waste of what he had thought was considerable intelligence, not to mention sexual talent. He'd often considered luring the comely young woman away from the staff of Henry Broome.

Henry. He'd been too trusting of Chang. Randall always suspected that Chang, an educated woman with access to most of Henry's affairs, knew about their mutual business interests. Henry should have had more self-discipline. Randall made the effort to ensure his own courtesans were content, but he would never give any of them entry into his professional dealings. That would be taking a great risk—for absolutely no reward.

Fortunately, Randall was able to contain the situation with a single phone call. The man with the raspy voice usually obtained results in a very short time. In this case, Tabula Rasa intercepted Chang's manila envelope before the day was over.

"Good-bye, Roberta," Randall said. "I'll miss your gentle touch."

He looked up to see her replacement, a tanned beauty, standing next to him with his morning coffee, naked as a jaybird.

■ ■ ■

The reporters descended on Henry as soon as the senator exited the limo near the Capitol Building steps. As usual, Henry was prepared. He held up both hands as the barrage of questions began concerning the death of Roberta Chang, Chief Aide for the senior senator from Hawaii.

"The death of Roberta Chang comes as a blow to myself and everyone on my staff," Henry began. "She was a competent aide who, given time, might have made a name for herself in the political arena. Most of all, she was a warm, caring human being who was interested in helping average Americans better themselves. As you probably know, Ms. Chang's mother died unexpectedly not long ago. Coupled with Ms. Chang's fight with bouts of depression, this terrible tragedy must have seemed overwhelming. Depression is a disease like any other, and this is just one more example of the need to show compassion, not judgment, to people suffering from this disease. I personally will never forget the contributions Roberta Chang made to my office and to the American people. Thank you."

The reporters did not throw their usual follow-ups at Henry. Given his words on his aide's depression, they didn't pester him for details.

It didn't hurt that they also knew that the senator would have roasted the first one who dared use the death of his aide as a fishing expedition for scandal.

■ ■ ■

The call came at 11:15 sharp, just as it always did.

"Good morning, Henry." The man coughed. The man must be a heavy smoker, Henry thought for the hundredth time. His voice was as raspy as sandpaper.

"Good morning, sir."

"Let's get right to the matter at hand, Henry. You've been careless, and you know I don't like carelessness."

"In what way have I been careless, sir?"

"Are you aware that Roberta Chang was attempting to leak sensitive information to Edward Karn, information held by Gregory Randall?"

"No, sir. I wasn't."

There was an ominous pause at the other end of the line.

"Did you know of Chang's whereabouts before her death?"

"She'd been taking considerable leave time because of the death of her mother."

"Well, Senator, she wasn't so distraught that she couldn't find time to sleep with Gregory. She took pictures of documents in his briefcase in the hotel room. Fortunately, Randall brought the matter to my attention in time. You dropped the ball, Henry. You should have had a much tighter rein on Ms. Chang."

Henry was a seething volcano, but he knew better than to erupt while on the phone with a man of such power. "Obviously, sir. I'm terribly sorry."

Henry was aware that Chang occasionally slept with Randall, and though he'd grown suspicious of his aide due to her aloof manner, he had no idea she was attempting to compromise operations.

"You need to redeem yourself, Senator."

"How would you like me to do that, sir?"

"Too many people are starting to snoop around. We have detained some of them. Others still pose a threat. I think it's time you pay attention to Mark Stern. He could be a formidable opponent."

"I know just what to do regarding Mr. Stern."

"Good. Have a pleasant day, Henry. And be careful."

There was a final cough at the end of the line before Henry heard a click.

"Goddamn!" Henry shouted. He wanted to strangle Randall.

Gregory should have notified Henry's office instead of going over his head. Henry had experience in taking care of such matters. Instead, he had been humiliated, receiving a rebuke from one of the most influential men in the country. He despised Randall.

But he also needed the corporate wizard and his connections. Henry made a small fortune from his dealings with Randall, and a small fortune was what it was going to take to put him in the Oval Office.

For now, he'd turn his attention to Mark Stern. On *Washington One-On-One*, Henry had refrained from commenting on Stern's counterculture background. Now, he'd leak the info at his disposal, with a little embellishment, and discredit the bleeding-heart liberal reporter.

"All in a day's work," Henry said, regaining his composure and once again assuming the persona of an amiable Democrat who cared for widows, children, and orphans.

46

Mark and Gwen spent a fitful night tossing and turning in separate beds. It was more than a little strange for Mark to have Gwen that close and yet that far away. *Easy boy. She's married and pregnant. They don't get much more "off-limits" than that.*

Up at dawn, they went to a coffee shop across the street and then returned to the room. Gwen showered while Mark went online and began doing research. He also placed a call to Lonny Reisman to see if his friend had been able to refine BioNet's original findings and another call to the paper to let them know that he was still alive, still undercover, and still "working on a killer story."

"So what's up?" asked Gwen, emerging from the bathroom wearing a fresh blouse and pair of denim jeans, her hair still slightly damp. Mark admired her for a millisecond—all that he would allow under the circumstances—before returning his attention to the laptop screen.

"I've just spoken to my friend at Active Healthcare," Mark said. "His company has stats in the form of millions of claims and doctors' reports. The seizure pattern goes far beyond what BioNet found."

Gwen's eyes opened wide. "How so?"

"The trend also exists in small to midsize cities. Muncie, Hattiesburg, Pensacola, Modesto, Carlsbad, Flagstaff, and dozens that you might not even recognize. Mandeville, Louisiana. Garden City, Kansas. Jamestown, North Dakota. Farmington, Arizona. Essex Junction, Vermont. The list goes on and on. There are seizure spikes everywhere, although the actual number of seizures, fatal or otherwise, is naturally much smaller in these populations. They would probably have shown up in a system as sophisticated as BioNet sooner or later, but Lonny's outfit has a much richer data feed."

"Then the crisis is far worse than we could have imagined." Gwen retrieved the pictures she had taken of Gene McMurphy's map. Red dots marked the cities, large and small, that Mark, BioNet, and the AE files had found. Gwen clenched her fist. "We've got to notify somebody, Mark, before this continues. I took an oath to protect the health and welfare of this nation's citizens."

"I know, I know. But we've been through this before. We don't know who to trust right now. We need some hard data."

"Showing what? That Marci was aware of a very dangerous man named Dieter Tassin? We already have that, and a sex slave story is not exactly going to provide the attorney general or the FDA commissioner with useful information on this case. I'd say we're way off course. We already have hard data on seizure activity."

Mark loved opportunities like the one Gwen just lobbed to him.

"Okay, then. Follow this. I've been using the *Wall Street Journal* database on consumer spending to find out what people have been buying during the last year. It's highly accurate. What Lonny Reisman's data does for medical trends, the *Journal's* database can do for spending patterns. It can pinpoint very specific data on almost any product that's out there."

"I can tell by the look on your face that you think you've found something."

"It appears so. First, my research indicates that cigarette purchasing patterns have remained very stable. The number of young people starting to smoke pretty much equals the number of people who quit or die from lung cancer or emphysema. There's just no trend indicating that cigarette sales are up."

"But that misses the point. The number of packs sold isn't as important as what's actually in those packs."

"Yes, and we need to continue to consider that. But one product that has skyrocketed in sales is coffee."

Gwen shook her head. "And I'm sure you could say the same for a thousand other products—various auto makes, appliances, iPods, clothing, what-have-you. Besides, gourmet coffee is popular these days. So what? There's just nothing in coffee that can cause a seizure. Caffeine is the active ingredient, and while it certainly alters metabolism, it just doesn't affect the seizure threshold."

"You're so sure that tobacco can be tampered with, but you won't entertain the possibility that—"

Gwen's cell phone rang. She pulled it out and flipped it open.

"No!" Mark said emphatically.

He was too late.

"Hello—"

Mark leaped up, grabbed the cell, and clicked it off.

"Shoot," said Gwen. "Reflex. That was dumb. I guess I was hoping it was the hospital since they have my cell number."

Mark looked at the number of the missed call. "The call wasn't from an area code anywhere around here."

"That means we hit the road again, doesn't it?"

"You got it."

They packed hurriedly, paid their bill, and got back in the Suburban.

"Do you have any idea where we're going?"

"Do you know of a lab where I can get a coffee bean analyzed?"

"I can't believe you just asked me that."

"Gwen, the plants at the bottom of the map in your pictures? It's hard to tell in the dim lighting, but they look like coffee plants."

Gwen leaned her head against the window and sighed in frustration. "The best place to go is Quantico. Jack has a lot of Secret Service buddies who work there. I think we'd get in with no problem, and they have a lab at the facility."

"Quantico it is," declared Mark. "Before we even get there, I'll have you convinced that coffee is behind all this."

47

The voice belonged to Peter Tippett. Jan was sure. She was no longer groggy from drugs, and the tinny little buzz coming from the brass button at the top of her jeans had an unmistakably British accent.

"Peter? Where are you and why am I talking to my belly button?"

"That's unimportant. Just do as I tell you. Tell your captors that you're sick. Feverish, nauseous, dizzy."

"But—"

"Just do it."

Jan took a deep breath and called out. "Hey! Somebody! Help me!"

There was no answer.

Jan stood and tapped on the door of her cell.

"Can anyone hear me?"

A small window at the top of the door slid open. "What's all the racket about?" The face outside the cell belonged to the man Jan now thought of as "pocket protector man."

"I don't feel . . . so good. I think I'm . . . spiking a temp. Queasy. Vision . . . blurred."

The window into the cell slid shut.

Thirty minutes passed and nothing happened.

Minute thirty-one, however, did not disappoint. The cell door swung open, revealing a bald man wearing thick glasses and a doctor's lab coat.

"Hello, luv. Ready to—how do you say it in America—blow this Popsicle stand?"

Jan laughed. "Peter? What . . . how . . . I mean . . . "

"I was detained in a small facility next to this one. The glasses belong to one of the idiots who brought us here, the lab coat was in a closet with medical supplies, and I decided to give myself the sexy Yul Brenner look." Peter glanced at the body on the floor and Jan's eyes followed. "Pocket protector man" was out cold. "Before I disabled my captors, that unfortunate man guarding you called my building and asked his colleague to summon a physician. I knew they didn't want us dead, so I gambled that they'd look for a doctor."

"How on earth did you disable them?"

"I have a black belt in tae kwon do. In technical terms, I kicked the crap out of them."

"And you just walked in here after that?"

"Essentially, yes. My impersonation of a doctor threw that little geek lying on the floor long enough for me to gut-kick him into next week."

Jan embraced the ersatz doctor, realizing instantly how good it felt to hold him. "You never cease to amaze me, Peter. I never would have guessed . . . "

She suddenly stood back. "And how is it that you can talk to me through a button on my jeans?" She sure was glad he was on her side.

"Just about anybody can buy a small radio like that online these days. Most bona fide spies use devices smaller than a pinhead. I put it on your jeans a few days ago as a precaution. Now, enough chat. Let's get out of here."

Jan and Peter left the building, enabling Jan to see she'd been held in one of three small buildings somewhere in the countryside. Peter escorted her to a white van, started the engine, and drove down a dirt road leading away from the compound.

"I had a disturbing conversation with someone, Peter. He said terrorists had infiltrated America's food supply and that we were compromising government operations to handle the threat. You know, I've heard stranger stories coming out of the government. The feds have done a great many unorthodox things since 9/11. This guy may have been a straight shooter."

Peter laughed and took out his cell phone camera. "Did the man look like this?"

"Yes!" Jan exclaimed. "That's him. How did you get his picture? And how did you get a cell phone. Weren't you searched?"

"I keep a very slim cell phone stitched into the lining of my coat. In case you haven't noticed, I'm a bit of a gadget guy. As for the man, he's not a straight shooter at all. He's a political appointee—Alan Jordan—who settled into the CDC in Atlanta about the time you started your BioNet study for Gwen. As far as my sources know, the guy has absolutely no legitimate function within the Centers. He's the Cost Overrun Liaison. How's that for a bureaucratic title? My guess is that he's the CDC's counterpart to McMurphy at the FDA."

"Damn. I knew he looked vaguely familiar. How badly do you think the agencies are compromised?"

"I don't think they're compromised at all, as a matter of fact. There's no way conspirators could corrupt entire agencies that employ people who have given their lives to public service. I think Jordan and McMurphy may be operating in tandem, but independently of anyone else at their respective agencies, except for a few subordinates such as Snyder, who really don't have any agenda of their own. That having been said, McMurphy and Jordan are obviously very well connected and can act with a certain amount of impunity."

"So what's our next move, Inspector Gadget?"

"I think we need to talk with Gwen as soon as possible and find out what's been going on."

"How do we find her?"

"Like I said, my dear, I have sources within my company. For now, let's get some clean clothes, a bite to eat, and find a motel room. I could use forty winks. Something tells me that we're in for quite a ride now."

Jan fell silent. She knew Peter was right.

■ ■ ■

Dr. Edward Karn sat in his car on a side street leading to the Reflecting Pool, rain pelting the windshield. He was very surprised earlier that morning when he got a phone call from an old friend. A rendezvous had been set up, and Eddie Karn now waited in his Prius, drumming his fingers on the steering wheel.

The passenger door opened, and Karn's friend, wearing a tan raincoat, hurriedly slipped into the passenger seat.

It was Dr. Bruce Merewether—the same Bruce Merewether that Henry Broome had unceremoniously heaved into a dumpster back at Princeton. When Bruce realized that majoring in the classics wasn't going to net him much revenue after graduation he'd efficiently switched to premed.

"Good to see you, Bruce."

"Same here, Eddie."

The two men shook hands.

"What's up?" asked Karn. "I sure didn't expect to hear from you, of all people. It's been years."

"This is what's up."

Merewether handed Eddie a sealed manila envelope.

"Is this what I think it is?" asked Karn incredulously.

"Probably. I was told by Roberta Chang to give this to you if you didn't get the original."

"Huh? How did you even know that there was an original?"

"The original envelope, had you received it, had instructions inside for you to call me as soon as you were in possession of it. I never got that call, and so here I am. I'm a backup plan, as it were."

"But how did you know Roberta Chang?"

"Actually, she knew me. Apparently, Henry is fond of bragging and recounting his exploits to any and all listeners. That naturally included Chang. I'm sure she heard the Cottage Club dumpster story on more than one occasion."

Karn laughed. "Do you know what's inside?"

Merewether shook his head. "There's a second sealed envelope inside the first. It's none of my business."

Karn sat back, his head resting against the top of the seat. "It's been a difficult few weeks. After the way Henry humiliated me, some people in this town back away when they see me coming."

"Having been humiliated by Henry myself, I know the feeling well. I'll be off now, Eddie. I'm guessing that whatever is inside that envelope is pretty important."

"I suspect you're right. Thanks, Bruce."

Merewether opened the door and stepped into the rain. In a moment, he was gone.

Karn started the car and headed home. Soon, he'd know why Roberta Chang had been so adamant about passing information to him. It might even have cost her her life.

48

Mark and Gwen traded Rick's Suburban for the congressman's Honda Accord. They drove right through Quantico, Virginia, however, deciding to find a new place to stay before doubling back and heading for the base that was home to a great many government installations. Feeling the need for something more comfortable than a motel, Mark found a bed-and-breakfast in Fredericksburg. They registered under assumed names.

"Now then," Mark said, creating a workspace on a mahogany writing table in the corner, "I need to access the *Journal*'s database again. We can head over to Quantico later."

"Be my guest," said Gwen. She stood there with a wistful expression on her face and Mark could tell that she had plenty on her mind.

"What are you thinking?"

Gwen smiled softly. "It was good to hear Rick say that Jack was doing better."

Mark felt for her. He didn't think he could hold up as well as Gwen was holding up if their situations were reversed. "Greater range of movement and improved articulation—I'd say that's better than better."

Gwen nodded, her eyes misty. "I should be there. Fitz rule Number Ten: Love is the most potent drug of all."

"Jack would understand."

"I don't think so. We had a huge fight before he collapsed. He probably . . . I don't know what he's thinking."

This was alien territory for Mark. He wanted to hold Gwen and comfort her, but he knew that wasn't the right thing. He was stymied. The only thing he could think to do was deflect her thoughts.

"Then let's take care of business, nail the bad guys, and get you back to your husband."

Gwen took a deep breath. "Okay."

Amazingly, that seemed to do the trick. Mark worked for nearly an hour before leaning back in the straight-back chair and stretching his arms over his head. "I want you to look at something," he told Gwen.

Gwen looked over Mark's shoulder at the data displayed on the laptop. "Numbers and pie charts," she said. "What's the bottom line?"

"You yourself said that gourmet coffee is flying high right now. We all know which coffee chain is the hottest in America. Pequod's."

"Can't argue with that."

"Here's the smoking gun, as far as I'm concerned. Every time Pequod's moves into a new market, seizure spikes occur, whether we're talking about Podunk or Pittsburgh. Simultaneously, sales of Pequod's competitors start to taper off—especially the small micro-roasters. In response, they usually scale back considerably and eventually settle for a much smaller market share or else go belly-up entirely after a few more months. The thing is, long before then, the seizure spikes stop."

"Come on, Mark. Everyone knows that if you throw together enough different types of information, you'll find patterns, even in the phonebook."

"Granted, but I wasn't on some fishing trip. I started out with the hypothesis that this was about coffee. You're the statistician here, not me, but this chart says the chance of error in the correlation is less than one in fifty thousand."

"Okay," said Gwen. "Let's suppose that there really is a correlation between Pequod's entering a new market and the seizure spikes in a community. Your theory of evildoing still doesn't hold water. The spikes stop long before the competitors go out of business. If Pequod's was doing something to the coffee to knock out the competition, wouldn't they keep doing so until they finished the job?

And let's go back to the simple medical facts: coffee can't cause seizures."

Mark scratched his head. "I admit I'm missing some pieces to the puzzle. If Pequod's is somehow responsible for the seizures, then the episodes should continue until the market is secured."

"Exactly."

"But the correlation, in and of itself, can't be ignored, Gwen. The chances are just too remote that seizure activity would happen, month by month, in only those cities that Pequod's enters for aggressive marketing."

"I'm not really debating that point, but as an epidemiologist, I'm saying that cause and effect can be a tricky business. Just consider the early days of AIDS. At first, it was supposedly a gay disease. That turned out to be totally false. After that, people tossed around theories about methods of transmission like crazy, with people afraid to be in the same house or workplace with someone who tested HIV-positive. True, there were some basic correlations, but they either didn't hold up or there was some other reason, far more scientific, that explained the correlations in a different way. It turned out, for example, that gay men had a higher percentage of sexual partners and didn't use protection as much as their heterosexual counterparts. It also was, and is, harder for women to give the disease to men than men to women because the exchange of body fluids isn't the same."

Mark sighed. "It's a valid analogy."

"And I could give you a dozen more. In Africa, villagers contract any number of tropical diseases, but because of poor education and sanitation, they attribute symptoms to what comes down to folklore and superstitious practices. In the case of Pequod's, people in my field would ask, 'What patterns accompany coffee consumption? Are there interactions between drugs, possibly a new drug on the market, and a perfectly normal chemical compound found in coffee? Or since Pequod's is so popular and so available, is the quantity of coffee being consumed affecting those individuals in the population who can be pushed over the seizure threshold by something ordinarily benign?' That doesn't make the company a culprit, assuming coffee's involved at all, which I still doubt. There are a lot of possibilities, Mark."

"I'm open to whatever theories you might have, but the seizure spikes shouldn't cease if coffee is interacting with something else. The correlation is still too weird."

"What does America enjoy most with a cup of coffee?" asked Gwen.

Mark groaned. "Cigarettes—yes, okay, but I've already told you how I feel about that."

"Cigarettes are known killers, and tobacco companies are known for deception. Fact, not opinion. Pequod's moves in, and people start to smoke more. I think we have to keep an open mind."

"You're still ignoring the spikes. People wouldn't stop smoking all of a sudden." Mark paused. "According to his files, Jack had some cigarettes analyzed. Let's make a simple call and find out what his friend at ATF found."

Gwen reached for her cell phone.

"Not so fast," Mark said with a grin. "We'll use my cell."

Mark got Todd Gimmler on the line and then handed the phone to Gwen. She talked for several minutes, asking many questions involving various chemical compounds, some which Mark had never heard of.

"The cigarettes came up negative," Gwen admitted, "but Gimmler's analysis isn't the final word."

Mark sighed heavily. "Come on, let's get to Quantico and have my coffee bean checked out. The analysis might give us some information."

"And if nothing unusual shows up?"

"I'll eat my words. Every journalist does it sooner or later. But I'm also relying on my instinct about Dieter Tassin. The man seems to be the quintessence of evil, and he just happens to be working at Pequod's. In newspaper work, that's the kind of thing that grabs your attention."

■ ■ ■

Mark was cruising on the highway when he turned on the radio, and adjusted the digital scan until he found a National Public Radio affiliate. The piece currently airing caught his attention immediately.

"Reports are now surfacing," said a female correspondent, "that noted author and newspaper columnist Mark Stern is a drug abuser who has been in and out of several expensive rehab centers since his twenties. Stern is also believed to be sympathetic with more than one ecoterrorist group—the proverbial 'tree-huggers' who have allegedly been linked to the bombing of several timber companies over the past decade. Stern, who is not yet considered a suspect in any of the bombings, has been unavailable for comment. Likewise, the *Washington Post* had no comment on the story, which first broke in *USA Today*."

"Wow," said Gwen. "You've been a lot busier than I thought."

Mark laughed. "An iconoclast makes a lot of enemies. If anything, this is rather suspicious as far as timing goes."

"How so?"

"Someone is taking pains to discredit me, which in turn means that the same someone thinks I might be on the verge of disclosing information that's not supposed to see the light of day."

"Have any idea who that someone might be?"

"Gwen, there are more people in New York and Washington who'd like to see me take a fall than I could list during the next five miles."

"So there's a price to fame and fortune, eh?"

"Most definitely, Dr. Maulder. There are many days when even I don't want to be in my shoes."

Gwen seemed to accept Mark's dismissive attitude at face value. He was thankful he had such a good poker face. It wouldn't help Gwen to know that he took attacks like this very personally. It also wouldn't help her to do the same math in her head that he'd just done in his.

They'd made extremely powerful enemies.

■ ■ ■

Using Mark's cell phone, Gwen called John Van Rankin, one of Jack's close friends within the Secret Service. She told him of Jack's hospitalization and spinal cord injury and that she'd like permission to visit Quantico. She didn't go into any detail—she and Mark had decided to play things by ear and decide what they'd tell Van Rankin later.

As they drove, Mark had a nagging feeling that he was forgetting something, something important.

Something to do with Dieter Tassin.

49

Anne Davidson Broome did not have to wait long for her call to be put through to Phillip Trainor, the congressman from Arizona who won the verbal fencing bout with Henry at the DNC Gala. The Broome name opened many doors and shortened considerable time on "hold."

"Anne, how nice to hear from you!" said Trainor. "To what do I owe the pleasure?"

"Most of the party is looking to you as its future, Phillip," said Anne Broome. "That's no secret. I'd like to sit down and talk with you in the next few days if you have an opening in your schedule."

Trainor laughed. "I'm flattered, Anne. And I'm constrained to point out that you may be overstating the case a bit when it comes to my future. There are quite a few who believe that Henry's ascendancy is inevitable."

"That may well be, but the only thing for sure in Washington is that nothing is for certain."

"Can't argue with that. What is it you'd like to talk about, if you don't mind my asking?"

"The future of the party. Long-range goals. What's doable and what's not. Things like that. I'll be more specific when we meet if you have the time. And by the way, Henry doesn't know I'm contacting you, and I'd like to keep it that way."

"I can always make time for you, Anne—and mum's the word. The Davidsons have been supporters of the party for a long time, and

I don't have to tell you that it hasn't been very common for oil interests to back the Democrats over the last few decades. My secretary will call you right back and set something up for early next week. How does that sound?"

"That's perfect, Phillip. I appreciate it."

"Anytime."

Anne put the phone receiver back in its cradle and sat down on her living room sofa. She was convinced that she could contribute to the party. Not financially, though. She was thinking more in terms of public office.

Her own.

50

Most people knew of Quantico as the nation's premier Marine training facility, but it was also the location of the FBI training Academy—and more. The CIA, NSA, and Secret Service all had training facilities and intelligence gathering units at Quantico.

Thanks to John Van Rankin, Mark and Gwen received visitor's passes immediately, although they had to pass through several checkpoints before arriving at the Secret Service facility. Gwen knew her way around since, in her capacity as epidemiologist, she'd been on the base a few times since 9/11 to consult with intelligence officials on the subject of bioterrorism.

As she was about to knock on Van Rankin's door, an explosive "Gwen!" nearly bowled her over.

"I haven't seen you since your Christmas party last year," said the forty-eight-year-old deputy director of the Secret Service base. "And this would be Mark Stern, I presume. Your face is on the side of a lot of buses in this area, Mr. Stern, ever since you started writing a column for the *Post*."

Mark smiled and shook hands with Van Rankin before the three of them sat in the deputy director's office.

Gwen immediately informed Van Rankin of Jack's condition.

"I'm terribly sorry, Gwen. You know that a lot of people here owe their lives and careers to Jack. The two of you have a lot of friends here and always will. We may not be the Marines, but as you know, the Secret Service has its own kind of Semper Fi."

"I know, John, and I'm very appreciative of your offer. It might be good for some of Jack's old friends to stop in and see him."

Suddenly, Gwen saw her opening and took it.

"In fact, John, I think Jack and I might be in danger. I'd like it if you could post a twenty-four hour detail at the hospital."

"Of course, Gwen, but tell me what this is all about."

Gwen proceeded to tell her host of how she and Jack had become suspicious of certain adverse health patterns across the nation. "We've been under surveillance for a couple of weeks now, and a good friend at the CDC has dropped out of sight. I myself was reassigned to AE files at Rockville."

Mark shifted uneasily in his chair. Gwen knew that he hadn't expected her to be so forthright in her explanation, but Gwen knew immediately that she could confide in Van Rankin. Sometimes you just had to go on instinct.

"So you suspect that someone inside the FDA or CDC is trying to conceal something?" Van Rankin asked.

"Or perhaps inside the government," interjected Mark.

Van Rankin leaned back in his leather desk chair and smiled.

"You're true to form, Mr. Stern. I'll give you that much. But I don't have to remind you both that there are probably many good reasons why the government might want you to step back from a sensitive issue that becomes more of a matter for the intelligence community than public health."

Gwen was already nodding. "I know, John, but all I really want to say at this point is that hundreds—maybe even thousands—of people are dying, and that the Public Health Service should be more proactive. There are patterns of seizure episodes all over the country, and for everyone who has died, thousands of others are having seizures but surviving."

Van Rankin looked troubled. What Gwen had just described was more than a sensitive issue that intelligence might want to keep under its hat. Indeed, if a nationwide health threat existed due to terrorist activity, he himself might well have been notified. If it were a case of some causative agent in food or drugs, then Gwen was right—the Public Health Service would be actively involved, with thousands of workers attempting to find answers.

"I have to admit that you've piqued my curiosity since I can't explain what's going on. I can ask around and see what's—"

"Please don't do that," Mark broke in.

"Mr. Stern, I should warn you that—"

"He's right, John," interrupted Gwen. "Think about it. If you start asking questions, then you might be sending out signals to some very dangerous people operating with impunity inside the government. We'd prefer to gather further data."

"And you think I can be of help in gathering this data?" asked Van Rankin.

Mark took the coffee bean from his pocket and tossed it on the Deputy Director's desk. "For now, we'd like your lab to analyze this."

Van Rankin leaned forward, elbows on his desk, as he stared at the bean with incredulity. "That's it? You want my technicians to analyze a coffee bean?"

"I'm asking for a bit more than that, John," said Gwen. "I'm asking for your trust. I know what it looks like from your perspective. We come in here with almost no advance notice, spin a tale of conspiracy, and back it up with . . . that." Gwen pointed to the bean. "But please, do it for Jack and me. There's something going on, John, and whatever it is, there are people doing some very unorthodox things to hide this from public health officials. If I'm wrong, I'm wrong. Just do an analysis to see if this bean is different from any other coffee bean."

Van Rankin looked at Gwen, then Mark, then back at Gwen again.

"I don't suppose you'll tell me where this bean came from."

"We'd rather not," stated Mark. "I'll be the first to admit that we can't fill in all the pieces right now."

Van Rankin sighed heavily. "I'll do it for friendship's sake, Gwen. There's no harm in an analysis, though I wish you'd share more of your suspicions with me. But for now, I won't press. With Jack in the hospital, I'll cut you some slack. Later, I may ask for more. And Jack will certainly get a round-the-clock detail. It will be very low-key. No one will know of our presence inside the hospital."

"Thank you, John. You don't know how much this means to us."

Van Rankin stood. "How can I get in touch with you?"

"We'll get in touch with you," Mark said. "I'm fairly certain that our phones aren't secure."

"Very well, but remember—I'll only go so far with this before you'll have to be a little more candid."

■ ■ ■

Mark and Gwen left and drove back to the bed-and-breakfast. He'd just sat down in front of his laptop when the elusive fact he'd been trying to recall hit him.

He smiled and reached for his cell phone. It was time to ask Charlie Nicholls up at the *Journal* for another favor.

■ ■ ■

The Fed Ex packages from Nicholls arrived at the bed-and-breakfast the following morning. Mark opened the slim packet and looked at the photographs that Charlie had gotten from Anh Nguyen. They were Polaroid snapshots of Anh's two daughters, Tuyen and Mai. Nicholls had apparently managed to communicate with Nguyen personally since he had scrawled the names and ages of the daughters on the back of each snapshot. Mark sifted through the two dozen pictures until he found the most recent. There were four that he plucked from the pile and arranged in a row on the edge of his worktable. Two of the photos had the ID of "Tuyen, age 29" and "Tuyen, age 34." The other two read "Mai, age 30" and "Mai, age 34."

What Mark had remembered was Randall's penchant for lovely Asian beauties, and Tuyen and Mai had indeed grown into lovely young women with long black hair, high cheekbones, and devilish, sexy smiles. They appeared to have had cosmetic surgery since they were a bit fuller of figure than most Asian women were.

The other package Charlie had sent contained copies of pictures and notes, archived at the *Journal*, that Mark had used when doing his profile on Gregory Randall shortly after the CEO's father died.

There had been an abundance of material on "Junior," as Mark had called him while working up the piece, and most of it amounted to what reporters called deep background. Randall's attraction to Asian women had naturally not made it into the profile—it wasn't really germane to anything Mark had to say—but there, before him, were the pictures he was looking for: Randall squiring women to various galas and parties for the ultrarich—Randall on a yacht, Randall at a Long Island home, Randall at the ballroom of a luxurious hotel. Several showed either Tuyen or Mai on his arm during the past three years.

It wasn't exactly a math problem—if A=B, and B=C, then A=C—Gregory Randall adored Asian women, Tassin worked for Randall, and Tassin had been in the business of procuring female sex slaves for men.

It seemed quite feasible that at some point during his acquaintance with Randall, Tassin had returned to New York and procured the grown daughters of his former Vietnamese wife. Indeed, it would have been far too coincidental for Tuyen and Mai to have gravitated to Randall on their own. There was obviously more to the story—for example, when exactly had Randall first met Tassin, and how had Tassin later coerced the daughters away from Anh? Mark Stern knew what the bottom line was: Tassin, chief roastmaster at Pequod's, served his master well. If this were the case, to what extent would Tassin go to satisfy his boss in matters relating to Pequod's coffee?

Mark reflected for a moment, recalling Tassin's remark near the roasting chambers about Hansel and Gretel. Assuming Tassin was an unusually spry man in his late seventies or early eighties, he could have been a German soldier in his late teens toward the end of World War II, a soldier who may not have orchestrated the horrors of the Holocaust, but one who would certainly have seen them firsthand, and may well indeed have been stationed at one of the death camps. It would be all but impossible to trace Tassin back to the war, but he would ask Charlie Nicholls to see what he could find. Either way, Mark knew that Tassin was a thoroughly evil man simply by what he'd seen in Marci's file and by the correlation of Anh's snapshots with the pictures in the *Journal's* archive.

And by the fiendish look Tassin had given him in Seattle.

Mark felt certain that Tassin's diabolic plans were somehow being implemented across the country, though the exact mechanism for killing people was as yet still an unknown.

And what of kindhearted, smiling Billy Hamlin, Mark wondered. How did he fit into any of this?

There was still so much to learn.

51

The last person from whom Mark expected to hear was Dr. Edward Karn. Karn e-mailed Stern's column, which Mark could access remotely and discretely. Over the years at various papers, this connection proved to be an effective—and surprisingly secure—way to make private contacts.

The message read:

Dear Mr. Stern:

I have information that might be of interest to you. Given that the proper authorities might not be so proper, I'd feel more comfortable sharing the information with you instead.

Sincerely,
Edward Karn

Mark had his hands full with the glut of conspiracy information that seemed to be multiplying on an hourly basis. Karn, however, was exactly the kind of story for which he'd been trolling when he'd first contacted Rick Mecklenberg to see what was "out there." Though he felt a bit guilty taking any time away from Gwen's story at this point, he sent a reply using the *Post*'s e-mail template directing Karn to meet him the following morning at a nearby IHOP.

■ ■ ■

Gwen opened the door of her room at the bed-and-breakfast and her jaw dropped.

"Jan?" She could barely believe the missing BioNet Director was standing in front of her, along with the man she presumed was the security specialist mentioned in the iPrive correspondence. "How did . . . where have—"

Jan laughed. "I'll explain all of it if you let us in."

Gwen shook her head briskly, as though doing so would make the world sensible again. "Of course. Come on in."

Jan walked into the room and hugged Gwen tightly. It was the kind of hug people gave when they thought they'd never see you again.

She stepped back and turned toward the man next to her. "Gwen, this is Peter Tippett. He helped me break into BioNet before we were abducted."

"Abducted?" Gwen said, alarm streaking her voice. "What are you talking about?"

Mark, who had been working on the laptop, drifted over to the front door. Gwen introduced him and then implored Jan to tell her what happened. What came next was a story Gwen would have considered inconceivable just a week ago—an odyssey of capture and escape that included a lecture by Alan Jordan on alleged food contamination by Islamic terrorists.

"This is incredible," Gwen said when Jan finished.

Jan chuckled humorlessly. "I only wish I were making it up."

"As you might have guessed from where you found us, Mark and I have been on a surreal ride of our own."

Gwen told Jan about everything from Jack's seizure to their encounters—or near-encounters—with an unknown foe. Then Mark relayed what they had uncovered, although Gwen was quick to point out that she wasn't buying into coffee as the cause of seizures.

"As a physician with the CDC," said Jan, "I have to side with Gwen on this one, Mark. Things aren't always what they seem."

Peter sat down and slumped in an oversized chair in the corner of the room. "I'm basically a security specialist," he said, "although my work mandates I keep close ties with the intelligence community, with whom I often consult. I suggest that Gwen and Jan continue to work the medical angles of this rather perplexing problem. But," he said, turning to Jan, "I think Mark and I need to check out any other leads, no matter how speculative. While coffee may turn out to be a benign footnote to this enigma, the correlations Mark obtained from the *Wall Street Journal*'s database can't be ignored."

"Looks like we have our work cut out for us," said Gwen.

"It certainly does," said Mark. "Before we go any further, though, I need to know something. How did you find us?"

"Those close ties with the intelligence community come in handy. A couple of former employees who knew Jack and Gwen now work at Quantico. When you showed up there, one of them followed you back here."

"We were that easy to track," Mark said, casting a worried expression in Gwen's direction.

52

The next morning, Mark sat in a booth at an IHOP trying to read the breakfast menu while his eyes scanned the room at the same time. Since Jan and Peter showed up, Mark felt even less secure.

Out in public, he saw enemies—real or imagined—around every corner.

A few minutes after he sat down, Eddie Karn slipped onto the leather bench seat on the other side of the table. "Good morning, Mr. Stern."

"Pleased to meet you, Dr. Karn," said Mark, extending his hand across the table. "I'm a big admirer of yours."

"And I like the way you think and write," said Karn. "That's why I contacted you. Like me, you're wary of established points of view. You're an independent thinker."

Mark graciously nodded his head ever so slightly. "Thank you."

"I have some information that I'd like to show you. It concerns Senator Henry Broome—or some of it does, at least. After breakfast, I suggest we go someplace more private."

Mark's ears pricked up. "I have a room nearby. We can go there when we're finished."

■ ■ ■

Karn sat in an antique chair. Mark, Gwen, Peter, and Jan gathered around as he opened the manila envelope given to him by Roberta Chang via Bruce Merewether.

"Bills of lading, customs receipts, cargo manifests . . . " said Mark. "You said they concerned Henry Broome and were sent to you by someone before she died. That would be Roberta Chang, I take it, since she was the senator's chief aide."

"Correct," said Karn.

"Where did she photograph these?" asked Gwen.

"I honestly don't know. They came with no explanation. I assume she gave them to me since I was Senator Broome's latest political victim. I recently learned that Ms. Chang was well aware of Henry Broome's background."

Mark had been studying the shipping receipts while Karn spoke. The bills of lading showed that large shipments of coffee regularly arrived at Pedregal, Panama from three Hawaiian cities: Kaumalapau, Kawela, and Numila.

"We need some maps," said Mark.

"I'll go online," said Peter, unfolding his laptop. "Have them in a sec."

"As you see," said Karn, "the coffee is shipped under the company name of Transpacific Coffee, Inc."

Jan and Peter exchanged quick glances. "Transpac," they both said at the same time.

"I saw that name on Gene McMurphy's PC in his office," Gwen said, perplexed. "How the hell is he tied into coffee shipments?"

"We already know that Jordan and McMurphy are communicating," said Peter. "The seizure stats were sent from the CDC to the FDA via Iceland and Panama."

"The other bills show coffee being shipped from Pedregal to Seattle," stated Karn.

"What's the connection between Seattle and Transpac?" asked Jan.

"If Pequod's buys Hawaiian coffee, why not just have it shipped straight from the islands to Washington State?"

Gwen examined the bills more closely. "We still have no evidence that the Hawaiian coffee is used by Pequod's."

"And yet these shipping receipts were grouped together by Roberta Chang," said Mark.

"As Dr. Karn said," remarked Gwen, "we don't even know where these photos were taken."

"My guess is that they're from the files of Henry Broome," said Karn. "It's the plainest explanation."

Gwen shook her head. "Maybe, maybe not. Making that assumption at this stage might be dangerous."

Peter turned his laptop toward the group. "Take a look at this. Numila is on the island of Kauai. Kawela is on Molokai. Kaumalapau is on Lanai."

"What about Pedregal?" asked Mark.

Peter turned the laptop around, hit a few keys, and displayed a map of Panama. "Not sure what to make of this," he said, "but Pedregal is on the west coast of Panama, on the Golfo de Chiriqui. I would expect most coffee to be loaded on the Caribbean side for shipment to the United States since the crops are pretty heavy in countries like Colombia, Venezuela, and Brazil. If this Hawaiian coffee is grown for any company other than Pequod's, it should logically pass through the Canal."

Mark went over to his own laptop and began accessing the *Wall Street Journal* database again.

"Dr. Karn, you said this had something to do with Senator Broome," said Peter.

"I'm not sure what to make of all this, but I do know that the island of Lanai has been owned by the Broome family for decades. I've kept my eye on Henry Broome over the years for several reasons."

"Which are?" asked Gwen.

"For one," began Karn, "Henry— "

"Look at this," interrupted Mark. "Transpacific Coffee is registered to Anne Davidson Broome. She's listed as the president of the company."

"That's Senator Broome's wife," Karn said. "She's the daughter of a former oil tycoon. As far as I know, she had nothing to do with Lanai until she met her husband."

"All the same," said Jan, "Broome himself may have no interest in coffee. His wife may just be a savvy businesswoman."

"Possibly," said Karn. "The plantations on Lanai formerly grew only sugarcane and pineapples. But Broome must be aware of his wife's activities. Henry has always made it his business to know the business of others. I doubt much happens on Lanai that he doesn't know."

"You were about to say something else, Dr. Karn," said Gwen. "Something about Henry Broome."

"Yes," said Karn. "I saw Henry do some rather disgraceful things to people at Princeton. Some might dismiss them as college pranks. I never did, though. In addition, Henry's roommate was killed by a truck in the fall of 1977."

"Can the death be linked to the senator?" asked Mark aggressively.

"Not that I know of, but I won't put anything past Henry Broome. When he wants something, he gets it by any means possible."

Peter raised his hand. "What does any of this have to do with coffee?"

Karn shrugged his shoulders. "I think all we can say at this point is that Roberta Chang thought these bills of lading were very important. The rest might be meaningful or entirely incidental."

"Let's not forget why we're all here, folks," suggested Gwen. "There's a serious health hazard in America, and we need to find the cause. Right now, we're talking coffee, shipping receipts, and events at Princeton almost thirty years ago. I think we're losing our focus."

"Maybe not," said Mark, looking up from his laptop. "My column just received an e-mail that said LOOK AT TRANSPAC FILES. The e-mail address is az7459gmp@wild.com. I sent a reply asking why I should do this, and a mailer-daemon came back saying that the e-mail was undeliverable. I think Peter and I need to go down to Panama and see what's going on in Pedregal. I'd like to see the files and find out beyond any doubt if there's a connection between Hawaiian coffee and Pequod's. If Henry Broome is indeed involved, it might be the government connection to the seizures we've been looking for."

Gwen frowned, picked up Mark's cell phone, and punched in a number on the keypad.

"I concur," said Peter. "There's nothing more I can do up here to access Transpac files by computer. They know I've been snooping, and the only way I might be able to get into their system is on-site."

A few moments later, Gwen addressed her colleagues, who were brainstorming as to how the assembled facts might add up. "I just spoke with John Van Rankin, a friend at Quantico. His team analyzed the Pequod's bean Mark got in Seattle. The result? That bean is no different from any other. Regardless of the source of the coffee, it cannot have caused any seizure episodes."

There was visible disappointment in the room, especially on the face of Mark Stern. After several moments of silence, the journalist spoke up. "As you yourself said, Gwen, coffee may not be the agent responsible, but there's some connection between Pequod's markets and the seizures. On top of that, we have the info that Roberta Chang passed to Dr. Karn, though we don't know why she sent it. And that information just may relate to Pequod's."

"Actually," said Karn, "I might know of a reason."

Everyone turned to stare at the doctor.

"I did a little poking around myself after Roberta contacted me since I had heard Henry comment on TV on how sad he was at the recent death of Chang's mother. It turns out that she died after a seizure episode."

Gwen threw her hands up as if in defeat. "Bon voyage, gentlemen," she said to Mark and Peter. "Pack your mosquito netting. I don't know if Panama can be expected to have a Pedregal Hilton."

"While we're gone, I think someone needs to talk with the parents of the senator's roommate who died," suggested Mark, "assuming they're still alive and can be found."

"His name was Jamie Robinson," said Karn. "His parents still live in Scranton, Pennsylvania. I'll be glad to drop in on them since I was at Princeton while Jamie was enrolled there and knew the boy's advisor."

"I'm going with you," volunteered Gwen.

"Guess I'll sit around and do my nails," Jan joked.

"Actually," said Mark, "I was thinking that you and a friend of mine, Rick Mecklenberg, should pair up and handle anything that might surface. At this point, we don't know what we might run into."

The air hung heavy with that notion.

53

Peter Tippett and Mark Stern stood next to a shack at the end of an airstrip cutting through pines in the Virginia countryside, watching Peter Tippett & Associates' Gulfstream III appear from the shimmering heat like a mirage. It descended quickly, touching down and rolling to a stop twenty yards away from the two men.

"The company usually keeps the jet parked at Manassas Jet Center," explained Peter, "but we occasionally have it flown here and then switch pilots before proceeding to our final destination."

"But you're just a security consultant, for crying out loud," said Mark.

"True, but our clients don't really want their competition, some of whom are foreign governments, to know that they're using our services. I can promise you that those who hire us are under a great deal of scrutiny. If they weren't, they wouldn't need us in the first place. It behooves us to play matters close to the vest."

A pilot, a young man in his early thirties, climbed down the short stairs that unfolded from the fuselage.

"It's all yours, Mr. Tippett."

"Thanks, Rick. There's a pick-up parked next to the radio tower behind the control shack so you can get back to D.C."

Mark turned around and saw a building that looked like a utility shed. "You mean that someone in there controls all takeoffs and landings?"

Peter smiled. "A single controller is all I need to help me know what's in the airspace within fifty miles of this location."

"You're going to fly us to Panama?"

"You want a qualified pilot, don't you?"

Mark laughed. "You've been flying a long time?"

"I was a pilot in the Royal Air Force, my good fellow. Flew Harrier Jump Jets with Prince Andrew in the Falklands, as a matter of fact."

"Enough said. Let's go."

Mark and Peter climbed aboard. Moments later, they were airborne, the Gulfstream banking gently as it climbed and headed south through wispy clouds.

■ ■ ■

Peter sat at the controls of the Gulfstream with Mark strapped into the copilot's seat. There had been little turbulence thus far, and they now cruised at twenty-five thousand feet over the Gulf of Mexico. Peter threw a few switches and banked sharply to the left, causing Mark to look at his pilot.

"What was that about?"

"Hopefully, nothing."

"We're climbing again?"

Peter didn't answer as he banked sharply to the right.

"Hey," said Mark. "I don't usually get airsick, but you left my stomach a few miles back there."

"Sorry. It appears we have a shadow."

"We're being followed?"

"That's the most logical conclusion. Could be a refection off the clouds below—even a flock of birds—but my guess is that we're being tailed by a small private plane."

"What are we going to do?"

"Remember that this plane is owned by my company. It has a few gadgets the FAA doesn't even know about."

"Such as?"

"This certainly isn't a stealth aircraft, but I can jam the radar of military jets if necessary." Grinning, Peter looked at Mark. "I don't think we're being pursued by a military jet, so he doesn't have fire system radar. The pilot is almost certainly following our civilian transponder, which I can turn off at any time I choose and switch to a military channel. And I most definitely choose."

Peter turned a dial in the center of the cockpit and descended into a thick cloudbank below. Once hidden, he changed course, flying due east for five miles before turning south again.

"So?"

"No more shadow," said Peter.

"Where are we going to set this baby down?" asked Mark.

"Obviously someone has an idea where we're going despite diverting the Gulfstream to your private strip before takeoff."

"We don't know that for sure. Regardless, there's a deserted strip in Panama. A Jeep will meet us, and we'll drive a hundred miles or so to reach Pedregal."

"That's just great."

"I thought reporters had a spirit of adventure."

"The New York subways give me all the adrenaline I need."

"We'll also be wearing what's in the carry-on back in the cabin."

Mark got up, made his way past two rows of light brown leather seats, and saw a black canvas bag sitting next to a row of very sophisticated electronic equipment. Unzipping the bag, he saw dark green camouflage outfits, berets, and aviator sunglasses.

"You gotta be kidding," Mark said when he returned to the cockpit. "We're going to impersonate Panamanian soldiers?"

"We can't very well walk into Transpac and announce ourselves as Mark Stern and Peter Tippett, now can we?"

"I try to help out an old girlfriend," Mark muttered, "and now I'm staring at a firing squad in Central America if we're caught."

"It's not so bad down there," said Peter. "They actually treat condemned prisoners very well in Panama."

"I don't even want to know how you know that," said Mark.

The plane emerged from the clouds, the blue waters of the Gulf far below.

PART V

54

“May I help you?” asked Alice Robinson timidly, standing behind a screen door in the center of her front porch.

“My name is Edward Karn, and this is my friend, Gwen Maulder. I was an acquaintance of Henry Broome’s back at Princeton.”

Alice Robinson smiled broadly through the dark mesh screen. “You knew Henry? What a lovely man. Please come in.”

Gwen was nervous as she entered the humble living room of the Robinson home. While Karn may have known Henry during their university days, she was worried that the Robinsons might know of Henry’s antagonism to the former FDA nominee. Alice was congenial, at least for now, but her husband might be another matter.

Alice led Gwen and Karn to a plastic-covered sofa. As they sat, a man descended a short, steep stairway.

“This man knew Jamie’s roommate,” Alice told her husband.

Tom Robinson stared at his unexpected visitors for several seconds before smiling weakly. The Robinsons appeared to be in their mid-seventies, and Tom was slightly hunched over. “Any friend of Henry Broome is a friend of ours,” he proclaimed. “That man has sent us Christmas gifts every single year since Jamie’s death. He even sends Alice flowers on her birthday. Salt of the earth.”

Karn smiled while Gwen breathed a sigh of relief. The retired couple did not appear to keep abreast of current political events.

“I’m a doctor, Mr. and Mrs. Robinson,” Karn said, “and I’ve been told by a friend of mine, Professor Kucherlapati, that your son was conducting some very interesting experiments. I was wondering if you had any of Jamie's research tucked away in the attic. Professor Kucherlapati said Jamie was something of a prodigy, and I'd love to look at his work."

Gwen knew that Karn had not yet talked with Kucherlapati, but he hoped it would help him gain the Robinsons' confidence.

"Professor K!" said Mrs. Robinson. "The students adored him."

"We've saved everything from Jamie's room," confessed Mr. Robinson in a more somber tone. "You're more than welcome to look at it. Jamie didn't keep information written down for very long, but he did put it all on an Apple computer. Nothing like the computers today, I suspect. Probably doesn't even work. It's been sitting on Jamie's desk upstairs all these years."

Gwen looked at Karn.

"May we see it?"

"Of course. Come on up," Tom Robinson said, standing.

"Excuse the dust and the stuffiness," said Alice Robinson when she opened the door to Jamie's room. "I guess we're guilty, like a lot of parents who've lost children, of keeping everything the way it was."

"That's perfectly all right," Gwen said. "I understand completely."

Karn seated himself at Jamie's desk after plugging in the old Apple—Gwen couldn't remember the last time she saw one of these. The machine came to life, but Karn was unable to access any files. The operating system was not only old, but also password-protected. "I don't suppose we could borrow this for a week or two so that some friends of mine in the computer field might be able to look at Jamie's data."

Alice Robinson smiled. "You can borrow it for as long as you need it, Doctor, although I don't know why the notes Jamie made on all those plants he was growing would be of interest to anyone, especially after all these years."

"Plants?" said Gwen.

"Yes," said the deceased student's father. "We took one from Jamie's dorm room, in fact, and tried to plant it on Jamie's grave, but it didn't do so well. We brought it home and Alice pressed it between two sheets of wax paper and put it in the family Bible."

"Could I see it?" asked Gwen. "I'm a physician, too. I work at the FDA, and I'm always interested in various kinds of plants."

Mr. Robinson got the Bible and carefully extracted the flattened plant from the middle of the large book.

"Do you recognize this?" Gwen asked her partner.

Karn shook his head. "Could be anything."

"We never knew what it was either," said Mr. Robinson. "You're welcome to borrow that, too, since it probably goes with whatever's on Jamie's computer."

"Thank goodness we gave all the rest of Jamie's plants to Henry," said Mrs. Robinson. "It's a comfort to think that they're growing somewhere."

Gwen's heart nearly stopped. Jamie Robinson, killed by a truck, had been growing plants that his parents gave to Henry Broome, future senator from Hawaii.

"Thank you both very much," said Karn. "I promise we'll take good care of the computer and the plant and return them as soon as possible."

Out in Rick's automobile, Gwen turned to Karn. "Do you think that plant could be tobacco?"

Karn rubbed his chin and thought. "It's little more than a seedling, it's thirty years old, and it's not much thicker than a piece of paper. I couldn't begin to venture a guess."

"I'm going to bring it to John Van Rankin at the Secret Service and let him have a look at it."

Karn looked pensive. "My hunch, Gwen, is that the Robinsons' plant is coffee, not tobacco. I know how you feel on this issue, but Broome probably took Jamie's plants and started growing them in Hawaii. Why else would Roberta Chang be so interested in bills of lading showing shipments coming from Lanai?"

"Coffee seems the logical answer for the plant," Gwen conceded reluctantly, "but Van Rankin has already assured me that the coffee bean Mark obtained in Seattle is normal. We're still missing any connection to seizures. There's something that doesn't fit."

"If Henry's involved, Gwen," Karn said, "you can be sure they fit all too well."

55

The Gulfstream touched down on dry desert near the town of Remedios, which was southeast of Pedregal. If a discernable landing strip lay beneath the jet's wheels, Mark didn't notice it as Peter reversed thrust on the engines, bringing the jet to a slow roll.

"How does one hide a jet?" Mark asked.

"The locals will help us."

"Huh?"

Peter pointed out the cockpit window to the three o'clock position. Two Jeeps were rumbling over the hardpan, kicking up a fine plume of dust behind them. "I radioed ahead and arranged for our transport."

Mark just nodded his head. He had no idea what to expect anymore.

What came next, however, was impressive, even by a reporter's standards. Peter, with the help of the two Panamanian drivers from the Jeeps, took a large piece of netting from the Gulfstream's cargo hold and draped it over the fuselage and wings.

"From the air, the jet will be virtually invisible and appear as part of the desert," said Peter. "It's fairly old technology. Even today, some countries have entire false landing fields, complete with dummy planes and painted runways, while the real fields are heavily camouflaged with netting, vegetation, or cloth. It was originally a Cold War tactic. Time to put on our outfits, by the way."

Minutes later, Peter and Mark stood next to a Jeep, wearing military fatigues and dark glasses. Before leaving the states, Peter had instructed Mark not to shave so that he would have at least a small bit of stubble on his face, and the reporter now had a respectable five o'clock shadow.

They climbed into the Jeep and rumbled off to Pedregal.

56

The adjacent chairs on which Edward Karn and Gwen Maulder sat were not particularly comfortable. They were in John Van Rankin's office at Quantico, and at this point Gwen knew what Van Rankin's words would be before he spoke them.

"You want me to analyze a twenty-nine-year-old plant that's thinner than tissue paper and hardly bigger than my hand?" asked Van Rankin. "You know I want to help you, Gwen, but—" Van Rankin paused and glanced at Karn, whom he obviously respected. Taking a deep breath, he tried to focus his thoughts. "You present me with information on seizure patterns and ask me to analyze a coffee bean, of all things—one that repeatedly showed nothing more than the normal constituents of coffee. Now you're asking me to run this plant through the lab, and I'll bet you a million bucks that you think it's coffee."

"Yes, that's exactly what we believe."

Van Rankin ran his fingers through his hair in exasperation.

"Gwen, you're a physician employed by the FDA. Do you really think that an everyday, household product like coffee could cause nationwide seizures? Forgetting the basic chemical properties of caffeine for a moment, do you believe that the major coffee companies in America would allow a tainted product to make it to grocery store shelves? Do you really think nobody—not consumers, not doctors, not public health authorities—would notice? The idea is preposterous."

"No, that's not what I'm saying at all, John, but—"

"Your ecoterrorist reporter friend thinks so."

The characterization of Mark stopped Gwen cold. "What?"

"The Senate Agriculture Committee decided it would like to question Mr. Stern on ecoterrorism."

Karn shot Gwen a quick, worried look. "That's Broome's committee," he said.

Gwen nodded, her face clearly reflecting concern. "Mark's not an ecoterrorist, John."

Van Rankin shook his head. "Regardless, I told you and Stern when you were here before that I'd reach a point where I'd need more information in order to help you. I'm afraid we're there."

Gwen sighed heavily. "Fair enough. Believe me, I appreciate what you've done and know how all of this must sound. I'll give you more information, but I need you to keep it close to the vest."

Van Rankin forced a smile. "I'll try, as long as you don't tell me Al-Qaeda is launching another attack."

"The cities where seizures are showing up are the very same ones in which Pequod's opens new stores and engages in aggressive marketing. The timeframes also match up perfectly."

"You think Pequod's is behind all this?" Van Rankin's voice had the distinct timbre of disbelief. "I'm more likely to think that there was a second gun at the Kennedy assassination."

"I personally don't think there's a chance in hell that Pequod's coffee is causing seizures," said Gwen. "Mark and I vehemently disagree on that particular point. I do think, however, that the correlation between the location of seizure episodes and Pequod's' marketing has a statistically significant relationship that's yet to be determined."

Van Rankin looked as though he'd eaten a bad burrito. "If I didn't owe your husband my life, we wouldn't be talking, you know. Gwen, you're not exactly a trained investigator for this kind of crime."

"You're right. I'm not a criminal investigator. I'm an epidemiologist with the FDA, and this is what epidemiologists do."

"Actually, Gwen," said Van Rankin, his voice softening, "you were an epidemiologist with the FDA. You've been placed on administrative leave."

Gwen's mouth hung open, blood draining from her face. "How do you know that? Did someone call you?"

"No. I simply made a few discreet calls on my own because of all the cloak-and-dagger associated with your last visit here. That's what turned up. But don't worry. I had a friend access your personnel file through a government database. No one can trace you back to me."

Gwen was silent, too numb to be angry. The government she'd served so well had pulled the rug out from under her. Her reassignment to the AE files by Snyder and McMurphy was one thing, but being relieved of all duties was another. She knew she shouldn't be surprised given the events of the last three days, but news like this was never easy to digest. She again wished Fitz were alive to help her make sense of the bizarre unfolding events.

"What do you think of all this, Dr. Karn?" asked Van Rankin.

"I think something smells pretty rotten here. Dr. Maulder and Mr. Stern have some outlandish theories and I'm normally as skeptical as you are. However, Gwen's job at the FDA was to run outlandish theories into the ground. That's precisely how one protects the public's health. Instead, the minute she starts investigating, all hell breaks loose and political types come out of the woodwork to quash her."

It was Van Rankin's turn to sigh. "Okay. Given the correlations between Pequod's and seizure patterns, I'd be running down leads, too, if I were in your shoes. I've seen too many young agents around here get dumped on for outlandish theories that turned out to be true. A decent supervisor would give them upfield cover."

Gwen nodded slightly. "Thanks, John. I appreciate that."

"I'll run the plant and see if it's coffee. I'll also see if it has anything in common with the bean. How does that sound?"

"Sounds good." Gwen looked deeply into Van Rankin's eyes. "I appreciate your being a friend here, John."

Van Rankin smiled. "You're welcome. And sorry about breaking the news to you about your job the way I did. You deserve better."

Gwen looked down at the floor. "I'm starting to learn to expect the worst."

Van Rankin sat up in his chair, which caused Gwen to look up at him again. “In the midst of all this shop talk, you’ll be glad to know that one of my men stationed at George Washington Hospital called a few minutes ago. Jack’s speech is showing definite improvement. I think he’s turned a corner. He can actually communicate a full range of ideas, though it takes him a while, and his articulation still needs some work.”

Gwen smiled for the first time since she’d set foot onto Quantico that morning. That smile faded quickly, though. She missed Jack. Meanwhile, he had no way of knowing where she was or what she was doing. For all he knew, she’d abandoned him in his hour of need.

“I wish I could see him.”

“That’s probably not a good idea right now,” Van Rankin said. “I can get him a message if you’d like.”

“I’ll do it,” Karn said. “No one is going to touch me even if they know what I know. I’m too high-profile, especially right now.”

Gwen nodded. At least Jack would hear that she loved him and wanted to be with him.

Suddenly she brightened. “You know, he might even be able to do a little bedside police work for us.”

57

"The town looks pretty good compared to what I expected," commented Mark as they drove past the Pedregal Power Company's thermoelectric plant. Though the town was small, most of the one- and two-story buildings appeared to be fairly modern and clean.

"Did you expect to find a quiet village with banditos sleeping in chairs tilted against the local cantina?"

"To be perfectly truthful, yes."

"So did I," confessed Peter, as Pedro followed signs that read Albergue de Pedregal—Pedregal Harbor.

"How do we know that Transpac is by a dock?" asked Mark.

"We don't, but it's the most logical place to look. I'd rather not stop and ask for directions. Might attract too much attention."

"So will riding around town indefinitely. This place isn't that big."

"Point well taken. À la puerta," said Peter.

The smell of saltwater was unmistakable now as the Jeep glided smoothly over a straight road that descended for several hundred yards to the Golfo de Chiriqui.

The harbor was small. Peter counted no more than eight warehouses bordering the dock. The fourth one, situated on the gently curving bay, had a large faded sign that read TRANSPACIFIC COFFEE IMPORTS. Pedro rounded the corner of the building, parking at the side of the warehouse.

That's when they encountered three men wearing white shirts and dirty slacks. Each held an Uzi, the first pointed at Pedro, the second at Mark, the third at Peter.

■ ■ ■

"Jack? Jack Maulder?"

Jack opened his eyes to see a familiar-looking man attired in a dark blue suit and red bow tie standing above him. Jack had seen him on TV but couldn't place his face.

"Allow me to introduce myself," said the man. "I'm Dr. Edward Karn, though I'm not one of your physicians."

Jack nodded and held out his right hand, which Karn shook lightly.

"First," said Karn, "let me assure you that Gwen is doing fine. I've met with her recently, and while she would have liked to accompany me today, we didn't think it safe."

"Been worried like crazy . . . has something else happened?"

"The important thing for you to know at this point is that she's fine—except that she misses you horribly. Things have heated up, but she's not in harm's way."

Jack nodded that he understood.

"Gwen is with Jan Menefee and Congressman Rick Mecklenberg right now. She's in good hands, although she impresses me as someone who can be pretty tough on her own when she has to be."

Jack smiled faintly and cleared his throat. "Yes," he said slowly. "She can be . . . head . . . strong."

"I've come to ask a favor," said Karn. "I'm aware of the recent investigations conducted by you and your wife. There have been some additional, um, complications. It's possible that you could help us out. If you're feeling up to it, that is."

"Complications?"

Karn shook his head. Jack got the distinct impression that the man was glossing over the facts. "Not complications necessarily. It's just that the area of interest has shifted from tobacco to coffee, and there's someone in the coffee industry who may be implicated in a death that occurred in 1977."

"A murder?"

"Possibly."

"Cold case files," said Jack slowly.

"Gwen thought of the same thing. She wondered if you had any contacts with the police department in Princeton, New Jersey."

Jack thought for a moment. His concentration was more than a bit fuzzy. "Princeton? Don't think so."

"That's too bad," Karn said softly.

"But New Jersey State Police . . . yes. They can probably look into old records."

Taking a notepad from the nightstand, Karn wrote several things down on a piece of paper.

"Here's what we have," said Karn, laying the paper on Jack's top sheet. "It's not much to go on, but if you can turn up anything, it might help."

Jack blinked several times, trying to think of what words he wished to articulate. "Not about . . . tobacco?"

"No one really knows for sure at this point. All we know is that there's a very real public health risk going unchecked. By the way, some agents from the Secret Service are guarding you, but you may not recognize them. They're not on the company clock, and they're unlikely to admit who they are. Apparently you guys never stop looking after your own."

"Understood. I thought some of those ugly male nurses looked a little weird."

Karn laughed and extended his hand once again. "Thanks, Jack. I'll be back in a day or two to see if you've turned up anything."

"Tell Gwen . . . I . . . love . . . her."

"I most certainly will, Jack. You're a lucky man. Take care."

Karn left and Jack looked at the paper. The words didn't make much sense to him right now. He'd look again in a little while after he got some more rest.

Gwen was okay. When he last saw her, they were in danger—or at least they might have been. Then she was gone. He didn't know what to think.

Jack was so glad to hear she was okay. Even though he knew there was more to the story than what Karn told him.

58

Op One landed his Lear 31A at Concepcion's small airport. The Gulfstream flown by Tippett had eluded him over the Gulf of Mexico, but it wasn't very difficult to figure out where the troublesome security analyst was headed. The agent's orders regarding the pilot were explicit: make sure he didn't return. As for Mark Stern, One's orders were equally firm: make sure he was apprehended and brought back to the States. The leader of Tabula Rasa was eager to have the reporter taken down several notches sitting on the hot seat in front of Henry Broome's Senate committee. Imprisoning Stern would be infinitely preferable to simply killing him in Panama.

The agent got into a waiting Lincoln Navigator and started driving to Transpac headquarters in Pedregal. For Tippett to send a file to Central America was one thing. For him to snoop around the many sensitive areas on actual Transpac premises was another.

The drive would take no more than ninety minutes. After that, Op One would eliminate Tippett and make sure that the Englishman spent eternity at the bottom of Golfo de Chiriqui.

■ ■ ■

"*Adonde vas?*" asked one of the armed guards holding an Uzi. (Where are you going?)

Pedro tilted his head toward the warehouse. "*Comercio,*" Pedro said. (Business.)

The two guards frowned.

"*Comercio*," Pedro repeated in a frustrated voice as he pulled folded papers from his shirt pocket and handed them to the guard. They were copies of the bills of lading given to Karn.

"*Pasele*," said the guards after examining the document. Pass.

Pedro led Mark and Peter into the warehouse through a metal door. The group was ignored by the dozens of workers driving forklifts or handling burlap sacks containing coffee. Mark was struck by the contrast between this warehouse and the one at Pequod's. Everything at the Seattle operation was conducted with military precision. Here, the Panamanian workers were clearly busy, but they laughed and joked and sang as they performed their various tasks. There were no lines painted on the concrete floor, no orderly procession of forklifts from one location to another.

"Follow me," Peter ordered. "I'm going to ask the man by the receiving door to show me his receipts."

"Isn't that a little bold?" asked Mark. "Why should he show bills of lading to a stranger?"

"Because we're federales. Down here, not much happens without the government's approval. And nothing—and I do mean nothing—transpires without some palms being greased along the way. The Spanish word for such bribery is *mordida*. You can bet that this operation, especially if it's in the least bit tainted, operates thanks to generous—how shall I put it—'donations' to the Panamanian government."

They walked to the receiving bay, Peter now taking the lead. In short, clipped phrases, he asked to see the bills of lading. The man before them, short and dark-complexioned, held a clipboard with papers on which he appeared to be tallying the number of palettes that forklifts brought into the facility. He looked at Peter and then at Mark for several seconds, after which he began to ask Peter numerous questions. Mark put his hands on his hips, trying to look the part of a tough soldier. The irony of the situation was not lost on the former hippie and antiwar activist. Peter's conversation with the receiving clerk seemed to last an eternity, but at last the short man handed Peter several papers, prompting Peter to utter a brief "Gracias."

"What was that all about?" asked Mark as they walked away. "I thought we were busted."

"Our friend Carlos back there was curious as to why he had never seen us before. Just as I suspected, it's apparently not unusual for the government to show up here, but he said that the same men have been coming here for years. He wanted to know where they were."

"What did you tell him?"

"I said the others had gotten drunk and been in a wreck in Concepcion. I told him we'd much rather be shaking down the local whores, but that we had our orders."

"What if he calls up to verify your story?"

"Then I'd say we're in for a spot of trouble. Meanwhile, I told him we were going to look around. He didn't seem fazed. I guess the local feds can do what they want as long as it doesn't interfere in warehouse activities without sufficient reason. Pedro's presence didn't hurt either. Let's take in the sights, but try to appear nonchalant. You still look uptight."

"It's hard with these leather boots. I can hardly walk straight."

"Relax. You'll do fine."

The impostors moved leisurely through the warehouse, their berets and aviator sunglasses in place.

"Look," said Mark. "Over there."

"I see it," said Peter. "They're transferring coffee beans from sacks with 'Transpac' stenciled on them to ones that say 'Pequod's'"

"Transpacific Coffee is a legitimate company," Mark pointed out.

"There's no reason to transfer the beans unless any tie between Pequod's and Transpac is supposed to remain completely off the radar screen."

"A company has the right to secrecy, and I don't know that any laws are being broken by such a maneuver," retorted Peter, "but it's certainly not the usual modus operandi for a corporate entity. The cost of this little deception must be absolutely enormous. Shipping the beans from Hawaii to Seattle without this detour would save millions. Roberta Chang obviously knew this was more than just a bizarre move to keep the location of the coffee plantations secret."

"Amen," said Mark. "Pequod's may be a lucrative enterprise, but having worked for the *Wall Street Journal*, I can guarantee that companies don't piss away millions of dollars on stunts like this."

“The point of origin on the bills of lading could be altered after the fact with a little ingenuity,” added Peter. “The transfer doesn’t make sense.”

“True,” said Mark. “Besides, in Seattle, no one can get anywhere near the sacks. No one could read whether they come from Transpacific or Timbuktu. But speaking of the sacks, there are two kinds, both for Transpac and Pequod’s. One has blue stenciling on the burlap, the other black.”

“Two kinds of beans?” theorized Peter.

“Perhaps, but according to Billy Hamlin, there’s only one kind of cherry that makes it to Pequod’s facility. What next?”

“We can try to look at the files. Isn’t that what your mysterious e-mail advised?”

“Yep. But where are the offices, and how do we get in and take a gander at the computers? Do we just say ‘pretty please’?”

Peter touched Mark’s upper sleeve lightly. “Look,” he said. “The answer is right here. All loaded and ready to go.”

Mark had no idea to what his companion was alluding, but at this point, he didn’t care. He just wanted to get out of Panama with all his body parts intact.

■ ■ ■

To Carlos Adenidos, two of the federal detectives he’d seen at the receiving door had appeared legitimate. The third, however, had looked nervous, fidgety. When the federales began their inspection of the warehouse, he picked up the telephone mounted on the corrugated wall and dialed a number.

“Op One,” said a businesslike voice at the other end of the line.

Carlos proceeded to describe his brief encounter with the suspicious men.

“You did well to call me,” said One in fluent Spanish. “But don’t—I repeat, don’t—do anything until I arrive. I’m about thirty to forty-five minutes away. I’ll handle matters when I arrive. Understand?”

“Sí.”

59

Rick Mecklenberg sat with Jan in the congressman's office. Peter figured that would be the safest place to be before flying south. No one was likely to conduct a hit in the hallowed, marble-floored halls of the Rayburn Office Building.

Jan and Rick sat in the corner of his office, where Jamie's Apple II had been stored for safekeeping. With Peter out of the country, Jan was the next most likely person capable of accessing the old operating system. As director of BioNet, she was computer savvy, though she didn't have Tippett's ultra-high-tech gadgets. Still, she could maneuver through systems that would make the average PC user's head spin.

"Any luck?" asked Rick after Jan had typed in several commands on Jamie's yellowing keyboard.

"None at all," she replied. "His password could have been anything. If this kid was a prodigy, he probably had enough sense to create a random alphanumeric password."

"Any alternatives?"

"Yes, though so far I'm coming up empty. The only thing to do at this point is to bypass the password protection altogether. I'm using a simple interface to allow my laptop to talk with the Apple."

"Wouldn't you need special software to do that?"

"The interface box is already loaded with software to allow binary systems to speak to each other. One thing hasn't changed since the computer revolution began: computers run on chips that convert all information into a series of zeroes and ones. The interface would normally be able to access any PC—even a 286 or a 486 with no Pentium—but this damned Apple is just too freakin' old. It's not even recognizing the connection."

■ ■ ■

Mickey Spangler was old. Too old, Spangler thought, to be carrying the burdens of a lifetime. He'd been a petty crook all his life, driving shipments from the Jersey docks or taking position as wheelman for the occasional getaway vehicle, but he always thought he'd kept his nose relatively clean. He never went near the rough stuff, or at least never intended to. The on-campus accident at Princeton had changed his life forever, though. All he'd known was that he was supposed to wait for a phone call on the corner or Nassau and Washington Streets. Make a right at the cabstand and then drive down Washington. He'd figured he was the getaway ride. One minute he'd been driving along, thinking of his wife Ethel and how they had two great sons, and the next thing he knew, his truck had killed a college kid, mangling the kid's bicycle in the process.

He could have almost convinced himself it was an accident if not for the guy in the rugby shirt. Immediately after the accident, Rugby Shirt had taken him aside before the police arrived and scared the hell out of him. Told him about how curious the cops might become about the whereabouts of a certain truckload of color televisions. In retrospect, Mickey felt he'd acted like a fool. He should have made his statement, should have told the truth to the police, but Rugby Shirt knew so much—too much. Once Mickey told the police the prearranged cover story, they seemed satisfied. Everything was fine that night until Rugby Shirt called him from a pay phone, making sure he was sticking to his story. If he didn't follow instructions, the cops would hear a different version of his story and would start connecting some very unpleasant dots that trailed back into his past.

Mickey had shut up, just like he was supposed to. It didn't help much in the end. "Three strikes and you're out" was enough to nail him. A hijacking gone bad, possession of stolen property, being an accessory to armed robbery—and here he was now, dying in a prison hospital while contemplating the true meaning of a life sentence.

The last bust was the most ironic. He'd been sitting by the curb with the engine running, waiting his turn for a fifteen-dollar blowjob by the most talented pair of nineteen-year-old lips he'd ever met. Who knew that someone was going to rob the 7-Eleven across the street and that the getaway was going to get spooked, running just before the cops got there? The would-be desperados spotted Mickey's car idling at the curbside and decided to carjack their own getaway car. Mickey's rented paramour did a quick exit stage-right as the police arrived from all directions. All the cops saw was the two armed robbers trying to enter Mickey's car. By the time they had their guns pointed at him, he had his pants back on and looked like any other getaway driver.

Wouldn't you just know it—the two kids were juvies who would say anything the DA wanted to avoid being tried as adults. With two strikes against him, Mickey was easy pickings for accessory to armed robbery. And just to make sure the cell door stayed shut, the authorities tagged Mickey for corrupting two minors he'd never met.

Twenty-nine years later, Mickey was dying of lung cancer in a prison hospital ward. Why couldn't he die at home with a little dignity?

Home. Ethel had long since remarried, but his son Tad and his wife would gladly take him in . . . wouldn't they? They hadn't exactly been regular visitors. Mickey was no threat to anyone now, so why couldn't he go home and turn up his morphine drip in the comfort of a regular bed with a family member by his side? He'd seen only pictures of his two granddaughters over the years.

This definitely wasn't the glamorous life of crime he'd signed up for.

60

Peter and Mark stood before the glazed door of the Transpac business office. Pedro stood outside to deter anyone who wanted to gain admission. Peter lifted the flap on his sleeve and produced three rings, placing them on the middle fingers of his left hand.

"What the hell are you doing?" asked Mark, not really wanting to know the answer.

"Each ring has a minisyringe attached to it. I just press the ring against flesh and voilà—the recipient of a little drug cocktail will be out for nearly an hour."

"Is there anything you may have forgotten?" Mark asked wryly.

"I once forgot my ex-wife's day off," Peter said with a grin. "That's how I got caught with the maid. Since then, I've learned to think ahead."

Mark shook his head at Tippett's cavalier answer. "Do we knock or just walk in unannounced?"

"Let's surprise the buggers," Peter said. "When we go in, let's throw them off -balance. Open your arms like you know them and are ready to issue a warm embrace. That will give me time to size things up."

"Go ahead," Mark said with resignation. *Did Woodward or Bernstein ever do anything like this?* "We've come this far."

Peter opened the door. Two men, each wearing a summer shirt and khaki pants, sat at desks in a small office cooled by a very old and very loud window AC.

"Compadre!" exclaimed Peter, smiling broadly, as he approached the man sitting to his left.

Mark opened his arms and stepped to the right. "Hola, señor," he said, sounding like a high school Spanish student.

Both workers seemed baffled, glancing at each other and then back at their uninvited visitors.

Peter walked forward and extended his right hand in greeting to the puzzled clerk seated at the desk. The man started to hold out his right hand tentatively, and as he did, Peter advanced quickly and pressed the index finger of his left hand against the clerk's neck. Within seconds, the man slumped over the wooden desk, motionless.

The other man sprang to his feet as Mark drew near and encircled him with his arms.

"Hold him!" called Peter.

Mark squeezed as the confused but angry man struggled to free himself from Stern's bear hug. "Hurry up!" urged Mark. "I can't hold him for long!"

Peter crossed the small office rapidly and pressed a different ring against the man's forearm. The man started to speak, but as with his office mate, he lost consciousness quickly. Mark eased his limp body to the floor.

"That wasn't so bad, now was it?" asked Peter.

"As far as offenses punishable by execution go, no—it was a piece of cake."

"To the computers," Peter said, sounding like Batman ordering Robin to the Batcave. From Mark's perspective, Peter was having far too much fun with this.

■ ■ ■

"There's no password," proclaimed Peter, sitting at one of the desks in the small office while Mark stood behind him. They had dragged the unconscious Transpac employees to the side, where they would be unseen should anyone open the glazed door.

"That's the first easy thing about this operation," said Mark.

Peter began examining Transpac files.

"Tell me what you're seeing," said Mark, feeling a bit useless.

"I'm in the financial files. So far, I'm seeing straightforward payments made by Pequod's, but not to Transpacific. According to these records, Pequod's is buying its beans from plantations in Colombia and Brazil. That contradicts what we just saw. Out there," Peter jerked his head, motioning to the warehouse, "Transpacific beans are being transferred to sacks reading 'Pequod's' Also . . . " Peter's voice trailed off suddenly.

"Also what?" asked Mark, impatiently.

"There are large sums of money being paid from Randall to Lanai, Inc., whatever the hell that is."

"Has to be a dummy corporation for Broome, and I'm talking Henry, not Anne. How large are the payments?"

"Substantial. Some are larger than the payments for the beans themselves. By extrapolation from these numbers, I'd say the senator is raking in tens of millions of dollars, and I'm just scanning these files quickly, not going through them in-depth."

"Gregory Randall and Henry Broome may share other business interests," speculated Mark, "but I'm willing to bet that Broome's getting a very nice price for selling his wife's beans to the high and mighty Randall. That means those beans must be very special. On paper, who's buying the Transpacific beans?"

Peter moved the mouse and hit the down arrow key several times. Laughing, he said, "Transpacific is being paid by several different West Coast companies—The Coffee Gourmet, The Perfect Cup, Roastmasters, A Finer Bean, and several more."

"I doubt those outfits even exist. Print out as much hard copy as you can. We should check out those names when we get back home. That's assuming, of course, we do get back home."

Peter leaned forward, planted his elbow on the desk, and dropped his chin onto the open palm of his hand.

"You've found something else?" inquired Mark.

"Indeed I have. An entirely different batch of files, all labeled 'Asian Trade'"

"Let me have a look," said Mark.

They switched places. Sitting at the computer, Mark started scanning the files. He knew exactly what he was looking for. "Holy crap, it's actually on file."

"What's on file?" asked Peter, standing near the door.

"Hundreds of profiles of young Asian women, ranging in age from sixteen to thirty-five. Each file lists name, nationality, age, height, weight, bust size, and a complete medical file. And every single one claims that the woman has been tested for STDs and is clean."

"Gracious," said Peter. "Transpac is a flesh-peddler, too?"

"No mention of Transpac, though the data's on Transpac computers, which is unquestionably weird."

"What's the affiliation then?"

"Give me a minute. There's so much here."

Mark heard heavy footsteps in the hall. He turned and looked at his colleague, who had already spread his feet, angled his body, and lifted his arms in a position that Mark associated with one of the martial arts.

The sound of the footsteps faded.

"I hope this doesn't take much longer," Peter said, glancing at the bodies on the floor. "Sooner or later, either someone is going to come in here or those two down there are going to regain consciousness."

"I know, but we flew a long way," said Mark, suddenly emboldened by what he was reading.

"All right, but just remember, time is of the essence."

Mark continued to work at the terminal. "No affiliation is listed, nor would I expect to find one. What I do see at the bottom of each file is a broker."

"I'm not following."

"The person who procured the woman, no doubt. I bet you . . . yes . . . there he is!"

"Keep your voice down," urged Peter.

"Tassin," said Mark. "Dieter Fucking Tassin is on dozens of these files, maybe hundreds. Let me try a quick search."

"For whom?"

Several seconds elapsed before Mark triumphantly said, "For Tuyen and Mai Nguyen, the daughters of the client Marci Newman was representing." Mark sat back in the chair, astonished. "I knew that Gregory Randall had a passion for Asian women, but the fact that he's actually providing them for other people and keeping records of it—this is absolutely incredible."

"Any indication where these women are being sold?"

"Yes," said Mark excitedly. "Some of the files are labeled as 'open' others as 'closed.' On those marked 'closed' there's further notation, 'designated recipient.'"

"A rather cold term for a cold business," said Peter, shaking his head. "I'm all for a robust sexual appetite, but this is disgusting by the standards of anyone decent."

"I recognize a good many of these 'recipients,'" said Mark. "Several of these men are CEOs of major corporations. And a very prominent senator—Henry Broome, to be specific."

"Get that printer working, and not just on the Asians," Peter advised.

For the next ten minutes, Mark printed files pertaining to both coffee shipments and the slave trading done by Randall. He kept Mai and Tuyen's file on top of the thick stack of papers that came out of the printer. A Fortune 500 CEO was their "designated recipient."

"Okay, let's get the hell out of here," said Peter. "We'll leave our friends on the floor and out of sight in case anyone opens the door a crack. With any luck, people will think they're on a coffee break."

Mark tucked the printouts underneath his shirt as Peter opened the door.

"Good afternoon, gentlemen," said a man—definitely not part of the crew—standing outside the warehouse office. "You've been very busy inside, I take it." He polished the toe of his boot on Pedro's inert form, slumped next to the door. His neck appeared to have been broken.

Mark and Peter froze where they stood.

■ ■ ■

"Get in the Jeep," ordered Op One. "And give me whatever you found inside the office—no games."

Without hesitation, the reporter removed the sheaf of papers from beneath his camouflage shirt and handed them over. A nine-millimeter pistol tended to make people cooperative.

Op One marched Stern and Tippett from the warehouse. He brought them to the army Jeep they'd arrived in.

"Get in and drive," Op One said to Tippett. "We're going into the desert. A little off-road trek to find a picnic spot. It's time we really got to know one another. Of course, you might have to do a little digging before lunch. And you might even be in the mood for a long nap afterward."

Tippett got behind the steering wheel. Stern got in the passenger seat while Op One climbed into the rear. A scowling Panamanian with a Glock automatic and two shovels climbed in next to him. Tippett fastened his seat belt and the reporter did the same.

"I'm glad mommy taught her children to be careful," Op One mocked as he leaned back in his seat to provide the maximum distance between his gun and the men in front. "It's always wise to use safety rules on the way to an execution."

Tippett started the engine. "Where to, mate? Wouldn't want to be late for my own burial."

"Very cute," said One. "I've always hated the glib sense of humor you English have. Just drive the way you came for now. I'll tell you when to leave the beaten path."

They drove for thirty minutes until the Jeep passed low hills to the north.

"Okay," said One. "Slow down, ease onto the shoulder, and start driving. We have ten miles of desert between the road and the hills."

■ ■ ■

Mark had no idea what Peter was planning. The man had signaled for him to put on his seat belt—Peter had made no such insistence on the ride down—but he couldn't imagine what could save them from an assassin's bullet now.

The Jeep had gone about five miles from the turnoff, the nearest hill looming large now. Mark wondered how his obituary would read. Would his colleagues assume he died on the trail of a Pulitzer-level story and eulogize him accordingly? Or would the people he pissed off along the way get the last laugh and relegate the news of his death to a couple of lines?

Suddenly, Peter cut the wheel sharply, sending the vehicle into a tailspin through the sand. A shot from the nine-mill shattered the windshield as their captor, attempting to squeeze a round at Peter's head, was thrown off balance.

"Hold tight!" Peter called to Mark.

He accelerated and cut the wheel again, sending the Jeep into a 360-degree roll. As soon as the Jeep righted itself, bouncing from the left tires to the right several times, Peter turned around to see if the gunmen were still aboard. The one who captured them was lying face down, making incomprehensible sounds in the sand about twenty feet away. His Panamanian colleague, however, had managed to keep his place in the Jeep—at least his torso had. The roll and the slide had left a bloody object the size of a soccer ball spinning on the white sand.

"Thank God for seat belts," shouted Mark.

"Get out and lie flat!" called Peter, running to the prostrate body of their captor, who was beginning to stir. As he approached, the other man gripped the gun, preparing to fire.

"Not today!" Peter said, lunging.

What ensued was a martial arts contest that Mark, raising his head from the ground, watched in amazement. Their would-be assassin was obviously trained in the same moves as Peter. Sand flew as the combatants struggled to their feet, arms and legs thrust forward in lightning-quick strikes as they turned, ducked, and postured. After several minutes, Peter managed to trip his opponent with a flying ankle twist. He then knelt next to his foe and administered old-fashioned punches until the man was dazed and bleeding badly from his mouth.

"Give me a shoelace!" Peter ordered, looking back at Mark.

Mark removed the long, thick lace from his right boot and handed it to Peter, who rolled their captor over facedown and tied his hands behind his back.

"Have a gritty little snack," Peter said. "It's good roughage. I don't mean to be rude, but we'll be off now."

"Is the Jeep okay?" asked Mark.

Peter was already in the driver's seat. He turned the ignition, and the engine started without hesitation. "Let's pick up our papers before we head on back," he said, letting the engine idle as he eased out of the driver's seat.

They collected the documents copied at the warehouse, got in the Jeep, and drove back to the road, where they turned east and headed for the Gulfstream.

"Does this happen frequently in your line of work?" asked Mark.

"No, but remember that I was in the RAF. I'm used to flying upside down."

An hour later, the Gulfstream was airborne, climbing over the Gulf of Mexico on a course toward a narrow strip hidden in the Virginia pines.

61

Gwen and Karn were at Quantico 7:45 the following morning.

"Did you find anything, John?" Gwen asked as soon as she and the doctor had been ushered into Van Rankin's office.

"Yes and no, Gwen. I've run a dozen different tests on that bean, and I see no evidence of any kind of adulteration. My conclusion is still the same. The coffee, which is Arabica as opposed to Robusta—the two main kinds of beans used by most of the world—can't produce seizures."

"And the plant?" asked Gwen.

"We have a bit of a mystery there. It's definitely a coffee plant and, like the bean, it's Arabica. Both have forty-four chromosomes. What's strange is that in both the plant and the bean, there's a dark band on chromosome number two. Never seen anything quite like it."

"Mind if I have a look?" asked Karn. "I've studied human genomes for a good portion of my career. I'd love to see what that band actually looks like under an electron microscope."

"Be my guest," answered Van Rankin. "I'll take you to the lab right now if you'd like."

Karn smiled graciously. "Thank you."

■ ■ ■

Karn looked at the slide made from the bean, then the one with a cross section from the plant. Just as Van Rankin had described, chromosome number two had a dark band across it on each slide. He looked up, knit his brows, and folded his arms.

"What is it, Eddie?" asked Gwen.

"I've seen something like this before."

"What is it?"

"I'd like to go back and check some old research before I speculate," he replied. "We have enough theories flying back and forth as it is."

Gwen smiled warmly. "My dad would have liked you, Eddie. He was a man of science who played the hunch and took chances once in a while, but he was also very thorough."

"Thanks. Listen, since Rick and Jan haven't been able to access Jamie Robinson's computer, I'm going to make a call to an old friend. There's a good chance he can at least speculate on what Jamie was doing. Is that okay with you?"

"Of course. I'm glad you're on our side."

"What's the old saying? God works in mysterious ways, his wonders to perform. If I'd been confirmed as FDA commissioner, I might have been far too busy to be helping you now."

"I still think you'd have been good in the job."

"So do I," said Karn. "So do I."

■ ■ ■

When they left Quantico, Gwen returned to the bed-and-breakfast while Karn drove to George Washington Hospital. Jack was asleep, but a male nurse approached, holding an envelope.

"Mr. Maulder said to give this to you when you returned," said the nurse.

"Thanks," said Karn.

Outside in his car, Karn opened the envelope and found that Jack had indeed gained information from the New Jersey State Police.

The others would find this very interesting reading.

62

Unshaven and decidedly ragged, Mark thought he looked like a felon. Maybe that was appropriate since he'd committed his share of felonies the last few days. He had taken plenty of risks in pursuit of a story before. The risks he'd taken recently, however, were off the charts. He wouldn't forget that ride toward his execution anytime soon.

He and Peter entered the bed-and-breakfast midmorning. Gwen, Jan, and Rick were already in the extra room they'd set up as their office. Mark had no idea what the owners of the bed-and-breakfast thought of their comings and goings. Like good innkeepers, they kept their thoughts to themselves.

"Sorry for our rather ragged appearance," announced Peter before anyone had a chance to say hello. "Mark and I haven't had much sleep. We landed in the middle of the night. We needed a bite to eat and a change of clothes after my company met us at the private strip."

"You guys look terrible," remarked Gwen.

"Thanks," said Mark. "Masquerading as Panamanian federales and getting shot at will do that to a fella."

Gwen's mouth hung open. "Are you all right?"

"Could you define 'all right?'"

Mark saw the concern on Gwen's face and could've sworn his heart skipped a beat. "We're fine," he said reassuringly.

Gwen nodded. "What did you find? Something that made your ordeal worth it, I hope."

Mark produced the files copied from the warehouse. "Long

story short? The beans are transferred from Transpacific sacks to Pequod's sacks once they arrive in Pedregal. Transpac records, however, indicate Transpacific Coffee is sold to other companies."

Peter had already gone to his laptop. "Those company names we saw—The Perfect Cup, The Coffee Gourmet, A Finer Bean, Roastmasters—they're real companies, but I just checked out their websites. There's nothing secretive about their roasting processes at all. In fact, they describe their operations quite openly. They all say they buy coffee from Brazil or Colombia, not Hawaii."

Mark continued. "Transpac also has records of payments going from Randall, Inc. to Lanai, Inc. Our guess is that Randall is paying Henry Broome a little extra for his—or should I say his wife's—Hawaiian coffee."

"There's no record of any Lanai, Inc. that I can find," Peter chimed in.

"Something's definitely rotten in paradise," said Rick Mecklenberg.

Mark and Peter yawned simultaneously and flopped down on the bed. "Anyone have a strong cup of coffee?" Peter asked.

Everyone laughed as Jan handed Peter a thermos of hot coffee. "It's Pequod's," Jan said with a chuckle. "If you're cruising around in the morning looking for coffee, it's hard to find anything else."

Gwen related how she and Karn had visited the Robinsons and procured Jaime's Apple II.

"Can't access it, though," said Jan. "Even using an interface. Thing's just too friggin' old."

"The Robinsons had an old plant pressed in their family Bible," Gwen continued. "One of several that Jamie had been growing, according to his mother and father. After his death, the rest of the plants went to none other than Henry Broome, the nation's illustrious chairman of the Agriculture Committee."

Peter let out a low whistle. "Wow."

"Eddie and I ran the Robinsons' plant over to Van Rankin," said Gwen. "Chromosome analysis shows that not only is it a coffee plant, it's also identical in chromosome structure to the bean Mark copped in Seattle."

Mark sat up straight and looked directly at Gwen, unable to

suppress a wide grin despite his fatigue. "Still want to deny that coffee's the culprit?" he asked.

"I'm not denying anything, but I want some hard data on how coffee can produce a seizure. I'm still sticking to what I've said before. Just because we have a connection doesn't mean coffee's the culprit. For all you know, there could be some additive in one of their flavor syrups, maybe even a sugar packet. It always pays to keep an open mind."

"Okay," conceded Mark. "I respect your scientific approach. And without some chemical data, we don't have anything to bring to the authorities. That said, I don't think Henry would have gone through the whole Transpac charade if the coffee wasn't at the center of this mystery."

Gwen had no response. Mark liked debating with her—especially when he won a point.

"You're leaving out the best part," said Peter, sipping the brew from Pequod's "special" beans. Mark didn't know how Peter could do it with so many questions raging.

Mark rubbed his bloodshot eyes. "Yeah. Almost forgot. Gregory Randall is running a sex slave business, and Dieter Tassin's name is on several of the files. He sold Anh's daughters, as a matter of fact."

"Damn," said Gwen.

"What do we do next?" asked Rick, standing up and pacing the room. "We've got a full plate here."

"We probably need to move again," suggested Peter. "We were followed all the way to Panama."

"We can either split up or together find someplace that's safe," said Mark.

"I, for one, am not going off on my own," declared Jan.

"I'll protect you," said Peter with a chuckle. He moved closer to Jan and put his arm around her shoulder. Jan beamed at him.

"I think it best if we all drive to the Capitol Building," said Rick. "There are literally dozens of tunnels and passageways under the building that should allow us to resurface and then drive to my home in Virginia."

"Okay," said Peter, "but where's Karn?"

"He went to check out some old research and to call a friend who might know what's on Jamie's computer," said Gwen.

Just then, there was a knock on the door and Eddie Karn entered the room.

"Eddie—good timing," said Gwen.

"Jack left this for me." He held up the envelope for them to see. "We've got some pretty incriminating information on our favorite senator."

The room went perfectly still in an instant.

■ ■ ■

"Jack is doing very well, by the way," Karn said before starting.

Gwen smiled and thanked him.

"Anyway," said Karn, "Jamie Robinson was hit by a truck in November of 1977. The police report on the matter is quite clear. The driver was a man named Mickey Spangler. No foul play, but the only witness was Henry Broome, class of '78. Henry's official statement was that Jamie had been talking with him and suddenly hopped on his bike and took off. Henry claimed he tried to reach out and stop Jamie but it was too late. The police never investigated further. Later, however, Spangler got in a few more scrapes. Being an accessory to armed robbery was the nail in his coffin, earning him a life sentence."

"I'd say we need to pay a call on Mr. Spangler," said Mark. "Where is he today?"

"He's in the medical wing of a New Jersey correctional facility west of Atlantic City."

"Medical wing?" asked Rick.

"He's dying of lung cancer."

"I think we'd better get moving," suggested Jan.

63

Gregory Randall surveyed the next batch of Asian beauties Transpac forwarded to his computer for inspection. They were all lovely, of course, but he needed to be as discriminating as his clients, many with whom he did business on a regular basis. Some of the young women in the profiles he examined had a slight blemish or a nose that was a bit too short, even by oriental standards. The face had to be perfectly symmetrical, the eyes narrow but alluring, the mouth thin yet sumptuous enough for a deep, passionate kiss. And then there were weight and height to consider. No matter how beautiful the face, the women had to be slender and at least five-foot-four.

As a child, Randall traveled the globe with his father, taking in sights that most children his age could never hope to glimpse in school textbooks. As a teen, when his dad was securing what would become the Randall empire, the teenage Gregory Randall was mesmerized by the beautiful women he saw all through Asia and the Far East. American girls his age were so tacky, with ridiculous hairdos conforming to the latest fad. Western females used sprays, mousse, and all manner of awful products to sully their appearances. And they still looked plain compared to the exotic fare he saw when in Thailand, Vietnam, or Taiwan.

More importantly, Asian women were dedicated to pleasing their husbands and mates. American women were traveling further and further toward independence with their ridiculous feminist movements. Asian women did not fear the virtue of obedience, a word that western women were actually deleting from traditional marriage vows more frequently with each passing year.

As Randall continued to look at the profiles, a red e-mail flag popped up on the corner of his screen. Opening it, he read the message, swiveled his chair away from the computer, and clenched his fists. From Panama, Carl Richey was notifying him of a breach in Transpac files. Analysis of a Transpac hard drive revealed that an intruder accessed many sensitive documents. Furthermore, Op One had been found in the desert, hands tied behind his back.

"Dammit!" screamed Randall. "How many incompetent people do I have working for me?"

He picked up the telephone and called the man with the raspy voice.

"Don't worry, Gregory. I'm already aware of matters as they presently stand. The situation is extremely serious, but I'm taking measures even as we speak to recover any documents that were obtained from Panama and to gather up once and for all those who would compromise our operations."

"But sir—"

"The rest of the Tabula Rasa force is moving into place right now," the man said, coughing.

Randall took a deep breath. "Yes, sir, but some of the troublemakers are important people. We can't just eradicate them, at least not all at once."

"Some can disappear, Gregory. A couple can have fatal accidents. Another is already in the process of being discredited. I don't like this any more than you, but I have confidence in my personnel."

"Of course, sir. I just thought I'd alert you in case you didn't already know."

"Good-bye, Gregory," said the raspy voice.

Gregory looked across his spacious, modern office, sunlight streaming through floor-to-ceiling windows. He reached across his desk, pushed a button, and curtains bunched in the corners automatically began to close.

Bright light was hell on migraines.

■ ■ ■

Mark put away his cell phone and glanced up at the people before him, all packed and ready to leave the bed-and-breakfast. "A friend in New York says that Henry Broome has stepped up efforts to locate me and serve me with a subpoena very soon if I don't step forward and testify before his Senate committee. The rumors of my alleged drug abuse are also starting to make the rounds of talk shows. I may become a liability to everyone here overnight."

"We'll just have to hope that we can make some serious headway as quickly as possible so nobody here has to stay in hiding for much longer," said Rick. "We've obviously disturbed a sleeping giant; either we'll play David with five smooth stones, or the giant's going to have us for lunch."

Rick, Gwen, Mark, and Karn decided to use Rick's Suburban, which the congressman had parked out front while Mark and Peter were in Panama. Jan and Peter would take Rick's Honda. They'd all go to the Capitol and then, as Rick had suggested, wind their way through various tunnels and passages until they could resurface and drive to the congressman's home in Alexandria, Virginia.

They stepped outside the bed-and-breakfast. As soon as Mark saw the two dark blue cars parked in the middle of the street, he knew things would not go as planned. Men wearing blue satin windbreakers stood on the sidewalk.

"Federal agents, Mr. Stern," said a tall, lanky man holding a bullhorn, indicating that he'd planned to order Mark from the premises if he had not soon appeared. "Come with us, sir. The rest of you, please continue on your way. This is a federal operation. Interference will be met with an arrest."

"What's the charge?" asked Mark.

"You've been subpoenaed to appear before the Senate Committee on Agriculture." The officer stepped forward and handed Mark the subpoena.

"Wait a minute, Officer," Mecklenberg interrupted. "I'm an elected member of the House of Representatives. Since when have officers of the executive branch done errands on behalf of the legislative?"

"Sorry to bother you with this, Congressman, although you may have some people asking you about the company you keep." The agent swept his eyes across the small gathering and then looked again at Rick. "Think of this as a kind of courtesy for the Capitol police. We have an arrest warrant for Mr. Stern based on the drugs found in a lawful search of his apartment. A Senate committee also wants to ask him questions on other matters. As soon as he's finished testifying, he'll be taken to a federal magistrate for arraignment." The tall agent turned to Mark. "At which point you'll be charged with felony possession of narcotics with intent to distribute."

Mark could barely believe what he was hearing. Getting in this car could make his recent Jeep ride seem like a Sunday drive.

"Better do as he says," Rick advised. "We'll spring you somehow."

Mark looked at Gwen. If she'd been concerned for him before, she was now borderline panicked. For the first time in his life, Mark genuinely believed he might never see her again. He wanted to say something, but his mind raced too much to form any words.

Rick stepped forward and shook hands with his friend, but said nothing. Mark palmed the folded piece of paper that passed between them like a rock star taking a groupie's phone number. Then, with one last glance at Gwen, he got into the car.

■ ■ ■

The blue cars disappeared, leaving the other five standing on the street stunned.

"What just happened here?" asked Edward Karn.

"Nothing legal," answered Peter. "Those men weren't federal agents. They showed no ID and they didn't read Mark his rights. Also, if they had a drug case against him, they wouldn't have told him where they found the narcotics. The whole thing was a charade to apprehend Mark."

"Staged by whom?" asked Gwen.

"The logical answer would be Henry Broome," said Jan.

Rick looked skeptical. "Henry may have something to do with it, but he's probably part of something much larger. Senators have enormous power, but I doubt that Henry is acting alone. He has to have some heavy hitters working with him."

"I'd vote for Gregory Randall," Peter said. "We know that Pequod's is somehow involved."

"Maybe," responded Rick, "but even Randall and Henry together couldn't hide seizures, plus the entire Transpac angle—the false receipts, the sex slaves. They've got to have some kind of government help."

"The intelligence community?" asked Peter.

"Perhaps," said Rick. "Four out of five Americans think the CIA whacked Kennedy."

"I don't know much about conspiracies," offered Karn, "but I think we'd better be on our way if those gentlemen who took Mark weren't on the up-and-up."

There were nods all around.

"Let's proceed to the Capitol," suggested Rick, "but once we're there, we'll have to change plans. They know I'm involved—whoever they are—so I'm going to see if we can crash at a friend's hunting lodge deep in the woods. My house isn't safe anymore."

"Can we stop off at my office so I can gather some additional research?" asked Karn.

"If you think it's absolutely necessary," said Rick.

Karn looked at Gwen.

"It's necessary," Gwen said. "Let's go."

64

"Gotta pee."

The tall man wearing the blue windbreaker turned around and looked through the wire screen into the backseat of his sedan. "What's your problem, pal?"

"Clean out the ear wax," Mark said condescendingly. "I have to take a leak."

"Hold it in, Stern."

"Now!" replied Mark defiantly. "I'll do it here on the seat or you can pull over to the nearest convenience store. How much escaping can I do with my zipper down?"

Mark knew that the only leverage he had was to create some confusion. If he could get the agents flustered, he might be able to think of something.

"I'm gonna count to five and then let loose," said Mark. "Unless you want the back of your car permanently marked as my territory, you're going to find a toilet for me, and you're going to find it fast."

Letting out a sigh, the man in the front seat looked at his driver.

"Pull over into that gas station on the right," he ordered. "We'll let him do his business and then get moving again."

The driver pulled into the Shell station and killed the engine. Mark and the man from the passenger seat walked into the station's convenience store. "Federal agent," proclaimed the man in the windbreaker to the cashier. "Got a can in here?"

The young girl behind the counter motioned to a door in a narrow hall to the left of the beer cooler without even bothering to look in their direction.

Mark walked into the tiny restroom . . . and so did his captor.

"What the hell are you doing?" Mark said sharply.

"I don't let anyone out of my sight when they're in my custody."

"Gimme a break. I'm pee shy."

"You are one massive pain in the ass, Stern," the man said bitterly. "I'll be standing right outside the door."

■ ■ ■

Three minutes passed. Then five. Stern didn't come out.

"What in the hell is wrong with that guy?" asked the lanky man, pushing open the cheap splintered door to the restroom.

The small cubicle was empty.

The man dashed to the counter of the convenience store, glancing quickly across the aisles. "Hey," he said to the cashier. "Where's that guy I came in with?"

The girl shrugged.

"Damn! Is there a back door?"

"Why do you want to know?"

The man flashed a wallet ID for a split second. It was enough to make the girl lose the attitude.

"There's a receiving door in the back. That's the only other way in or out."

The man's windbreaker spread like wings as he raced outside to his partner. "The son of a bitch is gone. You stay here and keep your eyes peeled. I'm going around back."

Stern was nowhere. The man looked everywhere—among the cardboard boxes and in between the stacks of heavy plastic delivery cartons used to hold gallons and half-gallons of milk. He looked left and saw a car wash. The wall of another store was to his right. Behind the convenience store was a wooden fence that separated the station from a residential area.

"Shit," he said, kicking angrily at a candy wrapper on the ground. "Where in the hell did the bastard go? Is he some type of freakin' magician? I was outside the door the entire time."

He hurried back to the front and ran through the car wash before returning to the blue sedan. "Let's roll," he said, hopping onto the front seat. "We'll make a pass up and down the block and then go through the neighborhood behind the store. He could have gone into any one of a dozen yards by now. I'm calling for backup."

He took out a cell phone and within minutes, there were two more cars on the search.

"Knock on every door if you have to, but find that SOB."

■ ■ ■

Mark could barely believe his gambit worked. He was certain neither Woodward nor Bernstein had ever done anything like this. Maybe a little bit of Peter Tippett rubbed off on him while they were in Panama.

When the tall agent turned away and stepped into the hall outside the bathroom, Mark held the door carefully by the protruding clothes hook on the back so that it wouldn't shut all the way on its pneumatic hinge. He watched his captor take a few steps away and reach into his pocket for a cigarette and a book of matches. When the guy struck the match, Mark grabbed what he figured would be his only opportunity to make a run for it. Holding his breath, his shoes in his hand, Mark slipped quietly out the bathroom, mere inches behind the man's back, praying that he wouldn't turn around, that the door wouldn't squeak, and that his footsteps couldn't be heard. Moving like a shadow, he took a sharp left down a long hallway, a quick right, took two steps, and came up against a dead end.

Shit. Now what?

Further exploration revealed that what Mark initially thought was a wall was in fact a filthy door obscured by all sorts of items that would be better off in the dump. Nervously, he cleared a narrow path as quietly as possible. Fortunately, the door was unlocked. Once outside, he climbed up by stacking several plastic cartons together; three minutes later, he lay on the flat roof of the convenience store.

He waited, peering over the edge. He figured he had about one more minute before the cavalry appeared.

He was right. They came in droves, agents everywhere. But they never even looked up at the roof.

After some time, he estimated half an hour or so, Mark could see that the search had progressed far into the residential neighborhood, away from the store's vicinity. He lowered himself over the side, dropped to the ground, and went back inside the 7-Eleven.

"Hey buddy," he told a man grabbing for a twelve-pack of Coors in the cooler. "I'll give you a hundred bucks if you give me your baseball hat and sunglasses and then trade shirts with me." Mark made sure his back was to the cashier—though he was relatively sure she hadn't seen him when he came in—and positioned himself behind the cola display.

The man reached for two more twelve-packs. "You're on, pal. Can I sell you my watch, too?"

"No, but you can rent me your pickup truck for an hour. It will be waiting for you at the Greyhound terminal in the next town."

Mark walked outside, wearing the cap, glasses, and dirty Hawaiian shirt. He stepped into the rusted blue Ford truck and was gone.

65

Anne Davidson Broome was no fool. She was well aware that Henry had his little flings on the side. She had long ago told Henry the price of his freedom: separate bedrooms, no scandals, and no questions about her frequent trips to the world's most expensive female-only spas. The problem? The rules had suddenly been broken. Her husband had not exercised proper discretion at the DNC Gala. She had seen his hands exploring the soft terrain of at least a dozen women, all of them young enough to be his daughter. Her own father and grandfather had not always been faithful to their wives, who looked the other way in order to benefit from the wealth generated by the Great Midwest Petroleum Company. It was an unfortunate family legacy: the men were allowed to sow their wild oats as long as the homestead was well maintained and no bastard children received the name of Davidson on their birth certificates.

Still, tolerance was one thing, and humiliation quite another. She put down the P I's report on Henry's latest mischief and walked to the living room of her well-appointed Washington home.

"I think we need to talk, Henry."

"I'm busy, dear." He had his feet up while he drank his thirty-year-old scotch on the rocks.

"No you're not."

Henry frowned. "What's that supposed to mean, Anne?"

Anne stood before her husband, looking down at him to give herself the psychological advantage of height. "Henry, your lack of discretion when it comes to women has become far too embarrassing. I see you have a new chief aide—a Ms. Virginia Soo."

"Yes, that's correct. Is that a problem? I can't work without a staff."

Henry shook his glass, watching the cubes rattle back and forth.

"It most definitely is a problem. You've already brought her to two different motels after lunch in the past week. Really, Henry. I would think that you could make it somewhat harder for my private investigator to spot you. If he can, then so can most of Washington."

Henry rose to pour himself another drink, but before he did, Anne could see the rage on his face. Good.

"I'll try to do better," Henry said, patting her derriere as he strode past. "And don't waste your money on an investigator anymore. If I catch one in the act, you'll both be sorry."

Anne stiffened at his touch, and then smiled. "Do not threaten me, Henry. And I'm afraid there won't be any more chances for you to do better. You humiliated me at the DNC Gala, and things have only degenerated. All those Asian women. At least one a week, according to the investigator's report. I'm guessing that they come courtesy of Gregory Randall?"

Henry turned back to her and headed toward the couch. "Don't tax me, Anne. You're stepping over the line."

Anne simply laughed as she pushed Henry back onto the sofa, causing his scotch to spill on the adjoining cushion. "I don't think you comprehend my meaning, Henry. You're out."

"Out?" Henry said, laughing mockingly. "Out of what?"

"The coffee business, for one, which I already technically own. The Senate, for another."

"And how exactly are you going to accomplish this coup?"

"Let's just say that a little bird e-mailed a well-known reporter about how to find information about the payments from Randall to Lanai, Inc. Suggested he look through Transpac files to verify it. I don't have to remind you that Transpac files store lots of information, even about that little hobby of handing around Asian women."

Henry stood, red-faced. "Listen here, Anne. There's as much damning information on you in those files as there is on me. You own Transpacific Coffee. You've got to be stark raving mad!"

"Mad? No, Henry, dearest. I'm just a housewife who does fundraisers for charity and occasionally signs on the dotted line—and someone who wants your Senate seat. Imagine the outrage I'll display when I find out that my philandering husband gave me enough shares to make me majority stockholder of Transpacific Coffee Imports, a company that sells to Pequod's, even though it doesn't say so on paper. Exactly what's so special about those beans anyway, Henry? Why all the subterfuge? They were your pet project when you first brought me to Lanai all those years ago, and you've kept your little secret for all these years."

Henry threw his heavy tumbler at a picture on the wall, smashing the glass inside the frame. "You think I would share that with you? You think you can topple me?"

"I don't only think, Henry. I know. Because I have an advocate. Phillip Trainor, to be exact, the next Democratic nominee for President of the United States. He thinks the sympathy vote for me will be enormous, plus the press loves a good sex scandal. I'm an upstanding, scorned woman whose father and grandfather were successful businessmen, a woman who had the guts to blow the whistle on her husband, one of the most powerful men in the world, simply because it was the right thing to do."

"You wouldn't—"

"Trust me, I would. Assuming it comes to that. Of course, it would be far easier for you to step aside for reasons of 'health.'"

Anne never expected what she saw next. Her comments hadn't flustered Henry. They hadn't caused him to slump on the couch. Instead, they seemed to embolden him. Henry put his hands in his pockets, and faced his wife squarely. "Let me tell you why you're not going to reveal anything more—not ever. And why that reporter is going to be worth nothing more than a three-dollar bill in a few days. And while I'm at it, let me also tell you about those plants I grow, the ones you 'technically' own."

Henry smiled his most arrogant smile.

"We have Mark Stern in custody—you didn't know that, did you?"

Anne tensed, but her face revealed nothing.

"And we have all the data he collected at Transpac. As for

Transpacific Coffee, its offices in Pedregal are already empty. Nobody in that port seems to have heard of the company. As for their files . . . what files? As of 11:15 this morning, there are no files, no Transpac . . . and no Mark Stern to cause trouble. Whatever you blab will be regarded as the ravings of a crazy woman. Might even land you in a rehab center if I pull a few strings. So many wives of congressmen have drinking problems. Now, as for the coffee . . . "

Despite her strength of character, Anne Broome suddenly didn't feel so confident.

66

In a '98 Nissan Quest with numerous squeaks and rattles, Gwen, Jan, Peter, Rick, and Karn bumped along a dirt road outside of Calverton, Virginia.

"I don't think I've ever been in so many different cars and rooms in such a short period," Gwen commented.

"I think our switch to the van back at the Capitol was clean," said Rick, who'd borrowed the Quest from Alex Morgan, a friend at the Department of Treasury. "No guarantees, but I'd be surprised if anyone knew where we are. We may still need another vehicle before this is all through, though. There's an old Ford Bronco where we're going, although I'm not sure it's been used in a while." Rick held the wheel tightly as he followed the ruts in the ground through a gentle turn. "Up ahead—that's Alex's getaway. Uses it for deer hunting, or for just some peace and quiet."

The van rumbled to a stop and the occupants emitted a collective gasp. The porch of the large pine cabin was occupied.

"What's he doing here!" exclaimed Jan.

"What took you guys so long?" Mark Stern said, getting up nonchalantly from the old wooden rocker and moving toward the Quest.

■ ■ ■

"You escaped?" cried Gwen. Once again, she had that look of genuine concern on her face and Mark's heart ached. If they managed to get out of this situation alive, he was going to have to figure out a lot of things.

Mark held out his arms as if to display the fact that he was indeed standing in front of his friends. "I'm all here, right."

"How'd you know where to find us?" Jan asked.

Mark nodded toward Rick. "A friend of mine gave me inside information before my unfortunate incarceration."

"But still—how did you dodge those morons?" asked Peter.

Mark grinned. "I pretended I was you?"

Peter guffawed. The others simply seemed mystified.

"Bravo," said Peter. "We need you if we're going to put all the pieces of this puzzle together. Pulling a story together for page one is your strong suit, isn't it? I mean, aside from dodging would-be captors."

■ ■ ■

They settled into the dining room of the lodge, gathering around a large table with their papers and computers.

"Now that we're settled—and unwatched," Karn said, "I want to show you what I went back to my office to gather. This came from an old friend of mine, Professor Raju Kucherlapati, who was Jamie's mentor at Princeton. According to the professor, Jamie was obsessed with trying to figure out how gene sequences in plants led to the synthesis of various optical isomers."

"I hope you're going to keep this simple," said Mark, laughing. "I already need a translation."

"Go on, Doctor," said Gwen excitedly. "I think I see where you're going."

"When you first take high school chemistry, molecules are just flat stick figures of atoms," explained Karn. "Later, you learn that they have three-dimensional form and that certain molecules, called chiral molecules, have mirror images of one another. The mirror molecules are made of the same atoms and are attached to each other in the same way, but they bend in a different direction. Let me offer an example. Your two hands work and look the same, and yet you can't put your right hand into your left glove. They're mirror images of each other."

"Yes!" Gwen called out. "Stereochemistry!"

Karn clasped his hands as he surveyed his audience. "Jamie was trying to create abnormal stereo isomers in his coffee plants, the ones that Henry Broome eventually took to Hawaii and apparently planted on Lanai. The direction in which an isomer bends or rotates light has nothing to do with its function, but it's the only way to distinguish one chiral form apart from the other. If light passes through a solution containing the molecule and bends clockwise, the isomer is positive, or dextrorotatory. If an isomer rotates the polarized light counterclockwise, it is negative, or levorotatory. To simplify matters, scientists use the shorthand notations of d and l for these molecules."

"What's the significance of the d or l?" asked Rick.

"At first glance, nothing," replied Karn. "But think about something like the newest artificial sweetener, which is just the optical isomer of sugar. It tastes sweeter than sugar because it hits the same receptors, but you can't break it down and get calories out of it."

Rick frowned. "That didn't help me as much as I think you thought it did."

Gwen stood, barely able to contain her enthusiasm. "With your permission, Doctor?" she asked, glancing sideways at Karn.

"By all means, Gwen," he replied. "We're obviously on the same wavelength."

"When molecules are synthesized in the lab, these isomers can sometimes be created in equal amounts, and result in what is called a racemic mixture. In nature, nearly all chiral molecules are created in the left-handed, or l form. The d form, or right-handed isomer, is usually inactive. There are exceptions, however. These exceptions surround molecules that bind to cell membrane receptors that are highly shape-specific. We're talking about mirror images of the same molecules. Here's the catch, though. Although the molecules are basically the same, the receptors don't care what they're made of, only their shape." Gwen hesitated before she continued. "Neurotransmitters are essentially keys that fit certain receptor sites in the body's nervous system. We've all heard of adrenaline and know its effect on the body. Adrenaline is just one of many neurotransmitters. Serotonin is another, one that seems to be intricately involved in sleep and depression. Most sleep aids and antidepressants now on the market affect serotonin levels in one way or another by blocking its receptor site."

"Okay," said Rick. "We understand that Jamie was a very promising chemist. What does this have to do with the mess we're in?"

"The important thing to remember is that neurotransmitters must fit like a key into a lock. But ask yourselves—would a mirror image of a key fit a particular lock? No. The teeth of the key would be the same shape and height, but the angles of the teeth would be backwards."

"What's going on in Henry's plants, Gwen?" asked Peter. "Are you saying that Jamie Robinson managed to alter the structure of caffeine, which is causing the seizures?"

"Not exactly, Peter, and here's the really tricky part. The two isomers are still the same chemical. If Jamie found a way to get coffee plants to manufacture a d form of the caffeine molecule, it's still caffeine."

Peter rubbed his chin, shaking his head. "Then aren't we back at square one?"

Gwen slumped. She rubbed her forehead. "I guess the first thing we need to do to find that out is confirm that Jamie's plants do in fact make a d form of caffeine," she said. "Then maybe we'll be able to see what square we're on."

"If I may interject," said Karn, "we also have the question as to how an undergraduate was able to pull off such an amazing feat as changing the basic isomer found in coffee. Even Kucherlapati, who was unaware of what plants Jamie was using in his experiments, said that he didn't think the research was very relevant—or that Jamie stood a chance at being successful in reversing the chiral properties of a molecule, for that matter. I have to admit, however, that I've looked at some notes that corroborate that chromosome banding is sometimes seen in genetically modified foods. I was reminded of this at Van Rankin's lab. Whether Jamie's manipulations constitute such modification is unclear. It's a gray area. I think we need to do two things. First, we need to access Jamie's Apple once and for all."

"I'll do what I can to get in there," Peter said.

"Second," continued Karn, "we need some lab work to examine the isomers of the plant and bean."

"Agreed," said Mark. "But speaking as a layman here, shouldn't we have Van Rankin analyze an actual cup of Pequod's for comparison's sake? After all, if coffee is the bad guy, then everything you and Gwen have outlined is going to show up in the actual product, correct?"

"I agree," answered Karn. "Analyzing the coffee itself is crucial now. But we want to compare the actual liquid to the plant to see if this can be traced to Henry Broome."

"Speaking of Broome," said Rick, "what about Mickey Spangler and Jamie's death? That doesn't sound so accidental anymore. I wonder if anyone else died to promote Broome's cause."

"We have a lot to do," Gwen said. "I'll go with Dr. Karn to the NIH, which has a more sophisticated set-up than Van Rankin. I think the good doctor's credentials should get us in with no problem. I'll disguise myself if necessary. Peter and Jan can work on Jamie's Apple here at the cabin. Mark and Rick can go to the New Jersey facility where Spangler is staying. Depending on what you find out, somebody may be calling on the attorney general very soon. We already have the Transpac files, which should be brought to his attention anyway. Surely there's enough in what Mark and Peter brought back to launch an investigation into the dealings of Transpac, Pequod's, Tassin, Randall, and Lanai, Inc."

Peter interjected. "You're forgetting that Mr. Stern here is currently regarded as a fugitive from justice, even though the federal agents were bogus."

Mark shook his head. "Doesn't matter. None of us should travel alone. I'll go with Rick—lay on the floor of the car if I have to—and Rick can go inside the correctional facility to talk with Spangler."

"Once more unto the breach," Peter called out. "Of course, Jan and I have the easiest job. We stay here and play with a computer."

67

"Mark!" cried Billy Hamlin. "I've been really worried about you. First you cut our Seattle visit short. Then you're on the nightly news every evening. I, for one, place no credibility in all this business about narcotics possession, but what the hell is going on? Don't you think it would be wise to hire a top gun lawyer and then turn yourself in?"

"Yeah, it's been quite a ride," Mark said into his cell phone. He was slouched in the backseat of the noisy Nissan as Rick drove to New Jersey to meet the dying Mickey Spangler. "But I'll be fine. Things are clearing up even as we speak. In fact, I was calling to see if you could make it over to D.C. in the very near future. I want to do another extensive piece with you before my competition catches up. Besides, I think I can finally beat you at racquetball."

"Just let me put you on hold a second, Mark, okay? You caught me in the middle of something."

As he waited, Mark seethed in silence. He really wanted to beat the crap out of Billy Hamlin, but not at racquetball. The CEO was either an imbecile or he had played Mark all along—surely the latter. It was time to confront the Pequod's head honcho and see what the all-American boy had to say for himself before Mark blew his company out of the water.

Billy kept Mark listening to muzak for several long minutes. Meanwhile, Mark imagined the conversation Hamlin was having with someone close by. "Yes, it's Stern. He seems to be in the Washington area. Wants me to fly there to meet him. What an ass.

Maybe the fool still trusts me. Thinks of me as an ally who'll help get him out of hot water." The minutes that elapsed told Mark that Hamlin was probably not his "best bud" anymore.

"Sorry, Mark," said Hamlin when he finally came back on the line. "You know how it is . . . Look, I'll be in Florida all day tomorrow, but I'm heading up the coast after that and I could swing up to D.C. on the way. How would that be?"

"That'll be just fine, Billy."

"Where will I find you?"

Mark laughed. "I'll find you, Billy. See you in a day or two. Keep your cell on."

Mark hung up quickly before Hamlin could offer any alternate plans. He couldn't wait to see what wonderboy looked like unmasked. Mark usually knew how to size people up, but somehow Hamlin had slid under his radar.

"You okay back there?" Rick called out.

"Yeah," said Mark. "Just dandy."

Mark was plotting revenge in its most potent form—the column inch.

■ ■ ■

Gwen and Eddie had received the dubious honor of using Alex Morgan's old Ford Bronco, left rusting away for years in the shed next to his lodge. It was even noisier than the Quest, and it shifted gears with a harsh grinding usually reserved for twenty-year-old farm trucks. Karn drove to SAMHSA, the Substance Abuse and Mental Health Services Administration laboratories housed on the NIH campus in Bethesda, Maryland.

"Are you sure we'll get in?" asked Gwen from behind her scarf and sunglasses.

"I worked pretty closely with the SAMHSA guys when I was with the FDA," answered Karn. "My friend, Ted Gallagher, runs one of the labs on the main campus. Van Rankin has a respectable analytic setup at Quantico, but if we're trying to figure out whether we're dealing with chiral forms of caffeine or trying to isolate brain stem activity—well, Gallagher's really the only game in town."

Gwen nodded. "But can we trust anyone anymore? I don't even feel safe being in public, let alone confiding controversial information to someone in the government. We already know that both the FDA and CDC have at least one person on the inside."

"I wish I could give you some kind of guarantee, but we sure can't make any headway back at the lodge. I can vouch for Gallagher, however. He hates political types. He'd never throw his lot in with people like Broome, nor would he compromise public safety."

"Like I said before—I'm glad you're on our side."

"Thanks. This is all too ironic for me. I've seen my career go up in smoke for advocating more stringent regulation of genetically modified foods. Now, if Pequod's is doing what we think they are, people might finally take the issue more seriously. It all depends on whether or not we can prove it."

■ ■ ■

"D-caffeine?" asked a startled Ted Gallagher when they'd settled in his office. "You're saying Pequod's coffee beans contain the dextro form of the molecule? I'm not sure we even know if d-caffeine has any interesting properties since no one I know of has ever isolated it in sufficient quantities."

"Exactly," said Gwen.

Gallagher cocked his head and took in a deep breath. "No receptor site's going to allow the little bugger to dock," Gallagher stated in his down-home manner. "Can't work."

"And yet," said Karn, "Pequod's isn't a national fad simply on the merits of its taste. The molecule is finding friendly receptor sites somewhere in the nervous system, probably in the brain stem, and that's what we need you to find out: how and where does the d-caffeine work?"

Gallagher scratched his head, which was covered in straight, fine hair that rebelled against the comb's attempts to keep it in line. "I'll look at that plant and what's left of the bean. Van Rankin had a run at this, you say? Good man. I like him. I'll also see what's in the actual coffee. I don't suppose you want to tell me why you're bringing this to me?"

Gwen explained the working theory that the mirror image of the caffeine molecule was causing seizures.

Gallagher's eyes opened wide as he walked to his office door. "Stevens!" he yelled. "Get in here!"

A slightly out-of-breath technician appeared at the office threshold within ten seconds.

"I've got a job for you and your team," Gallagher said like a drill sergeant. "Put it on your A-list, and nobody outside the division knows what you're doing. Do I make myself clear?"

■ ■ ■

Jan and Peter sat in front of Jamie Robinson's Apple II.

"It's actually quite amazing what this thing could do, considering that it was the first real computer to hit the mass market," Peter said.

"Even more amazing is what Jamie did to the machine using the expansion slots. Fingerprint recognition? A back-up drive? I would have hired this kid in a New York minute."

"But how do we break in?" asked Jan. "My interface didn't even recognize the connection."

"We use a binary unscrambler."

"Never heard of such a thing. But then I've never heard of most of your gadgets and techniques."

Peter smiled at Jan warmly. "That's why you need to keep me around."

The words hung between them for a moment before Peter turned back to the machine. "I'm presuming, as you yourself did, that Jamie used an alphanumeric password. The unscrambler breaks up the code into two bits of information at a time. Cracking the entire code could take weeks, but getting two characters at a time is very doable. There are ten numerical digits—0 through 9—and twenty-six letters in the alphabet. That's thirty-six possible digits to use in an alphanumeric code. Take any digit, and it can combine with thirty-five other characters."

"But how do we know which number or letter starts each pair of password characters?"

"Trial and error, my dear. We start with 0 and follow it with A through Z, seeing if we get a match. If we get no results, then we move up to 1 and proceed in the same fashion from A through Z."

"That's pretty cool. But what about the fingerprint recognition? At least Jamie's parents still had a key to unlock the machine, but this recognition interface he created presents a different problem. I was just going to disconnect it."

"My techniques are rubbing off on you already," Peter said, jerking the pad from its port. "Not many people would have known back in 1977, but the damned thing only makes a difference as long as it's hooked to the machine. Other than that—useless. Disconnecting it doesn't affect access in the least."

"Got it. So let's start unscrambling."

Suddenly the cabin began vibrating with a distant but deep penetration. Gradually it grew louder and louder until the bass rumble caused pictures on the wall to shake and a paperclip to dance across the desk where Peter and Jan were working.

"What in blazes is that?" asked Jan.

Peter put his finger to his lips, motioning for silence. He got up and went to the window, Jan following.

"What's going on?" she whispered.

"Get down," Peter said, pulling Jan away from the window.

The vibration developed into a thundering sound, growing higher in pitch before falling rapidly again.

"A low-flying helicopter," said Peter. "Very low. It may be nothing; this close to the nation's capitol, it's hard to say. Law enforcement has hundreds of bases in the area. But if we're buzzed again, I'm calling Rick."

"I'm worried," said Jan.

"Let's get back to unscrambling," said Peter. "If we're hassled, we need to have that information ready for the others."

They returned to the desk and applied themselves to the Apple.

Thirty minutes later, Peter's unscrambler had the first digit.

68

"You're taking too much of a risk," Rick told Mark as they neared the New Jersey correctional facility where Mickey Spangler lay dying. "Besides, you look like Indiana Jones on spring break."

Mark sat up straight in the back of the Quest, pulling the soft, wide-brimmed hat down over his eyes in the fashion that Harrison Ford made famous. He wore conventional sunglasses and zipped up a jacket despite temperatures in the high eighties outside the van.

"I have to talk to Spangler as well," Mark said adamantly. "I've spent my life getting information from people. This is my strength, not yours."

"If you say so, but it's your funeral if we're busted. Maybe mine, too, as an accessory to aiding and abetting a fugitive. And it was such a promising political career."

"Relax. I'll say I kidnapped you or something."

"I think the sun got to you down in Panama."

■ ■ ■

"What kind of deal?" asked Mickey Spangler.

"You get to go home," said Rick, "and die with a little dignity." Rick looked at the hospital ward. "It's not Alcatraz here, but you could do better. Like I said, we're just looking for some information about the death of that kid at Princeton."

"How do I know I can trust you?" Spangler asked, coughing.

Mark guessed the guy weighed no more than 110 pounds. Lung cancer, chemotherapy, and radiation had exacted a heavy toll on the petty thief who had taken one too many wrong turns in life.

"I have connections," said Rick. "Lots of 'em. Depending on what you have to say, I go to the one I think is in the best position to help you, and we cut a deal. Anyway, the police aren't looking to double-cross a sick man. Frankly, the Department of Corrections would rather let Medicare pay for your last days. The authorities are after a much bigger fish."

Spangler, his bloodshot eyes sunken and suspicious, looked at Rick and Mark. "What is it you want to know? You already told me you have the police report about the kid."

"Your statement is that you saw Jamie Robinson mount his bike and ride across Washington Street. Right?"

"Right."

"Who was the man standing next to Jamie?"

"Dunno. It's been a long time."

Mark was standing next to the bedside. He pulled up a chair and positioned it next to Rick's. This was going too slowly. "It's in the police report, Mickey. The man was a student named Henry Broome. Now he's a U.S. senator."

"Broome. Sounds about right."

It was unclear whether Spangler was reticent to talk or had genuinely forgotten a name from half a lifetime ago, a name he'd perhaps chosen to forget.

"Is this the man?" asked Rick, producing two pictures. One was a college picture of Broome, the other a shot from a decade back when Broome made his first foray into politics.

The breathing tubes in Mickey's nostrils made a constant, unnatural hissing sound. "Yeah, that's him all right. You still haven't told me what you want to know. It was an accident. I swear."

"We want to know— "

"The truth," Mark said, interrupting his friend. Anything that Spangler said would have to be the result of information volunteered. Neither Mark nor Rick could go on a fishing expedition, hoping to stumble onto the right scenario. Spangler wanted to get out of the ward, and Mark knew he would probably verify anything Rick said.

"What if I told you Broome is claiming you ran over the kid on purpose? What if I told you that good ol' Henry Broome says the kid saw you breaking into one of the buildings on campus and lifting some expensive scientific equipment?"

Mickey tried to sit up but couldn't. "That lousy bastard! I did no such thing."

"Broome's a politician," Mark continued. "Might even run for the White House. People check the background of someone like that pretty carefully."

"Then the lousy motherfucker is afraid they'll find out what he really did. I never killed no kid in my life—not the Robinson kid, not nobody."

Rick glanced at Mark. "Then what really happened, Mickey?"

Another cough. The slim green breathing tubes hissed. Mark wondered if Spangler was going to make it through the next few minutes, let alone have the chance to go home—wherever that was.

"Before the cops got there," Spangler said, "this guy Broome pulls me over and starts telling me that if I say what I really saw, he'll tell the police about a truckload of color TVs I helped drive away for a friend of mine. Hell, to this day I don't know how the guy knew I was in on that heist. But he had a crazy look in his eye. So I said it was an accident—said that Broome had tried to hold the kid back, but that the kid jumped on his bike and rode out into the street. Later that night, he called to make sure I was still on board with his story. Kept making threats."

"So what you told the police is not what happened?"

"Hell no. I've played the thing out in my head a million times. It all happened so fast, but I'm sure of it. Broome pushed the kid, plain and simple. Hand was on Robinson's shoulder plain as day. Broome was a big guy. Just pushed the kid right out in front of the truck. My orders were to drive down Washington Street. I didn't know anything like this was gonna happen, though. I swear on my mother's grave. I thought I was on my way to make a pickup, and don't ask me what I was gonna haul, because people didn't usually tell and I never asked. Jesus, the whole thing was awful. Broome outright threatened me is what he done."

Mark glanced down at the mini tape recorder in his hand, again making sure the green RECORD light was on.

"But look," said Spangler, now wheezing from agitation and exertion, "I didn't have nothing to do with them two cheerleaders that died a couple days later. That was Ignatz's number."

"Who's Ignatz?" asked Rick.

"Never did know his real name. He did the dirty work back then around Trenton. The real dirty work, if you know what I mean. Princeton was a pretty upscale place to work. I drove loads of cargo to the Pine Barrens for him but never messed with any of it. There was always guys with shovels waiting when I got there. You gotta believe me on this one."

"We do, Mickey," said Mark. "Did Ignatz get his orders from Broome?"

"I dunno. You'd have to ask Ignatz." Spangler was barely able to speak now. "I . . . I . . . "

"Go ahead and rest," said Mark.

"Yeah," said Rick. "Take it easy. I'm going to talk with some friends and see if the prison will cut you some slack."

Spangler swallowed hard and nodded his head. It was all he could manage.

Outside, Mark and Rick got back into the Quest.

"Who's the right person for this little bombshell?" asked Mark.

"To nail Senator Henry Broome? The attorney general."

"Of New Jersey?"

"Hell no. Of the United States. Before this is over, we might have even more information to give him. Let's head on back to the cabin and see what kind of progress our colleagues are making."

69

"I just don't think it's wise, Eddie," said Gwen. "We can't split up."

"Like I said before," Karn responded, "no one is going to take a shot at me right now. I'm still too controversial, too high-profile. If anything happens to me, there will be an immediate investigation. I just need to gather some research on genetically modified foods and then make contact with a few friends who are still doing research in that area."

"But— "

"Besides, I want to visit Jack again and tell him how much progress we've made."

Gwen, who was ready with a dozen reasons why Karn shouldn't wander off , suddenly dropped her protestations. "You really think you're safe?"

"Absolutely."

"All right," said Gwen, "but be careful. Call Mark's cell phone when you're ready and we'll arrange a rendezvous to bring you back to the cabin. You might lead our pursuers back to the lodge if you come on your own."

The two parted. Gwen felt uneasy. She didn't think Mark or Peter would approve, but she had to know how Jack was, and Karn was probably right about not being a target. It was unlikely that anyone would go after him so soon after his public appearance before Henry Broome's committee and the subsequent talk about food safety on political talk shows.

She got behind the wheel of the Bronco and prayed she'd made the right decision.

■ ■ ■

Karn entered his apartment and went straight to a file cabinet, removing three manila folders filled with documents. He would take the information and consult with a few colleagues about the d-caffeine. If Ted Gallagher isolated the anticipated isomers from Pequod's coffee—the mirror image molecules of caffeine—he wanted to know how to approach the problem. Circumstantial evidence indicated the molecule was producing seizures, and yet a mirror image of caffeine was still just caffeine—just like a mirror image of your right hand is still just a hand . . . until you try to place it in your right glove.

This was precisely the kind of dilemma that worried Karn over the years. On paper, genetically modified foods looked just fine. And they were everywhere. Every supermarket in America, except organic markets, carried genetically modified consumables. Karn knew all the arguments. He knew that every food consumed in America had been genetically modified, not by moving genes around in a laboratory, but by years of breeding and hybridization. But Karn remained skeptical.

And then there was the Chaos Theory to consider. Most people knew of this scientific principle from *Jurassic Park*. The dinosaurs weren't supposed to mutate and develop the ability to reproduce in the wild—they were originally cloned in a lab from prehistoric drops of blood found in amber—but they had found a way. As a mathematician had said in the film, nature always found a way of achieving its goals, defying the limits man puts on natural processes. People like Henry Broome could ridicule him all they wanted, but Karn felt that sooner or later GMOs might either mutate or, worse yet, find a way to work synergistically with hundreds of chemicals within the human body in unexpected and dangerous ways.

Karn needed his notes. And to talk with colleagues he could trust.

Outside his condominium, he got into his Prius and started the engine. He headed down Rock Creek Park. Normally he slowed down to enjoy the meandering stream on his right, but today its beauty passed him by. He thought he saw a car coming up behind him once or twice, but every time he slowed down to confirm its presence, to let it pass, it dropped back. Was he being paranoid?

Karn passed the old barn at Tilden Street, recalling the day when CIA operatives openly disassembled the listening post that had been set up there. The agency eavesdropped on the Chinese embassy for thirty years! Even in Washington, things changed.

Karn's musings brought him around the bend below Porter Street when he heard a loud pop under his hood. He attempted to steer left, but the car went straight. Straight into the creek, over the twelve-foot waterfall, and into the rotor pool at the bottom. As he spun down into the cold, he thought about the half-dozen drowning deaths that happened every summer at that very spot.

70

They were all back at the cabin, except for Eddie Karn. Mark thought that Gwen had made a critical mistake splitting up her team and with every minute that passed, he became more convinced that she'd blundered in the worst way. Was Gwen cracking under the relentless pressure? It was certainly possible, though Mark would not have thought it possible of Gwen.

He bit his tongue and listened to the details of her meeting with the NIH guy, Gallagher. Then he and Rick told the group what they learned from Mickey Spangler—information that, if corroborated, could easily take down Henry Broome.

"As a member of Congress," Rick said, "I'm not all that concerned about gaining access to the attorney general, but I'd like to get Gallagher's report first, so I can present everything to him in a nice, neat package. Nailing Broome is sweet under any circumstance, but if we have him linked to other illegal activities, it'll be icing on the cake."

"We may not have the luxury of time," Mark pointed out. "I'm not sure how much longer Spangler can hold on, and I want to keep my promise to the man, regardless of what he's done."

Rick nodded in approval. "How long do you think it will take Gallagher to conduct his tests, Gwen?"

"Something like this would probably take a week. My impression of Gallagher is that he's the kind of person who gets things done, though. He may have some preliminary info in a day or two. He's apparently got awfully good teams under him. Isolating an isomer from a racemic mixture isn't all that difficult, but figuring out how the isomer—our d-caffeine—acts on nerve receptor cells is a different story."

"Let's hunker down and rest," advised Peter. "We could use it. And unscrambling Jamie's password is turning out to be a bit more time-consuming than I expected. I failed to factor in that he could use the symbols above the top row of letters on the keyboard—dollar signs, ampersands, that sort of thing. That means there are thirteen extra variables to consider in my binary program."

They all agreed to get some rest. As he lay in the dark—they'd decided to use flashlights rather than turning on lamps—Mark thought about where this story was going. He'd never been involved in toppling a dirty national leader before. Another item to mark off his Woodward and Bernstein checklist. It still wasn't that multipart investigative piece on the plight of the tamarin, but it was pretty sweet.

Assuming the story got out, of course. After everything they'd been through, it was crazy to think they were home free even with so much damning information available.

Mark thought again about Eddie Karn. Was he okay? He hadn't called his cell, which was worrisome. Even if something slowed down his return to the cabin, he should have checked in.

It took a few more minutes for Mark to relax enough to succumb to fatigue.

The helicopters arrived an hour later.

■ ■ ■

"Everyone up!" Peter shouted.

Everyone stumbled into the main room, bumping into things in the dark.

"What's going on?" asked Mark.

"We have company," said Peter. "A chopper buzzed the cabin earlier today while Jan and I were working. Three are swarming now at very low altitude. Looks like the bastards have found us once again."

"What do we do?" asked Jan.

"There's no way out except by road," Gwen said. "We can't outrun helicopters, for God's sake. We're finished."

"Maybe not," said Rick as the vibration from the rotor blades grew louder and louder. A chopper was obviously directly overhead, with two others cruising in nearby airspace. "There's a barn about a mile from here. Straight down a very narrow path that begins next to the fence out back."

"Just a barn?" asked Mark, raising his voice to be heard over the din of the copters.

A spotlight from above played across the window.

"Don't know. Maybe a farmhouse nearby, maybe not. I don't know these woods as well as Alex."

"We don't stand a chance," cried Mark. "We can either bolt to a barn or the road. What's the difference?"

The spotlight penetrated deeper into the room, causing everyone within to huddle together in a corner. A glass windowpane cracked from the intensity of the vibrations.

"The difference," said Rick, "is that they'll chase any vehicle that heads for the highway."

"A decoy?" said Mark. "You?"

"Yes. I'm the most logical one. As a U.S. Representative, they'll be forced to take extra care with me."

"Agreed," said Peter.

"No way!" cried Gwen. "We stick to—"

"He's right," said Mark, "and we don't have much time. There may already be people on the ground coming for us."

Rick moved toward the door. "I'm going to get in the Quest and back up so that the rear hatch is right next to the door. Somebody open it and then slam it shut after thirty seconds. Let 'em think we're all trying to escape."

He opened the door of the cabin and ran ten paces to the van. The spotlight picked up his form immediately.

"Stop where you are!" ordered a harsh voice through a loudspeaker attached to one of the hovering craft.

Rick started the engine and backed up. Mark opened the hatch as instructed and then closed it. Rick lurched forward and then peeled out down the dirt lane, heading for the highway.

Peter already had Jamie's PC in his arms. "Grab the cords, connectors, and disks!" he ordered Jan.

Mark had remained by the door, gazing into the sky. After a full minute had passed, he turned to the others. "I think they're buying it. The two other choppers are following the first. They're fanning out on both sides of the van—I think that's so they won't lose sight of it under all those overhanging limbs. Now's our chance!"

The four hurried to the Bronco and Mark took the driver's seat.

"Hold on, everybody!" he said, and guided the Ford onto a path clearly not made for vehicles. It was barely wide enough to allow passage, and branches scraped at the side panels and windows. When they were traveling in what he thought was a straight line, he shut off the headlights.

"Any sign of the helicopters?" asked Mark.

"No," Gwen shot back.

The Ford crawled forward, the undergrowth clawing at the battered SUV.

"Wait a second," said Jan, "one of them is returning."

Gwen turned around and looked out the rear window. "It's hovering over the cabin."

"Hope they don't have heat-seeking detectors," said Peter.

Mark kept the vehicle moving straight ahead. "We've got good cover," he said, "but I might end up running us into a tree."

"The chopper's moving off," Gwen said excitedly. "Headed back toward the main highway."

Mark turned on the running lights every few yards, shutting them off again when he knew what was ahead.

"There!" exclaimed Gwen, pointing. "I think I see something."

It was the barn. Mark drove into a small clearing and straight into the barn, shutting off the engine as soon as he was beneath the arched wooden roof.

"Now what the hell do we do?" Jan asked.

"By morning, they'll know of our little charade," Peter said. "They'll comb the woods with dozens of men, and it won't be hard to find this place once they discover the path. Might even locate the barn from the air. This is little more than a staging area for whatever we do next. We have a few hours at most to make our next move."

"A move to where?" asked Gwen.

No one answered.

71

Henry was doing his best to get drunk. Anne was nowhere to be found, and the servants were also absent. Henry didn't trust either circumstance. He called all Anne's shopping friends, but no one knew his wife's whereabouts.

"Probably with that asshole Trainor," Henry mumbled as he poured himself another double scotch.

He slumped onto the sofa. Things had taken a turn for the worse. Though what he told Anne about the relocation of the Pedregal operation was true, he hadn't been privy to the location of the new Transpac offices—if they existed at all. And his recent call to the man with the raspy voice had yielded nothing but a ringing phone with no answer.

"It's my goddamn coffee they're using!" he said angrily.

But coffee wasn't Henry's only trouble. He returned from his midday meeting with three members of his Agriculture Committee to find that his new chief aide, Virginia Soo, resigned during the lunch break.

"Anne probably threatened her," he muttered. "I don't know what kind of power play she's making, but she's gonna lose—and she's gonna regret it the rest of her life."

Picking up the remote, he flipped on the television and went straight to CNN. According to the breaking story, Dr. Edward Karn had just died, the result of a tragic automobile accident.

72

The night was eerie, quiet. Mark sent the beam of his flashlight across the barn roof to check its integrity. It had a few holes where the wood was rotten, but for the most part, it looked solid and appeared to provide adequate cover. An owl hooted in the distance.

"Did we just land in a Stephen King novel?" asked Jan, huddling close to Peter.

"No," said Mark, "but I'm reasonably sure that we're in the middle of something that was supposed to remain a deep, dark secret."

Gwen sat off to the side, by herself. She hadn't seemed right since she returned to the cabin without Karn. Mark ached for her. What she was going through was exponentially tougher than what he was. He walked over to her and knelt on the hard ground littered with straw.

"You holding up?" he said softly.

Gwen's eyes touched his briefly and then dropped. "I just wanted to get to the bottom of Marci's death." She sounded like a penitent in a confessional. "I end up pulling in people I care about and putting them in all kinds of danger. Jack, Jan . . . you."

"It sounds like Jack is going to be fine. The word from the hospital is great, right?"

Gwen nodded softly.

"As for the rest of us, we're grown-ups and we chose to help you. We've all been in trouble before and dealt with it."

"Not this kind of trouble. You do realize we're not just talking about losing our jobs or even going to jail here. If someone like

Broome knows what we have on him, he could do anything to stop us. We know what he's done in the past."

Mark was of course aware of this. If you spend enough time exploring the dark side of humanity, your mind jumps to those conclusions fairly quickly. He'd been hoping that Gwen hadn't been thinking that way, though.

"Eddie's in danger," Gwen said softly, "isn't he?"

There was no reason to kid her. "He might be."

"If something happens to him, it's my fault."

"Or maybe whatever happened to him would have happened to both of you."

Gwen said nothing for a moment and then put her hands to her face. Instinctively, Mark reached for her hands and held them in his. Their heads were no more than a foot apart. Even in the dim light, Mark could make out every contour of her face—every bit of tribulation in her eyes.

"You're doing something important here, Gwen. You may have started this because of Marci, but you're doing it now for everyone."

"I never wanted to be a crusader. That was your job."

Mark smiled and held her hands to his face. "You've always been a crusader. It's one of the things I'll always love about you."

"Mark, I—"

"Of course not. Some things just need to be said, though."

A moment later, Peter came up to them, breaking whatever it was that just happened between Mark and Gwen.

"Look what I found," he said, holding a long, coiled orange power cord.

"Great," Mark said, "but there's no place to plug it in."

"Take a gander through the rear."

The barn's large rear door was missing entirely and, as Mark aimed his flashlight outside, he located a small home about twenty yards away. It was in complete darkness.

"What if the residents are asleep?" asked Gwen.

"Or what if it's abandoned?" added Jan, who'd come over to join them. "There may be no electricity."

"Only one way to find out," asserted Peter. "I discovered the place, so I'll volunteer to check it out. It would be great if I could finish accessing Jamie's information before the sun comes up and we have to decide where to go."

"Be careful, Peter," Jan urged. She gave him a quick hard hug. It was obvious to Mark that she had a major crush on Peter. Going by the way Peter looked at her, he knew the feeling was mutual.

■ ■ ■

Peter stepped lightly to the ramshackle house, the orange power cord looped over his left shoulder. He was keenly aware that people who lived out in the woods usually owned a twelve-gauge, so caution was paramount in his mind as he approached the side of the home. A heavy layer of dust coated the windows. Moving closer, Peter shone his light on the window for a split-second before sweeping the beam away and turning it off. There were no curtains. He clicked the light on again and directed its illumination into the room beyond the dusty pane of glass. Empty. Moving around the house, he peered through each window and found that the other rooms were empty, too. Now came the real challenge. Having circled the house, he stood on the narrow, ground-level front porch and tried the doorknob.

Locked.

Kneeling, he produced a keychain with a small cylinder on it no bigger than a stubby pencil. Pressing a miniscule button on its side, he accessed what looked like a thin shaft of graphite and inserted it into the lock. In reality, it was a piece of slender steel designed for picking locks, a rod with extremely small serrations on its tip. With no deadbolt with which to contend, Peter had the door open within seconds.

He searched for the smallest room so he could try a light switch. Luckily, a bathroom with no windows adjoined the home's only bedroom. Peter flipped the switch on the wall panel, causing a single light bulb over the sink to flare.

"Excellent!" he said in a whisper.

He retraced his steps and plugged the orange power cord into an outlet above the baseboard, one approximately three feet from the front door. He uncoiled the cord as he stepped outside and made his way back to the barn. Midway, he glanced up. A few clouds obscured the stars, but otherwise the skies were quiet. No choppers.

"Okay, mates," he said when he was safely inside the barn again. "I'm going to see if I can finish deciphering Jamie's password. Mark, I want you to cover the cord outside with grass, dirt, leaves, sticks—whatever you can find. If any choppers return with searchlights, they could easily spot the orange line. Jan and Gwen, I want you to sit around the Apple so that its glow will be contained."

Everyone went off to their assignments. By the time Mark returned, Peter had the decryption program up and running again.

"Any luck?" Mark asked.

"It's taking much longer than I expected. The unscrambler I'm using was certainly not designed with an Apple II in mind, but it's slowly but surely discovering each password character. It's tedious, though."

They were so absorbed in unlocking the Apple's secrets that no one noticed the shotgun barrel aimed at Gwen's head until it was too late.

■ ■ ■

"Everybody just stay nice and still."

"Whom do we have the pleasure of meeting?" asked Peter, polite to the end.

The old man was gruff, but without the gun, he wouldn't be too much of a threat. "I live across that there crik and saw the light, thought I'd check it out. You're no part of the Brooder family. So the big question here is, who the hell are 'ya?"

"Federal law enforcement agents," said Peter. "I'll show you my badge, but I have to stand up and reach in my pocket."

"My granddaddy taught me to shoot Feds and bury 'em in the holler back in Kentucky. Well, go ahead, but don't try no funny stuff."

From a cross-legged position, Peter got to his feet, bending over and dusting off his pants legs. As he raised the trunk of his body, he threw a stiff, flattened right hand into the man's neck. The man, a skinny farmer with thin white hair and weathered skin, toppled backward, unconscious, but his shotgun discharged as he fell, sending buckshot into the roof with a deafening roar, and leaving dozens of new holes in the old wood.

"That's not good," said Mark.

"No, not good at all," Peter reiterated. "If I'd had one of the rings I used in Panama, it would have been simpler."

"I wonder if there are other neighbors nearby," wondered Gwen.

"We'll find out soon enough, won't we," said Mark.

Peter knelt down and continued to work on Jamie's computer.

73

Mark found some rope and a not-too-dirty piece of cloth in one of the stalls and set about the task of binding and gagging the old farmer. He wasn't happy about it, but he had to do it. They couldn't have the old man blabbing about them until they were long gone—whenever that might be. No other intruders showed up and no nosy neighbors came to investigate the shotgun blast.

An hour passed, and a feeble gray light outside the barn told Mark and his companions that dawn was about to paint the sky crimson and orange

"Let me use your magic cell phone, Mark old boy," requested Peter.

"I need to call my company. You're all going to become consultants for my security firm."

"Why?" asked Gwen.

"Because we have a meeting with one of my former clients this morning."

"Who?" asked Jan.

"A fellow by the name of David St. Germaine. He's Security Chief at the National Institute of Health."

"And just how are we going to get there?" asked Mark. "What rabbit do you have inside your hat this time?"

"A very large one, my friend. In fact, it's a rabbit that flies."

Gwen, Mark, and Jan exchanged confused glances.

Peter punched in a number and requested a pickup, giving his employee precise geographical coordinates.

"Are you going to explain?" asked Mark.

Peter ignored the question. "There!" he proclaimed triumphantly. "I've got the complete password. I'm going to copy the files to an old floppy—the Apple certainly can't handle a CD—and I'll examine them from my laptop while we're en route."

"En route how?" Mark said insistently.

Peter looked at him as though Mark were spoiling a surprise party.

"I spotted a pasture behind the house last night. That's probably when the old man saw my flashlight beam. It's big enough for a helicopter to land."

"You've got to be kidding," said Mark. "You produce Jeeps and jets out of thin air, and now a helicopter as well?"

"Precisely. If my company has its own jet and private landing strip, there's nothing unusual about a helicopter or two now, is there? Security is a very exacting field, Mark. I'm in demand not only because I'm good at what I do, but because I'm accessible."

Peter turned to face the old man. "We apologize for your discomfort, sir. I can guarantee people searching the woods'll discover you later this morning. Just sit tight."

The group made their way to the pasture. Peter carried the Apple II in case he needed direct access to the files. Copying twenty-nine-year-old files was, in his estimation, pretty much a crapshoot.

The helicopter arrived half an hour later. A Bell Jet Ranger was relatively small, its cockpit designed to carry a pilot, three passengers, and a small amount of cargo. Being the smallest, Jan crouched in the cargo well behind the seats.

"Take us to the helipad at the NIH," Peter instructed the female pilot. "Radio ahead for clearance. If you encounter any resistance, tell the radio dispatcher to contact David St. Germaine's office and inform anyone who answers that our remote monitoring station has discovered a breach in their backup computer systems. Tell them it's probably just a false alarm but that my team needs to check it out."

"Roger that," said the pilot. She banked sharply and guided the helicopter over the pine trees below.

■ ■ ■

Gregory Randall picked up his phone at 11:15 a.m.

"Good morning," said Randall, sipping the steaming cup of Pequod's coffee placed on his desk moments earlier by an Asian secretary.

"I've got disturbing news," said the raspy voice.

"Yes?"

"I received a call from one of our chemists in Central America. Our competitors' beans from several plantations across South America are now registering d-caffeine."

"With all due respect," Randall said, "I don't see how that's possible. Unless Henry has started growing elsewhere without telling us."

"Henry knows better. Carl Richey is sending a team into the field to investigate. Even though shipments are now going straight from Hawaii to Seattle, we'll maintain a presence in Costa Rica for the time being, especially in light of this new development. Transpac files have been purged or altered. I assume you've done the same with those at Randall, Inc."

"Of course. QuantumSheet has updated the files, both at Pequod's headquarters and at our main offices in New York."

"Good. I'll call when Richey checks in. By the way, I can't get in touch with Henry. Where is our Senator?"

"I don't know. His office says he was in briefly this morning and then left."

The raspy man coughed, then sighed. "He is very aggravating."

"I agree, but we need him."

The loud click on the other end was the only response.

■ ■ ■

Eddie Karn was dead. His body was missing, but they'd found his car submerged in a lake near his home. Gwen could hardly believe what she learned when they arrived at the NIH. David St. Germaine had delivered the group to Ted Gallagher and one of the first things Gallagher had said was, "A shame about Karn," as though everyone in the world already knew about it. Actually, most of the world probably did know about it already—according to Gallagher it was the lead story on all of the news shows—but it had been an utter shock to Gwen and her colleagues.

They had all taken it badly. Mark had been more broken up about it than Gwen would have guessed. But she had felt overwhelmed by a combination of sadness and guilt. This had happened because she let him go off on his own. If she'd been more insistent, more responsible, Eddie would be alive now.

A part of her wanted to curl up into a ball. The stakes had gotten too high. She'd started something she couldn't stop. But another part of her—the stronger part—told her that she needed to see this through to the end. Eddie had died for this. She'd make sure the people responsible paid for that.

Everyone had needed a few minutes to pull themselves together after hearing the news. Now, though, it was time to learn what Gallagher had discovered.

"Pequod's has d-caffeine, all right," Gallagher began. "No doubt about it. And yet it's having no effect on lab rats. They should be seizing like crazy—maybe dying considering their weight as compared to even very small concentrations of d-caffeine."

"It has to have an effect!" said Gwen. It struck her that since Karn's mention of optical isomers she had completely reversed her position.

"Now I didn't say that the rats were sitting around reading Charles Dickens," said Gallagher. "No, they're going absolutely crazy. Their metabolism is amazingly high. It's like they're on speed. Stevens thinks the d-caffeine is binding to receptor sites that usually accept amphetamines or amphetamine-based substances. We'll have to cross-section rat brains to see if this is actually what's happening, but it's the best working theory we've got."

"Damn," said Jan. "That's incredible."

"Might explain the full-moon madness I was tracking before Gwen called me," Mark said. "People in various cities were getting hypomanic. I have dozens of news clippings on people behaving like speed freaks."

"Still," said Jan, "we can't explain the seizure deaths."

There was silence in the room for almost a full minute before Gwen shouted, "Nicotine!"

Everyone turned to look at her.

"Explain," requested Mark.

"People who use amphetamines are chain smokers. Nicotine causes a large release of neurotransmitters in the brain. That's why it's so addictive. It gives amphetamine users a little extra jolt, both when they're using and when they're not. It helps keep the metabolism up and satisfies the body's craving for norepinephrine to a certain extent."

Gallagher was already nodding his head.

"Administer nicotine and d-caffeine to the animals simultaneously," Gwen told the lab director. "I guarantee they'll start to seize. Do the cross-sections on the others as planned to confirm the receptor site theory. Then measure the cyclic AMP level in their brains. It's going to be off the charts, just like Marci."

"Agreed," said Gallagher. "And if the seizure spikes occurred in various cities at different times, we need to take samples of Pequod's coffee from around the country."

"From both existing markets and areas that they're just moving into," said Mark. "I can supply that info."

"Not a problem," said Gallagher. "We have field units in several locations."

"But where did the d-caffeine come from in the first place?" asked David St. Germaine.

"I think I can shed some light on that," said Peter. "The answer was sitting in Jamie Robinson's thesis proposal in Kucherlapati's old files. Even though he never finished his thesis, thanks to our friend Henry, the answer was there all along. Jamie was fascinated by a newly discovered mechanism by which agrobacterium tumefaciens, a bacterium that causes tumors in plants, could be used to transplant genes into plants. The finding had just been published by Montagu and Schell the summer before and Jamie saw it as analogous to Kucherlapati's work with somatic cell hybridization, except that improved plants would benefit all humanity, not just those with rare diseases."

"Jamie was fascinated by coffee because different varieties have different numbers of chromosomes, even though they appear to be the same family of plant. He was conducting numerous experiments in his dorm room because he couldn't grow enough plants in the laboratory. In one experiment, Jamie was using agrobacterium to transplant the caffeine genes from Robusta beans to Arabica. Robusta has only twenty-two chromosomes as compared to Arabica's forty-four, but it has twice the caffeine levels. He didn't succeed, but he did produce d-caffeine in Arabica. His notes describe a dark band on chromosome number two of Arabica."

"Just like the plant and the bean," commented Mark.

"Jamie knew he was onto something," Peter continued. "He started chewing the leaves, almost like the natives in South America, and noticed he got a slight buzz. He analyzed his plants more carefully in Kucherlapati's lab and found out why he was feeling so energetic. From then on, his passion was optical isomers. He wanted to refine his research and then offer his findings to the private sector."

"The private sector found him instead," said Mark, "in the form of Henry Broome."

Mark's cell phone rang. Whatever Mark was hearing caused him to break into a wide smile. His part of the conversation amounted to "Yeah . . . I see . . . that's incredible . . . okay."

"Well?" Gwen and Jan said simultaneously.

"That was Rick," Mark said. "He's safe and sound and—get this—was calling from the office of the attorney general. He said he'll explain everything to us when we get there. There's an SUV downstairs with four U.S. marshalls in it. We're now under the protection of the attorney general himself."

Peter let out a low whistle. "Can't wait to hear Rick's story."

"You folks go ahead now," said Gallagher, shooing his visitors away with a flick of his wrists. "Stevens and I will continue to work on the coffee and nicotine. I'll let you know when we've got something."

Gwen's head was still spinning when they got outside. This thing had ratcheted up to levels she never would have imagined. Maybe that meant it would be over soon. She could go back to Jack. She could put the mystery surrounding Marci's death to rest. She could get back to her job, whatever that might be at this point. And she could spend a lot more time thinking about decorating the nursery.

They got into a black, unmarked SUV. Another black SUV—an escort—was parked behind the first, its engine idling.

The two vehicles exited the NIH campus and vanished into the traffic, a sure sign that in Washington it was business as usual.

74

Mark thought the stress had finally gotten to him when he saw the "ghost" of Eddie Karn sitting in the attorney general's office.

"It appears I'm not quite as dead as the news networks seem to think," Eddie said to the dumbstruck group.

"Funny," he added, looking directly at Mark, "the news media rarely makes mistakes."

Mark was tempted to go to hug the man. Instead, he blurted, "What the hell happened?"

Dr. Karn sat in a leather chair next to Rick Mecklenberg in the well-appointed office of Lane Chase, attorney general of the United States. Karn's right arm was in a sling.

"Broke my wrist and I have some pretty colorful bruises up and down the right side of my body, but otherwise, I'm intact."

Gwen did hug Karn. "But the news of your death . . . I mean, how . . . what happened . . . did you— "

"To borrow from Mark Twain, the rumors of my death have been greatly exaggerated. You know those fancy hammers they sell? The ones with the seatbelt cutters? Well, they really work. I figured that as long as my car was sitting in the creek and people thought I was inside, I might as well stay dead. It was clearly no accident that my steering went out when it did, and I wasn't going to wait around for round two. I tracked down Rick here, who got me under cover. I know it must have been hard, especially on you, Gwen, but I thought it wise if the people on our tail thought I was out of the picture. It left me free to review some literature and talk with colleagues, as I originally planned."

Gwen's face fairly radiated with relief. Mark found himself nearly as happy for her as he was for Karn.

"And you, Rick," said Mark. "How did you escape the helicopters?"

"I was apprehended on the highway and put into a dark blue sedan by the same guy who picked you up in front of the bed-and -breakfast. But then the damnedest thing happened. I woke up this morning in an apartment building—didn't have a clue as to where I was—and my captors were gone."

Lane Chase was a fifty-two-year-old man who looked like a thirty-five-year-old George Hamilton. He wore a subdued gray suit, and spoke in careful, measured sentences. "Representative Mecklenberg has filled me in on the Henry Broome and Mickey Spangler situation. He's also detailed your suspicions about Pequod's coffee and the unorthodox practices of Transpacific Coffee Imports, as well as the files implicating Gregory Randall's involvement. It's only a hunch at this point, but my guess is that someone with a great deal of power decided to back off and let Rick go. They think that you have too much information and that they either had to kill all of you—not easy, as we've discovered—or implicate themselves further with whatever murders they manage to commit. I would imagine there are quite a number of document shredders working at maximum output right now . . . Oh, and I've already checked for a Transpac warehouse in Pedregal—it's no longer there."

"Makes sense," said Mark, who'd seen his share of nefarious activities from a reporter's point of view. When Enron started to resemble the *Titanic*, both people and documents had disappeared with amazing rapidity.

"We've got an update on the coffee, though," Gwen said. "Ted Gallagher over at NIH has confirmed that Pequod's beans have a mutation, one that Peter says originated from Jamie Robinson's experiments at Princeton in 1977. The caffeine molecule is the mirror image of the one that occurs in nature; it's called dextro-caffeine. Gallagher thinks that it might be acting similarly to an amphetamine in the way it binds to receptor sites in the brain. He's running further tests now."

Karn had a troubled look on his face. "I've been looking at the issue of caffeine as an optical isomer. I've also spoken to Mr. Chase about the matter. The verdict isn't in, of course, until we get more scientific data, but some might argue that, under the law, d-caffeine is still just caffeine. Everyone here knows where my sympathies lie, but coffee is a whole food. The molecule is organic, and Pequod's does absolutely nothing to it, as far as we know."

"I'm going to speak with the secretary of the Department of Health and Human Services," said Chase. "We're in uncharted legal territory here. There's no telling how high in the FDA this conspiracy goes. Right now, our more immediate problem is Senator Henry Broome."

Mark looked puzzled. "In what way?"

"He's disappeared," replied Chase. "No one can locate him."

"He may just be shacked up with one of his girlfriends," offered Peter.

"If he knows what's up with Transpac," said Mark, "I think he's busy taking care of business."

"By the way," Chase said, "I've released Mickey Spangler to his family. New Jersey authorities didn't argue with my decision given his cost to their hospital unit. They were even more accommodating when I told them it was related to a federal investigation. I have people looking for Broome, but I'm not going to go public with our suspicions regarding the death of Jamie Robinson or the two college cheerleaders since the only evidence we have is a few words from a dying man. Given Broome's complicity in Transpacific affairs, I'm inclined to believe Mr. Spangler. That said, we have to proceed with caution.

"If you'll excuse me now, I have some meetings to attend. I'll provide each of you with undercover protection, but my guess is that you aren't on anyone's hit list at this point. I suggest that we meet here two or three days from now and discuss where we stand. In the meantime, we will hopefully have a line on Senator Broome and some further reports from Dr. Gallagher."

"Thank you, sir, for your time," Rick said.

Chase smiled and stood, the sign that he had to move on with his scheduled appointments.

Rick turned to his colleagues. "Time to get some food and rest."

"I can finally visit Jack," said Gwen.

Mark smiled faintly as everyone filed out of the office.

75

Aboard the Gulfstream V, Henry concentrated on his drink. His fifth scotch on the rocks had done nothing but take the barest edge off his somber musings, and he was getting frustrated.

He thought about poor, stupid, dying Mickey Spangler. He paid employees of the New Jersey correctional facility well to keep him abreast of Mickey's status through the years. Even before that, Henry hired local PIs to keep Spangler in his sights. Now, in light of the latest news, Henry had to believe that the old truck driver and petty criminal had spilled his guts. Why else would he be released into the attorney general's custody? Spangler had nothing left to lose. Jamie Robinson meant nothing to him. He had no idea of how the events on Washington Street in 1977 had changed the course of so many lives.

The lone flight attendant served Henry his sixth scotch silently and left him alone. Henry peered out the window at the earth below.

The plane was cruising over the Smokey Mountains as it sped toward Oklahoma where Anne still maintained the Davidson family ranch. Henry vaguely recalled enjoyable moments early in their marriage when the two of them had used it as a vacation spot.

It was another lifetime.

Spangler wasn't Henry's only problem, though. Eddie Karn was back from the dead and getting cozy with the attorney general. Chase would no doubt want to question Henry about the botched attempt on Karn's life. Henry played no personal role in the accident—that was Tabula Rasa's doing—but he'd still be questioned and he'd still come out looking bad. With Spangler's testimony, it wouldn't help to have a suspicious auto accident on his doorstep, too. It would be all too easy to assume that Henry had perceived Karn as a threat to his commercial interests, and that he had decided to do something about it.

And then there was the debacle with that damned reporter stumbling onto Transpac files. Deleting files and shipping the coffee straight to Seattle was a simple enough adjustment, but Henry knew that Stern had seen sensitive documents and would stop at nothing to get to the nitty-gritty details about Transpacific Coffee Imports—and about Dieter Tassin's role as well.

He drained his scotch and chewed on an ice cube, signaling the attendant for another.

Then, of course, there was Anne. Henry still couldn't believe that his own wife had such boldness in her. Forcing his chief aide to resign, threatening to reveal his dalliances, and then meeting with Phillip Trainor—clearly, she was deluded enough to see herself as capable of filling Henry's shoes and carrying on the family business. Ridiculous.

He'd have to deal with all of it. On his own if necessary. He wasn't going to let anything in his past screw up his future.

■ ■ ■

The jet landed ninety minutes later on a stretch of flat terrain in the northwest corner of the Davidsons' two-thousand-acre Wildcat Ranch.

Henry's thoughts centered on how to get his derailed career back on track. The powers that be wouldn't let him fall all the way—they had too much at stake, but he'd have to call in every single one of his markers from over the years. Luckily, there were lots of them.

His plane was met by a Jeep, driven by a Mexican man who'd worked for the Davidson family since Anne's grandfather hired him three decades earlier.

"Hello, Señor Henry," said Reynaldo Rohin. "The main house, sir?"

"Yes, Reynaldo. The main house. How are your grandchildren?"

"Very well, Señor Henry. Very well, indeed."

Henry's BlackBerry buzzed as he entered the enormous recreation room in the main house. An e-mail from Eddie Karn. How the hell did that maggot get Henry's most private e-mail address?

Henry was too curious to delete it without a look at its contents. The brevity surprised him. Karn was normally such a loquacious bastard.

TEXT MESSAGE: Henry . . . who's in the dumpster now?

Henry dropped his BlackBerry on the mahogany desk and proceeded to open a bottle of thirty-year-old scotch. He poured two ounces into a glass, and went into his private study.

Karn's message got to him. More than he would have expected. It also made one point clear—the buzzards were circling overhead. Karn couldn't have gotten the e-mail address without access deep within Henry's organization—some of the people who'd covered for him in the past had dropped their protection.

With a chill, Henry Broome realized that they were setting him up to be the fall guy.

Well screw all of them. Maybe he'd never realize his dream of occupying the Oval Office, but he could leave his enemies guessing—and his "friends" as well. Henry hadn't allowed anyone to bully him at Cottage, and he wasn't going to allow anyone to do it now.

Henry finished his scotch. He reached for the bottle again, but it was empty. *Good thing I have such a capacity to hold my liquor,* he thought. *I don't feel a thing.*

He stood and unlocked a drawer, taking out his 1860 silver-plated Colt revolver. Oh, but it was a beauty. Very old, but impeccably maintained and rebuilt over the years. It was his legacy from Henry Broome I, who claimed to have taken it off a Union Officer in the last days of the Civil War.

Always clean, always ready.

Henry called the airstrip, ordered the jet fueled, and requested a flight plan for Lanai. The pilot with whom Henry spoke started to say something about his duty-day and FAA-required rest periods, but Henry brushed aside his objections.

Less than an hour later, the ranch car delivered Henry back to the airstrip and he climbed aboard the jet.

■ ■ ■

The trip promised to be a calm one, and Henry allowed himself to relax.

The Gulfstream V, fueled for an hour's reserve beyond its intended destination, navigated its way toward Lanai, the most distant of the Hawaiian Islands.

Henry's mirth was tempered only by occasional glimpses of his pilots' slumped-over bodies. They disturbed his sense of order. He sat in the owner's armchair, sipping scotch and feeling the power of the Rolls Royce BR719 engines behind him. As the cabin altitude climbed through fifteen thousand feet, he began to experience a sense of power and euphoria. Whether induced by hypoxia or by the knowledge that he was checking out on his own terms, Henry was at peace and satisfied to be playing the last act. He would keep them guessing forever.

■ ■ ■

At flight level 430, the jet leveled off, flying on autopilot toward Lanai. By that time, worried pilots in F-16's had formed an escort around the uncommunicative private jet known to be carrying a U.S. senator. Since there were no grounds for a shoot-down, all they could do was follow the craft as it crossed the Sierra Nevada and West Coast. The fighters refueled over the Pacific, seeing no alternative but to keep following. When the jet came within range of the Hawaiian Islands, fighters from Hickam Air Force Base relieved the exhausted escort.

The Gulfstream navigated its way to Oahu perfectly, but failed to begin its programmed descent. Henry had seen to that. Lacking descent instructions, the jet kept flying west. Finally, it flamed out over the Pacific Ocean, losing its wings and shattering its fuselage as it entered an uncontrolled Mach 3 dive and scattered itself, and the remains of the two pilots and of Senator Henry Broome IV, over nine square miles.

The ocean was far too deep for any but the deepest of submersibles to consider a salvage mission. Unlike the waters off Martha's Vineyard, the Pacific had a considerable population of sharks. Within a day, all that remained of Henry Broome were memories.

76

Jack was asleep when Gwen got to his hospital room. For a moment, she stood in the doorway watching him. He seemed weak, vulnerable. From the time she met him, she regarded him as a powerhouse, but in that bed, after what he'd been through, he seemed nearly delicate. She felt tears coming to her eyes and put a thumb and forefinger up to the bridge of her nose to stem them.

Taking a couple of deep breaths, she moved to Jack's side. She put her head down on his arm and allowed herself to revel in the nearness of him. Over the past few days, she'd wondered at times if they'd ever be this close again. Now, even though he seemed weak, she took strength from him. The three of them—Jack, the baby, and her—were a powerful family unit.

"Gwen?"

Jack's voice seemed strained, as though it took him an extended period to say the single syllable of her name. But when she looked up at him, his gaze was vivid. He was all there.

She reached across the bed and hugged him tightly, temporarily ignorant of the tubes and machinery around them.

"Wow, that's quite a grip," he said slowly but clearly. "Have you been working out?"

She kissed the side of his face, then his lips, and then sat back. "I've always been stronger than you thought," she said with a smile. "I've just been holding back."

"I'm impressed." He reached out a hand and she took it. "Is it over?"

"It's not over, but I think everything has been set in motion. Most importantly, my part in it—the part that's kept me away—is over."

He squeezed her hand. There was real strength there.

"Did you get the bad guys?"

"We're getting them. At least one of them. We aren't sure yet how far this goes."

"That's good."

Gwen smiled and pulled his hand up to her lips to kiss it. She thought she knew how much she missed him when they were apart, but she had been far off.

"You were a big help in this," she said.

"I got in the way."

"You didn't. You were . . . amazing through this. Even when you thought I was crazy."

Jack's eyes darted away. "I owe you an apology for that. You were right about Marci."

"You don't owe me anything, Jack. No—wait a second—you do owe me something. You owe me a new office."

Jack turned back to her, his gaze more vibrant as though someone had just plugged him in. "I'll get started on the basement as soon as I get home."

"Maybe a few days after you get home." Gwen reached down and produced a baseball mitt from a bag next to her purse. "You also need to work on your curveball."

"Kids can't hit curveballs until they're teenagers."

"Our kid is going to hit a curveball when she's two!"

"She?"

"Or he. Either way, Dad had better be in great shape."

Jack's eyes glistened. "He will be."

■ ■ ■

Mark and Billy Hamlin sat on a bench next to the Reflecting Pool extending from the Washington Monument. The day was overcast, causing the leaves in the nation's capitol to show their darkest shades of green.

"I liked you, you son of a bitch," Mark said sharply. "I don't like many people—especially corporate people—but I liked you. And you screwed me."

"I'm telling you, Mark, you just dropped several bombshells on me."

They'd been together for several minutes, during which Mark briefed Hamlin on everything he and his colleagues had learned—and the contents of an upcoming hatchet job of Pequod's in the *Post*.

"Do you really expect me to believe that you knew none of this? You're the CEO of the whole freaking operation."

Hamlin put up his hands, as though to ward off Mark's blows. "I didn't say that I knew none of it. I knew about Pedregal, but not the rest of it. Certainly not about d-caffeine or—jeez—the sex slaves."

"I find that impossible to believe."

"You can believe what you want, Mark, but I'm telling you the truth. Randall told me Pedregal was necessary to maintain our secrecy. There was a certain logic to this. Every successful company keeps some secrets to hold on to its competitive edge. If the competition thought our beans came from South America when they really came from Hawaii, that would keep them one step behind us."

"So you're saying you knew nothing about the nature of those Hawaiian beans? You had no idea they'd been manipulated in such a way that they could kill people?"

Hamlin tipped his head back, his expression pained. He was either an Oscar-level actor or Mark really had given him new information.

"I know it sounds ridiculous, but even as CEO I didn't get access to everything. Randall made that a condition of my employment from day one. I knew he was ruthlessly competitive, but I didn't know he was dirty."

"And you can have Tassin over to your house for dinner—and regularly, from the way it seemed that night—and have no idea that he's involved in all kinds of evil shit with your boss?"

Hamlin shook his head and laughed self-deprecatingly. "Makes me sound like the world's biggest fool, huh? I knew Randall and Dieter went way back and I knew I had to be careful with Dieter. That's why he came to dinner so often. Keep your enemies closer, right? I swear I didn't know about the 'evil shit' though."

"I guess that means you think I shouldn't crucify you in the press, right?"

Hamlin looked genuinely mournful. "You're going to do what you're going to do, Mark. My only request is that you trust your reporter's instincts here. If you do, I think you'll realize I'm telling you the truth."

"And if I do, what happens next?"

Hamlin gazed out at the monument. He didn't say anything for more than a minute. "I have some decisions to make."

It was Mark's turn to be silent for a long moment after that. Finally he said, "You know, there's something I still haven't been able to figure out, though the bio-wizards may have done so already. Why does the seizure activity go down after the first couple of months?"

Hamlin's brow furrowed. Then his eyes opened in recognition. "I think I might be able to help you with that."

77

"The Proprietor's Roast is the answer," Dr. Ted Gallagher said.

It was four days later when Gallagher summoned the group back to the main campus of the NIH. Mark had called him right after he met with Hamlin to give him the "anonymous tip" that Pequod's screwed with the coffee whenever they entered a new market. According to Hamlin—a tough guy to not believe, even though it was nearly impossible to believe him—Tassin concocted a special roast to be used during the first two months of a launch. Tassin said it was all about flavor and that it took too long to create to make it Pequod's primary roast, but that it was a great way to get consumers hooked. Mark guessed that the last part was true, though the rest of it was bullshit.

"It's taken a while to line things up, and even now, the results are only preliminary pending duplication and further study. Think of what I'm going to say as the rushes of a Hollywood film —rough cuts of the day's shooting before the editor and director can put it all together. What we have now is awfully compelling, though."

"Let us have it," Mark said.

"First," stated Gallagher, "using Mark's tip, I made sure my teams carried out an analysis of Pequod's beans, both in existing markets and those that represent new territory for the outfit. The coffee from new markets showed a higher concentration of the mirror molecule than coffee from established markets. Pequod's has obviously been titrating the d-caffeine level—raising it—in order to hook people and keep the competition down when it expands to new markets. The d-caffeine binds to receptor sites that usually receive amphetamines and the like—cocaine, crystal meth, and a host of other uppers."

"That explains the seizure spikes," said Mark.

"Not really. The d-caffeine is enough to cause people to experience a slightly higher and more pleasant buzz, but that's about all it can do . . . except in those very rare instances where someone might already be at risk for a seizure and in compromised health on top of everything else."

"Does it make it more addictive?" asked Jan.

"It's a lot more addictive than regular caffeine, partly because it makes you feel so great without the unpleasant jumpiness. It does raise the brain's cyclic AMP level, just like Gwen said it would."

"Then why do they scale back on the d-caffeine after a few months?"

"My guess is that a lot of it has to do with money. It's more expensive to titrate. Once Pequod's has consumers hooked on their brand, they can drop down the levels and keep their market. Moreover, as they drop the d-caffeine levels, people buy more coffee to keep the buzz going. Suddenly they start going for the extra shot in their latte. They start dropping in for an extra cup on the way home, instead of just at lunchtime."

"And what about the interaction with nicotine?" Gwen asked.

"Nicotine is indeed the rogue factor that comes into play when we start talking seizures. Smoking, of course, raises the metabolism. As we already noted, it gives people who already take amphetamines or coke an extra rush. What's happening is that nicotine and Pequod's coffee are acting synergistically, pushing some people over the seizure threshold. Most people can handle it, even smokers. But not everyone."

"Not Marci," Gwen said sadly.

Mark saw Gwen's pain and felt an immediate surge of anger. "We're going to nail those bastards with this."

"Don't jump to that conclusion so fast," Eddie Karn interjected.

"What are you talking about?" Mark said, riled and indignant. "They're invading our bodies and they've killed people."

"It might not matter. Caffeine is a legal drug regardless of its form—left- or right-handed—and people consume it for its stimulant properties more than for its taste. The FDA allows companies to put caffeine into headache remedies, energy drinks, and dozens of other products."

"But Pequod's' caffeine acts differently in the human body than ordinary caffeine," Peter pointed out.

"That's entirely correct," said Karn, "and I don't think anyone in this room would be surprised that I advocate the regulation of many substances—not just coffee—to ascertain what is called the 'mechanism of action' for various chemicals in genetically modified foods, just as we do with drugs."

"Mechanism of action?" said Mark.

"How a various chemical acts and metabolizes within the body. The effects it produces, if you will. Unfortunately, I and a few others are lone voices crying in the wilderness."

Mark didn't want to hear about politics at a time like this. "Pequod's is getting people hooked by mimicking an amphetamine. That's way over the line. You're telling me we can't skewer them for this?"

"The argument," said Gallagher, "would no doubt be that the drug is doing what it always does, just in a slightly different manner."

"Then why the bloody hell can't a warning be issued alerting people to the dangers of using the two together?" asked Peter.

Jan shook her head. "Issue a warning saying that drinking coffee and smoking are dangerous to your health? Assuming Americans would even care, the coffee and tobacco lobbies would be all over the government agency that will dare to float that little gem."

Mark could barely stay in his seat any longer. "Then we crush Randall and Tassin."

Karn held up a hand. "Mark, I don't think you've been listening to—"

"I get it, the legal system lets scumbags slip through the cracks. That's not exactly a newsflash. You're forgetting, though, that we have something at least as damning on Randall and Tassin."

Mark looked around the room as the others smiled in memory of the information they'd gathered on the sex slave business. There were no legal vagaries there.

"I only wish we could have busted Broome with the same

thing," he said, returning their smiles.

"That would have been something to see," Rick said, practically rubbing his hands together. He had never said anything about it to Mark, but Mark guessed the congressman had experienced the senator's "political will" more than once during their time in Washington.

"Trust the guy to go out in a way that'll leave people scratching their heads forever," Mark said. "Suicide or aviation tragedy—we'll never know. Could be that the pressurization failed at altitude and the pilots didn't recognize it in time to react. Could be that they just forgot to pressurize the cabin. Could be explosive decompression at altitude. Only a very few know just how convenient it was for Henry to exit the stage at this precise moment. History will certainly treat him with more care than if he had put a gun in his mouth or stood trial for murder. The irony is that his coffee empire will feed the next four generations of Broomes even if Pequod's loses its competitive edge."

"We'll certainly have to run all of this by the attorney general," Rick said. "But my guess is that Broome got tipped off that Spangler had been released. He then put two and two together and realized he had more problems than just coffee to worry about."

Several people around the room nodded.

"I think our first order of business," Rick continued, "is to talk with the attorney general again and get his thoughts on all this. He said he was going to be in touch with the secretary of health. Let's see what he says when we lay the entire story out."

"I'll be here if anyone needs me," declared Gallagher. "This is fascinating stuff. I'm going to keep working on it until somebody tells me to stop."

Jan and Peter laughed, but Karn leaned forward conspiratorially.

"I wouldn't be surprised, Ted, if your phone rings in the next few days and somebody tells you exactly that."

78

Gregory Randall liked to do favors for people. They always paid off in the end and you could never anticipate how. Who would have known, for instance, that agreeing to give a clerical job to the idiot son of a lawyer in the attorney general's office would lead to a tip that kept Randall out of jail? Lane Chase could try to indict him for his part in the "Asian Beauties" program, but Randall had far more friends in high places than Chase ever would. Of course, he would give Chase something to make him go away—that was always part of the deal. Dieter Tassin wasn't really necessary anymore, anyway. Chase could have had Henry Broome as well, but Broome had already turned himself into fish food.

It seemed as though they were going to leave Pequod's alone, though they wouldn't have had much of a case anyway. QuantumSheet had taken care of all of that. The titration thing might be harder to do in the future if Randall sacrificed Tassin, but he'd put a team of people on it. Worst came to worst, they'd get by without the "Proprietor's Roast." Pequod's had so much momentum that it hardly mattered anymore.

His moment of contemplation gone, Randall called in his assistant and dictated a memo to his PR department. His newly acquired AC-IV processing chip would be seeing the inside of more and more businesses and homes every single day. The coffee empire would pale by comparison. Might be time to start a new food company, however.

Maybe chocolate . . .

■ ■ ■

The old woman in Apartment 5G beat her eviction notice thanks to the kind young lawyer who had died in May. The judge had just said, "I'm prepared to put this issue to rest," and then Marci slumped to the floor. In the commotion that followed, Anh didn't get to hear what the judge intended to say that day. But someone at Marci's firm got a continuance and when they went back to court, Anh heard the judge chastise her landlord for violating building codes and attempting to break Anh's lease. The judge told the landlord that he had "a great deal to be ashamed of—and not only in this case." Anh had no idea what he meant by that. All she knew was that she won. She only wished Marci could have been there to enjoy the moment with her. She was safe in her home, even though it often seemed gloomy and empty.

A persistent knock on the door drew her out of her thoughts. She kept the chain latched on, but opened the door, tentatively peeking without her glasses through the small crack. In the dark hallway waited two figures, tall and slim, carrying suitcases. "Who are you? What do you want?" she asked.

"Mama, it's Tuyen."

"Tuyen? Is it possible? Is it really you?" Anh removed the chain and opened the door. She put on her glasses to see the figures better, as if suspect of their motives.

Tuyen and Mai stood before her, small suitcases in their hands and tears in their eyes. "Mama, it is us. We are home."

"Dieter," she whispered in rapid Hmong dialect. "He will find you. I love you, but save yourselves. Hurry. Go quickly." Anh began to close the door.

"But we're free, Mama," Tuyen said. "Dieter can't hurt us anymore. No one can. Men with badges from— "

"From the FBI," said Mai.

"Yes, men from the FBI threatened the man who kept us. They told him he could face imprisonment if he didn't let us go."

"You free now? You stay with Anh?" With that, Anh opened the door wide and pulled her daughters inside, hugging them to her. Having her daughters return was nothing short of a miracle. In whatever years she had left, she might yet learn to be happy.

■ ■ ■

Dieter Tassin stepped off the plane in Lima. Peru would serve as home for the immediate future. He'd settle on somewhere more permanent after he'd had a chance to consider new opportunities.

He wasn't surprised to discover through one of his many sources that Gregory Randall had ratted him out to the feds. He'd had a long working arrangement with Randall, but it had always been a relationship built on mutual distrust. What did surprise him was that Randall thought he could get away with it. Not only had Dieter gotten out of America before the FBI could track him down, but he also left a little "time bomb" as a present for Randall. He'd keep a close watch on the American media to ascertain when it went off.

He would have no trouble finding employment as a roastmaster in South America if he so chose. Even though his escape forced him to change his identity, thus preventing him from trading on his resume, he knew that he was a wizard with coffee beans and that someone would want his services. Or he might finally retire . . . from that business, at least. South American women were dark, sultry and mysterious. Maybe it was time to cultivate an appreciation for a different ethnicity.

He took a taxi to his new villa. It was cool, open, and fully furnished, as promised. A computer was set up on a wide desk of teak wood, booted up and ready. He decided unpacking could wait. He sat down at the desk and started a new file, labeling it "Señorita."

Absentmindedly, feeling the rumbling in his belly, he reached inside his suitcase and found the box of rice pastries the girls had thoughtfully packed for him. Parting had indeed been bittersweet and their gesture convinced him that they had cared for him more than they could comfortably reveal.

The pastries were delicately formed, perfect miniatures of fish and crustaceans in bright, true-to-life colors. They looked almost too good to eat, but Dieter's sweet tooth was far more powerful a force than his artistic sensibility. He popped a brightly colored one that resembled a puffer fish in his mouth, savoring the combination of sweetness and spice that is unique to Asia. He'd miss this and other

Asian pleasures now that he was in Peru—but he'd get used to it.

There was a hint of another, vaguely familiar flavor in the treat, but for a moment, he couldn't place it. Dieter surfed the Internet for a while, enjoying his snack and his search for local action, which was always titillating. When he began to notice a slight fuzzy feeling in his lips, he put down the pastry in his hand, and put his finger to his mouth.

The odd buzzing in his lips was spreading quickly, and now numbness followed, all the way to the tip of his tongue. He tried to swallow, but it was difficult. Had he caught a flu bug on the way down? His eyes fell on the pastry box, its pretty wrapping, the ribbons undone.

He grabbed for the box. His hand managed to grasp the lid, but now it, too, had become useless and it fell heavily to his side.

Far too late, Dieter remembered the subtle flavor he had tried to place. One of Mai's specialties was the preparation of fugu, the Asian puffer fish. A delicacy in Japan and elsewhere, the fish protected itself from predators by manufacturing a potent neurotoxin, concentrated in its liver and ovaries. A careless chef could contaminate a slice of fish with enough poison to wipe out a whole restaurant with one slip of the knife. The most sought-after fugu chefs knew how to put a miniscule amount of toxin on each serving—just enough to make the lips tingle for a few minutes. Belatedly, Tassin remembered the shape of the fish pastry he had just eaten, and Mai's now-too-obvious, falsely teary, good-bye. That one always did have a rather wicked sense of humor.

Part of Dieter wanted to grin at the joke of it all, but those muscles were no longer working. He pined for a breath of fresh air, but those muscles also refused to cooperate. As he slid to the floor, a little air managed to seep into his lungs, but exhaling was now impossible. His chest began to burn as his lungs screamed for oxygen. He fought with all his will to breathe, but his body was deaf to his command, as immobile as cement.

Dieter Tassin silently cursed the twins in several languages, regretted that he would never know a new bounty of available beauties, and, as darkness descended, wordlessly slid into death.

■ ■ ■

Unlike her hero Frances Kelsey, who blocked the approval of Thalidomide and was decorated by a president, Gwen would never get widespread recognition for her role in averting a public health crisis that the country would never know about. However, she did get called down to the Humphrey Building on Independence Avenue, where the Department of Health and Human Services is headquartered. Once there, she was surprised to find herself escorted to the secretary's suite. Sitting in the room were Attorney General Chase, along with the secretary of health, and the inspector general of the department.

The secretary opened the meeting, saying, "Captain Maulder, there's no question that the country owes you a large debt—one that we will never discuss again. Let's just say that you know, we know, and the president knows what you have done. You have been put in for the Surgeon General's Lifetime Achievement Medal, which is the highest honor this department has to offer.

"Some folks, your friend Snyder included, have realized that it is time for them to leave public service. As near as we can tell, Snyder was keeping tabs on you just to curry favor with his bosses upstairs. He never knew what he was doing in trying to muzzle you. We did, however, pick up an interesting trail in Snyder's office and it lead right through Gene McMurphy, all the way to the acting commissioner, Lionel Channing. By torpedoing Eddie Karn, the acting commissioner was kept in charge. A word here and a word there to Snyder was all it took for Channing to pull your strings. Our friend Channing, it turns out, did have a motive. He owned one hundred thousand shares of Pequod's stock that Randall had given him before Channing went into government. Seems Randall could always spot a man on the rise and decided to invest in Channing. Randall had a change of heart once he started visualizing the wrong end of Leavenworth, Kansas, and told us all about the relationship."

"So what?" Gwen said. "Channing loses his meager government pension and goes to work for General Mills. Sounds like there's no proof he consistently or directly told Snyder to interfere with me. At any rate my activities were unauthorized and outside the scope of my job."

"Ah, but you're forgetting the Pequod's stock," said Chase.

"So he owned some stock he shouldn't have. He wasn't part of an insider transaction. The most you can do is fire him for it and he's already resigned," said Gwen.

"Well . . . yes and no," said Chase. "The stock ownership wasn't a felony. Unfortunately for our friend Channing, he signed multiple financial disclosure forms for both the White House and the Senate under penalty of perjury in which he made no mention of the Pequod's shares. There's quite a good chance that Mr. Channing will take up residence in Kansas under less luxurious circumstances than he is accustomed to."

"What about McMurphy?"

"We're still looking at him. We have already figured out that he goes way back with Senator Broome. Worked on his staff right after college," said Chase.

"I see from the look on your face that you see some justice in this outcome," said Chase. "Naturally, in your case, we hope you will stay. Once you return from your maternity leave, we hope you will consider taking up the newly created duties of deputy commissioner and chief safety officer at the FDA, with promotion to assistant surgeon general. That is," the secretary added with a smile, "if you think your husband can stand having a rear admiral in the house."

Gwen was stunned, though it only took her a moment to acknowledge that she deserved everything they were giving her.

"Thank you, sir."

The secretary handed her a card. "Here's the private phone number to this office. The one thing I ask is that the next time you spot a major public health disaster in the making, you call me before organizing your own army."

Gwen, slightly embarrassed, looked down at the card. "Yes, sir."

Chase took over where the secretary left off. "We don't want that husband of yours feeling outranked or unappreciated. If he would like to keep his Treasury pension but come to work at the Justice Department, we can use his computer investigative skills at a senior level. Perhaps an assistant attorney general's badge might make him feel more equal when he calls you admiral . . . "

PART VI

79

They got together every Tuesday afternoon for lunch. There was nothing official about it. No one penned it into his or her calendar. But at the end of each lunch, they always made plans for the next. Mark hadn't realized how important the group had become to one another until they prepared to split up after their last meeting with Gallagher. It was a ragtag team to say the least—even the most creative networking specialist would not have thought to bring them together—but Gwen, Jan, Peter, Eddie, and Rick had become the first group Mark felt he could rely on since his college days. That felt very good.

It was Rick's turn to pick the restaurant, which meant overcooked burgers and soggy fries. In the three months they'd been doing this, Mark had learned when he could look forward to the food (Eddie seemed to have a direct line to the best chefs in the city) and when he should make sure to eat a big breakfast. Rick had always had terrible taste, and access to state dinners hadn't refined it. His favorite part of campaigning was probably getting a chance to eat his fill of rubber chicken. Today, though, the food was an afterthought. The day before, Gwen had a follow-up meeting with Ted Gallagher and received astounding news—d-caffeine was showing up in the coffee of other roasters.

"How can that be?" asked Mark. "The d-caffeine plants are confined to Hawaiian plantations."

"But that's just it. I'm afraid they're not. Gallagher analyzed beans from Central and South America. Many, though not all, are showing the genetic manipulation. If there were even one decent-sized coffee plantation south of the equator, the altered plant could have spread—and it looks as if that's what happened."

Mark was baffled. "How?"

Eddie interjected. "It could have happened in any number of ways. A competitor could have stolen some of the plants over the last few years. Or maybe scientists—corporate, academic, you name it—were experimenting with a new variety that turned up down there. Or simple cross-fertilization. Nature is now following what Jamie Robinson programmed the plants to do years ago. That's what happens when man starts tampering with things."

"So things are even worse than before," Jan said.

Gwen shook her head. In the past few months, her face had filled out a bit, though she hadn't put on much weight. Mark thought it made her seem warmer, more open. Jack Maulder and their future child were very, very lucky people. "Remember that we only ever connected seizure activity to titrated d-caffeine. Lower levels don't seem to have the same effect and none of the samples Gallagher tested showed anything more than that."

"It's entirely possible they don't even know what they have," Eddie noted.

"Even Pequod's has stopped doing it in new markets," Gwen added.

Peter guffawed. "That's because we scared the shit out of them."

Gwen smiled. "We did something good, that's for sure. Broome's gone and Tassin's gone. And even though Randall dodged prison—I'd love to know how the attorney general screwed that one up—he's out of the coffee business. The only thing you ever read about him these days has to do with his new computer chip."

It was time for Mark to make his announcement. He'd expected it to be the big story of the day, but Gwen trumped him. "Speaking of which, I got a call from Billy Hamlin this morning."

"Hey," Peter said, "what's your best buddy up to?"

"Relocating. He's leaving Pequod's."

"Please tell me he's not going to one of the other brands where Gallagher found d-caffeine," Jan said.

"Actually, he's getting out of coffee entirely. He cashed out his options and is going to work for the Disney Corporation."

"Makes sense," Peter said wryly. "He's already turned parents into addicts so it's time to go after the kids."

Everyone at the table chuckled and Mark let them have their laugh. "You know, I think he might actually have been entirely innocent in this. He told me that he'd spent the past few months trying to corroborate what I told him about Pequod's. It wasn't easy because, as we know, Randall doesn't exactly run an open operation over there, but when enough of what he found supported our claims, he decided it was time to get out."

Rick leaned forward in his chair, nearly landing his tie in a pool of ketchup. "That's the angle for your story! You didn't want to do it because you felt it didn't lead anywhere, but now it does."

Mark shrugged. "No, it really doesn't. Everything I said about this a few months ago is still true. Billy Hamlin leaving Pequod's doesn't change it. Beyond the few documents we possess, the trail suddenly grows cold. We don't have anything to support our conspiracy story, so I'm left with d-caffeine. The public isn't going to respond to an article on receptor sites. If it's not linked to a cover-up, it's going to sound like I'm preaching, and people don't read my pieces to hear a sermon."

"But if Billy Hamlin is willing to talk about Randall, Broome, and Tassin—"

"Who says he would be? Would you be willing to rat out Randall if he knew where your wife and kids lived? And anything he said would throw suspicion on himself. It's lose-lose for him."

"So are you going to cover Hamlin's move in any way?" Gwen asked.

"Nah. Billy called me first to give me the scoop. I sent him to my friend Charlie Nicholls at the *Journal* instead. I owe Charlie a few favors."

Gwen smiled. That answer seemed to please her.

After that, the lunch relaxed into the easy banter that Mark had come to appreciate. Jan and Peter made official what the rest of the group had surmised for some time—that they were a couple. Mark was hardly an authority on relationships, but even he knew there was some real heat between them.

Gwen told everyone about her upcoming ultrasound test. At this point, there was a good chance they'd be able to determine the gender of the child. Jack had come around to the notion that he could raise a female softball star as easily as he could a major league shortstop, but Gwen was still hoping he'd get his boy.

"If it's a girl, we're going to name her Marci," Gwen said, her eyes misting a bit. Mark knew that Gwen did all she could to get to the cause of her best friend's sudden death. Still, while she'd managed to address the mystery, she hadn't yet fully addressed the grief. "If it's a boy, we want to use some variation on her name for his middle name but we haven't come up with it yet."

"You could always use Mark," Mark said coyly.

Gwen patted him on the hand. "Thanks for the suggestion," she said with a little grin. "Jack and I will take that under advisement."

In the past few weeks, Mark had stopped feeling uncomfortable hearing Gwen talk about her pregnancy and started enjoying how much she was enjoying it. He wasn't quite ready to take her up on her dinner invitations to the Maulder home, but he was doing better with all of it.

Peter regaled everyone with a story about his latest client, a huge multinational—he wouldn't mention the name ("confidentiality and all that"), but dropped enough clues to make it obvious to all—with a virus on its intranet "that would make a porn star blush." That led to Rick, in can-you-top-this fashion, telling about a barely-unnamed congresswoman's lewd diatribe after a five-martini lunch. He had everyone at the table laughing so hard that no one seemed to mind that he'd made yet another dreadful restaurant choice.

Rick would be getting ready to mount a reelection campaign soon. Peter hinted at a potentially months-long assignment in Istanbul. Eddie had just signed a deal with a publisher for a book on GMOs. Jan was getting her team ready to explore Phase Three of BioNet. Gwen was up to her neck in meaningful work at the FDA and planned to take three months at home after giving birth. And Mark had recently received a call from the *Chicago Tribune* that was far too interesting to ignore without some exploration.

These Tuesday lunches might not last much longer. But Mark was convinced the friendships would continue indefinitely. They'd done something significant together. They probably saved lives—and nearly died trying. If that wasn't the foundation for a lasting relationship, Mark didn't know what was.

80

"Is everything under control?"

"I've done what I could, Wallace," replied Lane Chase. "The irony is that I've pretty much told our troublemakers the truth. The caffeine is legal and can't be regulated, plus people are going to smoke and drink coffee if they choose. Aside from creative bookkeeping, no real laws were broken as far as the coffee's concerned. Even we didn't realize the seizure problem created by the combination of nicotine and d-caffeine, at least not at first. We have Maulder, Menefee, and Tippett to thank for that. Our public servants certainly perform at exemplary levels sometimes. Hopefully, we've thrown them enough goodies to keep their minds off the last piece of the puzzle."

"And the reporter?" asked Wallace Pembroke, chairman of the Federal Reserve Board in his raspy voice.

"He's the wild card. I think I've convinced him that pursuing the story any further was likely to be dangerous somewhere down the line, though. He's not stupid either; he himself realizes that the trail has grown cold. It was wise to terminate operations so abruptly. That said, I think we should read his columns—maybe keep occasional tabs on the man—and try to feed him enough scandalous stories that lead nowhere to keep him fat and satisfied. He can't be trusted; I don't trust him."

"Neither do I," said Pembroke. "But we have accomplished what we set out to do. I think even Randall understands our higher purpose. Of course, Senator Broome was never one to look further than his own money and power to the bigger picture of the nation's productivity."

"Agreed."

Wallace Pembroke coughed and cleared his throat. "You remember, Lane, it was a lowly midlevel staffer at the Department of Labor who noticed that worker productivity seemed to spike up in each region that Pequod's entered."

"Yes, I remember," said Chase. "Carl Richey, the guy we made our chief operative in Central America."

"And the rest is history," said Pembroke. "The nation is finally coming out of its twenty-year manufacturing slump, isn't it, Lane? We're actually manufacturing steel in Cleveland again. Auto plants are about to gear up for increased runs. Consumer goods are hitting the shelves at an all-time record, and it's all because workers feel better and work harder with d-caffeine in their systems. They don't call in sick as frequently. Assembly lines run ten percent faster with fewer errors and half as many stoppages. Overtime hours have increased without the usual grumbling. It's almost reminiscent of a wartime economy, with workers turning out the necessary equipment to keep the nation strong, competitive, and on the move. You know, there's nothing new in all of this. It's how we won the naval battles of World War I. Admiral Josephus Daniels took away the rum ration from the sailors and substituted coffee. The navy calls the stuff 'joe' to this day. All thanks to a little juice in the java."

"You've done a masterful job, Wallace. What's become of the Tabula Rasa force, by the way?"

"They're playing cards somewhere in their bunker, I suppose, waiting for their next assignment. Well, it's time for me to go outside and have a smoke and a cup of coffee."

"Always good talking with you, Wallace. Take care."

Lane Chase leaned back in his chair. The country was on course. All it needed was a little juicing up. As a public servant, he was gratified to have played a small part in its destiny.

AUTHOR'S NOTE

As stated at the outset, this book is a work of fiction. I have sprinkled it with some real-life characters, both to add verisimilitude and to have some fun. For the same reason, I have expropriated the names of some of my friends and assigned them to entirely fictional characters. Any unscrupulous characters out there that think they may have been "outed," should look into their own consciences, since any resemblance between the evildoers in *Capitol Reflections* and living persons is entirely coincidental.

I will admit that Gwen's character is inspired by a real-life American hero, Dr. Frances Kelsey, who retired from the U.S. Food and Drug Administration in 2005 at the age of ninety, and who was awarded a Presidential Commendation for her bravery and tenacity. Dr. Kelsey was charged with granting approval for Thalidomide, a new German sleeping pill that was reported to be particularly good for combating nausea associated with pregnancy. The manufacturer reported to the FDA that the drug had no side effects and, therefore, Kelsey was under significant pressure from above to speed up the approval, with external pressure from both the German company and consumers. Kelsey just couldn't believe that any drug had zero side effects, and continued to demand more information from the company. When her supervisors ordered her to stop stonewalling, it is rumored that she called President Kennedy's office on a Saturday morning with her concerns. Clearly, her career was on the line and she put a target on her forehead as far as her supervisors were concerned. However, her actions triggered a re-review of the matter and during that period, the first tragic reports came pouring in from Europe of children born without arms and legs. Only because of her unselfish disregard for her own career was the United States the sole Western country to be spared the heartbreak of the Thalidomide disaster.

This book began entirely as a product of my imagination. However, as with many cutting-edge topics, truth has begun to overtake the fictional elements of the story. Clearly, the actions depicted in this story are illegal and reprehensible. With that said, they have become increasingly plausible as the science for genetic modification of foods rapidly overtakes our ability to implement regulatory safeguards. As this book was going to press, the first news stories appeared showing that much of the U.S. rice supply was contaminated with a genetically modified strain of rice that has never been approved for human consumption. Whether or not human harm might result from its ingestion is unknown.

Imagine how difficult it would be to determine whether subtle symptoms arising in a small number of people were attributable to the rice they ate at dinner. The complications to worry about are not immediate toxic effects, which can readily be recognized, but rather subtle interactions with medications people may be taking, other foods they may be consuming, and their underlying genetic ability to metabolize various classes of molecules. It is important to remember that the major initiatives in genetic modification of crops are for the purpose of increasing yields by rendering them more pest and infection resistant. This is generally achieved by inserting genes to enable crops to manufacture molecules that are toxic to insects and to various fungal infections. Ironically, this seems to be the reason nature evolved caffeine from the coffee bush to begin with.

Regulation of genetically modified food is further hampered by the divided nature of our regulatory apparatus. Field crops are regulated by the Department of Agriculture. The Food and Drug Administration only gains jurisdiction when those crops enter the food chain. Safety of prepared foods in restaurants is the province of multiple state and local health departments. Although the characters in this book took the liberty of enlisting some resources of the Centers for Disease Control, food safety is not part of their mandate. Thus, it is not at all clear whether our government has any effective mechanism for reacting to the type of threat hypothesized in these pages.

The seemingly miraculous leap of d-caffeine from Henry Broome's plantation to other commercial coffee crops is less unlikely than one would like. In the past five years, we have seen genetically modified strains of corn and rice that were supposedly confined to controlled laboratory environments unexpectedly appear in field crops. Recently, coffee farmers on the Hawaiian island of Kona destroyed experimental GM strains of coffee being grown by the University of Hawaii because they feared the same type of accident.

Moreover, and more worrisome, it is not at all clear that the genetic manipulation envisioned in *Capitol Reflections* is against the law in any way. Those skilled in FDA regulatory law may take issue with Lane Chase's final comment that d-caffeine could not be regulated. Obviously, were the FDA to determine that a food, even a naturally occurring food, posed a major health hazard, the FDA has ample regulatory authority to force that product off the market, even if it has to seize the product at the store. In this case, however, the deaths were being caused by the manipulation of d-caffeine to gain market share for Randall. Although the d-caffeine was certainly addictive, it's not clear that without deliberate manipulation it was hazardous to the point where FDA could have forced it off the market on public safety grounds without a major battle. Certainly, there are those who might argue the theory that inserting a gene for d-caffeine constitutes the addition of a food additive not generally recognized as safe. This theory has been used voluntarily by at least one company that successfully sought FDA approval to bring a rot-resistant tomato to market for human consumption. The fine points will likely be debated in law school classes and law review articles until Congress clarifies the issue.

The broader point is that there is currently no law that requires premarket safety review of genetically modified foods, the way there is for drugs. Moreover, there is no requirement that genetically modified foods be labeled as such. The above discussion was originally part of the narrative, but wise editors suggested that I move it here for those readers who are determined to read every word.

While the story is fictional, much of the background is not. The major exception, of course, is d-caffeine. Nobody, to my knowledge, knows the properties of d-caffeine and it is unclear as to whether it has ever been synthesized, much less mapped to a specific gene. However, the definitions of "adulterated food," which is the primary tool the FDA has for enforcement, certainly doesn't contemplate such a manipulation. When it comes to food safety, the FDA is hampered by a limited scientific workforce and a body of law that was written in the fifties and sixties, long before today's science of genetic modification was ever imagined. We owe it to ourselves and our children to design a twenty-first century basis for ensuring food safety that rewards innovation and scientific advancement, while protecting the public.

In case you are wondering, Gwen Maulder is not done with her adventures. Please stay tuned for more of her escapades. If you would like to learn more about the issues raised in *Capitol Reflections* or to contact me for any reason, please go to www.capitolreflections.com.

As stated above, this book began as a work of fiction. I can only hope that it remains so.

Jonathan Javitt

ACKNOWLEDGMENTS

I had a great deal of help in bringing this project to publication. First of all, I want to thank Billy Hamlin for his invaluable teaching and Lou Aronica for brilliant editing. Dan Troy, Mark McClellan, and Scott Gottlieb were generous in answering many questions about the FDA's inner workings. I also took merciless advantage of my friends Bill Botts, Jan McDonnell, Maury Dewald, Gwen Feder, Elena Neuman, my mother Suzanne, and my wife Marcia by making them read multiple versions. Other friends have had their names appropriated as characters here and there. Others were unwittingly pulled into the story as themselves, simply to add verisimilitude to the plot. Tess Gerritsen and Michael Palmer were kind enough to teach me what a McGuffin is. From Sterling & Ross I want to thank Rachel Trusheim, Anna Lacson, Nicola Lengua, Jessica Gardner, Wenny Chu, Heidi Ward, and Mimi Lin. Most importantly, I want to thank Drew Nederpelt, publisher at Sterling & Ross, for believing in this project and making it his company's first novel.